LEOPARD ASCENDING

A HELLION HOUSE NOVEL

EMMA JANE HOLLOWAY

When courage and a crack shot aren't enough

After violence shatters Miranda Fletcher's world, she swears to protect those she loves. An air captain's daughter, she has courage enough to battle hungry monsters. Now a different threat hides among them—one much harder to destroy.

Miranda seeks out her rebel brother, Gideon, for aid. A private inquiry agent, he's searching for victims no one else dares to find. When one of his father's airships is blown from the sky,

Gideon suspects his cases are linked to the disaster, and his family is the villain's new target.

Danger hides everywhere—in gaslit clubs and drawing rooms, in the secret halls of the mages, and among the monsters of the forest. Uncovering the city's dire truth could cost Miranda and Gideon their lives—or condemn them to a fate more terrible than the grave.

CHAPTER 1

Gideon Fletcher slipped a hand inside his greatcoat, reaching for his pistol. Moments ago, as he'd crossed the cobbled street, he'd become prey.

Instinct alone guided him. The hunter was invisible, but Gideon had felt its gaze like the prick of a stiletto.

He kept walking, the rhythm of his stride even. Carriages rattled past, dodging around the occasional steam-powered vehicle. On this street of tidy shops, clockwork displays rotated behind bowed windows, spinning and flashing to catch the eye. He ignored the distraction, focusing on the shadowed doorways instead.

Anger blunted his fear. He'd been on the way to the Mercury Café for a drink and conversation. Even at night, he *should* have been safe on these gaslit streets. After all, didn't magic protect the great wall enclosing the city?

Should wasn't worth a brass farthing.

Casually, he angled his body to the left as if peering through the window of a nearby café. A quick scan of the pavement behind him revealed little. The last of the afternoon crowds dotted the solidly respectable neighborhood, hurrying to their dinners and clubs. The men wore waistcoats and bowler hats, and the women had servants to carry their shopping. Outsiders would assume nothing but petty crimes happened here.

And yet the flesh along Gideon's spine shrank as if cold, dead fingers caressed his back. He'd felt the same invisible eyes in the wilderness beyond Londria's gate, where the Unseen roamed.

Gideon cursed softly, the frigid air turning his breath to mist.

Slowly, he resumed his journey, his gaze traveling up the old stone buildings to search for lurkers along the rooflines. Above, a passing airship caught the setting sun, the silks of its balloon turning the color of flame. He looked away before the brightness dulled his vision.

Movement flickered in the shadows of the nearest building, but when Gideon looked, the alley beside the old bank was empty. Without hurrying his step, he slid into the narrow passage, finally drawing his pistol.

"If you wish a fight, I'm all attention." His words ghosted in the frigid atmosphere. Heart pounding, he strained to hear the slightest footfall above the clatter of the street behind him.

The tail of his eye caught a pale blur. He spun, unable to track the movement. The creature moved unnaturally fast, a kiss of air against his cheek, there and gone.

Gideon sucked in his breath, pulse kicking into a gallop as he flattened himself against the stone side of the bank. He cocked the hammer of his weapon as nervous sweat cooled on his temples. He'd fought the Unseen before—and knew his chances weren't good.

Hugging the wall, he advanced a few steps, and then a few more. The darkness of the alleyway was a physical mass. The creature was ahead, but nowhere in sight.

The stone blocks of the bank gave way to the brickwork of the Regina Hotel. Space was costly in a walled city, and the builders hadn't wasted an inch between the two structures. No hiding places there.

The end of the passage ended in a heavy door framed by enormous trash bins. Unless someone opened the door, he had the creature boxed in. Gideon gripped his pistol in both hands, moving more slowly now. Sunset done, the light was fading fast.

He almost missed the dark shape climbing the shadowed wall of the hotel. It was already a dozen feet above the ground. Tension twisted Gideon's stomach.

"Stop," he said, not bothering to raise his voice. The things had uncanny hearing.

The creature dropped lightly, landing in a crouch. As it rose and turned to face Gideon, it raised its hands in a mocking gesture of surrender. It wore a white shirt under a dark suit, no doubt stolen from a human victim. It even had a pair of fashionable leather boots.

Gideon's chest tightened with fear. There were two kinds of Unseen—smart and crazy. The crazy ones were bestial, violent, and relatively easy to outwit.

This one was different. Intelligence glittered in the male's brilliant gray eyes. The tall, slender figure had a mass of silver hair, sharp features, and chalk-white skin. The ethereal pallor was common to the smarter Unseen, as if their beauty and cunning were entwined.

It smiled, baring a mouthful of pointed teeth. Regardless of their varied mental powers, the Unseen all fed on human flesh.

Gideon aimed and shot. The sound roared in the small space —or maybe that was his own enraged voice. The figure sprang toward him, seemingly untouched by the bullet. Gideon's back slammed to the cobblestones, pain lancing through his skull.

The Unseen's lips moved, but the shot had dulled Gideon's hearing. Clawed fingers gripped his jaw, the creature's strange eyes intent. Gideon sucked in a breath, ready to shout for help. Surely, someone had heard his pistol shot.

The Unseen bent lower, its wild, earthy smell filling the air as if it brought the forest with it. It stopped barely an inch from

Gideon's face, tendrils of silver hair brushing his cheek. This time, it was impossible not to make out its words.

"I am Masson," it—he—said in a cracked voice, as if something had gone wrong with his throat.

He spoke. For the barest instant, Gideon's mind blanked with shock. Words made the monster like a human. More like him. *He has a name.*

"You're the brother," the monster added with a tinge of curiosity.

Shock made Gideon flinch. "What?"

Carnivore's claws dug into his flesh, pricking deep. Pain seared through his surprise.

He thrust the muzzle of his pistol into Masson's belly.

A door banged open to Gideon's left, the sound of steel on brick ricocheting through the alley. Masson's shoulders hunched in reaction, his posture feline.

Gideon pulled the trigger. The gunshot muffled the Unseen's defiant shout.

Its recoil slammed Gideon back against the hard ground as Masson writhed away, hands cradling his gut. Dark blood spattered the ground, but the creature remained on his feet. Commotion rang from the open door, but Gideon didn't take his eyes off his opponent.

Masson sprang, fangs bared. Gideon launched from the ground, driving his shoulder into a bone-jarring collision. The impact drove Gideon back, feet skidding. They grappled, claws tearing the pistol from his hand and taking flesh with it. Despite his stomach wound, Masson was impossibly strong. Gideon punched the creature's temple, knocking him aside.

The reprieve didn't last. Teeth aimed for Gideon's throat, but he twisted and let the fangs bury themselves in the heavy fabric of his greatcoat. They scraped his collarbone, needle-sharp. Revulsion shuddered through him. He flung his opponent off with a guttural shout of disgust.

A figure darted into view, swinging a cudgel two-handed. The weapon connected with Masson's upflung arm. A feral shriek followed the snap of bone, and Masson shrank away.

A second figure appeared, this one brandishing a long knife.

Gideon tried to snatch up his pistol, but his right hand refused to work. He grabbed with his left instead, unwilling to be the only one without a weapon. The other figures were running now, chasing Masson toward the dead end of the passage. He brought up the rear, ignoring the flare of pain from his ruined hand.

The faint golden squares of the hotel windows shed feeble illumination from above. Gideon followed the scuffle of feet, navigating by instinct. The need to strike back, to finish the enemy, drove him like madness.

You're the brother.

There was only one thing that could mean. This was the Unseen who had murdered Gideon's twin sister.

He put on a burst of speed. The alley seemed endless, though he covered the distance in seconds.

There was a scuffle and slide of boots on stone.

"Sainted mother of plague rats." The man with the knife stopped.

Gideon nearly bumped into his back. "What's going on?"

"There." The figure with the cudgel—a woman—stumbled to a halt and tilted her face toward the roofline. He followed her gaze, barely making out what the two were staring at.

Broken-armed and gut-shot, Masson was swarming up the side of the hotel again, moving as if his injuries meant nothing. Cursing, Gideon aimed his pistol, but darkness made accuracy impossible. He fired anyway, sparks fountaining off the bricks. He swore again, this time with venomous fury.

Masson paused, taking one backward glance, and then silently vanished onto the roof. Rage pulsed through Gideon, making his wound throb. There was no point in pursuit—not when he was this far behind. The network of aqueducts that served the city's rooftop gardens could take the Unseen anywhere.

"Missed him again," the woman muttered.

"Again?" Gideon asked sharply. His pulse raced so fast, it left him lightheaded.

"That one's been here before," the man said. "We came when we heard your gunshot."

"It was a good thing you did," Gideon said, though resentment darkened his mood. These two had interrupted his vengeance.

"It's the first time anyone's drawn blood from that one." The man twirled his knife in one hand. "Congratulations are in order."

Gideon opened his mouth, but he couldn't form a proper response.

"I know what you're thinking," the man said. "Few citizens of Londria know the Unseen breach the city walls, and fewer dare to admit such heresy. Yet, here we are."

Yes, here Gideon was—furious and in agonizing pain. The only thing keeping him civil was unanswered questions. "Who are you?"

"Not so fast." The man offered a one-sided smile. "It's a dangerous game slaying monsters. The city fathers would sooner toss us behind bars than admit their magic can't keep the beasties out."

Gideon frowned. He'd learned the hard way that wasn't exaggeration.

His silence wiped the smile from the man's face. "If you want no part of this chase, walk away."

"I appreciate your caution. I've fought the Unseen beyond the wall. And inside, too. I've seen what they can do."

Something in his answer struck the right chord. The man visibly relaxed. "I've seen you around town. You're one of the airship family. You flew rescue missions into the Outlands."

Gideon nodded, equally reluctant and curious.

"Then let's swap stories. Perhaps we can help one another." The man stepped closer, the dim light showing his features. "The name is Ned Huntley."

He was a few years older than Gideon, clean-shaven and wearing round wire-rimmed spectacles. He wore a fashionable tweed suit, as if on his way to a shooting party. Only the long knife hinted his quarry was more than grouse.

"Why no guns?" Gideon asked.

"Not when we're in the heart of the city. Too noisy. The club has practical rules."

"Club?"

"Happy to introduce you, old fellow." Huntley extended his hand, welcoming but firm.

Gideon hesitated. This so-called club might prove to be a gang of raving crackpots. Who else hurled themselves at the Unseen with no more than a knife? Still, he raised his right hand automatically. Gideon had been raised a gentleman, and it would be churlish to refuse the gesture.

Huntley's eyes went wide. "I say, you're bleeding."

Gideon looked down, and pain roared to life with an agonizing throb. Grooves dug into the flesh of his palm and fingers, soaking his hand in a red glove of sticky gore. His vision tunneled, the last rush of battle-frenzy collapsing like a punctured balloon.

The woman had remained in the shadows, staring after Masson, but now she snapped from her reverie. She cast a look their way and drew in a hissing breath. "Mr. Fletcher! I should have known it was you."

The woman thrust her club into Huntley's hand and hurried to Gideon's side.

Recognition gave him a sudden start. "Layla?"

She caught his wrist, bending his arm for a better look. "Claws or teeth?"

"Claws."

"Good. We'll take you inside." She shot Huntley a look that crushed any argument.

Gideon wavered, still disoriented. The Layla he knew—tall and lovely, with masses of strawberry-blonde hair—favored frills and lace. He'd seen her many times wooing clients in the soft opulence of Hellion House, her laughter bubbling like the brothel's free-flowing champagne. Clubbing a monster seemed wildly out of character, and yet she'd done just that.

"What are you doing here?" he asked.

She cast him the same quelling glance she'd given Huntley. "Same as you, I suppose. Now, be quiet."

"I have questions."

"They can wait."

She used his handkerchief to wrap his hand, though the cloth soaked through as fast as she bound the wound. Wasting no more time, she led Gideon through a narrow door. It was the same one she and Huntley had burst through minutes before.

Their path led into the hotel, the passage turning into a servant's stairway that crawled upward in a never-ending series of landings. Gideon had lost track of the flights—perhaps eight? —when they finally emerged into a dark-paneled foyer.

This part of the hotel was for private suites. Whoever Ned Huntley was, he had money.

The name tugged at Gideon's memory. *Huntley. Ned Huntley.* There was something he should know about the man, but pain and exhaustion numbed his brain.

Huntley crossed to a set of double doors with shining brass knobs. He opened them with a flourish, and piano music eddied forth. Voices followed, along with a cloud of tobacco smoke and the scent of strong coffee. Gideon's gut twisted at the smell, his wounds making him queasy.

Huntley strode through the door, raising knife and cudgel in a victorious salute.

"Huzzah!" someone shouted from inside the suite. "The conquering hero returns!"

"Did you get it?" cried another voice.

"Almost," Huntley said with a theatrical sigh. "It went skyward before we caught it."

"Come on," Layla murmured to Gideon, taking his arm. "He'll be here all night taking his bows."

With that, she pulled him past their host and into the room. It was a vast salon, overdecorated in red velvet and far too many gold tassels. A drift of mismatched carpets muffled their steps as they entered, though any stray sound was drowned out as the female pianist struck up a triumphal march.

Besides the musician, a young man sprawled on a brocaded fainting bench. Across the room, two dandies played chess, the board balanced on the sofa cushions between them. There was a playful air about the group, as if they were ordinary young people whiling away the time. The pile of weapons on the lid of the grand piano said otherwise.

Layla seated Gideon on an ottoman. Instantly, the young man on the fainting bench rose and poured brandy from a crystal decanter, thrusting the glass toward Gideon.

Gideon set his pistol on the low lacquered table beside him and accepted the drink. At the other end of the room, Huntley regaled the crew with an account of the fight.

Layla helped Gideon out of his greatcoat, careful of his injury. "Stay here while I fetch water to clean you up." She left in a swirl of skirts.

Gideon did as he was told. Voices receded as he sipped the drink, pain and brandy filling his mind until Layla returned with a cloth and basin.

"Bad luck." The young man who'd brought the brandy produced a medical bag and began unpacking tools, arranging them on the table. "Have you encountered this monster before?"

Gideon submitted as Layla unwound the handkerchief

binding his hand. The motion hurt and made his palm bleed again, but forced himself to answer. Talking was a distraction.

"Possibly. I've fought the Unseen many times but never had leisure to study their faces. This one called himself Masson."

The medic looked up, large brown eyes wide. He had a thin mustache and goatee, giving him the air of a starving poet. "It spoke?"

Gideon gave a silent nod. Despite the loud conversation around them, everyone seemed to have heard. The noise faded as they gathered around. Blood dripped from Gideon's hand into the basin with a hushed *plop*.

"It was one of the pretty ones," Huntley said. "One of their ringleaders."

There were other terms for the smarter Unseen—masters, herders, kings. Some speculated they were another species from their bestial cousins. Gideon had never cared much, loathing them all equally, but now he had a name. Now he had an individual to hate.

"Masson won't be pretty for long," he said in frozen tones.

Huntley gave a low laugh. "Very good, Mr. Fletcher. I knew you were a kindred spirit."

A chorus of agreement ran through the group, and Gideon was briefly cheered. He raised his brandy glass in salute and drank the fiery liquid down.

In the meantime, the young man had finished organizing his medical instruments. "Just to reassure you," he said, "I am a resident doctor at Walton Hospital, so I know my way around a row of stitches. My name is Fitzwilliam Arden."

As he spoke, he slid into a professional manner. All at once, he didn't seem so young.

"Gideon Fletcher."

Arden took the washcloth from Layla. "Were you injured anywhere else, Mr. Fletcher?"

Gideon closed his eyes, suddenly exhausted. "The beastly thing bit my shoulder."

For an instant, he drifted, the soothing touch of the warm water prompting him to drop his guard. A mechanical click snapped him back to attention.

He opened his eyes to the sight of his own pistol an inch from his face. Huntley's grip was perfectly steady. All around them, the hiss of steel on scabbard whispered through the room.

There was nothing friendly in Huntley's expression now.

"Did the bite break your skin?"

CHAPTER 2

The muzzle of the pistol filled Gideon's vision. His nose twitched at the smell of spent gunpowder—or maybe that was the burn of his temper.

"Superstition." He said the word carefully. It never paid to insult a man holding a gun to one's head. "The worst you can catch from their bite is a nasty infection."

Science had confirmed the truth. Still, plenty of folklore said otherwise, and he'd seen airmen take a knife to their flesh to cut out the mark of a monster's teeth.

"That is the official line. I went to the same lectures given by the same experts," Huntley said, the words clipped with tension. "They claim a bite is painful and nothing more, but that only applies to the bestial Unseen. Their smarter masters, the ones who masquerade as humans, carry the essence of what they are in their blood."

"And what are they?"

"Mad. Hungry. Cursed."

Gideon raised a skeptical brow. "And I will somehow catch that like the pox?"

Huntley's features stiffened in anger. "Don't scoff at something you don't understand."

"I've fought and killed my share of Unseen. Perhaps I scoff, but you presume."

Huntley sucked in an offended breath.

"Their blood and saliva carries madness," Arden said, breaking in with an apologetic air. "Ultimately, it is fatal."

"That's folly," Gideon protested. "Are you certain the subject in question wasn't simply rabid?"

Arden nodded. "I would know the difference."

"It happened to one of our own in the course of an evening." Huntley's hand shifted on the grip of the pistol, a subtle warning. "Every one of us was there, watching."

Gideon swore under his breath. Anger was better than the icy fear stalking his mind. "Surely, even a virulent disease takes time to fester and spread."

He glanced toward Layla, but she turned her face away.

"Come now," the doctor said. "The best antidote to worry is facts. Which shoulder did it bite?"

"The left."

The doctor gave Huntley a hard look. The man took a step back, though the pistol didn't waver. Slowly, Gideon set down the brandy glass and unbuttoned his jacket. The garment was new and the buttons tight. Working them with his left hand was difficult. With a noise of distress, Layla pushed past the others and bent to assist.

"Be careful, woman," Huntley protested.

"Don't be daft," Layla retorted. "He's not foaming at the mouth."

With Arden's help, she removed Gideon's jacket and waistcoat, fingering the fine linen of his shirt to see if there were holes made by Masson's fangs. Gideon craned his neck to see his shoulder. The fabric was torn.

The cold, sharp pressure of panic rose in his throat.

"Did you feel the bite?" Layla asked.

"I didn't feel any pain," he said, but in truth he didn't remember. He wouldn't notice a minor wound during the frenzy of a fight.

"Take off the shirt," Huntley ordered.

By now, Gideon was in no mood to protest. He had to know.

Again, Layla helped him strip to the waist, bringing a murmur of appreciation from one of the chess players.

He felt Arden's sigh of relief against his bare skin. "Nothing more than a faint mark. It didn't break the skin."

Huntley lowered the pistol. "Very well. You may dress yourself again."

"Thank you." Relief and embarrassment sharpened Gideon's tone. What made Huntley think he had the right to give or withdraw his permission?

Gideon snatched up his shirt from where Layla had left it on the carpet. Blood from his hand smudged the pristine white. He shrugged back into his clothes with Layla's help, then surrendered his hand for the doctor to stitch. The ragged wound throbbed horribly from being dragged in and out of his garments.

"I won't apologize for caution." Huntley set the pistol down. "As I said, we lost one of our own."

"His name was Sanfred," Arden added, needle poised in the air. "He was a fellow resident at Walton Hospital."

"He wasn't Sanfred by the time he died," Huntley replied bitterly. "There wasn't anything left of him. Not the man we knew."

"I honor who he was before that night." Defiance simmered in the young doctor's tone. The needle stabbed Gideon's flesh with more force than seemed strictly necessary.

"As long as you understand he lost his fight," Huntley said after a long pause. "And that none of us was to blame."

Arden gave a tight nod. "Of course."

Tension sparked the air as Arden turned away and unscrewed the lid of a blue glass jar. The herbal smell of the contents instantly cleared Gideon's head.

Arden spread the salve over his stitches. He kept his gaze on his task, but tension stiffened his neck and shoulders.

"I'm sorry for your loss," Gideon broke in, hoping to ease the mood.

"I appreciate that," Arden murmured.

"It was a true tragedy," Huntley added. "And, it impacted us in more ways than you might think."

"How so?" Gideon asked.

"Sanfred's death forced us to abandon our last meeting place," Huntley said. "First, he destroyed those rooms before we—before the end. Then the landlord got involved. He took a dim view after we burned the body on the rooftop."

"You what?" Gideon asked, his head swimming with more than pain now.

Huntley gave a disgusted snort. "His objection was ridiculous. The fire was perfectly safe."

Gideon frowned. "But…"

"It's a crowded city. Cremation prevents the spread of disease."

"It's rarely conducted in a private residence."

"Given what we do, we could hardly hire an undertaker."

Gideon let the topic go, since it wasn't about to lead him anywhere sane. "Who are the members of your, uh, club?"

He accepted a second glass of brandy. Arden wrapped gauze over his hand, working with the speed of long practice.

"We are the members," Huntley said with a shrug. "Myself, Arden, and you seem to know Layla."

"I do."

"Those gents are Barnard and Wilmington." Huntley pointed to the two chess-playing dandies, who bowed in unison.

"And finally, may I present the charming Miss Telford."

The young pianist gave a demure nod. Small, pale, and blandly dressed, her one distinguishing feature was a cascade of golden curls that made her seem far too delicate for this company. After growing up with three sisters, Gideon knew better than to make assumptions.

"We call ourselves the Anathema Club," Arden said, tying off the last round of bandages. "In honor of the foul language our former landlord hurled at our heads."

Gideon studied the young man as he gathered up his medical instruments. There was a grim turn to his mouth Gideon recognized from his own mirror.

"How did this group come into being?" Gideon asked.

It was Miss Telford who answered in a calm, clear voice. "We have all lost someone to the Unseen. You, of anyone, should understand what that means, Mr. Fletcher."

A prickle of surprise cut through the numbing balm of the brandy, but it quickly vanished. His family was too well known for true privacy. "You heard about my sister."

"All of Londria knows she vanished on the way home from her betrothal ball."

Images flashed through his mind. The swirl of a gown. Fog in moonlight. A flash of bloody teeth.

A ripple of fury, old and deep, shuddered through Gideon's limbs. He swallowed more brandy, and it burned down his throat like liquid fire.

Unseen had dragged Sidonie from the carriage. He'd given chase until someone—something—had knocked him out cold and left him for dead on the heath. Failure still smoldered in his gut.

At first they'd prayed to find Sidonie alive, and then they'd hoped to bury her. The search had been pointless. The Unseen left nothing of their meals.

Pain twisted in Gideon's flesh, as if the death of his twin had left ragged flesh.

He turned the conversation away from himself. "I take it you have all lost a loved one?"

"In one way or another," Huntley replied, sprawling in an armchair.

All the club members had taken seats. Gideon remained on the ottoman with his bandaged hand and bloody shirtsleeves. His mind flashed resentfully to the pleasant evening he'd planned at the Mercury Café.

Huntley's expression grew intent. "We're a motley lot from all corners of Londria. What unites us is the promise of payback."

"And what's the Anathema Club's charter?"

"Keep our existence a secret. Fight to kill. Never leave a comrade behind."

"And no guns?"

"Stray bullets kill innocents, and too much noise attracts the authorities. That's how we knew you were in trouble—we heard your pistol shot."

"A bullet evens the odds."

"I can't kill monsters if I'm dead or in jail." Huntley's smile was grim.

Silence hung in the room, charged with memory and emotion. Gideon considered the man's words. There were others who hunted the Unseen, including his youngest sister, Miranda —but he'd never met another seasoned vigilante. Not like Huntley.

"There is something I've always wondered," he ventured. "If the Unseen can enter the city, why aren't we overrun? Why not kill us all?"

"I don't know." Huntley looked away. For the first time, his hard confidence seemed to fade. "Nor do we understand why they take our best and brightest, but they do."

A rustle passed through the room. The others had given Huntley the floor, but Gideon felt their unspoken losses. Perhaps grief produced sympathetic vibrations, like musical harmony.

"Who did they take from you?" he asked Huntley. He had no right to an answer, but it seemed important.

The man slid off his spectacles, as if he couldn't bear to meet Gideon's eyes. "My wife."

An oath slid softly from Gideon's lips. "I'm sorry."

"Oh, don't waste your breath." Huntley grimaced. "We'll all be in the grave before this battle is over."

"AND HOW DID you respond to that charming statement?" asked Detective Inspector Palmer several hours later.

They sat in Gideon's rooms before the fire, the night well advanced. After Gideon had failed to show at the Mercury, Palmer had stopped by to check on him. From there, the conversation had quickly turned serious.

Palmer was compact and fair-haired, his weathered face set with brown eyes. Though only a few years older than Gideon, he'd already established a sound reputation in Londria's police force.

The man flicked his gold lighter. With a whirr, a tiny clockwork dragon emerged to light his cigarette with a puff of flame. Palmer snapped the contraption shut and sat back, taking a slow lungful of smoke.

Gideon rose and opened the casement window of his sitting room, letting the frigid night air dispel the fog of tobacco fumes. "Huntley asked me to join them. I told him I work alone."

"Good. They sound deranged." Palmer sat forward. "But I would keep up the acquaintance. They might be useful informants."

"In what way?"

Gideon resumed his seat in the armchair opposite Palmer. The leather was worn, like everything in the rooms he'd rented above Dobson and Son Booksellers. He didn't mind, even though he'd grown up with money. The place was his, and that was all that mattered.

"You said yourself they've all lost someone to the Unseen. As a fledgling private inquiry agent, surely that piques your interest."

"It will once I recover from their hospitality."

Gideon adjusted his position so he could peruse the wall to his right. There, he'd neatly pinned an array of photographs and newspaper clippings, each representing a missing person. Most were cases like his sister's—closed by the authorities before the police could mount an investigation. Those not found quickly were presumed dead. Most times, that was true—but not always.

"I see you've located another one." Palmer waved toward the photograph of a young man. Gideon had penciled "found" across the forehead.

"He'd taken up with a mistress. He was out of money and ready to come home."

Restless, Gideon rose again, this time to stand before the gallery. There were both men and women, most from good families and all of them young. He'd found five of them, but there were two dozen cases still unsolved.

"Any other leads?" Palmer asked.

"A few. I'm fairly certain this one ran from debts." Gideon tapped a photo. "And I wager she eloped. I don't hold out much hope for the others."

"Isn't that Margaret Huntley in the bottom row?"

Gideon glanced at the woman's face. "Yes, it is."

That was why he'd known Huntley's name. In the madness of the evening, he'd forgotten the woman—the missing wife—was here in his collection of lost souls. Perhaps it was because nothing about her stood out—at least nothing that showed in the frozen lines of the portrait.

Now that he saw Margaret's face, he vaguely recalled the couple. Sidonie had known the Huntleys and their set—but then she'd made friends easily. When Margaret's parents had reported her disappearance, Sidonie hadn't believed the gossip about Ned Huntley and foul play.

And now Huntley had devoted himself to vengeance against the monsters. So had the rest of the Anathema Club, each member nursing a private grief.

Gideon stared at the portraits. How many more people were missing? How many had been taken by the Unseen?

"Tonight's monster had a name," Gideon said, half to himself. "Masson knew I was Sidonie's brother. What do you make of that?"

Palmer said nothing for so long that Gideon turned to face him. His friend's gaze was steady.

"You interest the creature," Palmer said at last. "Perhaps it followed you."

"Why?"

"As it said, you're the brother. It recognized your scent. Or your face."

"But why does that matter?"

"I have no idea." Palmer lit another cigarette, the flame masking his features in an eerie glow. "But take care, my friend. It's not something you want to find out."

CHAPTER 3

$\mathcal{W}$ind hummed in the cables as the airship passed to the north of the Citadel's tower. Sun flashed against the stained glass windows of the ancient spire, giving it the look of a flaming sword piercing the cloudless sky.

Miranda Fletcher gripped the edge of the airship's rail, leaning into the chill breeze as the vessel ascended with giddy speed. The Citadel was the tallest structure in Londria, and in moments, it would be a stomach-churning distance below the ship's belly. This high up, there was no recovering from a mishap.

Yet, as treacherous as wind and rigging might be, Miranda loved the sky and the ships that sailed it. The *Leopard* was an older vessel, but Norton Fletcher, Miranda's father and the founder of Fletcher Industries, had modernized the design during the last refit. He'd replaced the engine and aether pumps. Indigo sails now augmented the twin balloons, making use of every breeze. Finally, they'd painted the hull a deep blue and gold, giving the ship a regal air.

But the real innovation was the newest invention they carried aboard, a secret to all but the manufacturers and the crew. A lot rode on how the ship and its new equipment would perform this day.

At twenty-two and the youngest of her family, Miranda had taken her father's place aboard the vessel to review its performance. By day's end, she would report the results of the test flight and, based on her detailed observations, her father would decide whether to put out the call for investors or return to the drawing board.

Every worker on the shipyard's payroll awaited her recommendation. If all went well, future orders would keep Fletcher Industries in business for years. If there was a flaw, her father trusted Miranda—his daughter and a trained aeronaut—to report it. Maintaining the reputation of Fletcher Industries was an honor and a grave responsibility.

"I needn't ask you if you're comfortable, Miss Miranda," Captain Higgins said with a grin that took years off his leathery face.

The firm had recently appointed Higgins acting captain. It was a well-earned promotion, but also a reminder that Miranda's older brother, Gideon, had quit the family business, leaving a hole to be filled.

"This ship floats like a cloud," Miranda said, shading her eyes with one hand. "It's like flying on a cushioned sofa."

"Don't get too cocky." Higgins unconsciously smoothed the jacket of his fine new uniform, his fingers lingering over the golden feathers—the symbol of Fletcher Industries—embroidered on the collar and cuffs. "We haven't put the girl through her paces yet. You know the drill."

She did. Higgins had tried to teach the four Fletcher children to crew an airship and fight as fiercely as any aeronaut. She and Gideon had been enthusiastic; Sidonie and Olivia had quickly taken up other pursuits.

Flight was hard work. Back then, Miranda had worked as a simple crew hand with no special privileges. Each night, she'd fallen into bed bruised and exhausted, but grateful. She was her father's daughter, madly in love with the air.

Higgins watched her expression and apparently read her mind. "How is Mr. Fletcher?"

"A little better," she said, a touch too brightly. "He protests at being kept indoors like a hothouse plant."

Higgins laughed at that, no doubt because he knew her plain-spoken sire so well.

"So, when are we testing the equipment?" she asked, changing the subject.

"As soon as we're sure everything else is running." Higgins touched his hat. "With all due respect, Miss Miranda, I'm not taking her over the wall until I'm certain we'll get home safe and sound."

"You'll hear no argument from me on that point."

"Then why not retire to the cabin for now? Rutherford's Imports sent up a tea basket. You should take advantage of it."

Miranda had worn a woolen skirt and jacket rather than her usual flight gear, thinking it better suited her role as a company representative. Without windproof leathers she was cold, and hot tea sounded grand.

Still, she lifted a brow. "I take it Rutherford's is offering a sample basket because they want a provisioning contract for the passenger vessels?"

Higgins gave a slight shrug. "I don't question a free meal. If you'll excuse me, miss."

"Of course, Captain Higgins," Miranda replied. "Carry on."

He left her alone, and she lingered to gaze out at the living map of Londria. It was the largest of the great walled cities, and the only one she'd ever lived in. Streets ran from the Citadel's spire to Londria's perimeter wall like the spokes of a great, irregular wheel. The Tamesis River wove through it like a mirrored serpent, crossing heath and parkland as well as crowded urban sprawl. From such a height, the city was a riot of color and texture, the ceaseless movement of boats and people a complicated dance. Londria was dirty, dangerous, and lovely all at once.

Although now, after monsters had taken her eldest sister, the danger seemed predominant. Londria's perimeter wall, magically enhanced by the Conclave, supposedly kept the Unseen out of the city. To think otherwise—to doubt the mages' power—was treason.

Miranda and Gideon knew the truth. That was why her brother had become an inquiry agent despite their father's wishes —to understand how the enemy penetrated the walls and why it was covered up.

Pain surged through Miranda, cutting off her air as if a fist were squeezing her heart. It had been so hard to admit Sidonie was gone. Swallowing, she pulled away from the memories. She needed a clear head. An airship was no place to become distracted.

Miranda started for the cabin, where the basket from Rutherford's awaited. Tea always improved her mood.

She'd barely taken a step before a running crewman nearly bowled her over. "Begging your pardon, Miss Miranda."

"What's wrong?" she demanded, catching her balance.

He sprinted off without a reply.

"Crewman Yale?" she called.

He was sprinting toward the engines—never a good sign. She strode after him, her skirts billowing around her ankles.

As Miranda neared the engine room, she sensed the problem —both with her ears and from the vibrations pulsing through the deck. The thrum of the half-beam stationary steam engine had changed rhythm. Now it stuttered like a failing heart.

Panic jolted along her nerves. A failing engine was a serious thing. The steam-driven propellers at the fore and aft of the vessel provided the necessary lift. Without them, the ship would go down.

Higgins charged her way like a determined bull. He tried to push past her, but she stepped in his path.

"Captain, please tell me what's happening," she said.

"There's a problem with the throttle valve," he replied, his tone clipped. "Something's gone wrong with the governor, and she's running too hard."

Miranda stepped out of his way, having heard enough. Regulating the flow of steam was essential. Otherwise, things could go wrong in a dozen explosive ways.

Higgins ran down the short flight of stairs into the engine room, already demanding answers from the crew. Miranda shifted from one foot to the other, needing to act. A moment later, she was bolting for the cabin, her fine leather shoes skidding on the deck.

Manners forgotten, she banged through the cabin door. Fortunately, the emergency had emptied it of crew members. Miranda dove for the storage lockers, rummaging for spare gear. Pushing modesty aside, she stripped out of her clothes and pulled on a pair of leather pants, jacket, and safety harness. Then she grabbed a helmet and boots that were almost, but not quite, the right size.

She scrambled back onto the deck. Higgins was returning from below.

"What can I do to help?" she asked.

He did a quick double take when he saw her in uniform, but he understood her intentions at once. She was no longer an observer, but a crew hand he'd trained. He jerked his head toward the mainmast. "Prepare to release the auxiliary sails on my signal."

"Yes, sir."

The order made sense. Slight but strong, Miranda was a fast climber. She sprinted across the deck, barely stopping to adjust the helmet's goggles against the wind. She grabbed the ladder bolted to the mainmast and started upward. A few rungs up she stumbled, the unfamiliar boots tripping her up. Cursing, she regained her balance and forged on, keeping close to the mast to minimize the pull of the wind.

Above her, the balloons floated side by side, each emblazoned with the company's golden feather. The pale, oval forms contained concentrated lifting gas, but not enough to keep the large vessel in the air. The auxiliary sails would help compensate for the faltering propellers, but would they be enough?

Fear made Miranda's chest tight, as if a giant had her in a crushing grip. She cursed long and hard, letting the wind shred the words, and forced herself onward.

It was a bitterly cold climb. She'd found fleece-lined gloves in the pocket of her borrowed jacket, and she was grateful for their protection. The only mercy was that she could see her goal—a round structure surrounding the mast above her. That was the platform where she would manipulate the sails.

She was still yards away when the entire vessel shuddered and the prow dipped in a sickening lurch. She swayed dangerously, one foot dangling in the air. Yelping with alarm, she hauled herself back to safety and gripped hard as the mast bobbed with drunken abandon. Miranda closed her eyes a moment, desperate to shut out the horrible truth.

The vibrating pulse of the engine had stopped.

Cursing again, she broke from her stasis to scramble the last dozen yards to the hatch above. She crawled through it on hands and knees, kicking the trap door shut again before she got to her feet. A waist-high railing encircled the platform, which formed a narrow walkway around the mast. On one side was a metal cupboard as tall as she was, and she immediately pulled open the double doors to reveal two rows of long brass levers. Each was embossed with the name of the sail it governed: *The Devil's Tooth, The Lightning Chaser, The Zephyr's Child.* Two dozen in all.

Miranda pulled the first, feeling the strain in her shoulders as she worked the spring. Then the next and the next, clenching her teeth against the strain until every lever was down. Then she leaned over the platform's rail, shading her eyes against the sun as she searched for Captain Higgins.

His whistle shrilled before she spotted him on the deck below. Two sharp, short bursts followed by a long trill. She spun and slammed the plate-sized starter button with all her weight. There was a *ca-chunk* from somewhere high up and chains began rattling over gears hidden in the rigging above.

"Ha!" Miranda crowed, slumping against the rail to catch her breath.

Spars sprang from the deck and masts, telescoping outward at astonishing speed. Massive brass casings sprang open to unfurl the sails with clockwork precision, spinning wheels and ropes hauling the sails into place with a deafening clatter. Then, the indigo canvas billowed and roared as the wind caught it, surrounding the vessel in thunder. In one enormous crash, the long brass levers Miranda had pulled snapped back into their starting positions, locking the sails into place.

The ship weaved with the sudden pull of the wind. Miranda grabbed hard at her perch, falling to one knee. Why was no one steering? Then she remembered the mechanical system that governed these sails, like the propellers, operated on steam. Her efforts had bought them time to attempt repairs, but they were still adrift.

And if they couldn't repair the engine? Their odds were dismal. Tears of fright pricked her eyes.

Then, a bit at a time, the nose of the ship lifted. Barely believing it, she got to her feet again. The tension in her chest eased, but an unmistakable crackle of magic slid over her skin, raising every hair. That sensation meant they'd just crossed the limit of the Conclave's protective spells—the ones meant to keep monsters out of the city.

She stared as the great stone blocks of Londria's perimeter wall slid beneath them. Beyond lay the Outlands, the vast forest of her nightmares. Gideon had taken rescue parties over the wall to find stranded travelers, but many were nothing but gnawed bones when—or if—he located them.

In the far distance, a pair of wild dragons sported over the trees. They might charge an airship, but they were far from the most dangerous creatures out there.

And then she looked down. The Unseen—a dozen, and then more—lurched from the trees. They wavered as the ship's shadow crossed their upturned faces, then sprang into a frenzied pursuit.

They were tiny from where she perched in the clouds, but unmistakable by their crooked, shuffling gait. These were the mindless ones, the flesh-eaters who swarmed their living victims like carnivorous fish. She'd fought them before, but only when she could pick the time and place.

Now she was a rabbit dangling above the wolves. Even with the sails, the ship's altitude would eventually decay.

Miranda's heart pounded as the vessel drifted onward, helpless in the grip of the wind.

CHAPTER 4

$\mathcal{A}$ shout snapped Miranda from her horrified trance. Earsplitting clangs resounded from the engine, followed by a groan of gears. Someone roared a curse.

She'd done what she could up here in the rigging. It was time to join the others—perhaps the trio of crew hands heading for the weapons lockers. She hooked the carabiner on her safety harness to one of the lines and braced for a fast descent to the deck.

The engine belched a plume of steam, and the ship reeled. Miranda grabbed the line for support. Then the ship rolled to port, tilting almost flat. Miranda tumbled like a discarded toy, her legs kicking as she fell from the platform into empty sky. She grunted as the safety line pulled tight, dangling for an agonizing moment before gravity sent her plummeting.

With the instinct of long training, she flipped so her feet could catch her when she reached the deck. Wind pummeled her face as she streamed downward. Higgins was directly below her, shouting orders at the crew distributing aether rifles. Then the ship gave another sickening dip, and he stumbled, catching his balance only to slide across the tilting deck. His arms flailed, but there was nothing to grab.

Miranda's heart jumped as the captain snatched at the gunwale only to lurch over it, feet dangling above the deck as his hat sailed into the sky. For a sickening instant, he seemed balanced on his midsection, only a fluke of physics holding him in place.

Airmen lunged toward Higgins, but his long slide had taken him beyond their reach. Miranda had no time to think. She thumbed the release of the safety harness, feeling the click of gears through her gloves. Timing was everything—wind, speed, and the angle of the deck coming together as she dropped. It was a longer fall than she liked. Impact jarred her hips and knees as she landed in a crouch just yards from the captain.

She sprang up just in time to grasp the back of his coat, using all her weight to haul him to safety. The cloth tore just as Crewman Yale skidded up beside her to grab the captain's arm. The ship coughed and shuddered, the engines coming back to life with a snarl. Chains clanked as the gears that worked the sails began to spin. High above, a cable snapped with the sudden force.

With no more warning than that, the deck heaved to an upright position. Miranda and Yale collided as Higgins tumbled backward. They all landed in a heap.

The crew cheered, whistling and banging their wrenches against the steel pipes. Miranda lay still for a moment, her cheek pressed against the boards of the deck. The blessed vibration of the engine thrummed through her bones like a mother's heartbeat. She sucked in a long breath, unsure if she were about to weep or burst into laughter.

Then she rolled onto her back and let Yale pull her to her feet. He was grinning, but instantly sobered. Miranda glanced from Yale to Higgins, and her own mood sank. The captain was scowling.

"You are reckless, Crewman Fletcher," he said, loud enough for all to hear. "What is the protocol for releasing a safety harness during a flight emergency?"

Miranda's mouth went painfully dry. To Higgins, safety came before anything else, even the fact that she'd saved his life. "Don't do it, sir, unless both feet are on firm decking."

"Correct. And what would have happened if you'd miscalculated your landing?"

She fought the urge to hang her head. "I would have gone over the side, sir."

"And if you'd lived, you would have joined me for dinner with the monsters." Higgins gave her shoulder a gentle squeeze. "Just because you can do something does not mean you should risk it, lass. As your father's proxy on this flight, your safety is paramount."

With that, he strode toward the engine room. Yale followed after, but not before he'd given her a sympathetic wink.

Miranda turned away, avoiding the eyes of the other crew members. Some were congratulatory, others resentful because they were not the ones who would be the toast of the night's revelry.

She didn't care about the glory. She cared about her friends—and the danger still to come.

The ship was rising, but it remained on the wrong side of the wall. The Unseen ran in a pack beneath them, trying to keep up while the ship gathered speed. The howling leader made an impressive leap, snatching at the ship's shadow as if he could use it to reel them to the earth.

In her mind's eye, she imagined her sister falling as the creatures swarmed over her like rabid dogs. They'd beaten Gideon senseless, but left him to die. Sidonie had been the sweeter prize.

A familiar rage swelled inside Miranda, threatening to push and push until she could no longer breathe. She turned her back on the Unseen, forcing herself to focus. Every time she thought she'd recovered from Sidonie's loss, cold fury rose like an undersea monster breaching the waves.

Higgins was returning to where she stood, wiping his hands on a greasy rag. From his expression, something new was troubling him. At least the safety lecture was over.

"The engine will hold until we make it home," he announced.

"What happened?"

His bushy gray brows drew together. "A number of rivets failed."

Miranda frowned. "A number? Was there a quality issue?"

"No." His lips pressed together, as if reluctant to speak the next words. "We inspected the ship two hours before flight time. I personally checked the engine. The damage occurred between my inspection and our launch."

Miranda's stomach dropped. "Sabotage?"

"The metal was sheared through by a tool. An aether knife, by the look of it."

Miranda stilled, the anger still swirling inside her finding a new target. "Why?"

Fletcher Industries had rivals—every successful company did —but none were killers. At least, that's what she'd believed until this moment.

Higgins studied her. "I don't know, but for now we must return to the airfield."

"Is that what our saboteur wants?"

He straightened, unconsciously fingering the new captain's badge embroidered on his collar. "It's plain whoever harmed the ship meant the test flight to fail."

She forced a grim smile. "It will if we scamper home like frightened kittens. We'll lose the chance at good investors and employment for the workers."

"Safety comes first."

Miranda nodded, too angry to speak. She hadn't meant to question the captain's authority, but some truths had to be spoken out loud.

The line of his jaw hardened as he drew a watch from his waistcoat pocket. A brass key dangled from the fob, flashing in the sunlight. "Then again, no one has touched our new equipment. It's locked up, and I have the only access. It would be a shame not to see what it can do."

"Are you suggesting that we proceed as planned, Captain Higgins?"

"Five minutes. I won't risk more." His tone brooked no argument. "One pass with the weapon will say more than any written report."

Miranda didn't argue, glad he'd agreed to risk this much.

The ship had turned and was following a course along the outside of the city wall. There was just enough time to make ready before the ship's path took them past the twin watchtowers of Londria's gatehouse. The monstrous structure spanned the width of the river. Great brass doors rose the height of the city's enchanted wall, shut forever against the Outlands and its monsters.

On the *Leopard*'s main deck, the captain unlocked a massive iron-bound chest with the key on his watch chain. Six tall crew members had gathered, each hefting a small iron cannon and fixing it to a mount already bolted to the deck. Three were positioned amidships on either side, balancing the weight. Segmented brass tubing connected each cannon to a canister the size of a bass drum. The concentrated substance inside was indispensable to the trial's success.

Despite his earlier confidence, Higgins examined each piece of equipment while Miranda watched from the sidelines. She wasn't trained for this drill, and this was no time to get underfoot.

The ship's course had steadied, remaining outside and parallel to the city wall. Soldiers paced atop the watchtowers, small enough from this distance that they looked like game pieces on a board. They were just the right audience for what the crew of the *Leopard* meant to do.

As the ship neared the wall, magic prickled over Miranda's skin once more—evidence of the spells meant to lock the Unseen outside the city. The barrier reached to the sky above and deep into the soil beneath, fueled by the mages of the Citadel.

Despite this protection, previous generations had cut down a wide swath of brush between the wall and the forest, exposing anything that tried to creep close. Soldiers on watch preferred a clear line of sight on their targets—and no trees thrusting limbs over the wall, just in case the monsters could climb.

The problem was maintaining that open ground. It meant sending workers into danger to cut down fresh growth. Understandably, few volunteered.

Fletcher Industries had the answer to that problem, and in moments, the *Leopard* would be above the open ground before the watchtowers.

"Ready the fire pods," Higgins bellowed.

A pack of Unseen still followed the ship like hopeful dogs beneath the dinner table. Three of the cannons pointed their way. The rest aimed at the edge of the forest, where saplings encroached on open ground. Crewman Yale flipped a switch on the canister. It grumbled, releasing a plume of smoke.

They were near the gates now, where the square watch towers rose almost level with the ship. As on every sunny afternoon, visitors crowded the very top of the towers. A few waved. Miranda waved back. The towers were as close as most would ever get to the Outlands.

"Take aim!" Higgins ordered.

The river lay ahead. They only had a few seconds to strike before there would be only water below.

"Fire!"

With a strange grinding noise, the brass tubes jerked, and the cannons belched a bright liquid flame at the ground below. Spectators roared with amazement. The Unseen shrieked and scattered like rats, wavering in confusion when the shortest route to the woods was ablaze.

Another blast scorched the grass and half the monsters in a span of seconds. The people on the wall—and Miranda—whooped in triumph.

Then she had to turn away from the grisly sight below—ash and bone caught in the act of escape. And yet it was no worse than what the Unseen left of their living victims. Miranda had watched a man die from the bites—an ordinary man walking home in the full light of day.

After today, that would not happen again. A fleet of fire ships on patrol would keep the city truly safe. The *Leopard* would strike a blow big enough to matter.

Miranda's throat cramped with unshed tears. If this had come sooner, Sidonie would be safe. Married. Happy.

"Fire!" Higgins bellowed again.

The cannons belched again, delivering one last blast before the ship sailed over the broad gray serpent of the river. This time, the deck bucked with the force of the volley. Miranda turned toward the canister in time to catch the surprise on the captain's face as Crewman Yale bolted from the engine room.

"Order twenty-one," Yale bellowed over the roar of the guns.

Higgins fell back a step as if slapped, but Yale gave a short, sharp nod. The captain immediately straightened. "Order twenty-one affirmed."

Miranda went numb with fright.

Higgins signaled to the crewman at the pilot's controls. A moment later, the blare of the steam-powered klaxon tore through the air. The sound shattered Miranda's confusion as she spun toward the ship's side, her years of training taking over. She grabbed one of the parachutes from its webbing at the edge of the deck. The order was clear.

She jumped for her life.

CHAPTER 5

*M*iranda leaped, the soles of her boots pushing against the last hope of safety. The drop was immediate, the rush of air pummeling her face. She gasped, fighting for breath even as her vision filled with the expanse of the Tamesis River below. She pulled the parachute's cord, the silk unfurling from her back like wings. The wind caught her like an invisible hand.

Others fell or floated around her in a sudden rain of bodies. Each crew member was no doubt thinking the same thing: *We're on the wrong side of the wall.*

Bollocks.

The engine exploded, flinging shrapnel through the air. A scream rang to her right. Ragged iron kissed her side as a metal shard hurtled past. The force of it flipped her in the air. She glimpsed the ruined vessel—the ship's sails were aflame, the lines dangling empty. The gondola had vanished.

How many dead?

A spreading warmth said she was bleeding hard.

Then she faced down again, the river rushing to meet her.

There were already bodies floating there, red swirling out from their bobbing forms.

Pain screamed along her side.

Splash. Someone landed seconds before her, water fountaining up, drenching Miranda's face. Then there were two more. *Splash. Splash.*

Fire reached the lifting gas in the ship's balloons. A second explosion hammered against her in a wash of heat, fearsome even from that distance. Scraps of burning sail fluttered past like wounded birds. A spike of panic fought past her bewilderment, but there was no time to respond.

Miranda hit the frigid river, the sudden shock blackening the edges of her vision. She gasped and spit, barely remembering to shrug out of the parachute's harness as she tried to tread water.

Huge brass doors loomed atop the bridge ahead. Watchtowers rose on either side. Below the bridge, the iron spikes of a portcullis dove far below the waterline. She'd always known the gate guarded the waterway, but never thought she'd be on the outside desperate to get in.

The only path to safety was to swim through the bars. She knew without looking that the Unseen waited on the riverbanks for those unlucky enough to miss the water—a bloody gift from the heavens.

Drowning wasn't the worst option.

A hand touched her cheek. She surged forward in panic, realizing a moment later it was a corpse with a face burned beyond recognition. More figures bobbed ahead, only a few flailing toward the salvation of the wall.

Miranda kicked, but shivers swept over her. She was cold—so cold—that she could barely draw breath. She tried again, managing one stroke, then two, but the water surrounding her bloomed with blood. She could ignore pain, but not open wounds.

Darkness took her, and she slipped under the surface. Only

the pain in her lungs made her struggle to breathe again. She brushed against another hand. This time, she gripped it, unsure if it belonged to a living man. All at once, that mattered less than floundering alone.

One more ragged breath, and she went under a second time.

The cold soothed the pain in her side, but her lungs refused to fill, even with her head above the waves. All she managed was a strange, rattling wheeze as numbness seeped through her limbs.

Soon the waters would drag her down.

A chunk of the ship's side floated nearby, bobbing drunkenly. With her last strength, she surged toward it and clung on, nails digging into the pitted wood of the planks. Her head sagged, forehead resting on her arm. The world darkened with seductive exhaustion.

Awareness was fading when the wild, sweet note of a horn soared over the scene, incongruous in its beauty. Miranda lifted her head to scan the water, wondering what the signal meant. Then narrow black boats slipped between the bars of the river gate—ten, twelve, more fanning out from shore to shore among the wreck's debris.

They belonged to nomadic tribes the city dwellers called River Rats. Elegant, fleet crafts, they barely fit two rowers seated side by side, but each boat was forty feet long, curving upward at prow and stern. The crafts flitted over the waves, two or three pairs of paddlers to a boat.

The newcomers were pulling the living from the water. Miranda cried out, her voice cracking with the cold. She dared not loosen her grip on her makeshift raft to wave. Would they see her?

GIDEON.

Come at once. Your assistance is required.

Olivia.

The note, neatly penned on heavy cream paper and sealed with green wax, arrived at Gideon's rooms as the streets were growing dark. The sender disturbed him as much as the message. Olivia, his bookish middle sister, never asked for help. He left at once, foreboding wrapping him like a cloak.

He hopped from the hansom cab before Allington House, his family's grand abode in Londria's fashionable district. He preferred walking, but he'd taken the cab for speed—and out of consideration for last night's injuries. He'd changed the dressing on his hand, but the rest of him still felt black and blue.

Rather than approach the front door, he went around to the back, where deliveries came. This way, he could slip inside, speak to Olivia, and leave without encountering his father. Any meeting between them ended in a shouting match.

His father wanted him at home, head down, and out of trouble. Gideon wanted answers, and for that he had to defy the Conclave.

He paused as the quiet shadows of the street engulfed him. He hadn't expected the sudden pull of this old, familiar place. He caught the lingering scent of the butler's pipe—Jeffries thought no one knew he came out here to smoke. Beneath that was the smell of the potted herbs the cook kept outside the kitchen door. Everything spoke of home, but this wasn't his anymore. He'd left so it could remain undisturbed, safe, and quiet.

He couldn't investigate without endangering the family and its business, so a very public split between father and son had seemed the safest option. Then no one else could be blamed for his actions.

This stolen visit was all he could risk.

He slid inside and ascended the stairs to the main floor, avoiding the servants clearing the last remains of the evening meal.

Gideon paused at the door to the drawing room and turned

the handle as quietly as he could. He pushed it open to glimpse firelight, candles, and elegant fruitwood furniture upholstered in topaz brocade. As he'd expected, Olivia was waiting, a book open in her lap. She wore a simple burgundy gown, her dark-honey hair pinned up in a crown of braids. The style made her look older than her twenty-three years.

He entered, closing the door behind him. Her chin jerked up, and she shoved the book aside, as if weary of pretending to read.

"What took you so long?" she demanded.

Gideon frowned. "I came as soon as I received your note."

"That was hours ago," she said darkly.

"That was twenty minutes ago."

She looked at the mantel clock and swore softly. "I'm sorry."

"What's happened?"

Olivia jumped up, flinging her arms around his neck. "Everything. Thank you for coming."

He hugged his sister, realizing he'd missed her far more than he'd thought. Olivia was the least like him in character, but that's what made her necessary. They balanced each other out.

"You heard about the *Leopard*?" she asked, pulling away to pace to the window and back.

"What about it?"

She cast him a sharp look. "Didn't you hear what happened? It's all over town."

Gideon had stayed at home all day, nursing his wounds—but he wasn't about to admit it. "I've been busy."

Olivia glanced at his bandaged hand. "Apparently."

His temper rose at the barb in her tone, but he fought it down. He wasn't here to fence with her. "Very well, then, what happened?"

"The *Leopard* went down."

A long silence followed, filled only by the ticking clock and the rustle of coal shifting in the grate.

Gideon's gut turned to ice. "Tell me."

"It was recently refitted to show off some new toy. There's money involved, but I didn't pay attention to the particulars. This flight was a trial of the new technology—which obviously failed."

"What do you mean?"

Her mouth worked for a moment, betraying the emotion she refused to show. "The ship blew up outside the river gate."

That was Olivia—brief and blunt. Stunned, Gideon sank into a chair, not sure his legs would hold him. His mouth felt stiff, as if his entire face had frozen in shock. "Who was aboard?"

Olivia sat on the matching divan, close enough to reach across and touch his knee. "Higgins captained the flight. Father was too sick to go, so Miranda went in his stead."

Gideon blinked, struggling to understand her words. "What?"

"Higgins and Miranda survived, if barely." She held up a palm to silence his questions. "The River Rats rescued a dozen survivors. They were the only ones willing to venture beyond the gate."

As expert smugglers, few could match the Rats' skill on the water.

"Unseen?"

"Hovering like ravenous crows."

An involuntary shudder rippled through Gideon. "How is Miranda?"

Olivia heaved a frustrated breath. "Asleep. She'll recover."

Gideon sagged with relief. "Thank the gods."

Her smile was brief. "That's easy for you to say. With Father and now Miranda, I have two patients. You know how I adore playing nursemaid."

"And yet you're good at it."

She raised a brow. "I can love my family and still hate the necessity."

"Is Father any better?" he asked.

"No. He's lost his two eldest children and nearly lost a third today." Olivia narrowed her eyes. "I'm his last best hope."

Gideon made a face. "I'm still here, whatever he thinks."

"Refusing to take up your role in the business," she retorted.

Annoyed, Gideon rose to prowl the room, picking up objects and setting them down. A menagerie of carved animals paraded across the top of one bookshelf. Sidonie had made them for Miranda. He couldn't bring himself to touch those, as if afraid of disturbing the ghost of his twin.

He turned to glower at Olivia, who was still talking.

"Now with both Father and Miranda ill or injured, and you gone, and Sidonie...*gone*," she continued, "I'm responsible for keeping the business running through this crisis. I don't want the responsibility for account books and fuel statistics. Why don't you come home?"

Gideon frowned. "You're the one with degrees in mathematics and physics. You inherited Father's talent for engineering. I can barely grasp how the ships actually float."

She gave a slight shrug and looked away. "Practical applications bore me. I actually had to converse with a tea merchant the other day. A tedious man on a tedious errand. Abstract theory makes better use of my mental powers."

Gideon bit back a retort. "You asked me to come. Is there something I can help you with?"

She played with the fabric of her skirt, nervously twisting it between finger and thumb. "I've heard you're playing detective."

He bristled. "I'm doing more than playing."

Olivia met his eyes, her expression grave. "Something went wrong on that ship."

"That requires an engineer's report, not a criminal investigation."

"No," said a voice from the doorway. "It was criminal."

Gideon stared. "Good God, Miranda."

His youngest sister wore a blue silk dressing gown that should have been flattering. Instead, the color heightened the bruises along her cheek and jaw. She was smaller than Olivia, brown-haired and fine-boned. From the way she moved, she'd taken a serious blow to her ribs.

"What are you doing out of bed?" Olivia demanded, brow furrowed in concern.

"I heard voices." She slouched against the door frame as if it alone held her upright. "I thought there might be news."

Gideon took a step forward, but Olivia beat him to their sister's side.

"Is there any word about the others? The captain?" Miranda asked as Olivia eased her onto the divan.

"Nothing new," Olivia replied.

Miranda's face fell, but she clasped Gideon's good hand, drawing him down beside her. "I'm glad you're here."

"What do you mean that there was criminal involvement?" he asked, resuming his seat. "What happened?"

Miranda closed her eyes, obviously riding out a wave of pain. "Someone sabotaged the engine."

"As I said, there is a lot of money at stake," Olivia added, forgetting her earlier disinterest.

Gideon nodded. He knew how the airship industry worked. "I'll discover who was behind this outrage."

He kept his voice reassuring, but his hands shook with anger. He'd flown on his father's ships, led those crew, and called them friends. He'd served with Higgins a thousand times. Whoever struck at them, struck at Fletcher blood. His father. Miranda.

Fury swept through him, shattering in its intensity.

"It was better that I went through this than Father," Miranda said. "I joined the crew so he could rest. I felt a little guilty because it was such a simple task. Perfect weather, short distance, barely anything to do. There was even a tea basket. Now I'm very glad it was me on board."

His grip tightened around her hand. She opened her eyes to meet his gaze. Terror had left a shadow in her eyes. He could almost sense it, as if fear traveled through their touch.

Her gaze flicked to his bandaged hand. "You're hurt, too."

"It's nothing."

Her lips curved down at the lie, but she let it go. "Be careful. Whoever did this to the *Leopard* knew what kind of damage they'd cause. They knew there would be crew."

They weren't afraid to kill. "I realize that."

She shifted against the pillows, pulling herself straighter. "I'm serious. Higgins checked the engine. So did Yale. The equipment was under lock and key. Whoever did this was careful."

"You mean the window of opportunity had to be small?" he asked.

Miranda nodded.

"Was the saboteur on board?" Olivia murmured.

"One of the crew?" Gideon asked, incredulous. "No airman would do that. Not unless they were utterly suicidal."

Olivia gave a delicate shrug. "We've seen our share of unlikely horrors."

"I'll start with likely facts." He'd do a proper job of investigation, using everything he'd learned from Detective Inspector Palmer. He'd start by checking names. Someone had been at the airfield besides the crew the morning the *Leopard* took flight.

"Who would do this to us? To anyone?" Miranda asked, mirroring his thoughts. "What sort of enemies does this family have?"

Olivia gave a short, sharp laugh. "Secrets and gossip were Sidonie's strength. Of any of us, she was the one who'd know."

CHAPTER 6

"She's doing it again. Sidonie. Make her stop."

At the sound of Margaret's voice, Sidonie jerked from a stupefied doze. A wave of resentment tightened her shoulders. She hadn't had real sleep in—she had no idea how long. She simply passed out from time to time, too exhausted to carry on.

"Sidonie!" Margaret called from the other cell. "Did you hear me? She's started again."

"I know," Sidonie moaned. "I know. There's no need to point it out."

She pressed her palms to her eyelids. Oh, the dreamless, black velvet of sleep. She'd almost had that sweet oblivion, but Margaret had chased it away. She forced her temper down, hating the sick feeling her anger left behind. *I'm not a spiteful person.*

"She has to stop."

"Damn you, what makes you think I can do anything about it?"

The offender was the third prisoner—the nameless woman who had been in the cells before Margaret had arrived, and

Margaret had been there long before Sidonie. The woman never spoke a word—but they knew the sound of her screams.

As Margaret said, she was at it again—wordless shouts of agony and terror with barely a breath in between. Sidonie forced her eyes open, wondering why that was easier to doze through than Margaret's angry complaints. Maybe the cries were just too familiar now.

Each one began as a low, muttering whimper, like a dog in pain, and ended in a piercing crescendo. During her first days of captivity, Sidonie had been horrified by the woman's obvious distress. But there was nothing she could do to ease that pain, and only so much anguish she could withstand. Eventually, her own need to survive had dulled her senses. Otherwise, her heart and nerves would have broken.

Now she critiqued them the way she might a soprano's aria. Tonight promised a good performance.

"I can't stand it anymore." Margaret's voice dropped to a snarl that raised the hair on Sidonie's arms. "I'd strangle her if I got the chance."

Was that exaggeration? Hard to say. They were all going a little mad.

Slowly, Sidonie got to her feet, shaking out her stiff limbs. The sound rattled the shackle around her ankle, making her wince. Days or maybe weeks ago, the skin beneath the iron cuff had rubbed raw. She'd lost any sense of how long she'd been here.

Another scream ripped through the air, rousing an animalistic sense of peril. She clenched her jaw, biting down on the impulse to howl back.

She'd never seen the screamer—she had no line of sight into the woman's cell, which was somewhere to her right. The prison reminded her of a stable, with two rows of stalls divided by a narrow aisle. From what she could see, the cells had vertical bars facing the inside but no windows to the outside. Her cell had a bucket, a blanket, and straw covering the dirt floor.

Margaret was across the way and down a space, so they could glimpse each other at an angle if they both stood near the aisle. The sight of another human face—however slight—was the only comfort they had against choking fear.

Margaret struck the bars, making them rattle. "I can't stand it. I can't stand the noise. It's making us sick."

"Please, try to be calm." Sidonie strove to put sympathy in her tone, but wasn't entirely successful. They'd had this conversation many times.

Margaret didn't seem to notice, raising her voice to be heard above the cries. "I'm sick. I lost another tooth. I don't even know how many that makes."

"I'm sorry. Does it hurt?"

"What?" *Scream.* "What did you say?"

"Does it hurt?" Sidonie shouted.

"Of course it does. We're sick. Why is this happening to us?"

They had no answers, and there wasn't anything they could do. Escape—even if they managed it—wouldn't last long. This was the Unseen encampment, buried somewhere in the Outlands beyond Londria's walls. Sidonie had never been outside the city, not even on one of her father's airships. She had never been adventurous like Miranda.

The Outlands was a realm of bogeymen and ancient ruins. Monsters had driven humans from the countryside centuries ago, mostly by eating them alive. The survivors cowered in walled cities, moving between settlements by dirigible or riverboat. Only those with a death wish went by land.

A fugitive prisoner would be nothing but tasty sport. They were safer behind bars, like birds too feeble to fly.

Sounds came from outside—footfalls, a branch cracking, something heavy dragging across the ground. She smelled smoke from a campfire. At a wild guess, there might be forty or fifty individuals in the village—if that is what the Unseen called their habitation. Until now, she'd never thought about how they lived, much less imagined whole settlements hid beneath the lush canopy of forest trees. Most likely, they had built on the ruins of deserted human towns. At least, this prison was built on old stone foundations. Sidonie had uncovered them as she'd scraped away the dirt to see if she could dig her way out.

The screaming hit a lull.

"Why are they keeping us?" Margaret went on, her tone acid. "Are we their dinner?"

Sidonie leaned against the bars. "There are only three of us. They don't have much of a larder if that's the case."

Her friend's laugh was a sob. "That's not funny."

"It is. A little bit."

"I wish I could sleep."

"I know."

Scream. Ah, the woman had found her breath again.

"I can't remember the last time I closed my eyes for more than a minute," Margaret murmured. "Days? Weeks?"

"I know."

Scream.

They never glimpsed the outdoors unless someone opened the main door to the prison, so it was impossible to tell if it was day or night. To make matters worse, every cell was hung with a strange lantern that gave off a blinding blue-white radiance that made it all but impossible to sleep. That and the constant, constant fear.

Was the light a form of torture? Were the Unseen—flesh-eating beasts of the Outlands—subtle enough to enjoy slow pain?

"Why do you think we're here?" Margaret asked again, her voice almost child-like.

"I don't know, my dear. Don't think about it. Think about home."

"I miss Huntley. He was the best of husbands."

Sidonie said nothing. She'd met the couple a few times in this drawing room or that. Huntley was rich, but that hadn't kept his beloved wife safe anymore than Norton Fletcher's airship fortune had saved his daughter on the night of her engagement ball.

Sidonie was still wearing the same dress she'd danced in, made from layers of cream and white satin. Tiny crystals in the embroidery had glittered in the ballroom's chandeliers. Once, the overskirt had looped to her bustle in a cloud of Gallic lace. Now the whole thing was a muddy, tattered wreck.

Why am I worrying about a dress? She'd lost so much more—Richard Wilcox, the brilliant, gentle doctor she'd promised to marry; her beloved father; her two younger sisters; and, Gideon, her twin. *I'm worrying about the dress because it's the only loss that's remotely bearable.*

She'd cried at first—wept until her eyes would barely open. And then she understood the truth—she'd lost her life that night. She just hadn't died yet. After that revelation, grief fell away like the shreds of her betrothal gown. She was in a kind of defiant trance, shocked past ordinary emotion.

"This isn't even the stuff of nightmares," Sidonie murmured. "We didn't have that much imagination when we were dancing and drinking lemonade."

Margaret remained silent. Maybe she hadn't heard over the racket. Sidonie studied her friend between the bars of the cell. The harsh light wasn't doing the woman any favors. Her dark-brown hair appeared bleached by it, like a watercolor fading in bright sun. Plus, even from this distance, it was plain her eyes and cheeks were sinking into hollows. They were losing weight fast. The Unseen brought food, but who wanted to eat anything served by creatures who preferred a raw—and hopefully squirming—diet?

Sidonie had no mirror, but suspected she didn't look any better than Margaret did. She was wheat blond and milky pale to begin with. Now she must seem a ghost. Would Richard even recognize her? Would she recognize herself?

Scream. Scream. Scream. The nameless woman was in fine form tonight.

Memories threatened to choke her like a fist, crushing her windpipe. She'd danced with Richard the night of their ball, delirious in their love, drunk on the joy of their new beginning. Then Gideon, her twin, had escorted her home. Halfway home, the carriage had been ambushed. She'd fought and screamed like a fury, but the full measure of her terror had seeped in later when there was time to drown in it.

The fear here was a slow and fatal poison, a relentless despair that wore her down like water dissolving a stone. Her mind, her sanity—everything that made Sidonie herself—was growing paper thin.

The door opened. Sidonie turned toward the sound, relieved by the distraction from her thoughts. There was no additional light, so it was night. She seized on the knowledge, craving the certainty of at least one objective fact.

Her gratitude faltered when Masson entered—tall, slender, and as pale as a moorland fog. He'd called himself king of this place. As always, his chin tilted at an arrogant angle, but this time he walked stiffly, as if he hurt, and one arm was in a sling.

Good, she thought without remorse. He was the one who'd snatched her from the carriage that night. Who was she to argue if someone taught him manners?

He glided to a stop before the screamer's cage, who fell eerily silent at his approach.

"Too much noise," he said, as if admonishing a child.

It still startled her to hear the Unseen speak. His voice was hoarse, but the words were perfectly clear.

"How long?" he asked, shifting so he could look from Margaret to Sidonie. His pale-gray eyes seemed sightless at a distance.

"She began crying out perhaps fifteen minutes ago," Sidonie answered.

He shrugged. "Getting worse."

"Perhaps you should call a doctor." She couldn't quite keep the bite from her tone. Sarcasm was a flaw that came with nerves.

"Does the princess make demands?" His tone dripped with menace.

Sidonie desperately wanted to flee, but there was nowhere to go. Instead, she planted her feet wide, bracing for whatever came.

Abandoning the sick woman, Masson prowled closer. "You'll want maids, too. You look ragged, princess. A wounded deer."

He sidled toward her, graceful as a hunting cat, and wrapped one clawed hand around the bars. His features were stark in the blue-white glare of the lanterns. He smelled of blood and the forest.

Sidonie swallowed, refusing to cringe, though her knees shook beneath her ruined skirts. As if tasting her emotion in the air, he leaned in, refusing to break their gaze. Threat hung between them, as well as a strange magnetic pull, as if he were willing her to her knees. Sidonie's pulse thundered in her ears, drowning out the nameless woman's moans. The dark pools of Masson's pupils expanded as he stared, his lips parting to show the tips of his fangs. With a shudder, she realized their breathing had fallen into the same rhythm, as if she were under his spell.

"What do you want from me?" she asked. "Why am I here?"

His lips quirked. "Stay alive and find out."

With sudden energy, he pushed away from Sidonie's cage, making her jump. He strolled toward the door, lips pressing flat as he passed the sick woman. Then, as he reached the doorway, he raised his hand—the one not belonging to the arm in the sling —and snapped his fingers, like a monarch summoning his slaves.

A servant came at once. Usually, the attendant who saw to the prisoners was a tall figure who looked like an older version of Masson. This one was very different.

Sidonie backed to the far corner of her cell. She could almost stand the monsters like Masson, the ones who resembled humans. The other Unseen—those no one mistook for people—made her stomach lurch.

The newcomer didn't walk. It shuffled forward with its back bent nearly double, as if it really wanted to use all four limbs. It held a tray with plates and cups for two, the liquid sloshing as it lurched along. Pale-brown hair grew in random patches on a spotted skull. Its bulbous eyes were cloudy with cataracts, and its lips hung loose before crooked, needle-fine teeth. Something about it reminded her of a deep-sea fish.

According to Gideon, this kind of Unseen had only small traces of human intelligence. They hunted in packs, tearing their victim flesh from bone while their prey was still alive. Airmen who crashed in the Outlands rarely came home.

Yet in a bizarre reversal, here it was, carrying her dinner on a tray. As it passed Masson, he set a hand on the creature's shoulder for a moment, as if it was a youngster just learning its duties. The gesture made her squirm inside, as if she'd seen something perverse.

The creature stopped at her cell first, sniffing like a dog. Masson unlocked the door, and the creature set one battered pewter plate and cup on the straw with exaggerated care. Sidonie watched, fascinated and repulsed by the careful gestures and the mumbling, drooling lips. Eventually, it grunted in satisfaction and backed away, giving a strange little bow.

Sidonie glanced at the food. The water was just water, but the food was revolting. Only the chicken leg held any appeal, and not enough to taste it.

Masson locked the door again, and the pair proceeded to Margaret's cell.

But when the door opened and the creature entered to set down the plate, Margaret gave a bloodcurdling shriek and threw herself to the back of the cell.

The warped creature cowered, spilling the cup as it tried to bow and shrink away at the same time. Margaret broke into sobs, turning her face to the wall.

Unperturbed, Masson locked the cell door again. With one backward glance at Sidonie, he ushered his shuffling charge through the prison door and back into the night.

"Whatever is the matter?" Sidonie asked Margaret.

"D-don't you know who that was?"

"Who?"

But Margaret was crying too hard to make sense. "I knew him."

"Masson?"

"No." Margaret buried her face in her hands.

"You knew that shuffling wreck?"

"The Citadel guards the city," Margaret mumbled into her hands. "The Conclave protects us with its magic. We are safe from the Unseen, forever and ever. Praise be to the Citadel."

Except they weren't safe, prayer or no prayer.

"The Citadel guards the city," she began again. "The Conclave protects us with its magic. We are safe from the Unseen, forever and ever. Praise be to the Citadel."

"What are you trying to say, Margaret?"

She gulped back a sob. "Where do the Unseen come from?"

The question hung in the air like a poisonous gas. Sidonie clenched her fists to stop her hands from shaking.

"They come from the forest," Sidonie replied tartly. "Like badgers."

Like badgers that had language, built prisons, forged shackles, and knew how to dress in the latest of gentlemen's fashions. Margaret had seen and understood something, but Sidonie didn't want to face it yet.

Margaret delivered a savage kick to the tray of food, spraying it against the wall. Then she grabbed the bars with both hands and rattled them savagely. The noise set the sick woman screaming again.

Sidonie curled up on the floor and wrapped her arms around her knees, resting her forehead against the folds of her ruined gown. She shut her eyes as Margaret recited her prayer over and over again.

Time passed—an hour, maybe more. Eventually, thankfully, the sick woman went hoarse.

The door opened again. It had to be the middle of the night, but that meant nothing here. The Unseen were largely nocturnal.

This time, the Caretaker entered. If he had another name, Sidonie had never heard it. Like most of the smart ones, he was tall, lean, and white-haired. He had a long, aquiline face, and while it was hard to guess the ages of the Unseen, he was somewhere in middle age. His exquisite suit would have blended into any drawing room in Londria. At a casual glance, he might have passed for a human.

He didn't enter alone. Two of the bestial Unseen waited by the door as he strode forward, watching him with dog-like devotion. Margaret whimpered, shrinking into the shadows.

He stopped before the screamer's cell. "I understand this one is in considerable pain."

So Masson had sent for aid, even if it was just another monster. "She is," Sidonie answered.

"Unfortunate." Unlike Masson's rasp, the Caretaker's voice was hypnotic, almost silken. He'd obviously worked hard to mimic human speech.

Sidonie found her mouth had gone too dry to speak, but then he didn't seem to demand an answer. Instead, he drew a key from the pocket of his exquisite waistcoat and unlocked the woman's cell door. The angle was wrong for Sidonie to see what happened next, but a moment later he emerged again and gestured to the guards. They came forward, one walking on his knuckles.

A minute later, they bore the screamer—perfectly limp and silent now—from her cell. Sidonie couldn't see much, but one of the woman's arms drooped to trail in the straw as the guards bore her away into the darkness. Was it a funeral procession?

The Caretaker came to her cell next, unlocking the door so he could approach her. She froze, a rabbit before the fox.

"And how are you doing?" he asked in his cultured, beautiful tones.

"What's going to happen to her?" Sidonie asked, too weary to stand up.

The Caretaker lowered himself to one knee, bringing his gaze level with hers. His smile was careful, showing none of his sharp teeth. "She will get what she needs. Do not worry."

"What do you want with us?" she asked.

"Me?"

"The Unseen."

"Ah." A flicker of amusement crossed his features. "We refer to ourselves as the Gentry."

Sidonie frowned, not quite sure if he was making a joke. "Isn't that another name for the fairies?"

He gave a slight shrug. "Fairies aren't always charming creatures with gossamer wings. They are monarchs of air and darkness."

Was this how the Unseen saw themselves? Kings, not monsters? "Are you all Gentry?"

"Ah, not our less fortunate cousins. Those we call Goblins. It's merely a colloquial term, of course, but it's best to differentiate between our kinds."

Sidonie hadn't thought it was possible to dislike the Caretaker more, but she managed it. "You didn't answer my original question."

He rocked back slightly, a pleat between his pale brows. "What do we want? It's hard to know where to begin. After all, you have everything: food, comfortable beds, and fine garments. We languish outside your city, hoping for scraps, but your wall keeps us out."

"We have to protect ourselves," she replied.

"From us?" His silvery eyes glittered, and venom lurked beneath that satin voice. "We are the faces in your mirror, my lady. We are your creation."

Questions flooded her mind, but asking felt extremely unsafe.

The Caretaker snatched one of her hands, moving too fast for her to see. She tried to pull away, but his grip was like iron. Firmly, he turned her hand over to examine the palm and then the back, finishing with a close examination of her nails. They were getting long and ragged. His own, she noticed, were not the unkempt claws she normally saw on the species. He had buffed them to an elegant polish.

He touched her forehead with the back of his fingers. "You have a slight fever. Are you sleeping?"

"No," she replied. "Not with these lights and the screaming."

"That's to be expected."

He was speaking like a family doctor, like her Richard. Her mind veered away, desperately seeking something else to think about.

"Why am I here?" she asked.

He rose to his feet, done with his examination. Frowning, he flicked a piece of straw from the pristine fabric of his pant leg.

"Ask Masson. He chose you. In the meantime, you seem to be well enough, though you should try moving around more."

"There's not far to go."

"There is always somewhere to go for those with imagination."

With that, the Caretaker left the cell and gestured to the open door. Sidonie got to her feet, suddenly aware of how stiff she was.

He watched her with appraising eyes. "You are free to roam as far as you may while I am here. I suggest you take advantage of it."

As he went to look in on Margaret, she tentatively stepped

outside the cell on unsteady legs. It felt strange venturing beyond the bars, even if it was only a few steps. The chain dragged behind her, the heavy links clanking in her wake.

She took a deep breath, intoxicated by the crumb of added liberty—and of the fresh perspective it brought. She could see the screamer's cell now, the door ajar and a rumpled blanket in the straw. Outside, there was a slice of moon and stars. And she had a far better view of Margaret's cell, where the Caretaker was unlocking the door.

Margaret rushed him with a high, keening cry. He reached out, snake-quick, and caught her arm. She spun to a halt, but she had snatched up the thick pewter tray that had held her food. She brandished it, bellowing with rage, and flung it with desperate force. The metal object missed his head, instead sailing upward to smash the glaring light above. The lantern exploded in a shower of thick, glowing liquid.

The Caretaker sprang back with a snarl, landing in a feline crouch. Sidonie shrank away, too, but was already well out of range. It was Margaret who caught the full force of the blue-white fluid that splattered from the lamp.

Wisps of smoke rose as the liquid sizzled against her head and shoulders. With an earsplitting shriek, she lunged forward in a frenzy, windmilling her arms. She rushed toward Sidonie, dragging her chain behind her. Sidonie reached out, thinking to catch Margaret before she injured herself.

She'd utterly misread everything.

Margaret bore her to the ground like a runaway carriage. Sidonie fell backward, bruising her shoulder as she fell across her own shackles—but she barely noticed that. The true danger was the madness in Margaret's eyes—as if the pain and fear and whatever had been in the lamp had driven her over a precipice. Margaret lunged, trying to sink her teeth into Sidonie's arm.

Reflex drove Sidonie's forearm into Margaret's face. It was a clumsy blow—it had been years since she'd been in a fight, even with her siblings. Her body barely remembered the moves.

A surge of panic burned through her like strong liquor. Her head seemed simultaneously clear and blank.

Margaret snarled, the sound chilling and feral. Sidonie writhed, struggling to get free, but Margaret was fumbling for a grip on her throat. Nails scraped skin.

"What are you doing?" Sidonie rasped, prying at Margaret's fingers.

Her friend made a noise, but it wasn't words.

Sidonie bucked, flinging Margaret aside. They rolled, tangling in their chains and straggling skirts, but Margaret pinned her shoulders again, this time using her weight to force the air from Sidonie's lungs.

Pain shot through her ribs, making the edges of her vision go black. She felt the touch of Margaret's lips against her cheek. It was almost a kiss, until teeth scraped her flesh.

Sidonie seized a loop of chain and hooked Margaret's neck from behind, using the momentum to heave her off. The chain dragged them both together, but this time Sidonie wrapped herself around the struggling woman, pulling the chain tight. Margaret clawed, raking at Sidonie's flesh until deep, red stripes covered her arms. The pain and smell of blood infuriated Sidonie. She gave the chain a sudden jerk, and Margaret went limp.

She froze, not understanding what had just happened. Then she crawled backward and pressed against the bars of the nearest cage. Sickness swamped her.

"I—I broke her neck. Didn't I?"

"You stopped her from killing you," the Caretaker replied, almost sounding calm. "Did she bite you?"

"Not hard."

"Never mind. I think you're immune by now."

She drew a shaky breath, not even wanting to know what he

meant. Tremors coursed over her as the aftermath of panic seeped away. "Why did she attack?"

"The substance in the lamp drove her to madness. Contact with bare skin is ill-advised."

Bewildered, she looked around. He stood by the open door of Margaret's cell. Masson was back, too, just inside the prison door. They both studied her with unreadable eyes.

"Why didn't you stop her? Or me?" she demanded.

They didn't answer. *So the light was a torture. Or a poison. But why?*

Did it matter? In the end, she'd been the murderer, not Margaret.

Inexorably, her gaze returned to the woman, seeing her up close for the first time since arriving in this prison. Margaret Huntley had always been slight, but she was gaunt now. Transfixed, Sidonie approached the body, skin prickling with disgust. The woman's fingers were tipped in claws. Her mouth, hanging slack-jawed in death, showed the beginning of fangs where her teeth had fallen out. She even *smelled* wrong.

Sidonie's mind groped at the implications but shied back, refusing to calculate what she saw. What she had done. That a tiny part of her rejoiced in her survival.

Masson strolled forward, a key in his hand. He bent and unlocked the shackle that bound Sidonie's ankle and tossed the cuff aside. She watched without speaking, trying not to flinch as his fingers brushed her stocking.

Masson gripped her chin, tilting her face up to his. "You'll survive, princess."

CHAPTER 7

*M*iranda dreamed she was back in the river, the intense cold clenched around her like a fist. Her only thought, her only hope, was that the River Rats would find her.

Another airman plummeted from the sky, landing almost directly on top of her. He pushed her down, down into the steel-gray river. Stale air bubbled from her lips in a rush as she spun, her limbs tangling with his in a balletic embrace.

One glance said the full force of the blast had killed him. Fair hair floated around the mockery of his ruined face as the water darkened with blood. Horror and suffocation wove together. Gray spots blotted out Miranda's vision as she clawed free of the dead man.

Desperately, she swam toward the light. Pain hit like an ax in her ribs. Not even the freezing water could mask her wounds.

Her head broke the surface. She spit water and took a wheezing gulp of air, more pain burning her side. All around her, the rippling surface of the river reflected the unholy glow of the burning ship, turning it to a lake of fire.

The River Rats had disappeared. They'd paddled past her as she struggled below.

Despair ripped a wail from her throat, shrill as an angry hawk. Hands gripped her from behind. She twisted, certain the dead man had seized her.

Instead, it was the tattooed face of a River Rat, leaning from the side of his boat. They'd slipped up on her, as swift and silent as one of their conjuring tricks. The man grinned, teeth white through his ink-black beard.

"What are you doing in the water, little Scorpion?" He leaned closer, dark eyes intent. "I have a message for you."

MIRANDA JERKED AWAKE, panting and desperately thirsty. Her eyes searched the ceiling of her bedroom, but the after-image of the flame-kissed clouds clung like shadows. She blinked once, twice. What had the River Rat said next?

She couldn't remember.

Or had he spoken at all? The crash, the dead man, and the boats were all real, but she was less certain about the rest. Had he really spoken to her, or was that a dream?

"Miranda?"

She turned her head, pain lancing up her back. Olivia stood in the doorway. Her sister wore a plain, steel-blue day dress, the white of her cuffs and collar pristine. The shadow of the shipwreck vanished, replaced by the practical, everyday world.

Olivia had a way of squashing flights of fancy, and for once Miranda was grateful. Her presence—and last night, Gideon's—was the best medicine she could imagine.

"You're awake," Olivia said with obvious relief. She crossed the room, putting a cool hand to Miranda's cheek. "You're running a fever. No wonder you were talking in your sleep."

"I fell out of a burning airship." Miranda gingerly squirmed into a sitting position as Olivia wrapped a shawl around her, covering the thin fabric of her nightdress. The scent of Olivia's violet cologne enveloped Miranda, comforting and familiar.

Yet the agony of moving left her breathless. The doctor's pain medication had faded.

Olivia poured a glass of water from the bedside decanter and passed it to her. "You are entitled to one fit of complaining. Only one, so use it wisely."

Miranda turned her gaze to the heavens. "You're not the dreadful nurse you pretend to be."

"You say that because you need me. The truth will come out the moment you feel better." Still, Olivia looked pleased.

Miranda didn't stop drinking until the glass was empty. Despite all the river water she'd swallowed, she was horribly thirsty—possibly from loss of blood. "How's Father this morning?"

He'd stayed by Miranda's side until Olivia had forced him to rest for his own good. The illness that had claimed him months ago had lingered, and this latest blow hadn't helped.

"He's still asleep, as he should be," Olivia replied briskly. "On another note, one arrived for you by private courier. Please pause to appreciate my pun."

"It's truly noteworthy."

"Jeffries brought it in to breakfast with the newspapers."

"Who is it from?" Miranda asked.

"The delectable William Kitteridge. I'm uncertain whether he was shocked by your sudden fall from the heavens. Girls will do anything for his attention."

"Nonsense." Miranda felt her face heat.

"There, there, sweeting." Olivia patted the top of her head. "However tempted, I didn't actually read his love note."

She pulled the letter from her pocket and set it on the bedcovers. The pale-gray stationery and scarlet sealing wax was like the man himself—exquisite and understated.

Miranda snatched it up and sank back against the pillow, running a thumb over the fine paper. "This is no love note. He's just a friend."

"A pity. The family could use his fabulous inheritance after losing a ship."

"And the crew," Miranda said, pressing a hand to her temple to ease her headache. "How many were lost?"

"There were twenty-one aboard, counting you." Olivia's voice went cool, as if reciting the solution to a math problem. It was her way of keeping steady. "The boatmen recovered ten wounded and six dead. Another five are unaccounted for."

Miranda's throat closed, her breath suddenly thick and painful. Faces flickered through her mind, but she wasn't ready to ask who had died. "Their poor families."

Olivia was silent long enough that Miranda's eyelids drooped. She was deathly tired and aching all over. Her side throbbed as if a giant had tried to scythe her down.

"I'll send Shore up with a breakfast tray in a little while." Olivia slipped out, silently closing the door.

Miranda's eyes flickered open long enough to take in her white bed curtains and green walls. Then she drowsed again, images from the river creeping back. The gray, chill water. Burning wreckage. The black boats knifing through the waves.

What are you doing in the water, little Scorpion?

Once upon a time, Miranda had drawn the Scorpion card from a River Rat's fortune-telling deck. The image signified a hidden protector, an all but invisible creature with a powerful sting.

It was a role Miranda had grown into, using her skills as an aeronaut and marksman. Like Gideon, she'd hunted the Unseen inside Londria's walls. And, like him, she meant to unravel the truth behind her sister's kidnapping. At first, it had been dangerous but exhilarating, a focus for her anger at Sidonie's death. Though she'd kept her identity a secret, she'd gained some notoriety as the mysterious Scorpion, who hunted monsters by moonlight and kept the city safe. Once, she'd even saved Gideon's life.

Kitteridge had kept her secrets. She'd accepted his help and friendship while keeping her heart out of bounds. While he might have flirted and charmed, he'd never demanded more.

What are you doing in the water, little Scorpion?

I'm swimming as fast as I can.

The River Rat's face drew close, lips moving as he gave her a message. She was asleep before the words took shape.

GIDEON SEARCHED LONDRIA'S RIVERBANK, his breath misting in the cold, damp air. It was mid-afternoon, the sun already dipping behind the taller buildings along the shore. With a soft cry of triumph, he finally saw the weathered sign of a black cockerel above a ramshackle tavern door. He'd thought he'd visited all the seedy haunts along this stretch of water, but apparently Higgins knew a few more.

He approached, wary of the loungers propped against the side of the building. He was all for a good fight, but his hand still throbbed beneath its bandages. Besides, this was a secret meeting. The last thing he needed was a brawl.

He needn't have worried. As he approached the tavern, the only thing moving was the sign creaking on its iron bracket above the entrance. He stepped over the legs of a snoring drunk and pushed through the door. Inside, the sour fog of old beer and sweat made his eyes water, but it was reassuringly noisy.

"Guv'nor," said a familiar voice above the din.

Gideon caught sight of a hand waving above the mob. He bought a mug of red ale and threaded his way through the closely packed tables. Higgins and Yale sat out of sight in the corner furthest from the door. Both appeared to have lost a boxing match with a kraken. Yale's head was swathed in bandages, and a crutch rested next to Higgins' chair.

Regret twisted in Gideon's chest. Higgins had waited years for a captain's jacket, and his first command had literally gone down in flames. One more reason to find the villain responsible.

Gideon took the empty seat opposite Yale. The tall, lanky crewman was just a few years older than Gideon, but his hairline was already in fast retreat. Bruises purpled both his eyes.

"I don't think either of you should be out of bed," Gideon said.

"I'd rather meet here," Higgins said, taking a swallow from his pewter mug. "It's too loud to eavesdrop."

Given that they had to lean in to hear each other, that much was true.

"Plus," Yale added, raising his own drink in salute, "after all that, we deserve a tipple."

"How is Miss Fletcher?" Higgins asked.

"Injured, but she will recover," Gideon replied. "She was among the lucky ones."

The conversation flagged a moment as they all thought of the other aeronauts blown from the sky.

"What happened aboard the *Leopard*?" Gideon finally asked, hoping they could give more details than Miranda.

Higgins set down his mug. "Treachery, boss."

Gideon looked from one man to the other. He wasn't their employer any longer, although he'd been the heir to Fletcher Industries not so long ago. He'd piloted ships. He'd led rescue missions into the Outlands to save stranded travelers. His personal history was woven through the business, whatever his current standing.

"Please explain," he said. "Leave nothing out."

The two looked at each other as if bracing themselves, then gave a nod. Taking turns and interrupting one another, they recounted every moment until the crew tested the prototype of the new weapon. Then the tale broke off, as if neither could bear to say what happened next.

"I should have gone back to the airfield," Higgins said, his face grim. "But the engine was running again, smooth as the gait of a pureblood mare."

"And then I saw the bottom rivets along one panel were melting," Yale said, the words cracking with remembered dread. "Someone had replaced them with an alloy that had a lower melting point. We only had seconds before the steam pressure blew the whole thing apart."

Cold, greasy fear snaked through Gideon's belly as he imagined the scene. Explosions aboard were every aeronaut's terror. His friends—his sister—had been a whisker away from obliteration.

"So let me understand this," he said, leaning closer to be heard over the din. "Not only was the engine tampered with, but it had been tampered with in several ways."

Yale gave a slow nod. "If we found and fixed one problem, there was another waiting to catch us. The bastard that did this understood engines."

"And they were fast," Higgins added. "I gave the *Leopard* a thorough inspection first thing that morning. The mischief happened between the time I left and the crew arrived to make ready for a one o'clock flight. Not much time, given the extent of the damage."

"Was there anyone around who wasn't supposed to be there?" Gideon asked.

"We caught one fellow weeks ago," Higgins said. "But we put on extra guards after that."

Yale finished his beer. "The day of the flight, everyone was checked coming and going from the airfield. If we weren't expecting someone, we turned them away. We're hunting a phantom."

Gideon's mood blackened as the villain took form—clever, talented, methodical, and lucky. They also understood what a wreck could do to a shipbuilder's reputation and future orders. Whoever had done this had targeted Fletcher Industries, their employees, and the families who depended on the money the work brought in.

He needed to think. He signaled for another round.

"Was it an inside job?" he asked after the barmaid refilled their tankards.

Higgins shook his head slowly. "I knew every crew hand there, even your sister. This wasn't one of ours."

Gideon cursed. "Then who do you think rigged the ship to blow? A rival? An unhappy investor?"

Yale's eyes glittered with frustration. "You haven't been gone from the airfield that long. You know the names and faces as well as we do."

Gideon took a long pull of the crisp ale, running possibilities through his mind. Rivalry with the competition was aggressive, but not to the point of murder. "It's the chance details that matter. Who has come and gone? Who owes money? Who lost their position and might want revenge? Any crumb of information is a start."

"And that's why we asked you here," Higgins said. "You know the business. You know how to solve puzzles. I don't like your new choice of occupation, but maybe there's a reason for it."

Both these men had been his teachers, but now they were looking to him for help. He felt a twinge of pride frosted over with rage. "I'll find out who destroyed the *Leopard*."

"We weren't meant to get away," Higgins said grimly, "and it was pure chance the *Leopard* went down over the river."

The conversation stilled as all three digested the captain's words. The killer had left witnesses behind. Clearly, that hadn't been in the plan.

"Listen, boss," Yale clanked his mug down on the table and pointed a long finger at Gideon. "Do us a favor and find the bastard before we're murdered in our beds."

CHAPTER 8

y Dear Miss Fletcher,

I am newly arrived in town for the holidays. Imagine my surprise when the first news I hear is of the Leopard and that you were upon it. My informants tell me you survived and will soon recover. I am greatly relieved to hear it.

Your reputation as an interesting female was secure prior to your participation in a flaming explosion in full view of the entire city. While you are now certain to secure an invitation to every social occasion for the duration of the Season, I implore that you do not repeat this gambit. One spectacular escape speaks of elan. Twice would be vulgar.

I hope to see you as soon as visitors are welcome.

Do be careful.

With sincere amazement,

K.

THE NEXT MORNING, Miranda's maid arrived at her bedside with her morning chocolate and a troubled expression.

"What is it, Shore?" Miranda asked when the young woman shifted nervously from foot to foot.

The maid's lips thinned with tension. "If you please, miss, a black carriage pulled up outside."

Miranda sat up, automatically reaching for the blue silk dressing gown Shore held out for her. Instantly, pain stabbed her side. She tried to hide her grimace, but it still took her a moment to catch her breath.

"Who is here?" Miranda asked once her voice steadied. "Did the carriage have a crest on the door?"

Shore blinked unhappily, her eyes wide beneath a fringe of frizzy curls. "It does, miss. It's from *that place*."

That place. The young woman meant the Citadel, the towering spire that housed the Conclave. While the mages didn't technically rule in Londria, they had more power than the Church or the Prime Minister. And, while the mages protected Londria with their spells, an increasing number questioned who protected Londria from the mages. So far, no one had dared to act on those doubts.

For once, Miranda had a perfect excuse to avoid their visitor. She was still an invalid, battered and bruised by the crash. Still, she wouldn't rest without knowing why a member of the Conclave had darkened their door.

"It's early for anyone to pay a call." Miranda abandoned her cup of chocolate on the bedside table, her appetite fled. "Is Miss Olivia up and about?"

"I'm sorry, miss, but she's gone out. Do you wish me to alert the master?"

"No, my father needs his rest."

Her duty was clear. With an act of will, Miranda threw back the covers and stood up. Cold air made her bare toes curl in protest. "Tell Jeffries to have our visitor wait in the drawing room. Then come back and help me dress."

Miranda rarely lingered over her toilette, but aches and

exhaustion slowed her down. A burning pain shot through her ribs at the slightest pressure, so she donned a loose-fitting tea gown that required no corset. Shore brushed her hair and put it up in a simple twist. Powder dulled the vivid bruises along Miranda's cheek and jaw, but nothing could hide them completely.

"Not my best appearance," she admitted, catching Shore's eye in the mirror.

The maid fixed an ivory comb in Miranda's brown hair. "You've been through a disaster, miss."

"I look the part."

"You're fashionably pale, miss. Like a maiden in a painting. Maybe the one in the river with flowers in her hair."

"Ophelia?" Miranda might have laughed if her side hadn't hurt so much. "I'm much more likely to have punched Hamlet in the nose."

"But you did land in the river."

"True enough, though I doubt I looked as pretty in goggles and flight boots."

A brief vision of the floating carnage made her shudder. She'd been lucky, so lucky. Something—maybe a piece of decking—had clipped her side, cracking ribs and gouging out a strip of flesh. Her wound was long, but thankfully shallow. She'd have a scar, but she'd survive. Still, as she made her way to the drawing room, every muscle yowling in protest, gratitude was an effort.

Pale winter sunlight drenched the drawing room and its yellow brocade furniture. The cheerful effect lifted her spirits, until her gaze fell on their visitor. Councilor Ormond, one of the Conclave's most senior members, wandered from bookshelf to bookshelf, reading the titles of her father's books. Ormond was a heavy-jawed boulder of a man with small, wide-spaced blue eyes that nearly matched the azure color of his senior councilor's robes.

The last time he'd come had been in the autumn, shortly after her sister's disappearance. She remembered his words as if he'd just whispered them in her ear. *Your continued search is upsetting to many. Mourning is expected, but the true business of life must go on.* With that, he'd ordered Detective Inspector Palmer and his men to stop searching for Sidonie.

Now here he was again—another tragedy, another visit.

As she lingered in the doorway, Miranda watched him linger over one shelf near the window, where a herd of toy animals roamed. Sidonie had carved them, year after year, for Miranda's birthday and Christmas presents. They were brightly painted, more comic than beautiful, but they'd come from the heart. The idea of Ormond touching them was unbearable.

That gave Miranda the impetus she needed to face the man. She stepped into the room.

"Welcome, Councilor." She dropped as much of a curtsey as she could manage. "How pleasant to see you."

Ormond bowed over her hand with an ambiguous smile, as if forgiving her polite falsehood. "I understand you were aboard the *Leopard*."

Miranda rose quickly, taken aback by his direct manner. Even men like Ormond usually opened a conversation with a polite preamble about the weather. "Yes, I was."

His gaze swept the length of her lacey cream gown down to her silk slippers. "You seem much recovered."

Miranda wondered what he'd heard of her condition, and from whom. "I'm improving."

To her surprise, he took her free hand, so that he held them both. A frisson ran through her—hot and cold and tingling—that seemed to run through their clasped hands up to her elbows. She tugged to free herself, but he gripped her hard.

Members of the Conclave were mages and the only magic-users who could legally use their power. She could tell he was up to something now, but what? What was he trying to do?

Their eyes met, his challenging. A memory stirred of meeting

Ormond at Sidonie's engagement ball. He'd done something similar then, but not so boldly as this. When Miranda tugged her hands again, he let her go. A smirk curved his lips.

Motion behind Ormond broke the spell. Miranda looked up to see her father shuffling into the room. Norton Fletcher was neatly dressed, but his clothes hung loose on his frame. Miranda silently cursed whichever servant had informed her father of the Conclave's presence. He didn't need another worry.

"Councilor," Fletcher said, his tone affable but his expression wary. "To what do we owe this pleasure?"

"Good day, Mr. Fletcher. Rest assured that the pleasure is entirely mine."

Ormond sank into a wing-backed chair, his blue robes pooling like a miniature lake around him. Fletcher sat beside Miranda on the divan, possessively close. Had her father seen her struggle with the councilor? A flush heated her cheeks. She had no clue what Ormond's gesture had signified, but it left her feeling soiled.

Fletcher's breath rattled as if simply descending the stairs from his rooms had tired him. She laced her arm through his, wishing he'd stayed away and yet grateful for his presence.

"I know it is early in the day, but when your man offered refreshments, I asked for some of your excellent port," Ormond said. "I remember it from the last time I sat in this lovely room."

"Of course." Miranda remembered every detail of that visit—sympathy cards and flowers, and Ormond drinking their wine. *Grief has its season,* he'd said, *but no season lasts forever.*

Pain shot through her jaw, reminding her not to grind her teeth.

Jeffries, the butler, manifested like a summoned djinn with a decanter and a tray of glasses. Conversation shifted to polite inquiries after this person or that. Miranda listened with half an ear, wondering all the while if Ormond had meant to ambush her, or if he had simply seized an opportunity to…do what? All he'd really done was ask after her health. She shivered, earning a sympathetic pat on the wrist from her father.

The councilor held his glass of ruby port to the light, admiring it as if it were an elixir made of gems.

"I'm glad to see you up and about, Fletcher," he said to her father. "I'm less pleased to see your lovely daughter laid low. The work of an aeronaut is dangerous business."

"I've been fully trained," she replied. "In truth, I was one of the fortunate. Many crewmen died."

"So I understand." Ormond frowned. "I understand the *Leopard* was on a test flight. Would you care to explain exactly what it was that you were testing? I know nothing of it."

The annoyance in his tone convinced Miranda he spoke the truth.

"The crew was testing a device that shot a chemical compound from a tank," her father replied. "The compound could be set ablaze."

"Is this a weapon of war?" Ormond asked, eyebrows drawing together in a frown.

"Its purpose is to keep the forest from encroaching on the city wall. If it chars a few Unseen along the way, so much the better." A defiant note edged Fletcher's voice. He'd created the device recently, fueled by the loss of his eldest daughter. He'd made a weapon from his darkest emotions.

Ormond set down his glass. "And what made you think this invention was necessary? The Conclave's magic has protected Londria since the Great Disaster."

"No disrespect was intended," Fletcher replied, his tone quiet but unapologetic. "There is a commercial market for such added security when expanding a section of the wall, opening the gates to a large ship, or gathering timber from the forest."

"We supply mages to assist with such activities," Ormond said, his expression a cool mask.

Miranda winced inwardly, wishing her father was less logical and more diplomatic. The Conclave did provide protection, but often at a price and certainly as a means of monitoring what the citizens of Londria were doing. Providing an alternative to the mages treads on dangerous ground—but it would have paid well. Her father wasn't the only one craving independence from the Conclave and their iron control.

But now Ormond knew Fletcher Industries had pushed the boundaries of obedience, and that trial had ended in fire and death. There was no fabulous achievement to excuse their actions.

"I wish I knew what went wrong with the *Leopard*," she said, carefully keeping the panic from her voice. "Nothing should have failed. Our safety and security protocols were beyond reproach."

Ormond gave her a curious look. "Have you considered magical interference?"

CHAPTER 9

The councilor's question caught Miranda off guard. "Magical interference from whom?"

He shrugged. "An enemy, I would assume. One with great skill."

She paused, considering. "Is magical interference on that scale even possible? The *Leopard* was a large ship and sailing at high altitude."

She realized it was the wrong question the moment she said it. On one hand, Ormond would never admit such an act was beyond the Conclave's powers. On the other, he'd never confess if they had done it. He certainly hadn't offered to find the saboteur. That alone was telling—but of what?

His only reply was a shrug. "My advice would be for Fletcher Industries to cut its losses."

Norton Fletcher sat forward, the line of his shoulders tight with anger.

"Respectfully, sir, what do you mean?" Miranda asked before her father could speak.

"Return to the passenger vessels you build so beautifully. Leave our battle with the Unseen to those best suited to carry it out. The device you made is clearly too dangerous for use aboard an airship."

Fletcher's sallow cheeks flushed with temper, but Miranda quickly squeezed his arm. The quality of the device was irrelevant. Clearly, the mages weren't about to share the power granted by their monopoly over the city's defenses.

The councilor's gaze slid from Fletcher to Miranda, pinning her with his small blue eyes. "You're a good daughter, my dear. You take after your mother's people. Such a noble bloodline."

Fletcher, born a commoner, said nothing. A smile played on Ormond's lips as an uncomfortable silence settled over the room.

"Look after each other," Ormond said mildly, rising from his seat. "Family is a precious thing. Don't let it slip from your grasp."

That was exactly what Miranda feared, and what she would fight.

After a long moment, Fletcher got to his feet. "We appreciate your concern, Councilor, and always value your sage advice."

Ormond's smile widened. "But of course. And now I should take my leave."

He extended a hand toward Miranda, but Fletcher intercepted it, giving a hearty shake. "I am always pleased to offer the Conclave hospitality."

Ormond accepted the words—true or not—and took his leave. Miranda followed him into the corridor, intending to show their guest to the door. As they neared the front hall, the councilor abruptly stopped, turning to regard her.

"My dear," he began and then hesitated, as if searching for the right words. "Much of what the Conclave does is poorly understood. It is and has always been an instrument of protection against the horrors unleashed by the Great Disaster."

"I know," she replied, mystified as to where the conversation was headed.

Ormond was a head taller, so he stooped a little as he lowered his voice. "Keep your father from interfering in matters he can't possibly understand—do it for his sake, and for yours. You may choose not to believe this, but I regard your family with fondness. You care for one another, and that is purer magic than any other in heaven or on earth."

Miranda drew back a step, confused. "I see."

"I'm not sure you do. The next knock on your door will not be from me."

Her mind flashed back to the Conclave's guardsmen pounding on every door, searching for those who used illegal magic. "I remember Captain Hagen."

Sidonie had outwitted the man. That had been lucky, since she'd hired a River Rat named Madam Alma to tell fortunes at their house party that very night. It had been a hair-raising business smuggling the woman to freedom.

"It won't be Hagen, either. The Citadel has other, less mannerly, enforcers." The lines in Ormond's face seemed to deepen. "Don't attract their attention, Miss Fletcher."

With a jolt, Miranda realized he was afraid. It rolled off him like a foul scent. "I understand."

Without another word, Ormond spun on his heel and left, moving faster than seemed possible for such a large man. Miranda waited until his heavy footsteps faded before returning to the drawing room. She immediately poured herself and her father each a large glass of the port.

"That was less than pleasant," Miranda said softly, sitting down beside her father once more. Ormond's warning scrambled around and around in her head like a frantic animal. She glanced at her father, ready to tell him about it, but stopped herself.

He looked far too weary for that conversation.

She chose something trivial to discuss. "What did he mean when he said I was like my mother's people? I don't look like them."

Sidonie was the fair-haired replica of their mother, but

Miranda didn't say it. Even mentioning her sister robbed her father's strength.

Fletcher shook his head, seemingly in a daze. "It is best to forget every word that comes from Ormond's mouth. He thinks we're treading on the Citadel's territory."

"As if only one group of people has the right to protect the city," Miranda retorted. She sipped the port, but it was too sweet for her taste. She set it aside.

In contrast, her father tossed his drink back in a single swallow. For an instant, he seemed the robust captain of the air she remembered. His words, however, erased the effect. "It doesn't matter. The explosion destroyed the *Leopard* and its weapon. That puts an end to the project."

Miranda watched her father's energy fade before her eyes. Some of that was his health, but more was due to his mood. The *Leopard's* destruction had hit hard.

"Don't think of it that way," Miranda protested. "Whatever else happened, the weapon worked perfectly. Your design was successful, and we have the plans. There's another ship—a better one—that's almost ready."

Fletcher gave a dismissive wave. "No one will buy it now. Unfortunately, we need the money."

On the street outside, Ormond's black carriage pulled away, clip-clopping into the distance. Miranda breathed easier.

"Think of all our people," he said dully. "There won't be work for a while. Not like I promised them."

Miranda understood. The sail makers and engineers, and even the company sending tea baskets, needed their business. It would be a while before a project of such scope came along again. All because the Conclave wanted to preserve their exclusive right to protect the city.

Except they weren't protecting the city. She'd seen—and killed—monsters in Londria's streets. Frustration swamped her. She could bow to Ormond's orders if they were fair.

They were anything but.

Miranda steamed ahead. "We don't need to ask a fortune for the new ship to turn a profit. And once word gets out about such a remarkable weapon, more orders will come. People want to feel safe."

"They won't feel safe if the Conclave comes for them," Fletcher said softly. "You remember Joseph Ellery."

The name made Miranda catch her breath. Ellery had been an ordinary banker, but he'd inherited unusual powers. Despite efforts to hide his talent, eventually he'd been found out.

His public trial had taken place on the steps of the Citadel. She remembered the look on his face when he'd been dragged away into the stone belly of the Conclave's headquarters.

Her father was right. Fletcher Industries was literally playing with fire, and she'd heard Ormond's message clearly. She just didn't want to accept it.

Fletcher's expression hardened. "The prototype and refit of the Leopard was expensive. Our cash resources are currently low. We needed buyers to begin with, but the only way we could succeed now is if someone—with far more money and influence than we have—took an interest."

"An investor, you mean?"

He nodded. "Preferably a blue-blooded one. Even the Conclave tiptoes around the royal family. Sadly, people like that choose their battles wisely, and we're not worth that much risk."

"We surrender, then?"

He smiled at the disappointed note in her voice. "We must, however painful that will be. I'd rather see you safe than own all the air fleets in the sky."

"What about the business?"

"We will suffer a loss and perhaps sell some of our working ships. Reduce our passenger flights." He said it lightly, but stiffened as if the words had hurt him. "I will ask Olivia to do the necessary calculations. She's better at cold-hearted math. Forgive me, but I'm going to lie down for a while."

With that, he rose with a groan and cracking of joints and retired to his rooms.

Miranda went to hers in turn, but not to rest her aching ribs. Carefully, painfully, she pulled back the carpet and lifted a floor board to reveal a hiding place. Inside was a sandalwood box and a small, well-thumbed book. She took out the box and opened it, revealing a deck of cards wrapped in silk. Madam Alma, the fortune-telling River Rat, had given her the tarot cards in thanks for helping her escape the Conclave's guards. The book explained the meaning of the cards, but Miranda left it where it was. She had memorized every word by now.

She unwrapped the deck from the silk cloth, well aware she was committing a crime merely by possessing them. She thumbed through the deck until she found the Scorpion, then set the card face up on her dressing table. This was the image she'd adopted as her symbol. The sharp-tailed creature had frightened her at first, but now she relished its defiance—an invisible defender with enough sting to conquer towering evil.

Then she shuffled the deck, using the repetitive motion to calm her nerves. Ormond's visit had disturbed her—that went without saying. But just as unsettling was her rage at the Conclave's presumption. They had no right to tell her father what to do with his business.

Or to threaten them. Or to send Ormond to touch her with his magic that way.

The citizens of Londria deserved whatever protection they could get. The Conclave should welcome the fire ship as a new tool in the fight for survival. There were enough Unseen to keep everyone on their toes.

Her hands shook as she caressed the cards, anger aching like a dagger in her chest. She wasn't like Gideon, who buried his rage in cold logic. Attack those she loved, and the Scorpion would strike back.

One by one, she pulled cards from the deck and arranged them in a triangle around the Scorpion. To the left were the influences to come, to the right the forces that were fading away. At the top was the card about to dominate everything.

The ascending card on the left showed a fierce cat—a leopard—rearing up with claws extended. It was the card of truth, of cutting through illusion, the force that revealed hidden dangers and refused to bow beneath the force of lies.

Leopard Ascending.

Miranda folded her hands, too filled with emotion to continue. Whether or not the cards had genuine power, the coincidence of the big cat's presence shook her. She studied the beast, admiring its white fangs.

No. If the Conclave wanted Fletcher Industries to abandon its weapons, they were hiding something. Despite the danger, it was important to understand the nature of that secret. Lives had already been lost.

She spared a glance at the other two cards. The one to the right—a fading influence—showed a rabbit in its burrow. *Domestic comfort.* The card at the top—the influence about to dominate—showed a butterfly. *Rebirth.*

Rebirth.

The first *Leopard* had burned, but perhaps it could be reborn.

She picked up the card with the cat. It seemed to warm between her fingers, as if the image was alive.

Ormond had warned them. Father had surrendered. Miranda had agreed to nothing. She'd been the one to see flame pour down on the Unseen.

Leopard Ascending was the perfect name for the next weaponized ship. Its mission would be to burn away the Conclave's lies.

CHAPTER 10

Gideon folded Miranda's note and returned it to his pocket. He'd read her account of Ormond's visit three times as his cab clip-clopped through the streets toward the airfield. And each time, the words seemed more sinister.

Fletcher Industries had done their best to keep the prototype a secret until the day of the test flight. One reason had been the Conclave and their possessive attitude toward the city's security. However, from what his sisters said, their father had assumed that the Conclave would have no grounds to object once the prototype was public knowledge. That was why Higgins had tested the weapon in full view of the gate.

But the trial had gone terribly wrong, and the Conclave was displeased—as evidenced by Ormond's warning. If that was not trouble enough, his sister was among the survivors, and might well be targeted as a witness by whoever had sabotaged the ship.

Gideon arrived at the airfield with a fresh sense of urgency, ready to begin his inquiries.

The cab set him down at the iron gate that led into the Fletcher Industries airfield. Normally, there were no guards at the gates during the day, but now a pair of uniformed figures framed the entrance. Someone had given the order to tighten security. Fortunately, they recognized Gideon at once.

"Good day, sir," said the taller of the two, nodding him past.

"Good to see you, Oxford," he replied, before setting off down the long drive that snaked toward the administrative buildings.

The familiar sights and smells of the place sent nostalgia surging through his veins. Ships hung above the vast fields, tethered like giant, ungainly birds. He knew each intimately—the *Dragonfly*, the *Scorpion*, the *Absolute*, and a dozen others. He'd worked on each and captained most. More huddled in enormous hangars, under construction or repair. Every vessel had begun as a sketch on his father's study wall.

There were days when he'd felt like one of those drawings—a plan of the *Gideon* to be built and implemented as part of the company fleet. Fletcher Industries had been his only future until the family had broken apart—Sidonie lost and Gideon walking away. Had that only been months ago?

The workers he saw nodded or waved. If gossip had circulated about his estrangement from his father—and how could it not?—it didn't dim their smiles. He'd been one of them. Until now, he hadn't realized how much he missed that easy camaraderie.

Before long, Yale intercepted him.

"Glad to see you, sir," the aeronaut said, touching his cap. "Ready to investigate?"

"I'll start with the offices." Gideon had learned much from DI Palmer, including the value of a paper trail. Since he knew the workings of the firm so well, it was a natural place to begin.

The brick building was a plain, two-story affair, with the administration offices on one end and the medical personnel at the other. His father's domain was near the front, but one had to run a gauntlet of clerks to reach it.

"None of the office drones are in today," Yale replied. "Handy for privacy, but I don't have a key."

Gideon said nothing, wondering if the locks had been changed after he'd left. Happily, the key he'd kept turned beneath his hand. The door creaked open, and they ventured inside, their boots loud on the wide planks of the floor.

They passed by a row of tidy desks, eventually reaching a door with NORTON FLETCHER etched on a brass plate. Gideon had the key to this door, too. They went inside, Yale automatically removing his cap.

The space was cool and dim. Wishing to remain unobserved by anyone passing the window, Gideon left the curtains shut and lit the lamp on the desk. He could hear distant conversation from the fleet doctor's rooms at the other end of the building. Otherwise, the place was quiet.

"Any word on the injured from the *Leopard*?" Gideon asked Yale.

"Gubbins passed. Too badly hurt." Yale leaned against the door jamb. "Featherly has gone missing."

"Missing?"

"Left his house to test his sprained ankle and never returned."

Gideon sat behind his father's desk, running his hands over the heavy, scarred oak. "I know Featherly, but not well. Was he the type to walk away?"

Some folks did that after an air disaster, as if fear struck so deeply there was no response but to vanish. Others drank or gambled to fight those demons. Still others found prayer.

"Featherly was a family man. He had a wife and wee lad with another child on the way. He had a reason to keep a steady job."

"Have you spoken with his family?"

"Of course. They have no idea where he's gone."

"Then do we assume was it foul play? He was a witness to the events on the ship."

"It's possible, sir. We've spread the word to keep watch for any sign of him."

Gideon nodded, hearing the anxiety in Yale's voice. "Good."

Yale sighed, his long face growing longer, and rose. "I'll leave you to your work."

Uneasy, Gideon added the missing aeronaut to his growing pile of mysteries as he opened the bottom drawer of the old desk. He found a thick, leather-bound journal with the Fletcher Industries feather stamped in gold leaf on the spine. He set it on the blotter. This was where his father kept his daily records.

As he opened the cover, he caught the scent of tobacco and the subtler smell of new paper. He turned to the most recent entry, which was in Miranda's hand. He knew she'd taken over many of their father's duties but had never realized the extent of responsibility she'd assumed. He was impressed and a little chagrined. Miranda was, like him, better suited to action. It would not have been an easy transition for her.

Then again, she'd only made one notation. There were a few blank pages left in the book, but there was nothing for the last few weeks. She would have had little time to sit in this office, managing the clerks and merchants constantly knocking on the office door.

He flipped back several months, hoping to gather information leading up to the *Leopard's* launch. After a half hour of reading about correspondence logs, supply shipments, and taxes in his father's terse prose, he gave up on the journal and went in search of the accounts ledger. He hunted for unfamiliar names, unusual purchases, or companies he'd never heard of before. No one had seen anything out of place the morning before the *Leopard* burned. Therefore, the culprit had gained access to the airfield long before the event.

This absorbed him far longer, since there was more detail to examine. He'd completely lost track of time when Yale returned.

"There's someone here asking for you, sir," the airman announced. "I brought him down from the front gate."

He'd barely finished speaking when Huntley appeared in the doorway, peering over his green-tinted spectacles. His greatcoat was unbuttoned, letting the ends of his long, striped muffler dangle over a paisley waistcoat. His low-crowned top hat tilted at a rakish angle. He looked every inch the gentleman eccentric.

"I've been looking for you," Huntley announced. "The delightful old bookseller who runs the shop below your rooms suggested you might be here."

Gideon had mentioned his destination to Mr. Dobson as he'd left for the day. Next time he'd think twice. "I didn't realize you knew where I lived."

"Layla knows."

Of course she did. All the girls at Hellion House knew his particulars because their proprietress, Gillian Randall, was his friend and occasional lover.

"Very well, what prompts you to find me?" Gideon asked warily.

Yale, who stood behind Huntley, mimed tossing the intruder out. Gideon gave a negative sign, and Yale retreated from the office, leaving them alone.

Huntley flopped onto the chair on the opposite side of the desk, shoving his hands into the pockets of his long coat. "I thought you had left flying ships for the detection business."

"I have." Gideon shut the ledger he had been perusing. "This is an exceptional matter."

The corner of Huntley's mouth quirked up. "The fallen ship?"

Gideon shrugged, admitting nothing.

"I thought the explosion was the result of a malfunction. That's what the newspaper said."

"Fletcher ships do not malfunction."

Huntley's eyes widened with interest. "I see."

Gideon rose, not entirely comfortable with Huntley's presence here. The man was perceptive and persistent. He was also, judging by that night with the Anathema Club, slightly mad.

"Did you come alone or are your club members with you?" Gideon asked.

"Alone. My motley crew have their own projects to pursue."

"Am I yours?"

"For today." Huntley gave a winning smile.

"I was just finishing up," Gideon said, telling the truth. He'd found what he could for the day. "Walk with me and let's find a drink."

Huntley brightened at once. "Capital plan."

Gideon replaced the ledgers on the shelf and herded Huntley outside, locking the door behind him. He waved goodbye to Yale as they set out along the path to the main road. Yale saluted in return.

Gideon pointed out the various ships to Huntley as they walked along the drive to the gate. His visitor listened politely, but clearly had other things on his mind. As soon as they reached the road and were out of earshot of any bystanders, Huntley changed the subject.

"I'd like to answer your question about why I was searching for you," he began. "I recall you are investigating a series of missing persons cases."

"I am."

"Then I may have something of interest to you."

For the first time since Huntley's arrival, Gideon's curiosity outweighed his irritation. "Go on."

Huntley remained silent as they passed the guards at the gate and set off down the street. Gideon pulled on his gloves, suddenly aware of his breath fogging into mist. The afternoon light had lost its warmth and was heading toward an early dusk. He realized he'd spent longer poring over the company books than he'd expected.

"I took a hackney to get here," Huntley said, stopping abruptly.

"So did I," Gideon returned, wondering how that was relevant.

"Well, I told my cabbie to wait," Huntley grumbled, looking up and down the empty street. "I have the sort of tale that goes best with a good meal."

"Never mind," Gideon answered. "We'll find another cab about a quarter mile up the road. They congregate near the taverns."

They set off west with a purposeful stride, passing workshops and brick warehouses. This was a business district, more concerned with function than style. A bicycle rattled by, but there weren't many pedestrians to overhear their words.

"As I was saying," Huntley resumed, "I may have found a puzzle piece for you."

He fished in the pocket of his coat and produced a small object that he dropped into Gideon's hand. Gideon held it up to the wintery light. It was a brass button with an enameled crest—three birds over a blue wiggly line that meant water.

"I recognize the design, but I can't place it," Gideon said, sliding the object into his pocket.

"The university's rowing club," Huntley said. "I pulled it off what remained of a hideous striped waistcoat. Only club members have the dubious honor of wearing those garments."

Gideon cast him a sharp look. "And where was this waistcoat when you removed the button?"

He expected a witty comeback, but something up ahead had caught Huntley's attention. Three dark-coated men were leaning against the recessed doorway of a draper's shop. Two wore top hats, the brims tilted low to hide their faces. The third was folding a newspaper, as if he'd been reading it moments ago. One of them shouted, pointing Gideon's way. Gideon couldn't make out the words, though the tone was ripe with outrage.

The one with the newspaper tossed it into the gutter. Another cracked his knuckles. All three started toward Gideon and Huntley.

"Three on two," Huntley mused. "Not terrible odds. What do you say?"

They exchanged a look and nodded. A jolt of memory rose in Gideon's mind—tall, dark-coated men in the misty cemetery that night his sister had been taken. Their height and the cut of their clothes looked familiar. There was no way to tell if these were the same figures, but icy rage still surged through his blood.

Gideon unbuttoned his coat for a greater range of movement. A glance alone said the street was empty of bystanders. In this neighborhood, the locals knew better than to linger near a fight.

Now that they were closer, Gideon saw the men's dark coats were of an identical old-fashioned cut, double breasted and with a long, full skirt. The tallest man was in the lead. He was well over six feet, a pale figure with a weak chin and drooping mustache.

"What do you want?" Huntley demanded.

"None of your concern," the man replied. "We're here for your friend."

"I'm *concerned*." Huntley leaned on the word. "I'd like a word with your master about your manners."

"Not likely," said the leader. "If you ever meet him, you'll regret the day."

"Who are you?" Gideon asked.

No answer came. The leader was within a few steps now. Gideon held up his hands, palms out. He'd done his fair share of brawling in the streets, but he'd avoid it if he could. He still ached from the fight with Masson.

It was then the third of the dark-coated men, silent until now, rushed Huntley. There was little method in the attack—it was more as if he wanted to trample Huntley to reach Gideon. Huntley flattened the man with a single cross to the jaw.

He hit the ground, top hat rolling into the gutter. As if a starter pistol had fired, the other attackers surged forward. Gideon kicked the leader in the gut, knocking him back. The man sucked in air, then reached under his coat for a weapon.

"Stop this at once!" a voice cried from behind Gideon.

The attackers froze. Gideon didn't turn for several seconds, though he heard the scuff of boot heels behind him. Only when he was sure it was safe, he cast a glance over his shoulder.

The newcomer was a slight man with brown hair swept back from a narrow face, revealing a marked widow's peak. To Gideon's surprise, he wore the navy-blue robes of a junior member of the Conclave's Council.

Gideon recoiled, but the mage raised a hand with quiet authority.

"What is the meaning of this?" the mage asked.

The attacker with the mustache slowly removed his hand from beneath his coat. The youngest of the three helped his fallen comrade to his feet. All three looked sullen.

"Well?" asked the mage.

Mustache awarded Huntley and Gideon a scalding glower. "We were just having a chat."

"What passionate conversationalists you are." The mage folded his blue-robed arms. He was small, half a head shorter than Gideon, but there was no questioning his aura of command. "Begone, all three of you."

The man Huntley had hit picked up his hat, dusting off dirt and dead leaves. His eye was already swelling shut. The three shuffled off with far less swagger than a moment ago. Huntley gave a disappointed growl.

"Are they yours?" Gideon asked the mage.

The man shrugged his narrow shoulders. "The Conclave employs a smattering of civilians on an ad hoc basis. These were not hired for their mental skills."

It wasn't a direct answer, but that was no surprise. The Council was anything but transparent.

"What did they want with me?"

"I don't exactly know," the mage replied, brow furrowed in thought. "I believe they call themselves the Threshers, separating wheat from chaff in human terms. They are loyal to the Conclave."

Gideon immediately recalled Ormond's visit to Miranda. Did the Conclave know he was searching for the saboteur?

Huntley cast the mage a cautious look. "And these Threshers seek out offenders with their fists?"

The mage shrugged again. "Perhaps. That is no reflection on either of you. They are fanatics with their own definition of loyalty."

"And yet employed by the Conclave," Gideon said uncertainly.

"Employed is a strong word. Not all of us approve of the Threshers' presence or their actions." The mage's frown deepened. "They are obedient when ordered, but the remainder of the time they are like feral cats, picking fights and biting ankles. Their attack was not the result of any official instruction."

"I'm glad to hear it," Gideon replied, still doubtful. "And thank you for intervening."

"You are most welcome, Mr. Fletcher." He thrust out a hand to Gideon. "And Mr. Huntley. I am Councilor Latimer."

"You have fortuitous timing," Huntley said as they shook hands.

"Not as miraculous as all that," Latimer replied. "It's not the first time I've caught the Threshers making mischief in far too public places. This is not the first time I've scolded them for a regrettable lack of discipline."

"You're a long way from the Citadel," Gideon commented.

"My duties take me to every corner of the city," Latimer replied. "It's inevitable that there is occasional excitement."

His wry smile was unexpectedly charming. The man had a bookish air that reminded Gideon of a teacher he'd known—one that kept lizards and mice in the schoolroom to keep his students entertained.

Gideon thawed a degree. "You have an interesting definition of excitement."

"Hazard of the job, I'm afraid, and now I must return to the Citadel. Could I trouble you for an escort? I'm not entirely sure our friends won't double back, and I do not trust their mood."

They could hardly refuse. They turned their steps toward the main road. Frost sparkled in the shadows where the old warehouses met the cobbles, dusting the sooty bricks with glitter.

Huntley massaged his knuckles. "That fellow's head was made of rock."

"A fitting assessment," Latimer said, tucking his hands in the sleeves of his robe for warmth. "I will have words with the relevant officials about this incident."

"And you truly have no sense of what they wanted?"

The mage shook his head. "Undoubtedly, they have invented a narrative of their own. There is some grumbling about the wreck of the *Leopard*. A few bright sparks claim it was an attempt to set fire to the city."

"Unbelievable," Huntley grumbled. "If arson was the goal, it wouldn't have exploded over the river."

Gideon glanced back to where the Threshers had disappeared, but there was no sign of the men. He reviewed their faces in his mind, but he hadn't got a good look at all three.

"Oy, there's my cab," Huntley exclaimed, pointing down a side street.

The vehicle was parked a few doors down the road and in front of a tavern. The cabbie leaned against the side of his rig, stuffing the last bite of a meat pie into his mouth. As Huntley stormed toward him, the driver quickly drained his battered pewter tankard.

"I told you to wait for me," Huntley barked.

"Beg your pardon, sir, but I didn't see the harm. I only meant to be gone a tick. Three gents gave me coin for a meal and said you'd be a while. Said they had business with you."

"And you believed them?"

The cabbie made an expressive gesture with his tankard while

Huntley turned crimson. Gideon intervened before matters devolved into a second fight.

They put Latimer in the cab, by then glad to put an end to their escort duty. No one suggested they share the ride.

"Thank you so much, gentlemen," the councilor said as he climbed inside. "Your kindness won't be forgotten."

"Our pleasure," Huntley said, almost convincing Gideon. "It was the least we could do."

Gideon signaled the driver, and the vehicle rattled off, horseshoes loud on the cobbles. Gideon and Huntley walked on to find a cab for themselves.

"That was a strange episode," Huntley mused.

"Have you heard of the Threshers before this?"

"Yes." Huntley rubbed his chin. "But only the barest whisper. They're bully boys all right, but I've never heard they were connected with the mages."

"What do you think that means?"

Huntley shook his head. "I'm not sure. Could be nothing, like Latimer said. Could be someone at the Citadel wants a word with you."

That was what Gideon feared. Would Latimer have stopped them if there had been no chance of witnesses?

They arrived at the Mercury Café after dark. It was the haunt of the demimonde, students, and amateur philosophers. Conversation was lively and loud. Tonight was busy, and the place was filled with the scent of tobacco and coffee.

Gideon was famished. They found an empty table and ordered food and drink. Once the whisky arrived, Gideon brought out the button again. "So, you were telling me where you found this."

"On an Unseen we dispatched last night," Huntley replied. "Apparently, he had a taste for water sports."

After a puzzled moment, Gideon remembered the button bore the crest of the university's rowing team.

"He wore their waistcoat. An ugly striped thing." Huntley leaned forward, peering over the top of his wire-rimmed spectacles. "I understand the Unseen steal clothing, but don't you find that particular garment an odd choice?"

Gideon swallowed a mouthful of Scotch, briefly losing himself in the sweet burn going down. "Maybe it came from one of the young men who…"

He trailed off, recalling the pictures of the missing people on his wall. He reviewed them row by row, each sketch or photograph fixed in his mind. One wore a waistcoat with broad diagonal stripes and brass buttons. The detail on the enamel crest was lost in the image, but the general shape was the same.

"One of the young men who…what?" Huntley prompted, taking a sip from his own drink.

"One of the cases I'm investigating—I mean—one of the missing lads belonged to the rowing team." Gideon's voice gained energy. "His name was George Bagstaff."

"Hm. So is the waistcoat a coincidence?"

Gideon shook his head. "I don't know. If I did, I'd be far down the road toward answers. What happened to the Unseen's body?"

"Went to get help to cart it away for burning, but when we came back, it was gone. More Unseen must have been lurking nearby. They saved us the trouble of disposing of their dead."

A cold prickle ran down Gideon's spine. Huntley had been lucky to get away.

"I have a theory," Huntley said. "You said Masson knew you were your sister's twin."

"He said I was *the brother*."

"It implies the Unseen know more about their victims—or some of their victims—than we think." Huntley tapped the tabletop with his finger. "Perhaps they choose those victims with care. Perhaps they aren't random killings."

Gideon had wondered the same thing, but hearing it from Huntley made his blood run cold. "What are you saying?"

"Maybe the monsters want something from us. Not ransom, because we would have been contacted—but something that makes it worth keeping their victims alive for at least a little while."

"That's a ludicrous leap of logic," Gideon retorted, suddenly angry. "They're beasts, not people. They're not that organized."

If they'd kept Sidonie alive, even for a day, what horrors had she suffered? What had his failure to protect her cost?

"And yet Masson knows you. He knows your sister. That suggests his actions aren't entirely random."

Gideon remained silent, his hand tight around his glass to stop the tremor in his fingers.

Huntley pulled off his glasses, holding Gideon's gaze with his own. "Isn't there a remote possibility that some victims might still be alive? Maybe your sister?"

"She has to be dead by now." And yet, he'd always thought he'd feel his twin die. He hadn't.

Huntley held his gaze. "I choose to believe my Margaret will come home."

CHAPTER 11

Sidonie stood in the doorway of the one-roomed house that Masson had assigned to her as shelter. The place was downwind of whatever served as the local garbage pit. The Unseen settlement smelled of blood and rot mingled with the wild scents of the forest. The stink should have drawn bears or dragons—some sort of scavengers—but no animals dared to come near the nightmare village.

Trees towered over the dwellings, effectively hiding them from sight. The vast forest unnerved Sidonie. Life inside Londria's walls hadn't prepared her for a place so wild, so indifferent to humanity. Worse, no one at home—at least as far as she knew—was aware this village existed. With all the flights her father's airships had made, none had ever mentioned a settlement of monsters in the woods.

Any chance of rescue, already slim, vanished still further.

Shivering in the icy breeze, she scanned the treetops, trying to guess the hour. Shadows gathered, so it was evening—but time was elusive here. How long had it been since she'd left the prison? The claw marks Margaret had dug into her arms had

"

completely scabbed over. Did that mean one day had gone by? Two?

Time enough to learn the ugliness of this place. Enough to wonder repeatedly why she was still alive and—even more—why she they'd brought her to this hell. She'd asked Masson once, right before she'd killed Margaret.

Stay alive and find out.

She'd tried to bring herself to ask Masson again, but couldn't find the nerve.

The settlement crowded around a central gathering place, with individual dwellings closest to the middle and the common buildings like the prison further away. Here and there, remnants of ancient stone supported newer wooden structures. The monsters were scavengers, molding scraps together with a mix of mud and straw. No decoration softened the plain surface of the walls. Although the Gentry loved clothes and jewelry, their love of finery didn't go beyond personal adornment.

Then again, not every Unseen had a home. The most bestial slept out of doors, piled together for warmth. Only a handful like Masson and the Caretaker—the pinnacle of monster aristocracy—had houses with furnishings and proper doors. Her cottage, simple as it was, marked her as their leader's favorite. It had straw for a bed and a wash basin. By the local standards, it was luxurious.

Sidonie had wandered the village just enough to map it. The act had sorely tested her nerves. Whenever she ventured forth without Masson's protective presence, the others watched her like wolves sizing up a pet rabbit. Still, none dared to touch her or impede her exploration of the settlement—until she stepped over the invisible line that marked the camp's boundary. Then a tall guardsman named Sark had marched her back to her hut, fingers digging into the flesh of her arm.

Sidonie rubbed her bruises at the memory. She hadn't

expected to walk away unchallenged, but there had been no other way to test Masson's security.

A shout snagged her attention, dragging her to the here and now. A scatter of bestial Unseen—the ones the Caretaker called Goblins—scampered across the central square, their filthy clothes blending into the falling shadows. One hooted, the sound a cross between an owl and a baying hound. A shiver passed over her skin at the eerie, forlorn noise.

It had to be a signal. A murmur ran through the village like wind in the grass, the path of rising voices almost a visible thing. Light flared in the trees from the direction of Masson's house. He had the best dwelling, with glass windows no doubt stolen from behind the wall.

If Masson took notice of the disturbance, something was happening. Rising excitement made Sidonie fidget. She'd never been interested in ships and guns, despite her father's failed attempt to train her as an aeronaut. But after her battle with Margaret, she longed for a weapon. Masson had been careful not to provide her with one. The hut had nothing but a straw bed and the gray wool blanket she was using as a shawl. With an uneasy sigh, she folded her arms and watched the path that led deep into the forest.

Unseen could move without a sound, but this time she heard their footfalls before they came into view. A procession of six figures made their way to the central square, bearing an improvised litter made of saplings. On it was the body of an Unseen— one of the Gentry. Even from a distance, Sidonie could see his fall of ice-white hair, lighter even than her own.

As the figures approached, the villagers gathered, Goblins shuffling and loping around the procession in a constant swirl. Unmistakable grief filled their muttering, grumbling moans.

Masson emerged from his home, an oil lamp in the hand of his uninjured arm, and strode to the center of the clearing. He moved cautiously, as if whatever wounds he'd suffered still pained him. All the same, he seemed to recover faster than a human.

Sidonie swallowed uneasily. If one attacked a monster, apparently it was important to finish the job.

The grim parade approached Masson, wordlessly set their burden down at his feet, then retreated to a respectful distance. His lamp splashed color and shadow over the tableau as he gazed down at the remains on the litter, face impassive. Sidonie's breath hitched as one of the Unseen moved aside, giving her a clear view of the corpse. The death had been bloody and thorough, staining crimson across the crisp white shirt and striped waistcoat.

Memory sparked. Weren't those waistcoats worn by the university's rowing team? The random detail was utterly out of place, colliding painfully against the mud and horror around her.

The leader of the procession stepped forward, every angle of his body tense with fury. "The city crawls with hunters." He pointed a clawed finger at the body. "We brought Bagstaff home. His bones belong here, with us."

Up until that moment, Masson had kept his cool mask in place. Now he glared at the speaker, his features twisting in rage. "How did this happen?"

"A knife." The Gentry's tone was flat with disapproval.

Masson seemed to lunge forward, but in truth barely moved. The motion was all in his furious expression. "How?"

Sark pushed past the leader of the expedition. The guardsman was taller than Masson, his shoulders filling out the tattered blue coat of his stolen uniform. Still, he could not match Masson's lethal grace.

"You hold us back," Sark said. "Two go, three go inside the wall. If many went, we would be safe. A pack."

"Two and three can take food and supplies *without notice*." Masson's tone was Arctic. "If they have skill."

"Hunters wait for us."

"More than hunters will wait if too many go inside the wall at once."

The crowd rumbled. Not all the noises were words, but from the sound there was dissent among the ranks. Masson raised his head like a panther scenting the enemy.

Sidonie edged backward, retreating into the shadows of her cottage. If Masson lost his grip on the monsters, her luck would run out. She cast a nervous glance at the pathway into the forest. If Sark was here, who was guarding the perimeter?

But then the crowd shifted, blocking the path. Sidonie cursed softly, her throat tight with frustrated tears. She needed a weapon. No, what she needed was more courage and a weapon. And a great deal of luck.

"My king." Another voice broke into her thoughts. It was the Caretaker, who appeared at Masson's side. "Perhaps it is time to reconsider our strategy."

Masson snarled, the sound lifting the hair at Sidonie's nape.

"I do not challenge you." The Caretaker held up both hands, palms out. "But listening costs no blood."

Sidonie realized she was holding her breath, willing Masson to back down. The Goblins were growing agitated, shuffling and bobbing like a sea of rags and twisted limbs.

Masson's gaze narrowed. "Fools think in days. I think in years. I plan."

The silence that followed seemed to vibrate, broken only by the sudden flap and caw of a crow.

"We hold back now. Eat well. Grow warriors in number," Masson continued. "We attack when we will win. Then we feast."

A few of the Goblins cheered, but the ragged sound soon died.

Sark looked from Masson to the corpse and back. "While you dream, we die."

Masson struck. It seemed like a mere flick of a hand, but Sark sprawled in the dirt. The others shuffled away, as if eager to put distance between themselves and the guardsman's shame. With a curse, Sark scrambled to his feet and stormed into the trees, vanishing from sight.

The Caretaker shook his head, his long pale hair shining in the lamplight. "You are correct. We have found stable prosperity by keeping to the shadows. Now, that may no longer be enough."

Masson wheeled on him, eyes bright with anger.

The Caretaker gave a slow smile. "Are you going to hit me as well?"

"Not yet." Masson lifted his chin. "I still do not agree."

"You say you play a long game," the Caretaker said softly. "Long or not, perhaps it is time to make a different move."

"Is it a game when no piece survives the board?"

"When the final battle for supremacy begins, remember that I taught you the moves, not the reverse." The Caretaker made a slight bow, one hand to his immaculately buttoned-up waistcoat. "I prefer to think of you as the son I should have had."

Their eyes locked a moment before the Caretaker withdrew, vanishing into the dark. Night had fallen while the scene had played out, turning the forest into a vast, whispering void.

Sidonie pulled her blanket closer, suddenly chilled to the bone. Pieces? A board? What games did the Gentry play? Chess with the skulls of their enemies?

She studied Masson as he dispersed the crowd and ordered the body removed. He was strong, fast, and ambitious—a king among monsters. She'd been courted by more than a few such males.

Ambition was like liquor and cards—amusing in small doses; deadly as a habit. Smart men knew the difference. Dangerous men knew how to leverage the ambitions of others.

Remember that I taught you the moves.

The Caretaker was the one to watch.

～

Sidonie jerked to consciousness. She sat up, the bed of straw crackling beneath her weight. The haze of sleep slowly shredded as her breath fogged the chill air. Something had disturbed her, but what? By the light, it was near dawn, which meant she'd only been asleep for a few hours. She was falling into the same nocturnal rhythms as her captors.

A woman's cry split the air. Instantly, Sidonie scrambled to her feet, wrapping herself in the gray blanket and pushing her feet into her tattered shoes. There was no need to dress—she slept in her clothes. Cautiously, she inched toward the door, replaying the cry in her mind. It hadn't been the shriek of prey. It was the wail of a woman giving birth. She'd heard it often enough.

Curiosity drew her to the cottage door. Frost glittered on the grass, a reflection of the bright stars above. What was a woman in childbirth doing here? A dozen grisly possibilities rose in her imagination. She hurried outside, driven by a primitive need to protect the mother and babe.

One of the Goblins crouched outside Sidonie's dwelling. It raised his face and hissed as she swept past, making her stumble in surprise. She spun to face it, fearful but angry, too. She was tired, so tired of expecting the feel of teeth in her flesh at every turn.

It crept forward, baring a crooked mass of fangs. Sidonie's stomach flipped, but she stood her ground, giving it a steely glare. One didn't run from bad-tempered dogs. Maybe this was the same.

No, this was worse. If one of the shuffling beasts attacked, surely his friends would catch the scent of blood and join in. Masson had given orders to leave her alone, but he was nowhere in sight. She was on her own.

The thing snarled, shifting its weight to spring. Without thinking, she bared her teeth, hissing back with all the disgust and fury boiling in her heart.

The creature's eyes went round with obvious surprise. It dropped to all fours with a confused whine.

"Go!" Sidonie commanded, putting the imperious tone of a dozen Society dowagers into her tone. She pointed for emphasis, jabbing the air to her right.

The Goblin wavered, head tucked low, before it scuttled away, casting a confused look over its shoulder.

Sidonie remained frozen until it disappeared behind another cottage. Then she sucked in a rattling breath, fighting down the urge to vomit from sheer terror. She'd won against the bogeyman—a small one, but it still could have devoured her in a blink.

She'd been operating on instinct, but not any instinct she recognized. It was the same and different from her fight with Margaret. This time, she'd immediately taken the upper hand and won before the fight even started. That was a good thing, wasn't it?

Maybe, but it wasn't the act of a lady. Circumstances were stripping away pieces of her character, leaving her in tatters like her ball gown. A new kind of terror prickled down her spine. Who would she be by the time she finally—hopefully—found her way home?

The woman's rising wail pierced the forest. Sidonie broke into a run.

CHAPTER 12

Sidonie slowed when she reached the edge of the settlement. A dozen yards away, the trees rose in a wall of creaking branches. Beneath their canopy, dawn had no power yet. The darkness ahead was so complete it might have been the edge of the world.

Possibilities rampaged through her imagination—she remembered childhood tales of demons luring the unwary with the sound of a weeping child. Once, she would have called such tales nonsense. Now—wasn't she living a dark fairytale?

She stopped and stood very still, pulse thundering in her ears. Then a rustle came from somewhere to her left. She stared hard toward it, her eyes eventually finding a roofline in the shadows. As she cautiously approached, she tried and failed to match it with the buildings she knew. This was a place she hadn't been allowed to go.

A long, single-story structure emerged from the thick screen of trees. Wavering light glowed from small windows, where heavy curtains had been pushed aside to admit the chill air. There were no windowpanes to muffle the clank and rattle of pans.

The sound reminded her of how long it had been since her

last true meal, and visions of hot, thick stew danced in her head. For an instant, her mouth watered. The Unseen provided enough bread and lightly-charred meat to keep her from starvation, but she could choke down just one or two bites at a time. It barely mattered how much her stomach pinched with hunger. The bread was beyond stale and the meat— Well, the Unseen were not choosy about what—or whom—they devoured.

But as she drew closer, she saw this wasn't a house at all, with a family and a cozy kitchen. It was a much larger structure, as unappealing as all the Unseen's buildings. This had to be where the cries came from, but why would a woman and her baby be here? And why weren't the Unseen swarming around them, eager to feed?

Steps from the door, she stopped dead, her instincts warning that something wasn't right. What was she doing there, unarmed and alone? What did she think she could do for the mystery woman and her babe?

The door swung open without warning, revealing a silhouette backlit by a lamp. It was the Caretaker.

"How might I assist you, my lady?" he said with a touch of sarcasm.

As her eyes adjusted, she saw his jacket was gone and his sleeves were rolled up to his elbows. If she didn't look closely, she might have mistaken him for an ordinary man.

"I heard someone in distress," she replied, hating how nerves and cold made her sound breathless. "I wondered if I could help."

"No doubt your mother taught you to visit the sick and elderly. Good works are gems on the crown of a true lady."

She shrank under his withering tone, but forced herself to rally. "I won't apologize for good breeding."

The Caretaker made a soft noise, but she couldn't tell whether it was amusement or exasperation. "And if I told you there was nothing you could do?"

"I would ask for proof."

"And if I said the proof was unpleasant, would you still risk it?"

Sidonie's stomach sank. "I would."

"Very well. Perhaps you will learn something."

After a brief hesitation, he stepped back and extended a hand to usher her inside. Sidonie entered, expecting to find others— the expectant mother, at least.

There was no one. With creeping unease, she realized they were alone. She squared her shoulders, swallowing down the urge to bolt.

One glance told her that this place was better kept than the other buildings. A dozen beds—proper beds, with sheets and blankets—lined the walls.

"This is a hospital," she guessed.

"This is where I work," he replied. "None of us is invulnerable, not even my kith and kin."

She glanced up at him, the image of her fiancé momentarily obscuring his marble-white features. Her doctor—her Richard— had walked into the worst slums of the city to tend the sick. He'd sat up all night with patients and pored over countless volumes to find forgotten cures. That devotion had made him a hero, and not just in her adoring eyes.

Richard had promised his heart and hand the night Masson had kidnapped her. Her breath caught, her chest suddenly tight with grief. Remembered happiness was a knife.

It wasn't the weapon she needed. Sidonie pushed the pain away, forcing herself to the present.

The Caretaker's ice-pale eyes held hers, patient as a frozen lake. There was something in his manner—the inhuman beneath his humanlike facade—that scared her more than any Goblin. His monstrosity ran deeper, although she'd only seen glimpses of it, like a shark's fin on a still ocean.

She tore her gaze away and looked again at the beds, this time finding what she expected. The one farthest from the door was occupied. Instantly, she started toward it, but the Caretaker caught her arm.

"Slowly," he said, releasing her. "There is much you need to understand."

With that, he took the lead, walking before her across the well-scrubbed wooden floor.

"This place is kept in good order," she said, partly to flatter, partly because she was genuinely interested. "Where did you learn medicine?"

"Wherever I could," he replied, his tone dry. "As you can well imagine, the official schools were not welcoming."

He stopped at the foot of the occupied bed. As Sidonie came to stand beside him, she caught the scent of blood and bile. The human woman beneath the sheets was unfamiliar, her dark hair loose and curling from the sweat still slicking her forehead. By her intense stillness, she had to be dead.

"I heard her cries," Sidonie said softly.

His reply was just as quiet. "You were minutes too late to witness her end."

A wave of sadness coursed through Sidonie. The patient had been around her age, her skin fine and her thick hair soft. Whoever she was, she'd lived an easy life before coming here.

Just like me.

"Who is she?" Sidonie asked.

"I'm sure you recall your companion from when you first arrived."

Sidonie's first thought was of Margaret, but then she remembered the screaming woman from the other cell. "What ailed her?"

"By the time she was ready to give birth, she was too weak to push the child out."

She wheeled on him. "You kept a pregnant woman chained in that prison?"

His pale face was a mask. Of course, he had kept her there.

Sidonie had listened to the poor thing suffering day after wretched day.

Sidonie took another look at the woman's placid face. The blood had drained from her complexion, but nothing else was remarkable. "She appears unchanged. Not like Margaret."

"Looks are deceiving."

Quickly, Sidonie's gaze searched the woman, the bed, the space around it. There was a basin of blood-soaked rags against the wall, revealing what the pristine sheet covering the patient hid away.

The woman had been in pain. Excruciating, horrible pain that got worse as the baby grew. Something unnatural had been happening inside her.

"And the child?" The words barely made it past Sidonie's lips.

"The boy will live. She made the ultimate gift of life."

"Where is he?"

"He is being tended to."

Sidonie realized she was clutching the iron rail at the foot of the bed, her knuckles white. She let go and stepped back, her fingers aching. An idea—rank and unforgivable—took shape, leaving her queasy.

She swallowed twice before she could speak. "Is the child human?"

"Not entirely."

"What does that mean?"

"He will grow tall and beautiful like his parents, but as dangerous as wild magic can devise."

Dizziness swept through her. "I don't understand."

"No, you wouldn't." The Caretaker clasped his hands behind his back, his expression distant. "Potential for magic comes the way other traits do, from mother to daughter and father to son. Through certain gifted bloodlines."

"But only the potential?"

"Correct. Like a spark to tinder, untamed power touches

those with magic in their blood. Magic begets magic, and Gentry are born."

"And those without magic?"

"They become Goblins. We choose our guests carefully."

"Does that explain what happened to Margaret?"

"Not entirely. She wasn't what she seemed."

What did that mean? Blackness dimmed the edges of her vision as her heart pounded furiously. Sidonie squeezed her eyes shut. "What about me?"

The Caretaker didn't answer. Anxious rage swelled beneath her ribs, as if it meant to claw its way free.

"Why haven't I changed?" She pointed to the bed. "Or is that what you have in mind for me?"

When he still didn't answer, she drew closer to the side of the bed, her soles sticking to traces of blood on the floor. Her fingers itched to pull away the sheet covering the woman's wounds, to answer questions that she dared not put into words. Mesmerized, her fingers brushed the white cotton, feeling the faint and fading warmth beneath. Scarlet bloomed in spreading pools as the pressure of her touch pushed the cloth into the woman's wound.

Tears slid down her cheeks, but she couldn't say who they were for—herself? The babe? The dead?

"You are bold," the Caretaker said. "There is no denying that."

Sidonie's fingers flexed, aching to claw the cool indifference from his face. And yet he was the Unseen, a dozen times more savage, more powerful. He could kill her in a blink.

She sucked in a breath of the chill hospital air, ignoring the rich, coppery smell of the congealing blood. It did nothing to calm her nerves.

"You're not going to give me an answer, are you?" she asked, her voice cracking on the words.

"I have fewer than you think."

"Then when will Masson tell me why I'm here in the forest?"

"Maybe he is ready. I do not know."

Pushing down frustration, she retreated from the bedside. "Then I will go ask him."

At that, the Caretaker smiled, showing the tips of his sharp teeth. "He will enjoy that."

A scream hovered at the back of her throat, ready to choke her if she didn't let it out. "I bid you good night."

"Pleasant dreams."

She spun and strode toward the door, self-discipline the only thing keeping her from scampering away like a frightened child. She all but leaped over the threshold, sucking in the clean, cold forest air. The first streaks of crimson dawn sparkled on the frost-encrusted ground.

She finally broke into a run, soles slipping on the frozen earth. When she fell to one knee, pain lanced all the way up her leg and her silent tears broke into ragged sobs. For all her terrifying questions, the answers were bound to be worse.

Magic begets magic. The Caretaker's words swirled like poison. *As dangerous as wild magic can devise.* What did any of it mean?

All she knew about magic were the scraps she'd learned in school. After the Great Disaster, back in the time of Raleigh and Queen Bess, thousands perished when wild magic was loosed upon the world. Monsters roamed free until the Conclave rose to protect humanity with their Citadel and their city walls.

Magic brought doom and death. No wonder the monsters courted it.

Slowly, Sidonie got to her feet, shivering in the freezing damp. Someone was walking her way, feet crunching on the scatter of brittle leaves. Sidonie squinted into the gloom, trying to recognize the figure. The female was wrapped in a shawl and heading away from the hospital along a different path, as if she'd left from the rear of the building. Her route would cross Sidonie's in moments.

Wiping her wet cheeks, Sidonie drew herself up and faced the newcomer. No good would come of showing weakness.

The figure was taller than one of the hunched Goblins and carried a bundle wrapped in a threadbare plaid. Something about her seemed familiar. Sidonie looked closely as the woman approached, though the shawl shrouded the newcomer's face.

Then recognition struck. She blinked, numb with astonishment. "Margaret?"

Relief flooded her, followed quickly by apprehension. The shawl slid back as Margaret turned her head. Her face lingered somewhere between monstrous and human, the features contorted horribly by the change from human to…what, exactly?

She wasn't what she seemed.

"Very kind of you to speak to me," Margaret said, the words slurred by too many needle-sharp teeth. Still, there was no mistaking the bitter tone.

"Why—how are you here?" Sidonie said in astonishment. "I was afraid I'd killed you, strangled you with the chain. I'm so very sorry."

"Do you think I'm that fragile?" Margaret gave a dry laugh. "Not anymore."

Rising horror blotted out any possible reply. The woman's eyes had turned yellow like a cat's, and the hand gripping the bundle was tipped with blackened claws.

"How are *you* still alive?" Margaret asked. "This isn't a place for pretty dolls."

Sidonie shook her head, though she wasn't sure what she denied.

Margaret chuckled again. Sidonie's skin crawled as her former friend bared her ragged teeth. At the noise, the shawl squirmed. At once, Margaret fell silent, cradling her burden.

"What is that?" Sidonie asked, though she had already guessed.

"It's the boy. If you're coming from the hospital, then you know the tale."

"Yes, I do." A faint buzzing filled Sidonie's ears. Shock, she guessed. She'd seen too many nightmares in a short time. Still, she couldn't stop herself from leaning forward to view the child as Margaret uncovered its face. To Sidonie's immense relief, the baby looked pale but human, with the round, scrunched features of any newborn.

"The Caretaker gave him to me to look after," Margaret said, clutching the squirming bundle a little closer. "He trusts me to keep him safe. It seems I'm to be his helper now."

"Won't the baby need a wet nurse?"

"I'm taking him to her. Lord Masson anticipated the happy event."

"And did what?"

Margaret rolled her eerie yellow eyes. "What do you think? He sent his men to the city to find one."

"But…" Sidonie stammered. This child had to be fed, and that meant a human mother had been snatched off the street—leaving her own child bereft.

"But nothing," Margaret said, turning away. "There are only so many ways the Gentry add to their number."

"Is that what—?" Overcome with revulsion, Sidonie stopped talking.

"The Caretaker explained it all. They don't breed easily," Margaret said. "Sometimes they have to make their brood a different way."

With that, Margaret stalked off, taking the baby with her.

Sidonie remained glued in place until the departing figure vanished into the trees, heading toward the prison where they had all been kept—Sidonie, Margaret, and the dead mother. It seemed Masson had new prisoners now.

And she had new questions.

Panic swamped her, formless and overwhelming. Her heart pounded as if she'd sprinted the miles from Londria's gates to this nightmare place, squeezing the breath from her body. Suddenly unable to stand still, she ran from the forest, retracing her steps through the village, past the houses and the central square—until she found her own doorway. She burst into her cottage, chest heaving.

The small, sheltered space felt a little safer, though it took a long time for panic to release its talons. By the time it did, she was sticky with sweat.

She tossed aside the gray blanket she'd worn against the cold. As she did, she noticed blood on her fingers from where she'd pressed the sheet against the dead woman's wound. She looked around for water to wash, but her basin was empty. Without thinking, she licked her finger, hoping to scrub the stain away.

With a gasp, she pulled her hand away, but not before the taste had filled her senses. All the food she struggled to eat had been foul ashes compared to this.

Her stomach cramped with hunger. The dead woman's blood was like honey on her tongue.

CHAPTER 13

"**I**'ve come to join you," Miranda said to her father as she entered the dining room.

It was the first time she'd dressed for dinner since the accident, and lingering in her room had grown well past dull. She longed for the warm feeling of a communal meal.

"I'm delighted to have the company," Norton Fletcher replied, setting down his soup spoon.

Her father was alone at the table. This wasn't the formal dining room intended for guests, but a cozier chamber their family used every day. The walls were covered in embossed green paper, and the furniture and wainscoting were oak. It would have felt somber but for the gaslights suffusing the room with a gentle glow.

Miranda took a seat to her father's right. Once, there had been six gathered around the table, and then five after her mother passed. It felt empty with just the two of them.

"Where is Olivia tonight?" Miranda asked, trying not to sound disappointed.

"She's dining with some associates from the university. Evidently, there is something exciting about an integer that must be discussed." He gave a wry smile. "I didn't ask for details."

"Probably for the best." She spread a napkin across her lap. "In any event, this means you and I will have time for a good chat."

The footman set a plate of soup before her. Cream of leek wasn't her favorite, but she was hungry for the first time in days. She took it as a good sign that even this insipid dish smelled delicious.

"How are you feeling?" her father asked. "The story of the *Leopard*'s misfortune freezes my blood."

She swallowed her mouthful of soup. "The term *misfortune* implies that it was an accident."

He sighed. "It's safer to imagine that was the case, since an investigation is impossible."

"Impossible?"

He made a derisive noise. "I seem to recall you were in the drawing room when Councilor Ormond paid a visit."

"We can't give up that easily," she said, keeping her voice soft despite a rising indignation. "There can be another *Leopard*."

Miranda studied her father's worn face. He'd once been a loud, blustering man, his complexion weathered by years of wind and sun aboard his airships. Now he appeared colorless, as if he were a faded portrait of himself. Sickness and grief had taken their toll on a man she'd always imagined indestructible.

His brows drew together. "You know as well as I do that fighting the Conclave carries consequences. I won't put my children in harm's way."

"What if your children want to fight back?"

A flush crept up his neck. "If any one of us is accused of treason, we all suffer."

She set down her soup spoon. "You know that's why Gideon left, don't you?"

Her brother believed the public rift between father and son would keep the family from harm while he investigated Sidonie's disappearance. It had been a difficult sacrifice in every possible way. Would she have to do the same to avenge the *Leopard* and its crew? Was she being selfish?

Twin spots of color rose in her father's cheeks. "My son is a fool who will get himself killed."

With that, he turned back to his soup, angrily scooping it up as if it had offended him.

It was time to change the subject. "You asked how I am faring since the *Leopard* burned."

Her father wiped his mouth with his napkin, waiting for her to continue.

"I've had vivid dreams. Most of the details match my memories—I'm in the water and one of the River Rats is pulling me into his boat." She paused to sip her water before carrying on. "In the dream, I realize that I am being saved, but I can't remember the ending. It's the part I can't remember that fills me with such dread that I wake up stiff with fear."

Her father put a hand over hers, but he didn't interrupt.

She met his eyes. "Are dreams like this normal after an accident?"

His gaze dropped to where their hands rested on the table, all sign of his earlier irritation gone. "Air accidents impact each survivor differently. Sometimes it's a crystal-clear recollection that repeats over and over, no matter how many years pass. Other times it's a question that can't be put into words."

She studied him, realizing how little she knew of the accidents he'd survived. He'd only ever told his children tales of success. "What do you dream of?"

"I had a ship go down outside the wall. I wasn't on it, or I wouldn't be sitting here to tell the tale." He withdrew his hand to pick up a glass of straw-colored wine and take a long drink. "Afterward, I dreamed of your dead mother. She reminded me over and over to feed the babies, but by then you were all grown."

He paused, as if embarrassed to be caught saying something so personal.

"What do you think it meant?" Miranda asked.

"Dreams aren't literal." His reply was gruff. "No doubt it was a reminder to do better. I'd failed to protect my crew."

He rose, setting his napkin aside. "Forgive me, my dear, but I'm weary and need my bed. I believe soup is all the dinner I can face tonight."

Miranda got to her feet as well, enfolding him in an impulsive embrace. "I'm sorry. I had no right to ask something so private."

"No apology needed," he murmured, hugging her back.

If only he would remain as he'd always been—the strong adventurer of legend. Now she could feel in his gentle touch how that power had faded. Her universe teetered on the cusp of change, and she had no control over anything.

It terrified her. Anger stirred, its nascent flame an attempt to keep her warm.

"Goodnight, little scamp," he said, kissing her forehead as he had when she was a little girl.

"Goodnight, Father," she murmured as he left the room.

If sitting down to dinner with two was bad, dining alone was worse. She tried to eat the chicken dish the footman brought next, but her appetite had fled. It was almost a relief when Jeffries interrupted the course to announce that a visitor had unexpectedly arrived.

Miranda picked up the calling card from the butler's silver tray. When she turned it upright, the flowing font produced the last name she expected to see that night. "Mr. Kitteridge?"

She hadn't heard from him since he'd sent her that cheeky letter. She hadn't entirely expected to. Predictability had no part in his nature.

"Indeed, miss," Jeffries said with careful neutrality. "Shall I ask him to return at a more convenient hour?"

Miranda hesitated. The heir of his wealthy grandfather, Baron

Kitteridge, William was considered a bachelor well worth catching—but he was the Scorpion's friend, not Miranda's beau. A good thing, since he had a reputation for vaporizing as soon as he'd caught a female's heart.

She'd determined long ago not to be among his casualties.

Usually, they met at the Mercury Café, where the patrons were politely blind to a veiled woman meeting a handsome young buck. They talked about aether weapons and how best to kill the Unseen that strayed within the city walls. On the rare occasions when they met in Londria's drawing rooms, they were coolly polite.

"Send Mr. Kitteridge to the yellow drawing room," she said to Jeffries.

Jeffries frowned, clearly concerned. Among the best families, it was rare for an unmarried woman to be alone with an unmarried man. "Shall I send for the Master?"

"Don't disturb my father," she said with a slight shrug. "I'm sure Mr. Kitteridge's visit will be brief."

A few minutes later, Miranda arrived at the drawing-room door. Kitteridge rose when she entered, a faint frown creasing his brow.

Miranda's unruly heart lifted when she saw him. Kitteridge was irresponsibly handsome—tall, with sharp cheekbones, midnight hair, and gray eyes. As always, he was dressed as if he had nothing better to do than to spend his time at the tailors.

He bent over her hand with a flourish. "I am delighted to see you looking so well, Miss Fletcher."

"Did you expect to find me otherwise?" she asked.

"Word on the street says your tumble from the sky was not an accident." He straightened, brushing back a lock of hair that had fallen into his eyes. "I would have called on you sooner, but as I said in my note to you, I have just returned to town for the holidays."

Like Olivia, Kitteridge was a student, but he attended the

university in Stonegate, a walled city far to the north. The curriculum there leaned toward scientific inquiry, Kitteridge's area of interest.

"How go your studies?" she asked, retrieving her hand from his grasp.

"My time at the university has been far less interesting than your recent adventures."

"And how did you know that the wreck was anything but an accident?"

He gave a slow smile. "Gossip. Tell me truthfully, how are you?"

"Good enough."

"And your ship?"

"Destroyed. It was sabotage," Miranda said, stepping closer so that she could lower her voice.

"Magic?" he asked in an almost eerie echo of Ormond's words.

Miranda glanced toward the door. She had left it ajar to relieve any suspicions of impropriety. Unfortunately, that meant any passing servant could hear the conversation. All at once, the walls around her felt suffocating.

"Come with me," she said, abruptly pulling him by the hand into the hallway.

"Excuse me?" he said with a laugh.

"This way." Miranda steered him down the corridor.

"Are you going to imprison me in the attic until I stop asking questions? Will there be cuffs and chains?"

"I have far better plans than that." She turned the corner and headed toward a pair of metal doors to her left. They belonged to the steam-powered lift that ran through the center of the house.

"Then where are we going?"

"Your virtue and liberty are quite safe."

"Pity."

"Be quiet. There is a splendid view from the roof."

Kitteridge obediently followed, quickly catching on to her plan. In a walled city with limited growing space, almost every building in Londria had a rooftop garden. They were public spaces acceptable for entertaining guests, but there would be no eavesdroppers.

Miranda's quick pace left her hot and queasy, a sign she still had more healing to do. When she pushed through the door onto the roof, the slap of icy air was a welcome relief. They wound through the raised beds, Kitteridge surveying the view. Aqueducts ran up and down the streets delivering water to the rooftop plantings, though this late in the year there were only hardy root vegetables and winter greens under glass cloches.

Miranda drew to a stop once they'd reached her favorite spot. The streets below were quiet, families settled and pleasure-seekers not yet ready for the dinner clubs and opera. The stars above glittered like frost, and the sickle moon shone as sharp as any blade. Up here, she felt free. She was a creature of the sky.

Kitteridge studied her. "By the way you're holding your side, your injuries still pain you."

"I'm on the mend," she said quickly, unnerved by the concern in his eyes. "What was the question you asked?"

"Was it magic that brought down the ship?"

"I've been on a ship caught by magic. That felt as if a giant fist was pulling the ship down to the earth. This was nothing like that. The *Leopard* was destroyed by an explosion."

He paused as if pondering his next question before speaking again. "Do you believe the Conclave had a hand in it? They would have that kind of power."

"I don't think so. There were details about the events that surprised Councilor Ormond when he heard my story. Surely he would have known if his own people were behind the event."

Kitteridge did not reply.

Despite the intoxicating view, she wished she'd brought more than the light shawl that matched her gauzy dinner gown. She drew closer to Kitteridge, his heat like a beacon in the night air. This close, she caught the scent of his skin mixed with the smoke of Londria's many chimneys.

"You have a lot of questions. What do you know that you're not saying?" she asked.

He shrugged. "I am torn between two priorities."

"What are they?"

"Few people know you are the Scorpion."

His statement didn't answer her question, but it was true. Only Janey, her friend and pilot, knew her secret identity. And perhaps one or two, who lived at Hellion House with Janey, suspected. And maybe some of the personnel at the airfield, where she kept her ship, did as well. And her brother knew, of course. It was actually rather hard to keep the Scorpion's identity secret.

"Gideon knows," she admitted, "though he doesn't quite say it out loud."

"And the rest of your family?"

"I've never told them."

He looked out over the horizon, his profile pale and perfect. "And what is it you want most in the world?"

It was an unexpected question, especially coming from him. Kitteridge could be irreverent or flirtatious, but he was rarely serious.

"Tonight I sat down for dinner with my father." Her voice cracked unexpectedly. "There were only two of us in a place that just months ago was crowded and loud with chatter. I want my family back around that table. All of us, including Sidonie."

He turned his gaze to meet hers. "I'm sorry."

"I know she's not alive. I'm not foolish. But I can't help dreaming that she'll come back to us."

He said nothing, but it was an expressive nothing.

"I'm afraid for the rest of my family," she murmured, as much to herself as to him.

"I understand that."

The sadness in those words tore at her. Kitteridge had lost his parents young—though she wasn't sure exactly how young. He had been raised by his grandfather, a lone child in the baron's imposing manor at the edge of the heath. It wasn't a comforting picture.

"What about you?" she asked. "What do you want?"

He laughed softly. "As I said, I'm of two minds. I'm concerned for you and your family. I worry that the level of danger you face is increasing. I worry that this won't be your only injury. I even worry that Gideon is going to get himself in trouble by associating with Detective Inspector Palmer, who never met a rule he wouldn't break."

He thought about her far more than she'd expected. "Do my affairs dominate only one of your two minds?"

His smile was brief. "My other mind is anxious for the Scorpion to resume her work. Someone destroyed a significant weapon against the Unseen. Now she has a saboteur to catch, along with obliterating the monsters."

"So she does."

He gave her a sharp look. "Your near death puts the two halves of my mind at war. Should you be safe, or should you deliver justice?"

His intensity made her nervous. "Why does justice matter to you? I thought it was the notion of pretty debutantes with aether weapons that amused you."

"Always," he said, his customary lightness returning. "I can have multiple motivations. Inspiration is everywhere. The question is whether the Scorpion is well enough recovered to be inspired."

"And you visit because you are a veritable force for motivation?"

"Perhaps I am not only amusing, but a muse."

This was more like their usual style. She glanced away from

him, all too aware of his charisma. "Will you ever pick up a weapon yourself? After all, you helped to build my aether gun."

"Ah, my weapons and battlefield differ greatly from yours. But I am a willing warrior. You are not the only hunter in this fight."

"By hunters, are you referring to the Anathema Club? Gideon encountered them the other night."

He made a sound that was not quite a laugh. "That lot does an excellent job of lurking in alleyways, but one day their luck will run out."

That was what Gideon had said the night he'd come to the house, except that he'd included more sinister details. The club had put down their friend like a rabid dog and burned the body afterward. She shuddered at the thought.

Kitteridge put a hand on her arm, squeezing gently. "I am here if you need me."

"In the shadows."

"The shadows are where my ways and means make a difference." He released her arm, brushing her cheek with the back of his fingers.

Her breath caught at his touch. She meant to ask about his *ways and means*, but her thoughts succumbed to his magnetic pull.

He leaned forward, his lips brushing her forehead just as her father's had earlier that night. And yet, this wasn't a paternal gesture—not at all. The night air felt suddenly thick and charged, as if lightning might erupt. She wanted this intimacy, and yet she wanted Kitteridge gone. The sudden shift in their friendship had come too quickly.

As if sensing her discomfort, he stepped back, putting space between them. "Forgive me. I overstep."

The words were awkward, as if he were covering up the same confusion she felt.

"There is nothing to forgive," she said, aware of the cold again. For a few minutes, he'd made her forget the wintery temperature.

"I should go," he said. "You need your rest."

"Will you be returning to Stonegate?" she asked, glad the night hid her burning cheeks.

"I will be in town for a while. If you permit, I will call again to see how your recovery progresses." His lips curved in a wry smile that dispelled the serious mood.

"Certainly." Miranda gave him her hand, and he bowed over it.

This time, the gesture was ever-so-slightly stiff. The polite distance between them held a different quality now. He'd crossed a boundary, and the old comfort would never return.

Wordlessly, she led the way back to the elevator and down to the main floor. She'd accepted Kitteridge's aura of mystery as part of his nature, just as he'd accepted her less than ladylike pursuits.

If she let him get closer, she needed answers. Why didn't he pick up an aether weapon and hunt the Unseen at her side?

Why fight in the shadows? What did that even mean?

Why did he fight at all?

The queries made sense in her head, but she knew that somehow they'd never make it to her tongue. Not yet. Not until she knew what asking would cost their relationship. She valued it too much to risk a clumsy mistake.

If she couldn't ask, what kind of a bond did they actually have?

The elevator's engine huffed and stopped. Kitteridge opened the gate, allowing Miranda to get out first.

"I can find my way from here," he said, following her to the main hallway. "I'm sure Jeffries will be all too pleased to hand me my hat."

She chuckled. "No doubt."

His expression was troubled, as if he had read her every thought. "Retire and rest, Miranda. Right now, healing is your only task."

He'd used her first name—a familiarity he rarely employed.

She chose not to match his familiarity. "Good night, Kitteridge."

He bowed one last time. "Be well."

She watched his tall form retreat toward the front hall, his gait as easy and graceful as a cat's. Without knowing why, she shivered.

Unsettled, Miranda mounted the stairs to return to her bedroom. The long upstairs hallway was sparsely lit by gas sconces, the blown-glass shades shaped like seashells. The effect was more pleasing than practical—the corridor was still dark enough that the light spilling from beneath Olivia's door was plain to see.

On another day, Miranda would stop to chat. Tonight she kept walking, craving solitude so she could think.

Kitteridge had asked whether the Scorpion was well enough recovered to take to the skies. As he'd said, she had a saboteur to catch. Unseen to battle. Justice to deliver. She was still thinking about the tarot reading she'd done, with the Leopard card ascending to dominate the future.

Was she ready to take flight again, even in the small runabout ship the Scorpion used inside the city? Stargazing on the rooftop was one thing, but when she seriously considered leaving firm ground, she grew cold as death. The sensation was close to outright panic.

Never in her life had she feared the sky. This was a new assault on her world.

She could be forgiven for now, but soon she wouldn't be able to use her injuries as an excuse to remain on *terra firma*. According to her father, air accidents impacted each survivor differently. What if she'd lost her nerve forever?

Miranda reached her room. Shore was waiting to unlace her gown and take down her hair. As her maid wielded the brush in long, soothing strokes, Miranda closed her eyes.

Months ago, she'd invented the Scorpion to rescue Sidonie. Once the hope of rescuing her sister faded, both Miranda and Gideon had kept on fighting to protect Londria from the Unseen, each in their own way. But while the welfare of the entire city was important, she cared most about her family's safety.

Now, the danger was greater than ever. If she couldn't fly, couldn't be the Scorpion, what good was she?

"That's all for tonight," she said as the maid set down the hairbrush. "I'm ready for my pillow."

"Very good, miss," Shore replied with a curtsy. "Shall I put out the candle for you?"

Miranda rose from her dressing table. "Thank you, but I will read for a while."

Shore made her exit. Miranda stood beside her bed, looking down at the soft expanse of lace-edged sheets. The maid had turned the covers down, inviting her to rest. Her aching body welcomed the idea, but her mind still churned with self-doubt.

She turned back to her dressing table, retrieving a small brass key from beneath the false bottom of her glove box. Then she opened her wardrobe and pushed her dresses aside. A modest green leather trunk was in the back and out of sight.

She kept the contents of the trunk private for a good reason. The armor and weapons it held belonged to the Scorpion. Everything was ready and waiting, in perfect working order, except for her. She clutched the key, willing herself to unlock the trunk and ready herself for flight and battle.

She was unable to move, even to insert the key into the lock.

Shame crept through her, leaving a burning sensation in her chest. How many horrors would ravage the streets because she was here, safe in her bed?

A sudden sensation of falling engulfed her, as if she'd lost her footing on the safe, sane floorboards of her bedroom. Her skin pebbled. Shore had built up the coal fire, but not enough to extinguish the terror of falling from the sky.

Fingers trembling, she closed the wardrobe door, and returned the key to its hiding place.

Miranda dove under the bedclothes and pressed her toes against the heated ceramic water bottle Shore had left to warm the sheets. She was safe. Warm. Slowly, her tight breaths eased to a normal rhythm.

Then gray despair seeped through her. Who would she be without the courage to fly?

Pain and fatigue tugged at her, but she rolled over, fighting the pull. Gideon was hunting for the saboteur but had sent no word of progress. Someone had to watch her brother's back.

His encounter with the creature called Masson unnerved her. She trusted Palmer, but the detective inspector couldn't always be there. No one seemed to think Huntley's club was a good idea.

Miranda rolled over again, unable to get comfortable. Her ribs still ached with every movement. Another wave of tiredness left her drifting on its tide.

Fear cast a constant pall over every breath.

The saboteur would pay.

The Unseen would pay.

The...

She was in the river once more, frozen to the core by the ice-gray water. Boats sliced through the waves, the paddles dipping in the same rhythm as her pounding heart.

She was dreaming, and this time she knew it.

"Please!" she cried, reaching out to the boatman. "I don't want to drown."

A hand reached down and caught hers, but this time it was slender, the olive skin impossibly warm after the frigid water. Miranda struggled into the boat, water sluicing from her flight gear as if she'd brought the river with her.

The hand that saved her released her. Someone pulled off her helmet and goggles. Someone else flung a blanket around her. Miranda used a corner to wipe her face dry, shivering until her teeth chattered.

"Here, allow me," one of her rescuers said, taking Miranda's hands.

Councilor Ormond had grasped her hands the same way, but this time the effect was heavenly. The hands holding hers contained the same impossible warmth as the hand that had plucked her from the river. Warmth slid through Miranda, washing away every trace of cold, every scratch, every bruise. The sensation was exquisite.

It was then, in her dream, that she understood the boatman wasn't a man, but a woman. The female River Rat pulled back her black lace veil to reveal her face. Delicate tattoos curled around her temples and cheekbones. It was the fortune-teller, Madam Alma, who had given her the tarot cards.

"What are you doing here?" Miranda asked.

Madam Alma shook her head, a soft smile on her lips. "There is much you need to learn, and I fear there is no time."

"Time for what?"

"To act once you find the knowledge you seek. That is the only test that matters." The fortune-teller twisted, pointing one black-clad arm toward the horizon. There, a tower thrust skyward.

"The Citadel? The home of the Conclave? What about it?"

Fire erupted in the heavens as the lifting gas from the *Leopard* exploded in a burst of roiling flame, painting the water crimson and orange.

"Doomsfire," Madam Alma said.

Miranda bolted upright in her bed with a gasp.

Doomsfire.

She gazed around her chill bedroom, eyes wide. The candle guttered, the light splashing unsteadily around her.

Doomsfire.

The entire message she'd been meant to hear was that one, inexplicable word.

What the blazing hell did it mean? The sensation of falling returned and with it, panic.

Miranda scrambled out of bed, thrusting her feet into her slippers. She suddenly, desperately, wanted another human to talk to. Moments later, she knocked softly on her sister's door. "Livy?"

"What is it?" came the unenthusiastic response.

Olivia's grumpy tone instantly settled Miranda's nerves. She was being ridiculous. Maybe she'd simply had a nightmare.

Miranda turned the brass knob and slipped in, closing the door behind her. She'd wrapped herself in a warm robe, but she was still chilled by the memory of the river. "When did you get home?"

Olivia glanced at the carriage clock resting on the mantelpiece. "Nearly an hour ago."

When Miranda had been on the roof and Kitteridge had been complicating their friendship. For an instant, she envied Olivia her carefully regulated life, devoid of romantic entanglements.

Miranda drifted toward the room's small fireplace, stretching out her hands to warm them. The scene was comforting and familiar, just what she needed. Olivia was curled in an overstuffed armchair before the fire, her feet tucked beneath a tasseled throw. She'd unpinned her hair, and it fell around her shoulders, catching the golden lamplight. A stack of books sat on the table beside her and a large volume lay open in her lap. She looked contented as a cat, queen of her private domain. Olivia had the knack of conserving her energy, while Miranda had to burn it off if she ever hoped to sleep.

Of most importance, Olivia was the smartest person she knew. If there was anything to the message in her dream—if it was in truth a dream and not a scrambled memory from the crash—her bookish sibling would know. But approach was everything. Olivia dealt in numbers, not vague portents. She didn't tolerate fanciful thinking.

"How was your dinner?" Miranda asked.

"Typical. The club was too warm, the dinner too cold, and the conversation halfway between." Olivia marked her page with a ribbon and set the volume aside. "How was yours?"

"Leek soup."

"Alas."

Miranda smiled. "Alas."

Olivia gestured to an overstuffed stool, and Miranda sat, cupping her chin in her hands.

"Did you interrupt my reading for a particular reason, or just to chat?" Olivia asked, tracing the embossed leather of the book cover.

"Both, I think."

"How was Father tonight?"

"He didn't stay past the soup course."

Olivia's gaze fell to her hands. Her fingers moved from the book to twine in the tasseled fringe of the throw. "I wish Gideon were here to help with the business."

"I do, too. But I'm helping," Miranda said, a pinch of resentment in her tone. As the youngest child, she'd struggled to keep up with her siblings. Some perceptions never changed. "I'm doing the lion's share at the airfield when Father cannot."

"Of course," Olivia replied. "And you do your best with the administration."

Miranda flushed. She had no talent for contracts and correspondence, but she'd doggedly kept the flood of paper moving. "I know I'm better at practical things."

Olivia's expression tightened. "Risky things, you mean."

"You never wanted to be an aeronaut."

"No, and Mother didn't want that for us. Not that she wanted a bluestocking, either."

Plenty of women pursued careers, some advancing to the highest levels. Few, however, came from noble families, who still believed that a true lady did not work outside the home. Their mother had hoped her daughters would marry well, as befit the granddaughters of the Earl of Havelock. The only one who had come close was Sidonie.

"We're fine as we are," Miranda said with a half-smile. "You're brilliant, and Gideon and I are practical, like Father."

"Yes, Father is daring, ambitious, and built the company from nothing. A wonderful model, except that he is failing, Sidonie and Gideon are gone, and you nearly joined them." Olivia pulled the throw closer about her, as if a sudden draft had chilled her. "That would leave me with responsibility for Fletcher Industries."

"You're completely capable of managing the business."

"I'm better suited to an academic career. I said it to Gideon and I'll say it to you." She leaned her head against the back of her chair. "Think of that before your next daredevil adventure."

To another, the words might have seemed unfeeling, but Miranda heard the fear beneath them. It mirrored hers. "I understand. I want nothing more than to keep the family together. Tonight, when I walked into the dining room, Father was the only one there. It should have been noisy and full of life. Full of *us*."

Olivia nodded slowly. "I know." Her eyes glittered. Cursing softly, she looked away.

Miranda rose from her seat and bent over her sister, pulling her close in a hug. Olivia's hair was silken against her cheek. There were hot tears, too, but Miranda pretended not to notice.

Her sister was like a hedgehog, prickles on the outside but with a vulnerable underbelly.

Miranda smoothed Olivia's hair. "I suppose I should leave you to your reading."

"Please do." Olivia picked up her book, pointedly opening it to the place where she'd marked it.

Miranda noticed it wasn't in English. "What is that?"

"Pythagoras in the original Greek. I borrowed it from the university."

"It's fortunate they had a copy." Londria had printers, but they didn't specialize in rare academic tomes, and imports were expensive and hard to get.

"There was a waiting list."

Finally, Miranda had the opening she wanted. "Was it the Greeks who talked about Doomsfire?"

Olivia looked up sharply. "There was a weapon called Greek fire. Entirely different."

"Then what's Doomsfire?"

"Where did you hear about that?" Olivia's expression was grave. "It's not a subject for the likes of us."

Miranda ignored the question and dropped her voice to a whisper. "It has something to do with the Citadel, doesn't it?"

Olivia leaned forward, her words equally quiet. "I came across the term in an old tome from the time of the Great Disaster. The book was from the special collections and contained some of Dr. Dee's writings on alchemy. Someone had left the book in a reading carrel in the university library."

"And you couldn't resist a look."

Olivia shrugged. "The language was antique, and alchemists wrote in a kind of code. It's hard to tell if they're writing a chemical formula or if they're raving mad. All I could determine is that Doomsfire is a magical substance—solid, gaseous, or liquid, I don't know."

"The book didn't say what it was for?"

"I closed the cover and backed away the moment I understood what I was reading. The Conclave occasionally uses the special collections for research. I didn't plan to be caught snooping in their business." Olivia frowned. "You know how they are. Say—or know—the wrong thing, and end up in the House of Questions."

"You did the smart thing." Miranda knew without asking that the subject was closed.

Olivia shivered slightly and settled back in her chair. "I want to read now."

Miranda forced a smile. "I hope Pythagoras is everything you desire in a bedtime read."

"Good night, Miranda," Olivia said pointedly, turning the page of her text.

"Don't stay up all night," Miranda returned. "You must save some delicious pages for tomorrow."

Olivia gave her a withering stare, and so she left. She paused in the hallway, placing her palm against the oak of Olivia's door, as if she could feel her sister's heartbeat through the heavy panels.

No one should ever feel their world crumbling away—not the way Miranda had felt at dinner that night. Not the way Olivia feared would happen, with her family gone and all the responsibility landing on her shoulders. Olivia was just loyal enough to give up her dreams to keep the legacy of Fletcher Industries alive.

Miranda dropped her hand from the door and started down the hall, her chest aching. She was sick to death of shadowy plots she didn't understand, of fear, blood, and monsters. People she loved were hurting. People she loved were gone forever.

If the city wasn't safe, someone else she cared about—Olivia, Gideon, or the servants, or the neighbors—would vanish from her life, and that was intolerable. The fight for Londria had to continue, and they couldn't afford to ignore weapons like the *Leopard*.

She wasn't brilliant like Olivia—Miranda had been born to do, to act. Her courage was all she had. Fear or no fear, pain or no pain, she had to fly.

And now she had a destination.

CHAPTER 15

"That one is going to get you killed."

Gillian Randall, proprietress of Hellion House, made the pronouncement in a dire tone Gideon hadn't heard before. It made him think of a vengeful goddess, which was more alluring than it should have been.

Her gaze lingered on the chair where Huntley had been sitting moments before. Gideon and Huntley had been at the Mercury Café—drinking and discussing their encounter with Councilor Latimer and the Threshers—for hours. Finally, Huntley had stepped outside for some fresh air.

Mrs. Randall must have arrived after they had, but he hadn't seen her come in. That wasn't remarkable, given the crush of patrons. But it was unusual, given the woman herself. With Titian hair and delicate features, she had the grace and air of a duchess. She wasn't a female any man overlooked.

Maybe he was more drunk than he thought.

She circled Gideon's table and alighted in Huntley's chair. She was wearing a midnight-blue gown that, while not exactly revealing, suggested the lithe form beneath.

Gideon straightened as she reached across the small table and took the glass from his hand.

"Are you listening to me?" she asked.

"I am," he replied, not entirely amused by the loss of his drink.

She raised her head, looking around the Mercury Café to see who might be listening. There was no one within earshot sufficiently sober to matter.

"I know what the Anathema Club gets up to," she said in a confidential tone. "Layla keeps me informed."

"Is that why you let her join them?" he asked.

"She's a grown woman. She makes her own choices, and I appreciate the information." Her eyebrows rose as if daring him to contradict her.

"Information is a form of currency."

"It's the only one I count on. When I offer it for free, pay attention."

"I'm well aware that Huntley is unorthodox. He nearly shot me the night we met."

"Men and their bonding rituals," she sighed.

Gideon eyed his glass of whisky, still trapped in Mrs. Randall's grip. He would endure a lot at her hands—even this outrage. Still, he hoped the lecture ended soon because, where she was concerned, the sequel would be much more interesting.

She was a widow and older than him, but not by much. No one knew the details of her past or how she came to run Londria's most exclusive brothel, and Gideon knew better than to ask. He wasn't a client—they were friends with an occasional interlude of passion—and he knew exactly how fortunate he was.

"Huntley has a good idea about what's going on in the city," he said, getting back to the main conversation.

"Ned Huntley has a good idea of how to get you cut to ribbons. He acts without thinking. Furthermore, he does it with pointy objects."

"You say that as if you care," he quipped, finally retrieving his glass from her elegantly gloved fingers.

She tilted her head. The light caught the sapphire dangling from her earlobe. "If you choose to ignore my warning, don't invite me to your funeral."

"Someone has to come."

"I have far too many of the morally dead in my acquaintance to worry about literal corpses. Perish at your own risk."

With that, she rose and signaled for Layla—who stood at the front of the café next to the dessert case, devouring a slice of Sacher torte with obvious relish—to join her. The young woman scraped the plate clean and handed it back to the smiling—and obviously besotted—server.

"Tell me, Mrs. Randall, how is it that you trust Layla in Huntley's company, but not me?" Gideon chided.

She bent to whisper in his ear, her breath a warm caress. "She has more common sense than you do, Mr. Fletcher. My ladies know how to survive."

With that, she sailed from the café, leaving a hint of her amber perfume behind. Layla followed. Huntley was on his way back in. He touched the brim of his hat as he passed Mrs. Randall, earning a cool nod.

"A formidable female," Huntley said as he reclaimed his seat.

"Quite," Gideon said, not inviting further discussion on that topic. She was annoyed with him, and it stung.

Huntley gave him a quizzical look, but held his tongue. The silence made Gideon uncomfortable, so he reverted to safer ground.

"Everyone the Unseen takes—or that I think they take—comes from a good family—wealthy, well-connected, old bloodlines."

"That's only half-true of my wife. Her father had money, but it was all from industry. It was her mother who was from the baronial hall."

"My parents were the same," Gideon replied. "The titles are on my mother's side, but Sidonie was an earl's granddaughter. She fits the pattern, as does your wife."

"Almost. There was some question about Margaret's parentage, which I didn't learn until my ring was on her finger." Huntley gave a lopsided smile. "Yes, family secrets, but if there's a pattern, you need all the facts."

Gideon was taken aback. "It might be important."

Huntley shrugged. "I'm too drunk to care about pedigrees. I love her and want her back."

"Fair enough." Gideon pulled a woman's ring from his pocket, holding it up to the candlelight. The peridot at its center flickered with green fire.

"It's a bit soon to propose, don't you think?" Huntley quipped.

Gideon grimaced at the joke. "My sister, Miranda, took it off the hand of a dead Unseen, who no doubt took it from the hand of the prey it devoured. Do you recognize it?"

Huntley shook his head. "It's not Margaret's."

They fell silent as fresh drinks were delivered. Gideon palmed the ring and returned it to his pocket.

"It's my hope someone might recognize it so that I might return it to the rightful owner's family," he added.

"It must be a souvenir, like the waistcoat on my monster. They're adopting the trappings of human life. They want to become us." Huntley took another swallow of his drink. "There's a nightmare for you. Monsters playing happy families."

Huntley pressed his thumb and forefinger against his closed eyelids, as if holding back tears. They were both more than a little drunk. Perhaps they should have ordered food as well as endless drinks.

Gideon tossed back the last of his whisky. "Time to go."

Huntley nodded his agreement. They paid and left the Mercury Café side by side. If their path weaved a little, Gideon didn't much care. He appreciated the companionship, whatever Mrs. Randall said.

They turned south, aiming in the general direction of the Regina Hotel. Gideon yawned, wondering if he might invite himself inside the Anathema Club's suite to sleep off the alcohol. His own rooms felt desperately far away.

For a while, a pair of River Rats wandered ahead of them, smoking long clay pipes and chatting in their own tongue. The moment Gideon and Huntley departed from the main street, they were alone. Had he been more sober, Gideon would have been on the alert for danger.

"I didn't use to be so incredibly serious, you know." Huntley seemed to speak more to himself than Gideon. "I used to joke with my young cousins, telling them not to go down alleyways because there were ghosts in the dead ends."

"Pardon?" Gideon asked, wondering just how drunk Huntley was.

"That's where the Unseen play hide and shriek." Huntley grinned.

"That's dreadful."

"Of course it is. And there is far worse to come."

Gideon waved a quelling finger. "Don't.

"Do you know why the Unseen never use cutlery?"

"Please, no."

"They prefer finger food." Huntley laughed, a strangled sound that had more to do with despair than humor. "Think about it."

Gideon grabbed a wall for support. "I'm going to be sick if you don't stop."

He thought he might be sick anyway, but Huntley raised a palm. "Hush."

They were both instantly silent, their drunken fog ripped away.

At first, Gideon heard nothing but the usual night sounds of the city. Distant voices. The clop of a horse's hooves. The drip of water.

But then his senses tuned to more subtle signals—the way they had when he'd been on rescue missions in the Outlands. There, the difference between life and death might be the rustle of a single leaf.

Barely moving, Huntley raised a finger, pointing to the street where they'd just been. The enemy was behind them. Gideon heard the soft susurration of panting breath. Their stalker was closer than he'd thought.

Without a word from Gideon, Huntley turned so they were back-to-back. Gideon wished he'd brought his gun, but his hand was still bandaged and clumsy.

"Anything?" Huntley asked.

"Nothing visible."

Huntley touched his arm. "Forward?"

"Go."

They ran toward the busier street ahead, keeping close to the buildings. Gideon glanced backward, watching the rear, while Huntley took point. Soon their path broadened, the darkness thinned by illumination from the apartments above.

Gideon saw their two pursuers the instant they stepped into the light. They were the same Threshers who had attacked earlier that day. First came the tall leader with the drooping mustache, then the one Huntley had knocked down.

A tiny part of him relaxed. "They're just humans."

Mustache pulled an aether gun. The weapon hummed as he flipped a switch to power it up. Pale golden light pulsed around the barrel, as if it had swallowed flickering gaslight.

Gideon bumped into Huntley's solid form. His friend had stopped without warning. Gideon spun, putting his back to the wall, trying to look ahead without taking his eyes off the threat behind them.

The third Thresher stood in Huntley's path, a revolver in his hand. Their opponents closed in from both sides, eating up the ground with purposeful strides. Gideon smiled inside. Smarter opponents would never throw away the advantage of remaining out of reach. Not when they were the ones with firearms.

"Go," Huntley said, the word pitched so that only Gideon heard.

Gideon sprang at Mustache before he could aim. The man fell back, but he had come too close to escape. Gideon grappled him, driving his knee into the man's gut hard enough that he doubled over and dropped his weapon. Gideon kicked it aside, then aimed a two-fisted blow to the back of the neck. The man went down, but rolled to his feet almost at once and reclaimed his gun.

Gideon was already in motion. He ducked down a narrow passage between buildings, using the high brick walls for cover. He hadn't seen Huntley's part of the fight, but his friend was behind him and breathing hard. Gideon slid between another pair of buildings, realizing that he knew this neighborhood well. Another turn, and he found the metal staircase zigzagging up the side of an office building. He swarmed up the steps, heading for the aqueducts above. Vanishing among the city's rooftops was the easiest escape.

Huntley followed, moving just as silently. When Gideon reached the top, he crouched, moving slowly and carefully. They were four stories up with no handholds, scrambling along a strip of brick and iron not much wider than his foot. The aqueducts sometimes ran beside the rooflines, but more often stood a little higher, using gravity to channel the water downward to rooftop gardens.

That was the case here. He put one foot before the other, well aware the narrow iron channels weren't meant for walking—especially not while drunk.

Once he was a dozen yards from the stairway, he jumped down to the nearest roof and crouched behind a chimney, signaling Huntley to do the same. Curses rose from below as the

Threshers circled like mystified bloodhounds. With a wicked grin, Huntley held up the revolver he'd taken from the third Thresher.

Euphoria—stronger than any liquor—left Gideon giddy. They'd not only survived—they'd outwitted their enemies.

After a minute, they moved on. Their escape had pushed them back toward Maudlin Way, which made Hellion House the easiest place to hide from pursuit. Gideon led the way from one roof to next using the aqueduct. The Threshers still wove through the streets below, determined as sharks who'd scented blood. So far, they hadn't searched the world above, and Gideon meant to find safety before they did.

As an aeronaut, he was used to operating at extreme heights, but Huntley was not. They were balanced on an expanse of iron-work that stretched between buildings when he heard the man slip and catch himself, cursing loudly.

Moments later, an aether gun whirred below. The enemy had found them.

Sweat broke out along Gideon's spine. "Move faster."

A white-hot blast sparked off the iron edge of the aqueduct, inches from Gideon's feet. He kept going, alert to every breath of wind that might skew his balance. In this stretch, there was no rooftop where he could leap and hide. The only chance of losing their hunters was directly ahead, where two aqueducts crossed. From there, they could change direction.

Gideon sped forward, using momentum to keep his footing. Another shot sparked a yard in front of him, close enough that the heat flared against his face. He flung up an arm to shield his eyes and ran through the fading ghost of the flame. Huntley's footfalls thundered behind him—they had both given up on stealth.

They were nearly at the junction. It hovered above a cobbled courtyard where two roads met. Iron braces secured the two aqueducts to a supporting pillar.

The next shot struck directly under Gideon, shattering the iron and brick from beneath. He flew forward, landing on the next section in a stumbling, slithering attempt to keep his balance. He fell sideways, grabbing at the tangle of ironwork that formed the junction—and missed.

Years of working the sails saved him. As he slid off the aqueduct, he snatched one of the braces holding the junction upright. Using that handhold, he swung forward and wrapped his legs around the iron pillar that supported the intersecting ducts. His heel caught the edge of the maintenance ladder that ran up the pillar. He hooked a foot in a rung and pulled himself closer, just as if it were the mast of an airship. From there, it was easy to grab the rails that ran along either side of the ladder.

"Are you insane?" Huntley bellowed from above.

"You're a pigeon on a wire up there. Get out of sight!"

A volley from the aether gun passed inches behind Gideon, the heat like a slap against his shoulder blades. It hit the iron above, raining down sparks. From the angle of the shot, their pursuers were a slight distance to the south. Not much, but there was still a chance for Huntley to escape.

Gideon needed a better plan than clinging to a ladder on a post. He might get back on top of the duct, but not while he was under fire.

He braced his feet against the ladder rails and loosened his grip. Instantly, he slid downward, picking up speed as his palms burned from the friction, even through the bandages on his right hand. Just as he was about to hit the ground, he flung himself loose and rolled. The impact made him grunt. Not a perfect landing, but good enough.

Huntley dropped down beside him, stumbling and swearing, a few moments later. "I hate you."

"You could have kept running."

"And leave you behind? What kind of a mate would I be?"

They both staggered into a run, but Gideon pulled Huntley to a stop around the first corner. They were both panting hard. The street was empty, but their pursuers would be there soon.

"What now?" Huntley growled.

"This lot won't give up. If we don't get them tonight, they'll be back tomorrow."

Like clockwork, Mustache burst from the shadows. His gaze was fixed on the pillar, as if he expected to find his quarry still there. Gideon slid from his hiding place, delivering a chop to the man's windpipe. The man dropped to the ground.

Huntley dove for the aether gun, scooping it from the cobbles as the other two Threshers pounded up. At the sight of the weapon, one flung up his hands and veered away, vanishing back into the murk. The second—the youngest one—wasn't so quick to adapt.

Gideon wheeled, ready to catch him. Only then did he get a good look at the young man's face. Although the lad's nose was broken and his eyes badly bruised, it was familiar enough. This was Featherly, the missing aeronaut who had survived the wreck of the *Leopard,* only to walk away from his growing family.

Had he been the one to allow the saboteur to access the ship?

Gideon lunged, grappling him. Featherly grunted with the impact, but slithered free with a ferret's agility.

A firebolt of pain lanced through Gideon's side.

The lad had a knife.

CHAPTER 16

Gideon woke disoriented and queasy. He pried open his eyes, blinking as bright light assaulted his vision. Daylight. It took another few seconds for his pounding brain to conclude it was morning.

Pain wandered like a cat from muscle to joint and back, pausing to admire the view. His skull felt monstrously heavy and packed with cotton wool—no doubt a parting gift from last night's drink. Pieces of his memory had vanished. He recalled racing along the aqueducts, fighting, and then…what?

With blurry eyes, he scanned his surroundings, noting marine-blue walls and a golden jacquard carpet. A vast bed stood at the opposite end of the room. Four mahogany posts twisted upward to hold a canopy of Brussels lace that fluttered in the air currents. The burgundy velvet coverlet was flung back, revealing delectably rumpled sheets.

Sheets he clearly hadn't occupied last night, though this was Gillian Randall's bedchamber. In a disappointing development, he was exiled to the daybed at the far end of the room.

An attempt to sit up tore a groan from his throat. Glancing down toward the source of his pain, he realized he was naked, a blanket drawn up to his chest. Lack of clothing wasn't unusual in a brothel, but this was different. A wide bandage wrapped his aching abdomen. Someone had tended his injuries and, apparently, left him to recover in Mrs. Randall's private rooms.

He tried to recall how he'd come by the wound, but no memory got past his thundering headache.

"Ah, the young knight awakens from his enchanted repose," Mrs. Randall said from somewhere behind him.

He tried to speak, but he was incredibly thirsty—was that from the hangover or the blood loss?

"It's pure luck you aren't dead," she added, her tone as dry as his parched tongue.

The day bed was at the wrong angle to see her, so he attempted to turn without angering his wounds. That only increased his sense the room was slowly rotating without him.

She sat at a dressing table putting on her pearl earrings. The intimacy of the image scattered his every thought. Their eyes met in the gilt-framed mirror, and she crooked an eyebrow.

"How is your head?" she asked.

"Hurts." It came out as a phlegmy croak, and he cleared his throat. "It hurts like the devil."

"Do you remember much?"

He began to shake his head, but the pain was blinding. "No."

"The story goes that your opponent had a knife. You disarmed him before he entirely removed your entrails."

"Good for me."

"Not quite. You hit your head on the iron footing of the pillar while wrestling with him on the ground. Sadly, knife-boy got away."

"Featherly." Details were reluctantly creeping back—the young man's bruised face and the blade in his hand. In retrospect, Gideon was shocked. He'd never said a harsh word to the lad—or received one from him. "He used to work for Fletcher Industries. We joked about his name, how he'd been born to work in the air."

Mrs. Randall spun to face him. "You knew your attacker?"

He had, and now Featherly was with the Threshers. Why?

A wave of exhaustion pushed him back onto the cushions. "How did I get here? Where's Huntley?"

"He left once we were certain you'd rise to fight another day." She approached and touched a cool hand to his forehead. "He brought you here. You were barely conscious. He was most unhappy that saving your skin meant the Threshers got away."

The scent of her—warm skin and that delicate amber perfume —wrapped around him like an embrace. Gideon closed his eyes, feeling the weight of her worried gaze.

"I told you that Huntley would get you killed. Grief over his lost wife makes him reckless, and I think you find that kind of bravado contagious."

"Huntley fought well. He probably saved my life."

"Perhaps he did. Perhaps you would have been more careful alone."

That much was true, but he didn't say so. Something in her expression struck him silent.

She touched his cheeks, then his forehead again, the gesture almost maternal. "Didn't I tell you that when I offer information for free, you should pay attention?"

"You did."

"Then don't ignore me again," she said. "All news in Londria finds its way to Hellion House sooner or later."

"Such as?"

"Everything that matters. Those who visit are often eager to unburden their minds. My ladies are great listeners. Often, that is the exact service our guests require. A companion who will not judge them."

"I know." His head hurt, and he was growing a touch impatient.

"You don't know. Few truly understand how this place works because the affairs of fallen women are irrelevant to anyone but us. Some entertain our guests; some serve the house in other ways. How they contribute is up to them."

The tone in her voice caught his attention, as she'd no doubt intended.

"Explain." Gideon struggled to a sitting position.

"This place was exactly what it seems when I came here. Now it is not."

She poured a glass of water from a rose-colored pitcher and handed it to him. He drank until it was empty, then returned the glass.

"Is that all you're going to say?" he prompted.

She sank to the foot of the daybed, resting a hand on his shin. "I give my women a choice. They give me absolute loyalty."

Gideon finally understood her point. "They tell you everything their clients say."

"Not everything. Their personal affairs remain so."

"That's a relief."

She gave a brief smile. "My women are the best at what they do, and I reward them accordingly. My aim is that they build a life of their own design. Half the fashionable modistes in Londria are my alumni."

"And your clients are the ranking figures in Londria," he said. "Politicians, nobles, merchants. If information is currency, you have access to everything."

She gave a slight shrug, looking away. "I'm a good businesswoman."

He wondered, not for the first time, who she had been before Hellion House. "You trust that I will keep this information to myself?"

"I do." She gave him a long look. "You are an aspiring investigator, and I am a treasure trove of fact. Besides, we like each other."

Gideon nodded slowly. He had reservations, but could examine those later. Her hand on his leg was more than distracting. "I assume you are telling me this because you have information about Huntley?"

"No, about the Threshers. Huntley said you'd met Councilor Latimer, and that he told you the Threshers were in the Conclave's employ."

"Latimer said the mages employ a smattering of civilians on an ad hoc basis."

"That isn't the entire story."

"Somehow, I am not astonished."

Gideon sat up, remembering to adjust the blanket that covered him at the last moment. Her gaze drifted the length of his torso, igniting his flesh with her silent appraisal.

"You make it damned hard to concentrate," he muttered.

She rose and plumped his cushions, encouraging him to lie back. Sadly, it was the gesture of a nurse, not a lover. "You're going to listen to my advice before you gallop into more trouble. I want you alive and well, Mr. Fletcher." Dimples formed beside her lips, but her eyes were serious.

Gideon drifted on that gaze, momentarily mesmerized. "Go on."

She paced a few steps, folding her arms across her stomach. "The Threshers have existed for about five years, perhaps a little more."

"I thought everything the Conclave did went back to the Great Disaster."

She shook her head. "Not the Threshers. They are not mages, nor are they officially sanctioned. They do not report to the Council. Not all the members approve of their existence."

That corresponded with what Latimer had said, but it left him curious. "How do you know?"

She was silent a long moment before she answered. "You must be aware that much of Londria chafes under the Conclave's rule."

"Of course."

"There are those who meet to discuss contingencies. Don't ask who they are."

He desperately wanted to know, but patience would serve him better when dealing with Gillian Randall. "Very well. Then where do the Threshers fit?"

"I would say they are a private army, except they are more thugs than soldiers. The term I heard was enforcers."

"Latimer called them loyal fanatics. Who gives them their orders?"

She shook her head. "I don't know. Why were they after you and Huntley?"

"I wish I knew. Featherly was an employee, an airman on the *Leopard*. And I'm investigating its wreck, so I assume I'm the target, not Huntley."

"Someone connected to the Conclave wants your investigation to end?"

"Councilor Ormond visited Miranda," Gideon replied. "The Conclave seems to have been in the dark, both about the *Leopard*'s purpose and its demise."

Her laugh held no mirth. "The Conclave is an organization riddled with factions. Someone cut Ormond out of an important conversation."

He tried to lean forward, but regretted the movement and sat back again. "So someone created the Threshers to pursue a private agenda? Sabotaged the *Leopard* without official sanction from the Council? Why?"

"There are only three reasons that I can think of—money, vengeance, or love. Most of the ugly things in the world come down to one of those three." She said it with a weariness that touched him.

A soft knock came at the door. At Mrs. Randall's summons, a maid appeared with a pile of folded clothes. She laid them on a footstool, curtsied, and left the room, closing the door behind her. Mrs. Randall shook out the top garment. Gideon realized it was his shirt, washed and mended.

"It will never be quite the same," she said wryly.

"I understand the sentiment," Gideon replied. The throbbing in his head had eased a notch, but the knife wound hurt like the blazes, leaving him shaky. He would say nothing of it, though. Not to her.

"Here," she said, holding up the shirt. "Let me help you into this."

Before he could protest, she worked the folds of fine linen over his head. He thrust his arms through the sleeves, discovering fresh discomfort in the movement.

Her fingers smoothed the cloth over his shoulders and down his chest. The gesture brought her face close to his. The scent of her hair was intoxicating. As their lips touched, heat against heat, his hand found the petal-soft skin of her cheek. She sighed softly, mingling her breath with his.

"Thank you," he said.

"For the shirt or the kiss?"

"Both are restorative."

Her dimples flashed again. "As intended." She returned to her dressing table and picked up a jeweled comb, arranging it in her crown of curls. Most women relied on maids to dress their hair, but he knew she did much of her toilette herself.

She was wearing an elegant afternoon dress suitable for the best drawing room in the city. Her appointments were none of his business, but he wondered what she had planned.

It was hard to play a convincing lover tucked up on the daybed like a child with the sniffles. He swung his feet to the floor, pushing the blanket aside. He rose, hiding his aches as best he could, and crossed to where the maid had left his clothes. He dressed slowly, careful not to open his wound. When he got to his coat, he checked the pockets for the ring and button he'd been carrying. Both were still there, despite the ring's value. As Mrs.

Randall had said, her ladies were loyal. They would not steal from their mistress's favorite guest.

"Tell me this," he said, fumbling with his boots. "The Threshers all wear dark coats and most have top hats."

"It is their unofficial uniform," she said. "What of it?"

"There were men who were similarly dressed in the graveyard the night Sidonie was taken. I assumed they were creatures like Masson."

Mrs. Randall turned from the mirror. Her eyes flared wide. "What are you saying?"

"Heresy, maybe. Or perhaps nothing. I don't know." He suddenly felt foolish, as if he'd allowed his search for patterns and connections to wander too far. He began fumbling with his necktie.

Her hands took the ends from his fingers. She'd moved so quietly he hadn't heard her approach. With deft movements, she knotted the cloth. Her face had gone pale.

"Beware of what you say, even here. Heresy will land you in the Citadel," she said. "In the House of Questions."

He searched for an answer but couldn't find one he liked.

She smoothed his collar. "Be careful. Please. I don't want you hurt again."

"I need to know the truth."

"Is it worth your life?"

"Someone took my twin. My youngest sister was on the *Leopard*. This is personal to me."

She tilted her head. "Martyrdom is a luxury most can't afford. You still think like the heir to a great fortune—one who can pay another to tend to those he leaves behind. The rest of us can't soften the blow of our demise. We're forced to keep fighting."

Gideon flinched inwardly. "Perhaps."

The corners of her mouth turned down. "I'm worth living for, Gideon."

She returned to her dressing table and picked up a fan and her gloves. Her features settled into the cool mask he recognized as her public face.

"I must go," she said. "Feel free to stay until you're rested."

"Where are you going?" he asked, unable to stop himself.

She waved her fan in a negative motion. "You have your investigations. I have my own concerns."

He pictured her at a racetrack or some den of the demimonde, on the arm of some wealthy gentlemen. A pang of heartache surprised him.

Taking her hand, he bowed, kissing her fingertips. "A thousand thanks for your hospitality, madam."

A smile softened her features. "Be a good boy and go home to bed."

With that, she left. Gideon watched her slim figure vanish through the door. He barely quelled an idiotic impulse to follow. Jealousy would ruin everything. Neither of them was the type to make promises.

CHAPTER 17

letcher
     A mutual friend informs me you have information I require. Come to the park at the end of Hambly Street immediately.
     ~Palmer

GIDEON FLIPPED a coin to the rat-faced urchin who delivered the message. The boy ran down the steps from Gideon's rooms, through the bookshop on the main floor, and out the front door with a chiming of bells. He was no doubt headed for the pie shop across the street for his first solid meal of the day.

Still half-awake, Gideon reread the message. He'd returned home from Hellion House, bathed, and fallen into bed. He'd managed a few hours of sound sleep before the messenger's knocking had roused him. Now, it seemed, he was back into the fray.

He dressed and made his way to the park as fast as his injuries allowed. The twenty-minute walk turned into a chilly forty-five. The frigid, gray weather promised rain or even snow.

As he went, the houses grew tidier, then grander, with holiday garlands around the windows and doors. The park wasn't large, comprising an ornamental lake surrounded by trees and bushes. Palmer and his men milled around the bushes at the south end of the water. Gideon joined them.

Palmer crouched at the water's edge, studying the muddy ground. A flock of ducks paddled and bobbed on the lake, leaving ripples in their wake. A quiet hush hung over the scene, ruined only by the body on the bank. From the general sogginess of the corpse, someone had recently pulled it from the water.

The detective inspector rose to greet Gideon. "You look like yesterday's tragedy served cold."

"I'm still doing better than your friend on the grass."

The detective inspector made a face. "A cook's helper cut through this morning on the way to market. Found this sod dumped in the shallows."

Palmer pointed to the body, clearly expecting Gideon to inspect it. "Tell me if he looks familiar. Trample the grass if you need to. We've already looked for clues."

After last night's whisky, Gideon's stomach was unenthused by the stench wafting from the corpse. He approached reluctantly. The man was on his back, limbs spread. Gideon hung back, stopping just short of the man's outstretched fingertips.

"I'm always happy to gain experience in the art of investigation," Gideon said, "but who told you I had information?"

Palmer joined him beside the body. "I crossed paths with one of Mrs. Randall's girls late last night. She said you ran afoul of the Threshers. Is that one of them?"

Gideon steeled himself as he closed in for a better view. His insides lurched. The man's face was bruised and bloated on one side, a ruin of meat and shattered teeth on the other. He jerked his eyes away from the obscene grin.

"A powerful weapon, close range," Palmer said. "He let his attacker get near."

Gideon forced himself to look closer. The firearm that had

killed the man had blasted away his flesh, but hadn't burned it. Not an aether weapon, then.

His gaze moved to the periphery of the horror, noting the hair and clothes, item by item. No hat. He wore good quality leather boots—unlike the river, this man-made lake lacked a current strong enough to tear footwear from a victim's feet. The rest of his ripped and muddy garments had likewise been expensive. How much of the damage had come before the man had died?

Gideon looked closer at the mass of crumpled coat. The black cloth was sodden, bunched up beneath the man's body, but the garment was definitely like those the Threshers wore.

Now he understood why Palmer had summoned him.

He circled the corpse to get a better view of the man's remaining features. Bruising evidenced a recent fight, maybe the same one that had torn the knees of his trousers. That would have taken a fall to a hard surface—the road, not this sward of grass.

Gideon took yet another look at the face, trying to match the features. A memory rose from the night before—the man who had run from the sight of Huntley holding the aether weapon. Huntley had already left bruises during the skirmish earlier that day.

"Well?" Palmer asked, fidgeting with his gold lighter.

"This was one of the three I encountered last night."

"The cook's helper identified him as Robin Vortigern. He lived with his parents on the next street. The father came around earlier and confirmed it. Poor sod took off afterward like a grouse in shooting season."

A name and address made the death more real—and more confusing. "The Vortigerns are a wealthy family. Respectable. They made their money in manufacturing engines—my father did business with them. I knew the older son at school, but not

Robin. He was a few years younger, and that means more when you're a boy."

"Was he the black sheep?" Palmer speculated.

"Not that I know of," Gideon replied. "Even if he liked women and whisky, why would he spend his time brawling like a common tough? Why would anyone shoot him?"

Palmer cast him a sidelong look. "You come from his world and are better suited to answer those questions than I am."

Gideon turned away from the corpse, unable to stare at it any longer. "I had nothing to do with him, outside of the occasions when he tried to bash in my skull."

Palmer pulled out his cigarette case and gestured toward the next street, where presumably the Vortigerns lived. "Then let's find out why he was running with the Threshers."

"Are you sure you want me there?" Gideon asked. "I'm not official police."

"You speak rich bastard."

They set out on foot for the Vortigern address, Palmer smoking as they walked.

"So, which of Mrs. Randall's ladies did you speak to?" Gideon asked.

"Layla," Palmer replied.

Something in his tone caught Gideon's attention. "Did she mention I was with Ned Huntley?"

"No." Palmer frowned. "Now there's a storm crow. How do you know him?"

"Long story."

Palmer exhaled a plume of smoke. "Don't be dragging his lot over to Hellion House. They don't need that kind of trouble."

His protective tone took Gideon aback. "You do know Layla is part of Huntley's club?"

Palmer visibly started. "What?"

Gideon suppressed a smile. "There's more to the lovely Layla than we knew."

"Bloody hell," Palmer swore. "I'll have a word with Mrs. Randall."

Gideon bit his tongue. That promised to be an entertaining conversation.

The Vortigern residence was large, with a broad porch and pediment supported by Corinthian columns. Palmer paused at the gate, studying the house for a long moment before striding up the walk. Gideon knew that in most wealthy households, the footman who answered the door would direct the police to the servants' entrance. They wouldn't dare to insult a Fletcher that way.

Gideon mounted the steps first and rapped with the heavy brass knocker.

Instead of a footman, a young and flustered housemaid opened the door. Her shell-shocked pallor said news of Robin's end had already spread through the house. In moments, the place would be sunk in mourning.

"Gideon Fletcher," he said to the girl. "And Detective Inspector Palmer of the Londria Constabulary."

She dipped into a curtsy. "I'm sorry, sir, the master and mistress aren't at home to visitors."

"I understand," he said. "There has been a terrible tragedy. That's why we're here."

"They'll be at home to us," Palmer added. "That's how the law works."

Minutes later, Gideon and Palmer were shown to a drawing room to wait. Thin winter light filtered through the drapes, showing off the spare, tasteful furnishings. Palmer sat, fidgeting, while Gideon prowled the room. A family photograph in a silver frame sat on a shelf. There were three Vortigern sons plus the parents. The image was a few years out of date, but further confirmed the identity of the corpse. The dead Thresher had been the youngest child.

Vortigern entered the room in a rush, his expression

promising a storm of anger. Palmer rose to his feet, and the three of them stared at each other for an uncomfortable moment.

"Mr. Vortigern," Gideon said. "My—"

"I know you, Fletcher," he replied, cutting Gideon off. "And you must be the police detective."

Palmer nodded, making no attempt to shake hands. "Detective Inspector Palmer."

"What is it you want from me now?" Vortigern said coldly.

"I'm sorry to intrude again," Palmer said, quietly taking the reins of the conversation. "It is our duty to investigate. Naturally, we would appreciate your assistance with a few questions."

Vortigern inhaled, as if about to object, but then waved a hand at the chairs. His eyes glittered, betraying his pain. "Keep it brief."

"Thank you."

Vortigern looked from Palmer to Gideon. "I understand the police, but what's your interest, Fletcher?"

"I've been of use in some investigations," Gideon said, improvising. "I understand the necessity of discretion in these matters."

Vortigern nodded. No one of any social standing wanted common constables blundering through their private affairs. A Fletcher—however much a black sheep—was more palatable.

They all sat.

"Do you know why your son was at the park before dawn?" Palmer asked.

Vortigern cleared his throat. "Not specifically."

"Generally?" Palmer gave an apologetic smile. "Any detail could be important."

The man sighed. "Robin was troubled. It was the usual story—some of his acquaintances did not have the best influence on him. I should have put a stop to it."

"How did he meet them?" Gideon asked.

"Does it matter?"

"It might."

"The university. He was a student there. Everything went well until about a year ago."

Palmer had pulled a notebook from his pocket. He flipped it open, pencil poised. "What happened then?"

"A friend of his disappeared. I assumed he simply ran off, but the boys—Robin and his other friends—seemed to think the Unseen snatched him off the street. A ridiculous idea. None of those venture inside the wall."

Gideon's pulse quickened. "Who was this boy who disappeared?"

Visibly annoyed, Vortigern rose to pace the room. "What does this have to do with Robin's death?"

"Perhaps nothing," Palmer replied. "But it could be important. Please bear with us."

Without warning, Vortigern stalked out the door. Gideon exchanged a glance with Palmer, who shrugged. "Your question might have triggered a memory."

Vortigern returned with a framed picture about fourteen inches across. He thrust it at Gideon. "There, in the front. His name was George Bagstaff. He probably fell prey to the River Rats. That's who you should be questioning. Smugglers and card sharps, the lot of them."

The photograph captured a group of about twenty male students arranged in three rows—two sitting and one standing in the back. Bagstaff was at the center front, an impish smile beneath a shock of straight dark hair.

Excitement swept over Gideon. The young man featured in his gallery of missing persons. "I know this case. Bagstaff is still missing."

"Yes, he is."

Other details caught Gideon's notice. Robin Vortigern sat at the end of the bench, an upright paddle in his hand. This was the university's rowing team, and they all wore the ugly striped waistcoats. His thoughts flew to the Unseen Huntley had killed, and the button Gideon still carried in his pocket.

Then he noticed a figure in the back row. The tall man with the drooping mustache—the one who had been with Featherly and Robin Vortigern—glowered from the picture.

"Who is that?" Gideon asked, straining to keep the eagerness from his voice. "He looks older than the others."

Vortigern frowned. "Dr. Strang. He is the faculty member who oversees the team. Unsuitable choice, if you ask me. He is a professor of an unwholesome branch of natural philosophy. Cutting up the dead or some such nonsense."

"Is he still the team's sponsor?" Palmer asked.

"Regrettably," Vortigern curled a lip. "He has an unhealthy influence over a few of the boys, Robin included."

Palmer made a note in his book. "What do you mean by unhealthy influence?"

"Filling their heads with odd ideas. I'm all for giving the mages due respect, but Strang is fanatically loyal to the Conclave. A true reformer."

That echoed Councilor Latimer's words.

"Did Strang do it?" Vortigern demanded, his mask of calm finally slipping. His shoulders rose, an unconscious signal he was ready to fight. "Did Strang kill my son?"

"That's impossible to say," Palmer said with deliberate calm. "It's far too soon to narrow our enquiries."

A polite knock came at the door, followed by an elderly butler.

"What is it, Lawson?" Vortigern asked irritably.

"Apologies, sir, but the mistress requires you."

Vortigern visibly mastered himself, then cast a dismissive glance at Gideon and Palmer. "We'll continue this another time."

"Indeed, sir," Palmer replied. "I'll be back if I have more questions."

"Very well." Vortigern left the room, almost at a run.

The butler politely waited for Gideon and Palmer to leave.

"What do you make of that?" Palmer asked as they descended the steps of the Vortigern house.

"Huntley killed an Unseen wearing a waistcoat identical to the club uniform," Gideon replied.

Palmer cocked an eyebrow. "Did he, now?"

"It doesn't close the case, but it's suggestive. I'm inclined to agree that the Unseen carried off the lad."

"And about Robin?"

"His friend's disappearance drove him into the arms of Strang and the Threshers. The question is, what went wrong?"

They'd reached the sidewalk. Watery sunbeams were breaking up the clouds. Palmer lit another cigarette.

"The father blames himself," Palmer observed. "Parents always do."

"Is there anything in that?"

"Normally, I don't rule out family. But I don't think the father did it. Not this time."

"Then where do we go next?" Gideon asked.

Palmer blew a smoke ring. "I'd like a word with the professor."

CHAPTER 18

"I know Strang's type," Palmer said. "Men like that are smart and ruthless, but they're also conceited."

"How does that work for us?" Gideon asked.

"He imagines himself above the rest of us. In his mind, he'll never be caught."

They had returned to the park after visiting the Vortigern house. Along the way, Gideon recounted his adventures with the Threshers, giving more information than Palmer had got from Layla. The detective inspector listened without interrupting, his frown deepening as they walked.

By the time they arrived at the park, a horse and wagon had come to take the remains of Robin Vortigern to a police surgeon for further investigation. Only a few personnel remained at the scene.

Palmer commandeered a police carriage, smelling of tobacco and damp upholstery, and a brace of constables to escort him and Gideon to their next destination.

"How does Strang's nature dictate our next move?" Palmer asked.

Every time Gideon accompanied him on a case, the detective

inspector treated it like a tutorial. As he'd only just begun his career as a private inquiry agent, Gideon gratefully soaked up the instruction.

He considered Palmer's question. "If Strang thinks he's untouchable, he won't vary from his usual routine. That's why we're headed toward the university."

"Exactly." Palmer stared out the window, frowning as if the scene outside troubled him. "We know the Threshers, officially or unofficially, are acting on behalf of someone connected to the Conclave. Strang thinks he's in the right."

"We don't know for certain that he killed Vortigern."

"No, but he knows something. Dr. Strang recruited his students. When someone woos another person to their cause, they study their mark in advance."

"How does that help us?"

"If he did his job, the good professor will have details about Robin Vortigern his family will never know."

"Such as?"

"Weaknesses, debts, and desires. Recruitment—or seduction—is all about answering a need."

The University of Londria was in the west end of the city. It had begun as a single old pile encrusted in gargoyles and tradition. Over time, the institution had engulfed a crowded snaggle of buildings on the north bank of the river. Palmer directed the carriage to the far end of the campus, where the rowing team had its clubhouse. They left the carriage at the curb with orders to wait.

"We'll start here," Palmer said. "Two members of this rowing team met with misfortune, and that means something. I want a feel for who they are when they're together. From there, we can move on to Strang's classroom. With luck, we'll find him in one place or the other."

The sun had come out during their drive, and Gideon glimpsed the sparkling river. Given the wintery cold, there weren't many rowers on the water, but the clubhouse itself was full of people.

"How do you wish to proceed?" Gideon asked as they approached the door.

"Quietly. There's no point in causing a fuss before our quarry is in sight."

"Then allow me to do the honors."

As soon as Gideon gave his name, the doorman admitted them. The main room was vast, the space divided into clusters of gaming tables, a refreshment area, and couches. Of all the university's sporting clubs, the rowing team attracted the cream of Londria's society. Liveried servants ferried food and drink to the occupants, most of whom were loud enough to be comfortably drunk.

At first glance, Gideon recognized many of the faces—these were the children of Londria's best families. Most were male, but he recognized some women, too. All combined, the cost of their clothing would have supported Palmer's constables for the next decade.

The detective inspector gave a low chuckle as he scanned the card tables and velvet-covered chairs. "And here I'd expected a boat shed."

"I'm sure there are boats here somewhere," Gideon replied. "The servants will know where to find them."

It was an exaggeration—serious athletes lavished time and care on their equipment. However, most people there were not members of the team.

William Kitteridge lounged against the wall next to a potted palm. Gideon had seen the man around town, making eyes at Miranda whenever the two crossed paths. Gideon's immediate instinct was to punch the man. However, he fixed his face into a friendly mask and approached.

"Well, well," Kitteridge said, looking down his nose even

though he was slightly shorter than Gideon. "Did you come to try your luck on the water?"

"Not quite. I'm looking for Dr. Strang. I understand he's the faculty sponsor of the rowing team."

Kitteridge cocked a brow. "I have no idea where he is." He said it as if Gideon had asked him to locate a garden slug.

"Not a friend of yours?" Gideon asked, a little amused.

"He runs with a different set." He said it with finality, as if that explained everything. "I stopped in here on my way to a faculty lecture on aether extraction using refracting crystals and the power of the sun. Ground-breaking theories."

"Indeed." That almost tempted Gideon to ask more, but Palmer appeared at his elbow.

"Found him," Palmer said. "Down by the water telling some River Rats to shove off."

"Oh, yes," Kitteridge broke in. "The club has strict policies about who can tie up here. Strang is rabid about it."

Palmer cast him a cool glance. "Hello, Mr. Kitteridge. I hadn't realized that you were back in Londria."

"Just for the holidays." He gave a thin smile. "Now, if you'll excuse me, I must find the lecture hall."

Kitteridge set his half-empty brandy on the tray of a passing footman and left, his step unhurried, though he covered the distance to the door within seconds. Gideon glared at his retreating back. What did so many women see in that fop?

The clubhouse had a second set of doors that faced the river. Gideon and Palmer made their exit, and Palmer led the way to the piers. After the brandy-scented crush inside, the air felt cold and pure. Palmer made a direct line to a man haranguing three River Rats, who were attempting to tie up their boat. Gideon was too far away to hear the man's words, but the haughty tone was clear.

A moment later, Gideon recognized the tall, drooping mustached Thresher. His fists clenched.

"I take it that's Strang?" Palmer asked, his tone light.

"Yes." The word came out harsh and clipped.

Palmer stopped, one hand on Gideon's arm. "I'll keep the professor here. Be a good lad and go get my men."

"What if he runs?"

Palmer glanced toward the River Rats. The leader had his arms folded and a sneer across his broad, dark face.

Palmer grinned. "I'll have help. It might even be fun."

Reluctantly, Gideon obeyed. He would much rather have watched Strang's face as Palmer put him under arrest. Sadly, by the time Gideon returned with the constables, Palmer was already escorting Strang to the carriage. The fun, if it had even occurred, had been brief.

Gideon rode up front, beside the driver, so both constables could sit inside with Palmer and Strang. The police station was in the city's administrative district, half a dozen blocks from the Citadel. The carriage circled to the back, and when the passengers alighted, Palmer escorted Strang through a small door and into a long, narrow hallway.

Gideon followed. This was a part of the station he'd never seen, even more drab and worn than the rest. A distant, metallic banging hinted at cell doors he couldn't see.

Their destination was a windowless room with a table and two chairs. Palmer sat closest to the door, obliging Strang to take the opposite side of the table. It was a tactic Gideon understood —the position afforded a quick exit if the prisoner attacked. Palmer pulled out his notebook while Gideon stood to one side of the door, a young constable to the other.

Now that they were nearly face to face, Gideon studied the professor. He'd straightened his broken nose, but bruises still circled his eyes and ran down his jaw. His lips were slightly parted, as if he had to breathe through his mouth. Gideon wondered what tale he'd told to explain the injury.

When Strang finally noticed Gideon, his eyes widened, and a

flush crept up his cheeks. Gideon suppressed a grin. Surely, they had the bastard.

"Detective Inspector Palmer," Strang said, sitting back in his wooden chair. "Why is that man here? He is not a member of the constabulary."

Gideon stiffened, accusations on the tip of his tongue, but he'd learned to follow Palmer's lead. The detective inspector continued jotting in his notebook, barely raising his eyes. "Mr. Fletcher is here today in a supplementary role."

Strang opened his mouth to launch further objections, but Palmer cut him off. "Mr. Fletcher was, along with myself and my officers, present at the scene where Robin Vortigern's body was discovered."

There was only one way Strang could go after that. His frown deepened, going from discomfort to shock. "Vortigern is dead?"

"Murdered." Palmer twirled his pencil between his fingers. "Now you understand why I asked you here, Dr. Strang. This is the second tragedy to strike your rowing team of late."

Strang's expression smoothed to a bland mask. "George Bagstaff was never located. He may yet live."

"Unlikely. I have it on good authority that a hunter killed an Unseen recently that wore a university rower's waistcoat."

"Mythical nonsense. The forest addles men's wits."

"This occurred in town."

Strang blinked. "Impossible. No Unseen cross the wall."

"It seems we are faced with a contradiction," Palmer waved a hand. "Please, explain it away."

Gideon cast a glance at the constable, who had gone ashen. Apparently, this youngster—he barely looked old enough to shave—hadn't yet heard about, let alone seen, the monsters roaming the streets.

"Where is Bagstaff's body?" Strang demanded. "Where is the proof? And—beyond mere coincidence—how is that connected to Robin Vortigern or to me?"

Gideon stepped forward, depositing the button on the table. Strang snatched it up, turning it to the light. Deep creases of tension framed his mouth. "Where is the rest of the garment? I see no evidence here."

Once more, Gideon wished Huntley had recovered the Unseen's body. Strang was right—a single button was a tantalizing nothing. Palmer snatched the button from Strang's hand and passed it back to Gideon, who returned to his post by the door.

"Bagstaff's disappearance affected Vortigern, didn't it?" Palmer asked.

Strang waved a hand, regaining a little of his poise. "Of course. We were all distressed. Bagstaff was a favorite of all who knew him."

Palmer scribbled, as if this was critical information. "So tell me, what is your field of study?"

The sudden change of topic startled Gideon, but Strang took it in stride. "I teach physical anatomy at the university. My true area of research is experimental biology."

"What does that entail?" Gideon asked, unable to help himself.

Strang turned toward Gideon. There was a spark of excitement in Strang's pale-blue eyes, as if they'd finally reached a subject of interest. "We all know a caterpillar turns into a butterfly. I want to know why. I also want to know why it does not become a goat instead, and if I could make that happen given the proper tools."

Gideon wished he had not asked.

Palmer cleared his throat. "Between your classes and your, um, research, is the rowing team your only other contact with students?"

"Officially, yes."

"Unofficially?"

"Londria is not infinite, Mr. Palmer. Two individuals of equal social standing are bound to cross paths."

"That's *Detective Inspector* Palmer. Let's be civil, Dr. Strang."

"Apologies."

"Tell me about the Threshers. Can anyone join?"

Strang shifted slightly, as if bracing himself for the questions to come. "If a man is fit and leads a wholesome life, any can apply to join."

"By fit, do you mean good with your fists?" Palmer said with a lift of his brow. "You seem to have been in a scrap, professor."

"We are an entirely reputable social club. We pursue sports—wrestling, boxing, and singlestick, among others. I got the worst of a bout, nothing more than that. Ask any member."

"Even Featherly?" Gideon asked. "He isn't a student like the others."

"As I said, anyone can join."

"Where can we find Featherly?"

Strang shrugged. "I'm not party to his personal affairs or his domestic arrangements. Perhaps you should ask the men at your father's shipyard."

"Why did you attack Mr. Fletcher last night?" Palmer asked.

"Mr. Fletcher must be mistaken." Strang spread his hands. "I am a respected member of the university's faculty. Why would I attack a man I don't even know?"

"And yet you did. Twice," Gideon said coldly, shaken by the bald-faced denial of the truth. "Along with Featherly and Vortigern."

Strang's eyebrows shot up. "You just told me Robin Vortigern is dead."

"He was alive last night."

"Are there reliable witnesses to this encounter?"

Gideon flinched. Huntley was a wild card, far less believable than a university professor.

Strang huffed with impatience. "Perhaps Mr. Fletcher should be the one answering questions about poor Robin's murder. Perhaps Featherly's, too, since the lad can't be found. Or perhaps Featherly was Robin's murderer and is now on the run."

"What would his motive be to kill Vortigern?" Gideon asked.

"What would mine be?"

Palmer held up a quelling hand. "Dr. Strang, can you offer any ideas as to why someone would harm Robin Vortigern?"

The man dipped his head, as if studying his hands. "Robin gambled. Surely you saw the crowd at the clubhouse today—William Kitteridge and his set. Men with deep pockets and icy nerves."

"Are you saying Robin's creditors killed him?" Palmer said.

As little as Gideon liked Kitteridge, he couldn't see the man dirtying his hands with common murder. He also knew Kitteridge was rarely in Londria. Strang was still lying.

The professor shook his head. "I'm saying Vortigern got himself in trouble by gambling. That is a certainty. I suspect he kept it from his parents. His father despised weakness."

That Gideon believed. "If one has to possess good character to join the Threshers, wouldn't a taste for cards and dice have disqualified Vortigern from membership?"

Strang laughed, a high-pitched sound that scraped over Gideon's nerves. "We all have weaknesses. Vortigern was ruined. Featherly is as poor as a church mouse. Debts inherited from his father, if I remember correctly."

"And you?" Palmer asked.

"I'm a scientist. I don't have the usual vices."

The detective quirked a smile. "But you have unusual ones?"

"That is always a matter for debate."

Gideon swallowed. Strang had an answer for everything. "If you all have weaknesses, how do the Threshers define good character?"

Strang drew himself up. "Loyalty to the Conclave. Loyalty to its laws that keep order across the land. We abhor cowardice in the face of our duty."

"Vortigern ran last night," Gideon said. "He proved himself a coward."

Strang gave him a burning look.

"Professor," Palmer interjected, "I understand Councilor Latimer warned you off the first time you attacked Mr. Fletcher and his friend. If a member of the Council doesn't agree with your actions, then in what way are you loyal to the mages?"

"Have you listened to nothing I've said?" Strang asked coldly, but this time he seemed amused.

"Indeed, I have," Palmer said, closing his notebook. "You're a skillful liar. I'll grant you that."

"Think what you wish," Strang replied. "But in your work, as well as mine, evidence is king. Without it, you are no more than a jester."

Palmer's jaw tightened, but there was nothing left to say. It was clear the interrogation was getting nowhere.

Gideon tried one last throw of the dice. "Were the Threshers in any way involved in the destruction of the *Leopard*?"

Strang sprang up with a noise that was almost a snarl. "I've heard enough baseless accusations. Arrest me or let me leave."

Palmer waved toward the door. "The constable will show you out. Thank you for your time, professor. It was most appreciated."

Strang crossed the room in three strides, drawing up short when he came close to Gideon. "Step aside, Mr. Fletcher."

The man was about to get away. Furious, Gideon continued to block his path. "You still haven't answered the inspector's last question, Dr. Strang. Are you loyal to the Conclave, or do you just do their bidding when their aims overlap with yours?"

Strang's blue eyes held his. "The Conclave is a living organism. New, strong shoots perpetuate growth while the old, lifeless husk falls away. Emulate the strong, Mr. Fletcher. Any student of natural philosophy will tell you that is the first law of survival."

With that, he pushed past Gideon, banging open the door as if he meant to tear it from its hinges. Gideon stepped aside, allowing the constable to escort Strang from the building.

After they'd gone, Gideon turned to Palmer. The latter lounged against the table, a thoughtful look on his face.

"And they wonder why so many despise the mages," Palmer muttered.

"He killed Vortigern," Gideon said. "I'm certain of it."

"I know," Palmer said.

"Then why didn't you arrest him?"

"I will, as soon as I have evidence stark enough that not even the Conclave can bury it. And unfortunately, Mr. Featherly is still a distraction. We can't eliminate him as a suspect."

"Not yet," Gideon agreed. "Still, my instinct says it wasn't him."

Palmer picked up his notebook, sliding it into his pocket. "This will be a long game. Watch your back in the meantime."

Frustrated, Gideon folded his arms. "Then what's the next move?"

"As a representative of the law, I say we watch and wait. Strang is going nowhere without a shadow. I don't care how long it takes, we'll catch him." Palmer's expression was grim. "Meanwhile, as the lawless private investigator beyond customary restraints, what do you say?"

"I can follow the thread that connects Strang and the Threshers and Vortigern and even the Conclave," Gideon said, "but Featherly doesn't fit. He's the connection to me, but why was he in the mix? Why is my family and its business involved?"

"I'm still not sure," Palmer mused. "But I saw Strang's face when you mentioned the *Leopard*. Your exploding airship is the key."

CHAPTER 19

Word of Robin Vortigern's death reached Miranda at almost the same time as a note from Gideon bringing her up to date on his case. Events were gathering steam.

Miranda had to get back in the sky. Otherwise, those events would leave her behind.

She arrived at the Fletcher Industries airfield well after the dinner hour. The night guards on duty were used to her appearing at all hours in her two-wheeled curricle. She'd taught herself to drive it a few months ago when it became clear the business required her presence at the airfield several times a week. That left the family's other vehicle—and the coachman— for the use of Olivia and their father.

After turning the rig over to the stable hand on duty, she walked the rest of the way to her ship, her equipment bag slung over one shoulder. The weight of the gear hurt her ribs, but she refused to acknowledge it. Her time as an invalid was over.

The ship was named the *Scorpion*. She'd named the vessel after the tarot card from Madam Alma's deck, and if the ship shared that name with the swashbuckling figure also named the Scorpion, that only made sense. Miranda knew how to fight, but her real strength was her aim with bow and gun. She worked best in the air, patrolling the streets, and picking off the Unseen she found skulking in the shadows. The woman and her ship worked as one unit, with one identity.

If a few men and women of Fletcher Industries drew a connection between Miranda, her ship, and their exploits, they kept her secret. Like Gideon, she was an aeronaut and one of their own.

The vessel emerged from the darkness as Miranda approached. It was small and nimble, with twin balloons positioned one above the other. Their silk was striped midnight blue and silver, and the high-prowed gondola was inky black. Its narrow profile allowed it to slip between tall buildings and along city streets, swift and silent as a ghost.

She'd launched the *Scorpion* dozens of times, but tonight she was as nervous as if this were a maiden voyage. Her heart galloped as she stepped between the mooring lines to the rope ladder dangling down the starboard side.

"Coming aboard," she called into the darkness.

Immediately, light flared. Miranda shielded her eyes to see her pilot, Janey, holding up a lantern. The woman lifted her goggles and peered down at Miranda, her breath a plume in the cold air. "Are you sure about this, boss?"

"I can't lie in bed forever."

Gritting her teeth, Miranda made her way up the ladder. If she moved at half her usual speed, at least she got to the top without complaining.

Janey helped her over the top. She was about Miranda's age, with blonde fringe over brilliant green eyes and braid down her back. She had a talent for mechanics and a taste for flight that matched Miranda's own. Her maker's workshop was in the back garden of Hellion House.

"It's barely been a week since the *Leopard* went to pieces,"

Janey said, tightening the collar of her flight jacket against the cold. "You don't have to push yourself so hard."

Janey was being kind, but that wasn't what Miranda needed. Flight was the only true cure for the sickness in her heart. She needed to believe the sky cupped her in its palm like a protective mother. Aeronauts walked on wind, and she was here to regain her stride.

Sadly, her body only remembered the terrified betrayal of the fall. She clutched her kit bag to stop the tremor in her hands. She saw Janey pretend not to see.

"Right," the pilot said, hooking her thumbs in the safety harness of her flight gear. "We'll take her out, nice and easy, and see where we go."

"I know where we're going." Miranda's words were firm. "I'm looking for something specific."

Janey caught her tone. "Then go suit up. I've a few things to check, and then we're off."

Miranda retired to the small cabin and loosened the flap of her bag. On top was a high leather collar studded with brass, perfectly suited to guard one's throat from slashing fangs. Under that was a walnut-brown leather coat that hugged her form yet allowed room enough to fight. Paired with an airman's trousers and boots, she could run and climb as freely as she pleased. She dressed quickly. The cold air was a fine motivator, but so was the fear she would back out of her plan.

At the bottom of the bag was a hard-sided case, plain black and bound in brass. Miranda unlatched the lid. Inside was a beautifully etched rifle, awaiting assembly. Canisters of aether distillate were packed in gauze, waiting to be mounted on the weapon. One blast could vaporize an Unseen from three hundred yards, if conditions were on her side.

Kitteridge had given her the collar and coat, but Janey had designed Viper, her aether rifle. Miranda ran a hand along the ornate barrel, loving its beauty and hating her need for it. Then, with deft movements, she assembled the weapon and slung it across her back.

The ship bobbed as the engine gathered steam, straining against the mooring lines. Miranda braced herself against the cabin wall, certain she would be sick. She leaned her head back, concentrating on her breaths. She'd intentionally skipped dinner, giving her stomach nothing to fight. High wind or hail, she was going back into the sky.

The moment passed, but not before her chemise was soaked through with nervous sweat. Angry with herself, she gathered her wits and went back on deck. After the *Leopard*, the space seemed minuscule.

"Releasing the mooring lines," Janey called as she pulled a lever.

As one, a dozen brass clamps loosed the lines that tethered the ship to earth. The *Scorpion* wafted upward, buoyed by lifting gas. Once it reached altitude, the propeller coughed to life.

Miranda hung on to the heavy cables that ran from the deck to the rigging above. Normally, the ship's motion felt natural. Now it seemed exaggerated, every bump and shimmy enough to kick her pulse into a gallop. She forced herself to let go and crossed to where Janey worked the controls.

"Where to?" Janey asked, shouting over the hiss of pistons and the hum of wind in the lines.

Even in the lantern light, Miranda could see the rosy flush of cold spread across Janey's cheeks. Still, the pilot laughed into the wind, exhilarated by flight. A little of that joy crept into Miranda's mood. It was a fine, starry night.

"Make a loop toward the Citadel," Miranda ordered. "Pass the river gate and make it wide. When we sail overhead, it should look accidental."

With a nod, Janey turned the wheel. "What are we looking for?"

Doomsfire, Miranda thought, but how would she recognize it?

Could she see it from the sky? She wasn't even sure where to look. In the past, she'd avoided flying too close to the Citadel, so her mental map of the grounds was sketchy.

"Reconnaissance," she said.

Janey cast her a curious glance but didn't ask more. In the light of the lantern that hung above the controls, her expression was intent but untroubled. Miranda moved to her customary spot on the port side of the airship, just behind the prow. This ship stayed low, skimming the rooftops and trees. She unslung her rifle and scanned the ground for quarry. Habit was taking over, soothing her nerves as the *Scorpion* silently prowled the night.

The river appeared below, a black shimmer streaked with light from the boats moored along its banks. The cold depths mesmerized her, the pull increasing as they neared the city gate. For an instant she choked, the sensation of drowning strong enough to be real. Then Miranda jerked her gaze from the water, studying the gate towers instead. Only the guards were present, marching an endless patrol along their stretch of the wall.

Miranda huffed in impatience. The great iron portcullis of the river gate grinned back.

The *Scorpion* drifted in a slow curve, veering northward away from the river. She knew this part of the town well, especially the cemetery where Sidonie's coach had been ambushed. Miranda had hunted there on a dozen occasions, taking her revenge on the Unseen two or three kills at a time. She inched closer to the side, peering down at the frosted graves. The headstones looked pale and brittle in the winter night, glittering with frost.

Miranda softened her gaze, taking in the scene as a panorama of black and gray. It never paid to search for the monsters—they were too clever for that. If they showed themselves, it was as a ghost at the edge of her vision.

There. A flutter in the shadows ahead. Miranda raised her fist, signaling Janey to change gear. The pilot shuttered the lantern and dropped closer to the frost-crusted grass. As details grew clearer, the ship seemed to speed up, rocks and bushes becoming a blur.

The Unseen panicked, breaking cover. Viper flashed, the pulse of aether flaring as it blasted the twisted creature to ruin. Two more followed, hunched and hairless. One spun to face the ship, baring its teeth in defiance.

Sidonie's image filled Miranda's thoughts. They'd sat together as they'd readied for her engagement ball. The future had been a wrapped gift, placed in their laps by the angels. The Unseen had turned that hope into an empty grave.

Miranda fired, and the Unseen's snarl turned to a cartwheel of limbs and fire. She dropped its companion a heartbeat later. A quiet settled over Miranda as she lowered Viper's barrel, and her stomach unclenched for the first time since she'd climbed the *Leopard's* mast.

The ship rose on a graceful incline, clearing a line of trees at the graveyard's edge.

"Another pass?" Janey asked. "I can circle back."

"No," Miranda said, looking wistfully behind them. There were likely more Unseen to chase—if nothing else, they always arrived to remove the bodies of their dead—but she had other priorities tonight. "Remain on course."

The ship ascended as they neared the heart of the city, rising above the highest buildings to remain out of sight. From there, it was possible to see the spokes of the city's main streets radiating from the Citadel's plaza to the wall. Silver strips ran down the center of those streets, carrying protective magic from the Conclave's home to the boundary circling Londria.

That power wasn't visible on the ground, but it was from the air. An evanescent shimmer glowed in the starlight, marking the web of mage-power below. The Conclave might not be as all-powerful as some believed, but it would be foolish to underestimate them.

Miranda left her post and joined Janey at the wheel. "How low can we go without being seen?"

The pilot frowned. "How should I know? They're magic folks down there."

It was a good point. "If they weren't magic?"

"Below the tip of the spire is easy. Closer to the main roof might be hard."

"Go between the two."

"Are we spying?"

"We're looking. Stay alert for watchmen. Or magical wards aimed skyward."

"Wards against an airship?" Janey scoffed. "Who would mount an air attack on the city?"

Miranda shrugged. "We can't assume what the mages are thinking."

The Citadel's spire was still distant when Janey cut the engine, guiding the ship lower. Miranda worked the sails, using the breeze to steer instead of the propeller. Bit by bit, they drifted closer to the pavement, the streets like crevasses of stone and glass beneath their keel. Soon the towers of Londria rose beside them. There was an eerie, underwater quality to the journey, as if they were a small fish swimming through jagged shards of rock.

"Here we are," Janey said in a voice just above a whisper.

The Citadel loomed against the pale, patterned stones of the enormous plaza. Miranda scanned, wondering who below might spot their ship. During the day, the Conclave guards patrolled the grounds around the building, but tonight the plaza appeared empty. Either the shift was changing or someone was lazy—or they wanted snooping airships to think they were safe.

There were few lighted windows in the building itself. Although the Citadel held hundreds of occupants, the graveyard had shown more life. What did the mages do with their time? Was the answer safe to know?

They were close enough now to reach out and touch the spire.

Hundreds of years before the Great Disaster, the Citadel had been a cathedral. The huge, ornate tower, with its belfry and spire, was visible from anywhere in the city. Buttresses arched upward to support the Citadel's roof, which was encrusted with mysterious carving and grotesques. As the ship sailed by, gargoyles leered at eye level, stone faces twisted like the Unseen. Despite herself, Miranda shuddered.

"I don't like this," Janey said.

"I agree. Let's finish and move on." Miranda turned her attention to the scene below, absorbing every detail she could.

The Citadel might have started as a cathedral, but had sprouted additional wings that gave it the shape of a many-limbed beast. Miranda counted several entrances, including one on the roof probably used for maintenance. On the side opposite the main doors, a lump of melted rock marked the place where the old House of Questions had stood.

The ship circled the front of the building. Only members of the Conclave went up the broad staircase and through the heavy, brass-paneled entry doors. Visitors were not welcome—and no one Miranda knew had ever complained of the fact. No one ventured willingly into the Conclave's lair.

"Do you see what you're looking for?" Janey asked, circling to the other side of the plaza.

What did Doomsfire look like? Miranda could see no flickers or flames. The only sign of magic was the glow on the roads that led to the wall—but that magic had been there since the Great Disaster.

"No," Miranda replied with a heavy sigh. "It was a longshot anyhow."

"Where to, then?"

"The airfield. There's nothing more we can do tonight."

Without warning, a piece of the roof flung itself onto the *Scorpion*'s deck, landing with a feral snarl. Miranda spun. The hunched shape of an Unseen crouched only yards away. She'd mistaken it for one more gargoyle.

"Bloody hell," Janey cursed.

Miranda had left Viper at her station by the prow, where she'd been shooting. She dove for it, but the monster was fast. In desperation, she dropped to her knees, hands outstretched to grab it, but the horrible thing landed on her back. Miranda fell flat beneath its weight as it sank its teeth into her protective collar.

Something fell behind her with a meaty *thunk*. The creature let go and squealed, so loud and high that Miranda's right ear throbbed. At a second blow, the weight of the Unseen's form rolled away. She scrambled to her feet and snatched up her rifle.

Janey stood near the pilot's station with a heavy wrench gripped in both hands. The freckles stood out along her cheek-bones, a sure sign that she'd gone pale. Her gaze flicked to Miranda, then back to the monster who stood between them, blood pouring from its scalp.

With a jolt of surprise, Miranda realized it wore the gray robes of a Citadel menial. Not even the Conclave was safe from the creatures they'd sworn to keep out.

Janey hoisted her improvised weapon. "Come near either of us again, and you know what you'll get."

The thing hissed like a furious cat. Janey flinched but stood her ground. It was all the distraction Miranda needed to kick the creature in the jaw, then cracked the rifle butt into its skull. Stunned, it staggered back against the bulwark. Miranda shoul-dered the weapon, taking careful aim. One misfire and she might hit a balloon filled with explosive gas.

The ship made a stomach-heaving lurch.

"Damnation!" Janey pounced on the ship's wheel, braid swinging with the motion.

"What happened?"

"We hit something, but I swear nothing was there."

They'd tripped a protection ward. Miranda glanced up just long enough to see the Citadel spire loom huge before the prow. The Unseen chose that moment to rush her.

Janey spun the wheel to port, but the sails fought her, causing the airship to roll violently, the gondola barely missing the corner of the spire. Miranda pulled her hand from the trigger just as she lost her footing and slid into the monster. They landed in a heap.

Miranda scrabbled away, repulsed by the Unseen's putrid smell. It lurched to its feet, eyes wild with panic as the gondola swayed with the ship's motion. It staggered, clearly disoriented.

As if rage was its only response to fear, it sprang at Miranda once again. This time, she was ready. As the ship tilted another degree, she caught the creature's robe in both hands and used the Unseen's momentum to pitch it over the side.

She fell against the gunwale, nearly following her opponent into thin air. The creature's scream held confusion and betrayal that found an answering note in her soul. Shadows veiled its wide gaze and open mouth, but not quickly enough. Its terrified rictus remained when Miranda closed her eyes.

The gondola swayed like a pendulum.

Bones cracked when the monster hit the pavement of the plaza. Miranda's stomach heaved.

Someone yelled from below. So there was a patrol, after all.

The engine came to life in a hiss of steam, followed by the *thwop* of the propeller. Moments later, the *Scorpion* regained altitude and sanity.

"Sorry," Janey said. "Stealth had to go. I couldn't pull out of this without power."

Miranda got to her feet, aware of Londria shrinking as they mounted toward the stars. Her breath came in puffs of steam. She'd forgotten the cold during the fight, but now it came back like a hammer. She picked up the rifle.

"Are you all right?" Janey asked. "Did it bite you?"

"No, I'm fine." Reflexively, Miranda touched the leather collar. She'd have to thank Kitteridge again for his gift. "And you?"

Janey gave a hollow laugh. "It's whisky for me tonight. Lots of it."

The ship was making good speed now, as if it had already forgotten their close call. Miranda shuffled into the cabin, sitting heavily on a stool as she put Viper back in its case. Only when she was done did she notice the tears wetting her cheeks.

The fall from the *Leopard* had been bad, but she'd told herself it was a one-time disaster. Yet, here was another.

She'd dropped a dead monster on the Conclave's doorstep, and the mages might have seen her do it. There would be consequences.

Miranda felt hollow, like a gourd with everything pulled out. She'd gone beyond fear to a vast gray nothingness. A giggle erupted from her throat, but she swallowed it down before Janey could hear. She wasn't hysterical, but she was overtired and her wound had reopened, soaking through her clothes.

Miranda buried her face in her hands. Her luck in the sky had clearly run out. Worse, she'd glimpsed the battle to come.

CHAPTER 20

"What's the current count of survivors from the *Leopard*?" Miranda asked Captain Higgins the next morning. "Any change?"

They stood huddled on the frost-whitened grass of the airfield, along with Gideon and Crewman Yale. A hundred yards away, Fletcher Industries' newest ship swarmed with crew members, readying the vessel for its shakedown flight.

"Three of the injured succumbed," Higgins replied.

"I'm very sorry to hear that." The number tallied with the reports her father had received from the company doctors. She trusted their medical men, but Higgins had a knack for knowing everything first.

"It's been a week now since the *Leopard* went down," he added. "Those still with us ought to survive."

"Nine dead then," she said. "I assume five are still missing?"

Higgins nodded. "No more have been recovered, dead or alive."

They had expected none, but hope died hard. Miranda shifted, easing the pain along her ribs. "So of twenty-one souls aboard the ship, only seven still walk the earth. Three of those seven are standing here. What of the rest?"

"Featherly joined the Threshers," Gideon said, prompting a curse from Yale.

After questioning the crew—including Miranda—Higgins had discovered that no one had actually seen Featherly aboard once the ship was in the air. There was a strong possibly he'd slipped away moments before the *Leopard* launched.

"I wonder who might have known Featherly had business with the Citadel's men?" Gideon mused. "His family, perhaps?"

"I know his wife, sir," Yale replied. "We grew up on the same street. I don't think she knew anything, but let me speak to her again. She might talk to me."

Gideon nodded his agreement.

"The others are still in the hospital under the watchful eye of our own men," Higgins said. "We're gathering their reports as they're able to talk."

"Have there been any incidents?" Gideon asked.

"A few black-coated men skulking about, but we've been careful," Higgins replied. "None of us walk about on our own."

"And no one fancies a scrap with our lot," Yale added with an evil smile. "The crew are in a mood."

"A mood is fine," Miranda replied, "but I'd rather not hear about any more casualties."

Yale touched his cap. "I promise you, miss, that no one will start a fight he can't finish."

"Begging your pardon, Miss Miranda," Higgins said. "But has Mr. Fletcher approved a name for the new vessel?"

She hesitated a moment, considering her reply. The men and women of the airfield, family included, needed a symbol, a rallying cry to bolster their spirits. "My father has not chosen a name, but I've proposed one. I'd like to call our new vessel the *Leopard Ascending*, in honor of the fallen. No one can keep a good ship or its people down."

"I like it, Miss Miranda," Yale said softly. "It's fitting."

They parted then, Higgins and Yale to their duties and Gideon and Miranda to the offices. She'd dressed soberly that day in a manteau of wool and velvet over a navy gown. After leaving the airfield, she intended to pay her respects to the Vortigern family, even if just to leave her card. It was unlikely they'd be receiving visitors yet, and their families had been nodding acquaintances, not intimate friends.

Still, she and Robin had been nearly the same age. They'd danced a few times here and there, and he'd been cordial. What had happened to the handsome young man? What trouble had he landed in?

She linked her arm through Gideon's, pulling him closer to her side as they walked across the grass. She needed to feel her brother's solid presence.

"Give me your thoughts," she said. "We can sell the new ship, but it won't make the profit we might have realized if the trial had gone forward as planned."

He furrowed his brow in concentration, but Miranda didn't expect a quick answer. Gideon was smart, methodical, and curious, but woefully uninterested in finance.

"What does Olivia say?" he asked.

"To generate more business." She sighed. "As if that wasn't obvious."

They'd reached the administrative building. As Gideon opened the door, the smell of ink and tea wafted over them. They wove their way past the bustling clerks to Norton Fletcher's office, shedding scarves and gloves as they went. Gideon closed the office door and settled into the chair where Huntley had sat just days ago.

"What ships are popular at the moment?"

"Runabouts like the *Scorpion*." Miranda pulled off her coat and hat and sat behind her father's desk. "But even they take time to make. Given my recent luck in the air, perhaps I should let the *Scorpion* go."

"Don't even consider it," Gideon said flatly. "You'd miss it too much."

"Maybe not."

He gave her a puzzled look, maybe because she hadn't yet told him about the previous night's flight. She'd been trying to force it from her mind.

"Will you be aboard the new ship for its test flight?" he asked.

A sting of shock coursed through her, as if he'd poked her with a pin.

"No." The answer came out faster than she'd intended. "No, definitely not. Higgins can manage it."

Gideon gave a sympathetic frown. "Still reeling a bit from the fall?"

She looked away, studying the few raindrops spattering the window.

"It'll pass," he said, with big brother confidence.

She barely resisted the impulse to smack him. He'd struck a tender place in her soul.

"We can come back to money problems in a moment," she said, struggling to keep her voice steady. "Tell me about your investigation."

"I can't find anything of note in the company books." His gesture encompassed the office.

She folded her hands on the blotter. "The latest records are at the house, not here. Father wanted to go over them, but he never seems to find the energy."

"I need to see them. I'll come by later, after he's retired for the night."

"What are you looking for?"

"Something new. Something out of place." He shook his head. "Featherly probably let the saboteur onto the ship, but they still had to pass through the gate. No one enters the airfield without a plausible reason."

"True."

"If they were a tradesman or a supplier, or even if they were a fraud posing as one, we'd have a record. At the very least, we'd have set up an account with the company who sent them."

"Well reasoned," Miranda said, and meant it. This was what Gideon excelled at—linking cause and effect and one event to the next. She'd never been able to keep secrets from him, even being the Scorpion.

"It's not much," he admitted.

"It's better than nothing. What do we know so far? Go over it all, even if you've told me before. I might be able to add a point or two."

An office boy knocked and entered, bearing a tea tray. He left and Miranda poured out the thick brew. The staff called it mouse-trotter tea—hearty enough to support the weight of a small animal. She handed Gideon a cup, the steam making lazy curls in the cool air. There was a fire in the grate, but so far it hadn't heated the room.

Gideon took a sip, his dark hair falling forward as he bent his head. He'd let it grow long, though probably from neglect rather than a fashion choice.

"Who knows when this really began," Gideon said. "But what we know is that Father threw himself into making a device to keep the area outside the wall clear, both from Unseen and any vegetation they could use for cover. He saw investment potential, which made the cost of the prototype a worthwhile gamble. However, someone objected and sabotaged the test flight. After that, Councilor Ormond visited to warn us off pursuing the project further."

"Yes," Miranda said, "but we're uncertain the Conclave is behind the sabotage, even if they claim protection of the city is their job and no one else's."

"We're uncertain the *Conclave's ruling Council* is behind it, which might mean something else." Gideon set down his cup. "Enter the Threshers, who report to someone in the Citadel who believes the old guard isn't up to the job anymore."

"There was something Ormond said—that the Citadel has other enforcers besides the guard." Miranda frowned. "He didn't seem happy about it, as if the mages themselves might be subject to discipline. But aren't the Threshers just ordinary civilians? Surely they're no threat to a mage."

"I don't know," Gideon shrugged. "A bullet will kill anyone. Or maybe some Threshers have magical talent?"

"Have you seen signs of any?"

"No, but either way, they have no scruples about shedding blood, even from one of their own. Vortigern lost his nerve and was dead by morning. Clearly, they can't abide failure."

Sick dread rolled through Miranda. She pushed aside her cup of bitter tea. "And you think the Threshers were after you because you were investigating the *Leopard*?"

"That's my best guess, which leads us back to the mages as prime suspects for the sabotage."

Something was missing, but she couldn't quite see it yet. "You would think the mages would welcome something designed to make their job easier. Besides, even they aren't truly safe. I was on the *Scorpion* last night, taking a good look at the Citadel. An Unseen dropped off the roof right onto the deck."

There was a moment of perfect silence, broken only by the muffled voices of the clerks beyond the door.

"Bloody hell, Miranda." Gideon's voice cracked. "Were you hurt?"

"Janey and I got a good scare, but we're fine." She rubbed her hands, the memory adding to her chill. "The Unseen took a long step off the ship to the plaza. It won't be bothering anyone again."

"Were you seen?"

"There might have been a guard or guards on the plaza, but they were too far away for a good look at us."

"Are you certain?"

"Mostly. I was busy." She hated the defensive note in her voice. "We had trouble with the ship. I think it was a ward, but we got free before it did any damage."

Her brother stared, his face turning scarlet as his gaze flicked over her face. Miranda forced herself not to squirm.

"Why were you flying over the Citadel?" he said in a careful voice. "The mages don't take kindly to spies."

"I know that," she said with equal control. "I'm sorry, but I finally remembered what the River Rat said. The message from Madam Alma."

Gideon raised his dark brows as Miranda leaned close.

"Doomsfire," she whispered. "It has something to do with the Conclave's power—old alchemy from the time of the Great Disaster. Olivia confirmed that much, but she knows nothing more about what it means."

Gideon sat back, pinching the bridge of his nose as if he had a sudden migraine. "And you thought you'd just fly over the Citadel and have a look for it?"

His fury grated on Miranda's temper. "Why not? It was a start. I had no way of knowing it would rain monsters."

He sighed, lowering his hand from his face. It was then she saw his fear for her, and that softened her mood.

"I would say you're lucky," he said, "except I know you're one of the best aeronauts in Londria. You had the skill to survive but —bloody hell, don't do it again. The consequences aren't worth it. If they'd caught you..."

She flushed. "The strange thing was that the Unseen wore a menial's robes. It must have stolen them right from the Citadel."

"That's what makes so little sense to me." Gideon made a face. "If the Unseen are robbing the mages—or killing the menials and taking their robes—the Conclave must know there are monsters in the streets."

"Of course they do," she replied softly. "It's the only thing that does make sense."

Gideon sprang to his feet, pacing to the window. "The Conclave's authority rests on their ability to protect us. Except they can't stop the Unseen incursions across the wall any longer —at least not entirely. What does that mean for the city?"

Miranda cleared her throat, finally voicing her suspicions. "Or do they have a reason not to stop the monsters?"

Gideon turned, his gaze meeting hers. His expression said he'd been thinking the same thing. "That's why they destroyed the *Leopard*. They have no intention of keeping them out."

Miranda's mouth went dry. "Why not?"

The question stopped their conversation cold, as if it was simply too big to digest.

"I don't know," Gideon finally said.

"Who would know?"

He shook his head. "Again, I have no idea. It's not a safe subject to bring up in conversation."

Heavy silence returned as Miranda grappled with Gideon's words. It was as if everything she knew had been turned inside out. She could feel her mind shrinking from the idea, as if the very notion burned her thoughts.

Could she believe the mages voluntarily allowed Unseen inside the walls?

Did she want to?

"I need to think," she said.

"I understand," Gideon agreed. "I keep searching for another way that this makes sense."

And after that, it was impossible to discuss something as mundane as investments and receivables. After a half-hearted attempt at drinking his tea, Gideon left to keep an appointment with Palmer, and Miranda went to pay her call on the Vortigern household.

Since the heavy clouds had threatened rain or sleet that day, she'd requested Jackson, the family coachman, to drive her in the brougham. It was enclosed against the weather where her curricle was not. When they reached the Vortigern's, several vehicles already crowded the curb. She asked Jackson to set her down at the end of the street, and she walked the rest of the way.

The curtains of the house were drawn and a black ribbon festooned the brass door knocker. A footman wearing a black armband opened the door before she'd reached the top step. Clearly, he'd been receiving visitors all day.

The black crepe and hushed voices reminded Miranda of the weeks following Sidonie's loss, reviving old pain. She left her card and note of sympathy without lingering. The time for a proper social call would come when the first shock of loss was past. Perhaps by then she would have insulated herself from unwanted memories.

She'd turned to go just as Kitteridge mounted the porch. She wavered, glad to see a friend and yet wanting time alone with her thoughts. The conversation with Gideon felt like a pressure inside her skull.

Kitteridge tipped his top hat to her. "Miss Fletcher."

"Mr. Kitteridge," she replied, waiting while he passed his card to the footman.

Kitteridge turned and offered his arm as they descended the steps. "Damned shame," he said. "That shouldn't have happened."

"Did you know him well?"

"Not really. We were in some of the same clubs, but I haven't been in town much. It was my grandfather who knew the family."

Miranda wondered who had come simply for Robin's sake. She had a sudden, awful suspicion he hadn't had many real friends.

Kitteridge interrupted her thoughts. "Shall we walk a little?"

Her first instinct was to refuse. Their last meeting had rattled her.

"Come," he said. "Your expression says that I'm terrifying."

"No," she objected. "I have a great deal on my mind, that's all."

"Then unburden yourself. I'm a talented listener."

They passed through the iron gate that separated the Vortigern property from the road. Kitteridge pulled her aside so that the next visitors—a pair of older women—could proceed up the walk. Miranda cast a glance to where Jackson waited with the brougham.

"Just a few minutes," she said. "It's cold."

He smiled as if he'd won a prize. "Come this way. There's a park at the end of the street."

She balked. "That's where they found him—Robin."

Kitteridge grimaced. "I know. We'll avoid that side of the water."

He led her down the street in silence for a few paces.

"Do you know what Robin got tangled up with?" she asked.

"He had a taste for cards," Kitteridge said, his voice grim. "Sadly, he had no talent for it. After a time, those of us with a conscience would not take his credit."

"So he ran up debts?" It was a depressingly common story.

"Of course. It made him vulnerable to predators."

Once again, she marveled at how Kitteridge picked up gossip with enviable ease.

"Like the Threshers?" she ventured.

"You are full of questions today." His gray eyes grew sharp. "Yes, the Threshers have a talent for recruiting those at a disadvantage. I take it your brother mentioned them?"

"In passing," she replied, suddenly unsure how much to say. "Gideon had an altercation with them. He thinks they attacked him because of his investigation of the *Leopard*."

"Maybe." Kitteridge didn't sound confident.

"Why else would they target my brother?"

They'd reached the end of the street. The entrance to the park lay ahead, framed by two waist-high stone urns planted with hydrangea bushes. A few of the blooms were still there, beautiful even in decay. An unexplained dread came over Miranda, as if the park teemed with dark secrets.

Of course, Kitteridge wanted to take her to this lovely, brooding place. This was the man who'd given her armor and told her how best to kill Unseen.

Wordlessly, he guided her through the entrance, keeping to the white stone path. Willows dusted with hoarfrost framed the ornamental lake, trailing their branches through drifts of golden leaves. The water was still, edged with wafer-thin shards of ice.

Miranda matched Kitteridge step for step, aware of the coiled tension in his lean form. Her skin prickled where they touched, as if he radiated a magnetic charge.

"I will answer your question this way," he said. "Have you heard of the One Hundred?"

The way he said it, she could hear the capital letters. "No."

"It's an old story that when the Conclave was formed, it was made up of one hundred families with magical talent bestowed by the magic of the Great Disaster. They were the families who became the noble elite, and who gave their most talented children to the service of the mages."

Miranda stopped in her tracks, forcing Kitteridge to halt as well. He turned to face her, ignoring a scatter of ducks waddling past.

"I've never heard of such a thing," she said.

He shrugged. "You wouldn't. It implies there are descendants of the original families who are not mages and yet have the potential for magic. The Conclave doesn't approve of hobbyists."

His smile was all charm and apology, as if he was sorry to trouble her with silly tales. She forced herself to look away before she drowned in it. "Then how did you hear this tale?"

"I spent my childhood reading my way through my grandfather's library. It was full of ancient history."

She didn't doubt that, or that the old pile had a dozen ghosts as well. "How is this story relevant?"

He reached out, taking her hand and giving a slight bow. "Your mother's father is the Earl of Havelock, and he is descended from the One Hundred. Generations back, one of your ancestors had talent."

She had a sudden memory of Ormond holding her hands, the feel of his magic swarming up her arms. She pulled away from Kitteridge, appalled. "That can't be true."

And yet, she'd felt the mage's touch. She always knew when a ship passed over the wall. And what about her dream about Madam Alma and the Doomsfire?

She had no grounds to dismiss Kitteridge's theory, however dangerous it might be. "The mages execute people for gifts they can't control."

"True." Kitteridge remained perfectly calm, as if he'd expected this reaction. "Still, all acolytes descend from the One Hundred."

"How do you know that?"

He gave a brief laugh. "It's a hard fact. I checked, but I was quiet about it. And here I grow near my conversational destination."

"Thank heavens." She meant to sound tart, but the words trembled.

They began walking again, the muted gold of the fallen leaves burning against the soft gray light.

"Your brother investigates like a young bull trampling a garden," Kitteridge said. "It's possible the Threshers came after him because of his missing persons investigations."

She'd seen the photographs pinned to Gideon's wall. She knew many of the missing—young, respectable sons and daughters, most with titles and fortunes. "Why? How do those cases matter to anyone but their families?"

"I suspect the police have orders to bury those files, but Palmer, renegade that he is, passed them on to Gideon to solve."

"And why bury these particular files?"

"Not all acolytes arrive at the Citadel willingly."

Miranda fell back a step in surprise. "Acolytes? I thought Gideon's missing persons were victims of the Unseen."

"Perhaps some were. But some were not. I don't know the entire answer, but your investigating sibling has to look deeper. As I said, they're all from families whose ancestors had magical talent. That is the single theme that ties the disappearances together."

Back at Sidonie's engagement ball, she'd heard about Simeon Blanchard, who had inexplicably broken his engagement to one of the Morton sisters to join the Citadel. If he'd been forced, that would explain everything.

And what had Ormond said? *You're a good daughter, my dear. You take after your mother's people. Such a noble bloodline.* If there was magic in her blood, it had come from her mother's family. As Kitteridge had observed, Miranda's uncle was the current Earl of Havelock, a title that dated back before the Great Disaster.

Kitteridge's theory fit like a key sliding into a lock. If he was correct, Gideon's investigations would reveal something the Conclave wanted to conceal. That agreed with what her brother had said.

Was she in danger? What about the rest of her family? And what bearing did this have on Sidonie's death?

Miranda's thoughts grew sluggish, as if too many new ideas were clogging their flow. How were the Conclave's dealings with the One Hundred, the missing, and the Unseen related? She touched her face experimentally. It had gone numb from cold and shock. "I don't know what to do with this knowledge."

He took her hand again, moving slowly as if afraid to spook her. "You're the Scorpion. You've fought by killing the Unseen, but they're not the entire story. I'm no investigator, but I know family trees. There's a pattern."

"You said family ties the disappearances together, but not all the missing became mages."

"No, they didn't."

She studied his handsome, solemn face, with its full mouth and straight black brows. "What about the rest? What about my sister?"

He lifted her hand to his lips. His breath warmed her, even through the fabric of her gloves. "I have no answer for you, Miss Fletcher, only one question. Why are the Citadel and the monsters fishing from the same pond?"

She laughed, but there was no mirth in it. "I have a better question, Mr. Kitteridge. What do they have in common?"

CHAPTER 21

"It's the baby," Margaret said, an edge of pleading in her words. "Look at it. Hold it."

Sidonie lay on her side, her knees drawn up to her chin. She'd lain in the same position for so long that the scratchy straw had packed down. Each lump and stone of the hard cottage floor beneath was intimately familiar to her bruised flesh.

The temperature was frigid, but she no longer felt it. Her plan —or lack of one—was to lie there, an inert mass, until she ceased to exist.

Margaret's breathing signaled impatience. "You can't stay there forever."

Sidonie disagreed, but she didn't bother speaking. She didn't care. Or perhaps she cared too much.

Her gums ached. They'd bled, but—thank whatever unholy gods ruled this place—none of her teeth had fallen out. When she poked with her tongue, they weren't even loose, although her mouth felt strange. Perhaps she was losing her mind and imagining a change. No one could blame her if her sanity had slipped a degree.

There were no mirrors, which made her glad and wary. Her

limbs were straight and her hair was as thick and long as ever—but she'd felt sick, cramped, and fevered. Most of that was over now, except for rampaging horror over what she might have become.

If she got away from this place, got back to a normal existence, would she recover? Her mind shied away, afraid of the answer.

Margaret's feet scuffed over the floor, coming closer. "Look. It's a beautiful boy, just like I wanted. He's perfect."

The woman—or creature or whatever Margaret was now—obsessed over that child. Its existence was her joy and the cure to all problems. All Sidonie could think of was the mother's still, bloody form.

"Sit up and look," Margaret persisted.

"I'm not interested," Sidonie croaked, her voice hoarse from lack of use.

It was the nicest thing she could think of to say.

"Learn to survive," Margaret said, each word careful. It was as if she had to think harder now to recall the complexities of educated speech. "Make the best of what's happened. I prayed for a baby for years without luck. Now I have one to love."

Sidonie's patience snapped. "Take that creature and go."

Margaret hissed her displeasure. Sidonie didn't care. Margaret filled her with disgust, but not because of her snarl.

Sidonie settled deeper into the straw, wishing there was enough of the dry, scratchy stuff that she could burrow out of sight. "Maybe it was human once, but it changed faster than the woman bearing it. It destroyed her as it grew. What would you call a specimen like that? A parasite?"

Margaret's foot came down on Sidonie's back, pressing her into the ground. "Masson was right to call you a feeble princess."

Sidonie bucked under Margaret's weight, lashing out with one hand. With a squeal, Margaret hopped away. Sidonie finally sat up to see the woman cradling the infant in one hand and lifting her skirt with the other to inspect her leg. Blood trickled down her shin.

Sidonie looked down at the gore under her sharp nails. They were more like translucent claws now, hard and sharp. The sight of them made her gut heave, but there was nothing in her gut but foul-tasting bile. She flung herself back to the straw, turning to face the wall and hopefully die.

Margaret whimpered like a chastened dog.

"Go now," said the Caretaker's voice. It sounded muffled, as if he stood just beyond the threshold of her cottage. "It must be time for the baby's next meal."

Sidonie heard Margaret mumble something and leave. The Caretaker took her place inside, pacing from one end of the cottage to the other, as if examining Sidonie from every angle.

"It is not unusual to feel out of sorts," he said. "Most go through a period of adjustment."

She pretended to sleep. Why would they not leave her alone?

"You've been alone for three days." The Caretaker seemed close now, beside the bed.

She said nothing.

"Do you not like children?" he asked. "Most of our female newcomers respond to the young when nothing else coaxes them from their beds."

She stiffened with fury. Of course she'd envisioned the children she would have with Richard. They'd imagined four—two girls and two boys. They would have been beautiful, smart, and wonderful. Now those shining faces receded like sailboats vanishing over the horizon.

"Are all your Gentry children born in blood and death?" she ground out. "By corrupting innocent mothers and their young?"

"Occasionally," he said. "Some are born of two Gentry parents, like Masson. Those births are too rare to keep our tribes whole."

That echoed what Margaret had said.

"Some are of mixed parentage, but they are extremely rare." The Caretaker's voice changed subtly, and she wondered what that meant. "If the mother is human, she finds it hard to carry the child to term."

Bleak images streamed through Sidonie's mind, but she couldn't form a response. She'd run out of dismay to spare.

"But I believe you're curious about yourself," he said, the words growing intimate. "How you've been reborn as one of us. I told you before, wild magic calls to those with power in their blood. Your ancestors were richly gifted, it seems, for you've come through this passage extremely well. Masson is pleased."

"Leave me alone," she whispered. When she saw him, she would tear Masson's eyes out with her new, sharp claws.

"The first law of survival is to face the unthinkable and make it your servant."

Tears leaked from beneath her lashes, trickling down her cheeks and into the straw.

"We are celebrating the midwinter tonight," the Caretaker said. "Won't you come join us?"

Midwinter? She'd been in the forest for a while.

She didn't move.

After a minute or two, the Caretaker went away. Sidonie remained still, afraid to learn what the Caretaker had meant by *reborn*. If she didn't stir from this nest of straw, she'd never have to find out.

Time passed. She dreamed or dozed, but woke to someone else's footfall inside her sanctuary. Three visitors in one day. Was she supposed to feel honored?

"The weak give up," Masson said in his rough voice. "You can do better."

Hate sparked, but so did fear. Sidonie opened her eyes just enough to see his form at the foot of her makeshift bed. He carried a candle stuck to a broken plate, which he set on the floor. The light sent his shadow snaking across the wall.

He held something in one hand.

"I brought you shoes." He tossed them onto her blanket.

She pulled her feet away as they struck the bed. She wondered if they were from the baby's dead mother. "What do you want from me?"

He crouched beside her, staring like a cat watching prey. His pale, alien features were striking but strange, as if the proportions were subtly different from a human's face. Even silent, he radiated a primitive force. Despite herself, she met his pale-gray gaze. This close, she could see his eyes weren't one color, but silver rimmed in black.

Her fingers flexed, sharp nails digging into her palms. Much of her was still eager to tear into that weird, beautiful face.

"I chose you," he said, as if that was self-evident.

"Why?" she ventured.

"I saw you."

Her lips trembled with the force of her anger. "That's not reason enough to destroy my life."

"We pay in blood for what we take from the city, but we must take to survive. We die. Humans die. It is fair."

That wasn't a chain of logic she cared to examine. "Why me?"

A corner of his mouth turned up, showing an edge of fang. "You were pale like us, proud as any warrior. You were born mine."

Her hand flew, impossibly fast, to shred those eyes. Just as fast, he caught her wrist, holding it in a painful grip. She barely covered her flinch of scathing revulsion at his touch.

"You do not like my answer?" His grin was sharp, as if accepting her fury as a challenge.

She bridled, hating that smile even more. "I had no idea the Gentry were romantics."

Masson narrowed his eyes and flung her back to the straw. With a heavy sigh, he ran a hand through the ragged mane of his silver-gray hair. She knew that look—the frustration of a male unfamiliar with rejection. But here, she couldn't count on the rules of polite society. He wouldn't accept her dismissal with grace—or even tolerance.

Sarcasm had always been her vice. She'd never dreamed it might get her killed.

Bowing his head, he seemed to come to a decision.

"You ate," he said softly. "I know this."

His words unlocked the memory. She'd been hiding from it like a child afraid of a ghost, shaking piteously whenever it took form.

Margaret had brought the flowered china plate of red flesh, arranged in a ring of small, dainty pieces fit for a garden tea. It had smelled intoxicating and sweet, like the dead mother's blood on her fingers.

Her hunger had been monstrous.

"I tried to vomit it up," she whispered. "It didn't work."

The confession shook her. Tears stung her eyes and throat. She forced them back, refusing to be weak in front of the creature who had destroyed her.

Masson's expression held a mix of pity and satisfaction. "Your body knows not to waste good food. You will survive."

"I can't. I will go mad."

He shrugged. "Many who come here choose a new name. It makes things easier."

"Did they believe that would absolve them of what they'd become?" she snapped. "My name is my own. I will own my sins."

Her sins might be all she had left.

Masson rose, his moment of sympathy done. He pulled off her blanket, tossing it to one side. "Put on the shoes."

Sidonie glanced at her feet. Her slippers were in tatters, the soles splitting at the seams. The shoes Masson offered were actually black walking boots with a small heel—practical without being ugly. It was a good trade, but she wanted nothing he gave her. It would create an obligation. Still, if the Unseen refused to let her quietly starve herself into oblivion, she was better off being able to run.

She toed off her slippers, ignoring the holes in her fine-knit stockings. She laced up the ankle boots as Masson watched, an unreadable expression on his face. When she was done, Sidonie wiggled her toes.

"The fit is not bad."

He grabbed her arm, claws scraping through the tattered fabric of her sleeve. "Good. Get up and be strong."

Sidonie stumbled, her legs cramped from inactivity. "Where? What if I don't want to?"

Masson didn't slow. He dragged her from her abode, refusing to let her lag behind. Night had fallen, but she could see perfectly well.

As the Caretaker had said, a celebration was underway. A bonfire occupied the middle of the square, already large but growing as Goblins hurled sticks and branches into the blaze. Unseen were gathering in numbers she'd not seen before— Goblins and Gentry appearing from the edge of the forest, some bearing odd-shaped bundles on their backs.

"All come here in summer and winter," Masson said as he pulled her closer to his side. "When the sun turns, we give the dead rest. It is the time to pay debts and make challenges."

Sidonie had never imagined monster festivals. It was the stuff of horror tales. Then again, how many were like her, raised in a world where high holidays marked the cycle of the year?

Anticipation thrummed through the settlement. The bonfire was just a fire and yet it wasn't. It grew as she watched, the heat and crackle speaking to something restless deep in her chest. The hands and feet of Goblins drummed on hollowed chunks of wood, a steady, insistent pulse. Once, Sidonie would have dismissed the primitive noise, but now it made her edgy, as if she wanted to dance or fight. Above all, she wanted to be free of the crowd. After the solitude of her cottage, there was too much to take in.

All her senses had grown sharper, but smell was the most noticeable—rotting meat, dirty flesh, smoke, the heady loam of the forest. It was a dizzying, nuanced kaleidoscope. Most strange of all, she could identify individuals by their scent as easily as by their looks.

Masson still hadn't released her arm, as if he feared she might run. Turning her nose toward his shoulder, she inhaled as discretely as she could. She didn't have words for his unique signature. It made her think of wet stone and woods, but that wasn't all of it.

He caught her sniffing and raised a brow. Sidonie looked away, pretending she hadn't noticed his reaction. She thought she heard a dry chuckle over the din. The urge to hurt him grew physical, like a taste upon her tongue.

A Goblin hunched beside the great bonfire, using a rock to crack bones so it could suck out the marrow. Sidonie caught the aroma of a particularly large thighbone. Her mouth watered, and she wasn't the only one to detect the delicacy. Two other Goblins bounded up and began grabbing for the same bone like quarreling dogs. With his free hand, Masson smacked the closest on the back of the head. The Goblins scrambled away, cowering before him. The first one snatched up his prize and ran.

Unfortunately, the scene made her think of food. Now that she was up and moving, she was aware of how hungry and thirsty she was. Ever since she'd wolfed down that plate of meat, she hadn't stopped dreaming of the flavor. Wanting it sickened her, even as the craving itched under her skin. Would there be refreshments at this party? What would she do if there were?

The idea made her stumble. Masson steadied her.

"New shoes," she muttered, looking away.

"Look proud and strong," he whispered. "It is safer."

Sidonie caught her breath, suddenly understanding what was

happening around her. Masson was on display for his people—Sidonie had seen the same look on many a politician. As he continued on, circling the blaze, he tilted his chin to show off his good looks, but there was more to it than vanity. His swagger was about strength, but also ferocity. A handful of females studied him the way a glutton studies cake. Most of the males stood aside as he passed. Masson challenged the rest with a glare and won every time.

He was the king, and Sidonie was part of his show. She was new and novel, like a fine carriage or a well-cut coat. Possession of her gave him prestige. She'd been courted by such men before and had despised them, too. But she'd had power then—her father's fortune, the protection of her family, and the rules of her class.

Things had changed. The regard of other males ran like scalding fingers over her skin. With galling clarity, she realized all over again that Masson's presence was the only thing keeping her safe.

She needed weapons. She'd never heard of the Unseen using them, but surely they must?

Masson finally slowed to where a pile of bones were piled at the rear of the bonfire.

"What's happening here?" Sidonie asked, a fresh trepidation creeping over her flesh.

New arrivals from the forest squatted beside the heap, untying the lumpy bundles they'd been carrying on their backs. Each one contained yet more bones. All had been stripped bare, without a scrap of flesh gone to waste.

Queasiness made her hot. There were many, many bones.

"We burn what remains of the dead to give them rest," Masson replied. "Our own, and those of the ones we hunt. We give their ash to the forest."

"And you do this twice a year?"

Masson nodded. "You listen. That is good."

Sidonie bit back a tart remark and counted skulls instead. All of them looked human.

"Who were they?" she asked.

"They walked alone," Masson replied. "They forgot about wolves."

She couldn't begin to calculate a year's tally, but far more humans perished than had ever been mentioned in the newspapers. They had to be the poor, the unwanted, and—as Masson said—those who strayed from the safety of the crowd. Someone inside Londria had to know or guess there were predators stalking the streets. The citizens, her friends and family, had been fundamentally betrayed.

Her anger twisted into a new shape. As Masson said, the Unseen did what they had to in order to survive. But for that to be possible, the Conclave's impenetrable wall had to be breached, goods stolen, and humans taken. How long had that gone on? Why had no one heard about it?

A shudder ran through her as rage mounted. Of course, people had to know. Londria's masters silenced the truth. But why?

The thought had barely formed before a new sight distracted her. Sark crouched beside the bone pile, dipping his fingers into the glowing embers of the bonfire. Then he wiped them over his face, painting himself with the ash of the dead. When he looked up and saw Masson, his lips flattened into a hard line.

He rose, anger furrowing his heavy brow. "You have ruled too long, Masson. You talk, but you do nothing."

"You want blood now," Masson replied. "I offer you endless bounty later."

"Later is never. Now is now."

"You are a fool, Sark," Masson sneered. "Your mind is weak like an ancient who cooks his meat."

Sidonie knew an insult when she heard one. Sark snarled from deep inside his chest.

Masson finally released Sidonie's arm. She stepped aside, rubbing the place where he'd gripped her.

"This is the time of challenge," Sark said, flexing his shoulders. "You die. I will lead."

Sark pushed forward into Masson's path. A handful of others crowded behind the guard. They'd clearly been waiting for this moment.

Masson slowly unbuttoned his jacket and cast it aside, drawing out the moment to demonstrate his lack of concern. With an airy wave, he summoned his followers, who were all miraculously close.

Sidonie gave a soft gasp. He'd expected this encounter. The parade around the fire had been a prelude to this moment.

Irritation crashed over Sidonie in an icy wave. This was as bad as pistols at dawn. Worse. A duel had a strict conduct and a physician in attendance. She searched for the Caretaker, but he was nowhere to be seen. Damn him.

From the fury in Sark's eyes, this would be a duel to the death.

Panic mounted. She loathed Masson, but he was the unholy abomination she knew. If he lost this fight, what would happen to her? Would she be Sark's property? Sark's dinner?

The bone pile drew her gaze like a magnet. Was that her next destination?

There had to be a way out of the forest.

CHAPTER 22

Sark and Masson faced off.

A silent signal rang through the settlement, for all the Unseen rushed in to glimpse the action. The supporters of the two opponents formed a circle, keeping the others out of the way. Sidonie tried to move, but the crush blocked her escape.

The crowd was a living, pulsing thing, vibrating with eagerness for blood. A Goblin pushed forward, only to be shoved back by one of Sark's guards. The creature squealed with frustration, biting his neighbor. A squabble followed that had to be put down with blows.

The mayhem distracted Sidonie, and she missed the first attack. As she looked back, Sark lunged, shoulder down as if he meant to bowl Masson over. Masson moved like water, using the bigger man's momentum against him. Sark thumped to the dirt, getting a hard kick to the gut before scrambling back to his feet. Masson was barely rumpled. Despite herself, Sidonie cheered with Masson's supporters.

A clawed hand fell on Sidonie's shoulder. She spun around to receive a hard blow to her cheekbone. Sidonie's head snapped to the left, pain flaring through her skull and spine. Someone grabbed a fistful of her hair and hauled her to the back of the crowd, finally tossing her to the frost-hardened dirt. Stunned, Sidonie shook her head to clear it.

When her vision focused, she saw her attacker was one of the females who had been making eyes at Masson. She had the same inhuman, angular beauty as he did. Was that the mark of pure Gentry blood?

"Such a pretty toy," the female said, her tone acid. "Masson needs more than a toy."

"He needs you, I suppose," Sidonie said dryly.

The creature bared her fangs. "I am Nalin. I fight beside warriors of quality."

A roar went up from the Unseen clustered around the main fight. Both women looked over to see Masson mount the bone pile, lifting a gory trophy to the sky in triumph. It was Sark's head, the ragged stump of his neck making it plain it had been ripped away. Sidonie gaped. How much strength did it take to do that?

Nalin curled her lip. "Sark had no bite."

The crowd rippled, then surged in a single wave, descending to feast on Sark's fallen corpse. Unseen could go for days without eating, but eventually their hunger overcame all else. A bloody corpse was too much temptation.

No one looked Sidonie's way. No patrols rustled in the woods behind them. She was on her own, without Masson's protection. She got to her feet, cheekbone throbbing.

Her opponent turned away from the macabre feast, her grin that of a cat who has cornered dinner. "Toys break."

Instinct took over. Sidonie bolted for the trees, wasting no time on a fight she'd never win. The crunch of leaves behind her warned that Nalin wasn't far behind. A hard weight crashed into her back, but Sidonie had braced for it, her feet skidding but keeping her balance. An arm hooked around her throat in a choke hold.

Sidonie was no fighter, but she'd had a twin brother, and this had been one of his more annoying moves. Sidonie squirmed and twisted, using her dead weight to slip her chin beneath Nalin's grip. Then she bit down on the bare flesh inside Nalin's forearm, tearing meat.

Nalin screamed in hot fury, but let go. Sidonie let her attacker's blood flow over her tongue before she released her grip. Triumph pulsed through her as Nalin backed away, her eyes wide with surprise.

"This toy has bite," Sidonie snapped, licking blood from her lips. The taste reminded her she was hungry. "Tell your friends to keep their distance."

She edged deeper into the forest, not ready to turn her back on Nalin. Another Gentry approached from her right, but his loping stride had no urgency.

"No one leaves," he said with vague irritation. "Go back to the fire."

Sidonie grabbed his hair and smashed his face into a tree. A rain of dead leaves fell as he slid to the dirt, unconscious. She gave a surprised laugh. She was stronger than she used to be.

With a glance, she saw Nalin had vanished. Sidonie sprinted into the woods, keeping her footing despite the darkness of the path. This was her best chance of escape, with so many of the Unseen drawn to the bonfire and Masson's fight. The perimeter guards would be thin, and she'd already disposed of one.

She kept to a narrow track that carried Masson's scent, hoping it would lead to the city. Longing filled her for her bedroom at Allington House. She could fill her bathtub with steaming water and scrub away the filth of the forest with sweet smelling soap. She had drawers full of clean, soft clothes. She could sit down to dinner with her family.

A vague dissonance filled her mind about the meal, but there were other bright thoughts. Midwinter meant it was almost Christmas, and for many years she'd spent the shortest night of the year making Miranda's gift. She'd carved and painted one animal figurine each year. The tradition began when they were both impossibly young, and those clumsy carvings had become a beloved family jest. Even once she'd had money to buy presents, she'd kept the tradition up for fun.

An ache formed in her chest. Soon, she could put her arms around her kin, kiss her father, and find Richard, especially Richard. He was a doctor and would help her heal. But how was she going to find her way into Londria?

She finally stopped running, her steaming breath like prayers floating up to the starry sky. A wide swath of shallow water trickled before her. She knelt and drank, washing the last traces of Nalin's blood away before confronting her next problem. She'd been following the path—and Masson's scent—but the stream cut through it, and there was no sign of a track on the other side.

Moonlight shimmered on the water, broken as something— an owl, or maybe a small dragon—crossed the sky. Rocks dotted the stream, allowing her to cross without soaking her new boots. Once she'd scrambled up the far bank, she studied the direction of the stream. The Tamesis passed through Londria, and wouldn't the stream run into the river?

She followed the bank until she picked up Masson's scent once more. Before long, she reached the edge of the trees and saw the wall looming ahead. A stretch of scrub grass separated the trees from the stone structure. From this side, the mages' famous barrier was impressively high.

Along this stretch of the wall, bushes and saplings had been allowed to grow within a dozen feet of the barrier, giving her cover as she approached. When there was nowhere left to hide, she sprinted across the grass to its base, hoping no guard saw her darting form. None did.

Once she was close, she could feel the wall's magic like a stinging pressure against her skin. It kept out the Unseen, and at the moment that seemed to include her. And yet somehow Masson had a route inside—that meant she did, too.

Stubbornly, she searched for Masson's scent, circling to her right. To her surprise, she found it where the stream broke above ground again, thinner and deeper, only to dive beneath the wall's foundation stones.

Legend had it that the mage's protection extended far above the wall and deep into the earth below. Sidonie had a vague memory of Gideon worrying about whether hidden waterways—especially ones that shifted over time—disturbed the barrier's security. She smiled wryly at her twin's obsession with such puzzles. Maybe soon she could tell him whether he was correct.

Wild grasses grew tall along the base of the wall. Careful not to touch the spell-soaked stones, she pulled the vegetation aside to reveal where the waterway vanished. There, the jagged mouth of a natural tunnel had formed where the stream eroded the ground.

Sidonie crouched, studying the passage. It went on for at least twenty feet. That was twenty feet in which the mage's magic might turn her into a pile of smoking ash. Also, it looked as if there might be spiders.

The alternative was never going home. Sidonie sucked in a breath and slid inside. The water filled up most of the tunnel, but she could duck walk along the edge as long as she was careful not to crack her skull on the base of the wall. Magic prickled along her skin, growing sharper as she approached the other side, but she wriggled out of the tunnel behind a sprawling clump of heather. She shook out her clothes and hair, certain she'd encountered at least one spiderweb.

She was safely back in the city. It took another moment to realize that she was in the Grove of Angels Cemetery. This was where she had been kidnapped the night of her engagement ball.

Moonlight silvered the landscape just as it had that night. Disoriented by the memory, she took a few stumbling steps.

There was the road where the carriage had stopped. Over there, Gideon had fallen when he'd tried to rescue her. She'd always assumed he'd survived, but she didn't know for certain. She'd had no word of her family since that awful night.

With a sudden sense of urgency, she sprang into a run once more. This time, she knew exactly where she was going. She had to find her way home, but first she'd find Richard. He'd know how to make her right again.

She was grateful for the new boots now, and her added strength. She ran for miles, eating up the ground with her long strides. Anyone who saw her would think she was a madwoman, but that didn't matter. She made it most of the way before she had to stop and lean against the side of a building to catch her breath. The clock from a church tower chimed, telling her it was three o'clock in the morning. No wonder there were so few people on the streets.

She walked the rest of the way to Richard's surgery, allowing her loose hair to fall forward over her face. She did not want to be recognized before she reached her destination.

Richard's father, Dr. Charles Wilcox, ran a hospital, but Richard himself had set up his practice in this modest part of town, where he could help those with less money to spare. Most nights, he slept in a room above his offices in case someone came calling late. His endless compassion and devotion to duty were among the many things she loved about him.

Her eyes sought the streetlamp that stood at the corner of his block, her heart lifting when she saw its glow. Without meaning to, she raised a palm to catch its brightness, then gave a soft laugh. She was literally fleeing the darkness of despair and coming into the light.

But she wasn't fit for it yet.

She edged into the shadows, aware there were more people on the street ahead. The late hour was nothing on this street, which was near the city's most infamous brothels. She only knew the name of one—Hellion House—because Richard sometimes doctored the women there, but she'd never gone down that road to see it for herself.

Farther along was a pub with patrons spilling onto the cobbled street, their conversation salted with snatches of song and shouts of greeting and goodbye. The smell of cooked animal turned her stomach, but the scent of human was another story. She watched the drinkers intently, instinctively looking for strays. Her mind glossed over what she might do to a lone human, but she was too nervous to approach, anyway. After so long in the woods, the loud voices startled her. It would take time to feel part of Londria again. It would take time to feel safe.

She reached the surgery door, her chest fluttering with expectation. The entire building was dark, but then Richard was likely asleep. She reached for the bell. It was then she saw a hand-lettered sign hanging inside the glass panel of the door. The surgery and rooms above were available for rent.

The street, with its noise and lights, receded into a haze. A cry stuck in her throat, aching to be set free. She tried to swallow past it, but something inside her tore. This had been her harbor, where she could finally rest. Finally come back to herself. She pressed a hand against the window where letters still spelled out Richard's name, but she found only a cold, hard chill.

She made a soft keening noise as she pressed her forehead to the glass.

Footsteps were coming her way.

She shrank into the deep shadows, away from the light. It was a woman sauntering toward the crowd of drinkers at the end of the block. By her gaudy dress, Sidonie guessed she'd come from the street of brothels. Hunger rose, but a deeper need pushed it aside.

"Excuse me," Sidonie called out.

The woman stopped and squinted into the dark where Sidonie stood. "Yes, love? Do you need something?"

She sounded kind and chatty, as if she took in kittens and waifs. Motherly, but not yet matronly.

"Do you know where Dr. Wilcox has gone?" Sidonie asked.

"Only bad news, I'm afraid," the woman said. "He's gone back to his old family home—somewhere far away, from what I heard tell."

"Oh." Shock numbed Sidonie, stealing away her power of speech.

"I know," the woman said with a tragic note. "Bad for us, but worse for him. He was never right after his sweetheart got herself killed. Try Dr. Leonard down on Fuller Street. He's not as good, but he doesn't charge much."

With that, the woman walked on. Sidonie stared after her, feeling oddly disembodied. Richard's great-grandfather had come from a continent away. If he'd risked traveling that far, he wasn't coming back.

"I'm sorry your heart broke, my love," she murmured to the night air. "But I came back. I'm right here."

She clamped a hand over her mouth, holding back a sob. She didn't dare to let it go, because beneath it was a howl of betrayal. She needed him, but he wasn't here to help her. It wasn't fair, and it wasn't his fault, but her heart hurt anyway and wailed with the desolation of an orphaned child.

A gale of laughter rose from the drinkers, the sound echoing down the street. The need to eat came flooding back, pushing everything else aside. It was time to go. She turned, and as she did, the lamplight fell over her. Her reflection stared back from the darkened window. Sidonie froze.

She was herself, and she was most certainly not. Her eyes, once blue like Gideon's, were now nearly translucent and reflected a silvery-gray light. Even in the darkness, she could see her deathly pallor, though one cheekbone sported a bruise from Nalin's blow. With the shadows tracing the bones and hollows of her features, she looked as famished as she felt.

She slowly lowered her hand, afraid. Her claws disturbed her, but she'd seen them before. It was a long moment before she scraped up the nerve to part her lips. No wonder her mouth had felt strange to her. All her teeth had grown longer and sharper, but her corner teeth had become fangs. Part of her had known this, but had kept that truth buried from her waking thoughts.

Strangest of all was the way she moved, every gesture quick and alert as a hawk. She was still herself, still the debutante who had ruled Londria's balls and assemblies, but she had joined the monsters.

Her heart thundered, a tide of fear pulling her under. Each breath stuttered, leaving her faint as she finally grasped that there would be no recovery, no safety, no reunions. She'd fallen into an abyss with no bottom.

A man strolled her way, humming to himself. She shrank into the shadowed recess of the door and let him go by. As he passed, she caught a whiff of the beery sweat on his skin and, with a sharp jab, realized he was prey, and that she desperately wanted to eat him. Horror should have made her retch, but it only made her stomach pinch harder. She wouldn't last much longer without a meal.

Lucky for him, there were too many potential witnesses. Lucky for him, she hadn't quite surrendered.

She slid around the corner, finding a street with less traffic. She knew this block—she'd shopped here once or twice when she'd been looking for something a hair on the disreputable side. The familiarity only reinforced the fact she had no idea where to go or what to do.

She'd counted on Richard to love her enough to help her. Now that she'd seen herself, she couldn't deny the truth she'd pushed away. It was fortunate that he'd left, because he would have tried and tried. So would her family, if she let them. But the hunger was too great, and there was nothing the household cook could serve that would satisfy the abomination she had become.

She could not take that risk. She was never going home.

The realization was an amputation of everything she'd known and loved. It would bleed as long as she walked the earth, but she knew she had to act swiftly and with purpose. She stopped, panting because she couldn't suck in enough air. Tears streamed down her cheeks, the salt stinging the scrapes and scratches in her skin.

What future did she have? She was clever, educated, used to leading her social set. She'd lost none of that, and yet she was doomed to that nightmare in the woods, where the monster who'd kidnapped her just tore his enemy in two.

Cart wheels rattled over the cobbles in the next street. The day started early for the merchants of the city. Soon she would have company, and that would end badly. If she chose to survive, she would have to grieve later.

What had the Caretaker said? *The first law of survival is to face the unthinkable and make it your servant.*

Sidonie wiped her cheeks on her sleeve, grabbing at anything that might form a practical plan. She looked from shop window to shop window until one caught her eye. A dark velvet dress hung in the bay window, long-sleeved and dramatic in its simplicity. It was exactly what she needed to replace the ruins of the gown from her betrothal ball. Power had a language, whether in words or symbols, and no one understood the nuance of fashion like Sidonie Fletcher.

She'd learned how to pick locks as a girl, but at that moment she lacked the tools and patience. She elbowed through a narrow pane of glass beside the door, then reached through to let herself in. Guilt and exhilaration followed as she roamed the store, which sold a better kind of second-hand goods. The air hung with a fog of stale perfume.

She picked up a carpet bag and began filling it with necessaries, working quickly in case the watch making their rounds saw the broken window. Under the glass of the front counter, where errant light caught a constellation of paste jewels, she found a lady's pistol and a stiletto in an enameled sheath. Both were fancifully decorated as accessories—clearly for those who fancied themselves wicked. Nevertheless, on inspection, they functioned perfectly well.

Weapons, at last.

When the bag was almost full, she took down the velvet dress, running her hands over the soft, rich folds. It was a garment fit for any dark queen.

She would show the monsters who had bite.

CHAPTER 23

Hospitals perturbed Gideon, as if a miasma of infection followed him for days after a visit. Still, the airship industry was fraught with hazards, and he'd spent plenty of afternoons visiting the wounded. This time, it was the invalids still recuperating after the explosion on the *Leopard*.

With a slight change in circumstance, it would have been him dead or broken. Guilt walked with him when he finally fled the stench of old bandages and lye soap.

He emerged onto the street, the chill wind tugging at his coat. None of the three crew he'd visited had known anything of use. Then again, their injuries were grave. One had broken bones and might lose a leg. Another had suffered a large fragment of metal perforating his chest, barely missing the large vessels of the heart. All would survive but would not live well. He could forgive them for a slipshod memory.

Deep in thought, Gideon nearly missed the sound of his name. He looked up to see Councilor Latimer standing just steps away. The small man wore a cloak over his blue robes, the hood pulled up against the wind. His eyes crinkled as he smiled.

"Good day, Councilor," Gideon said, stopping to greet the

man. He couldn't help but think about his earlier conversation with Miranda, and of his suspicions about the Conclave. Was this an opportunity to get even one of his many questions answered?

"Good day, Fletcher." Latimer rubbed his gloved hands together. The wind had turned his narrow face pink, making him look more youthful than ever. "I swear it is too cold for snow."

Pedestrians streamed by, passing in and out of the fitful sunshine. The hospital stood on a main road that led through an open market. Many in the crowd carried shopping, reminding Gideon the holiday was close. There had been no time to think about celebrating, much less garlands and presents.

"Are you visiting?" Gideon asked, nodding to the hospital.

"No, but I expect you are," the mage replied. "There are some of your former crewmates inside, are there not?"

"Yes. I'm afraid all I can do for them is to show my compassion."

"Good of you to do so, especially since you're no longer part of your father's business."

The words stung, but Gideon covered it with a polite laugh. "My interest is genuine, not a matter of obligation."

"You are an ethical man. That's rarer than you know." Latimer gestured with a sweep of his hand. "Walk with me a while?"

Gideon nodded his agreement. They strolled side by side, part of the midday rush.

"How do your friends fare?" Latimer asked.

Despite the councilor's easy manner, the question piqued Gideon's curiosity. It was both natural—they had met outside the hospital—and opportunistic. Was it a coincidence that they had crossed paths in this exact place?

If the mage was fishing, Gideon could do some fishing of his own. "My old friends are not improving as quickly as I would like. It's been a disappointing morning."

"Indeed?"

"Before coming here, I visited the home of another crew

member, Mr. Featherly. He hasn't been seen or heard from for many days. Do you know where he might be found?"

Latimer's expression faltered. "Why would I know the whereabouts of this man?"

They crossed an intersection, hurrying to avoid an oncoming hackney cab.

"It seems he joined the Threshers," Gideon said when they reached the safety of the curb. He kept his tone conversational. "In fact, Featherly was one of the three whose attack you interrupted when we first met."

The mage's face remained placid. "Are you certain?"

"The three found me again that night, and Featherly did his best to put a knife in my guts."

"Thank heavens he failed," Latimer said, his brow furrowing with concern. "Was that the same night young Robin Vortigern perished?"

Gideon suspected the mage already knew the answer. "You are well-informed, Councilor. Are you sure you're not aware of my missing man's location? Given Vortigern's fate, I'm concerned for his welfare."

"Even though he tried to hurt you?"

"I fear many of the Threshers are under coercion from those who recruit them. If such is the case with Featherly, some of the responsibility falls to Fletcher Industries, who did a poor job of meeting the needs of an employee's young family."

They'd reached the market, where a large square held wagons and barrows of produce, as well as a great many pigeons. A cider seller ladled out cups of the hot brew. The spicy scent tickled Gideon's nose.

"Mr. Fletcher, shall we stop fencing?" Latimer stopped walking, his expression sober. Where he'd seemed affably charming before, now Gideon could see the mage. Even if he was only a junior councilor, that still put him near the top of the Citadel's hierarchy. That made him dangerous.

"Please," Gideon replied.

"As you say, I am well informed. I know your detective friend questioned Dr. Strang. I know you were present. I know you suspect him of the murder but have no proof."

"Is Strang guilty?"

Latimer began walking again, and Gideon fell into step beside him. The councilor picked an apple off a barrow and tossed the vendor a coin. He bit into it with a crunch, chewing and swallowing before making a reply. "Strang believes in the Thresher doctrine of obedience."

"He believed Vortigern deserved to die because the lad ran from committing homicide? I had a weapon, and he didn't. He was smart to run."

They walked a little further. It grew colder at the far end of the square, where the shadow of a building blocked the sun.

"Cowardice," the mage said, as if that explained all. "Desertion. Failure. It can't be tolerated."

"Is it necessary to be so ruthless?" Gideon asked. "Robin Vortigern was a feckless boy."

So was Featherly, for that matter, regardless of what he'd done.

Latimer waved an arm in the direction of the market. "What do you see?"

Gideon grew uneasy. They weren't talking about Strang any longer. "I see commerce. People busy at their errands."

Latimer finished his apple and threw the core to the birds. "You see prosperity. If there is chaos, prosperity fails."

"So you believe in the Thresher doctrine? You seemed to scorn them before."

"They have a sound argument, for all their brutish manners. Many among the Council are too lenient when it comes to managing Londria's affairs."

If the existing Council was lenient, Gideon didn't want to be part of Latimer's world. Fear stirred inside him. "Why did the Threshers come after me? Why did you stop them?"

"I stopped them because I have no wish to see you murdered in the street. I don't approve of undisciplined mobs."

Gideon wondered if a quiet death like Vortigern's might have been acceptable. "Who wants me dead?"

"There are those who wish you would stop asking questions and pay attention instead," Latimer said, his tone sharp. "All the answers you require are in front of you."

"Meaning?"

"Londria's future always teeters on the edge between fear and safety." Latimer stopped and faced Gideon, his arms folded. "Too much fear among the populace breeds rebellion. Too much safety breeds disrespect. The Conclave has carefully preserved that balance for centuries, but your family's ship threatened to destroy it."

Gideon sucked in a breath. "The *Leopard* perished, along with all those lives, because a fire ship designed to keep away the Unseen would make citizens feel too safe?"

"You heard me perfectly well." Latimer's words were flat.

In a twisted way, that echoed what Ormond had said to Miranda. Still, Gideon still couldn't believe sane men had come to such a conclusion. Gideon gave a low, incredulous laugh.

"Is something amusing, Mr. Fletcher?" Latimer asked.

"No," he replied. "It's really not. Besides the destruction of a ship and crew, my sister nearly died. Plus, there have been two attempts on my life, not to mention the murder of a misguided young man."

"The Conclave requires obedience, Mr. Fletcher. It's best that the city remembers how much it needs us."

"And you think the *Leopard* would make Londria forget what it owes the Conclave?"

"I believe you already know the answer. Consider this a final warning, both for you and your family."

Gideon said nothing.

"This was not the conversation I meant to have with you today, but here we are," Latimer said. "I would far rather part peacefully, so consider my words. Now I bid you good day."

The mage headed toward a side street. He hadn't gone two steps when Gideon asked the question he'd been holding back.

"Isn't the real danger posed by the *Leopard* that it works too well?"

Latimer turned, his eyes dark with warning.

"The Conclave doesn't want the Unseen barricaded from entering the city. Why is that, Councilor? Why are you letting them in?"

Latimer's gaze swept the area, looking for anyone who might have overheard Gideon's words, but no one was near this end of the street. "Good day, Mr. Fletcher. Don't buy trouble you can't afford. You've seen the consequences."

With that, he vanished between the buildings.

Puzzled and frustrated, Gideon retraced his steps through the market and turned up the main street. His mind felt stuffed with questionable matter, as if Latimer had dumped the rotten sweepings of the market into his brain. The councilor had given few genuine answers and repeated what Strang had already implied. Latimer was guilty—just as the Conclave was guilty—but specifics were scarce. Evidence was nowhere in sight.

The one true thing was that Latimer wanted Gideon's investigation to stop. That meant Gideon was likely to uncover something useful. His best move would be to keep on his present path—no distractions or cutting corners.

His next stop was Allington House. He'd written ahead to determine a good time to visit, and that afternoon Miranda was taking their father to see the new airship. It was the perfect opportunity to see the rest of the company books.

When he arrived, Olivia perched behind the desk of their father's study with the ledgers open before her.

"Miranda told me you were coming," Olivia said, barely looking up from her work. "I thought it best to go over the entries she made for the sake of clarity. I'm certain our sister studied arithmetic, but it appears to have dribbled out her ears."

Gideon sat across from Olivia and pulled one ledger his way, flipping it open to review the most recent pages. "Have you noticed anything of interest?"

"Such as supplies for the crew lavatories?" Olivia asked dryly. "Or biscuits for the medical staff tea breaks? I tell you, it's a grand thing that I have access to the finest scientific minds in our hemisphere. I love putting my education to use."

He'd heard all this before. "You are an insufferable snob. Biscuits have deep emotional value for our office staff, especially those with jam."

She gave him a withering look. As if on cue, the housekeeper came in with a tea tray, setting it on a side table.

"Hello, Mrs. Trencher," Gideon said. He missed the staff at Allington House, and not just for their work. He'd known many of them since boyhood.

"Hello, sir, a pleasure to see you." She bobbed a curtsy. "Will there be anything else, Miss Olivia?"

"No, thank you, Mrs. Trencher." Olivia scratched out a total and carefully penned in a new string of numbers. "You may leave us."

The housekeeper departed, closing the door behind her. Gideon surveyed the tea tray, which sadly had none of the cook's excellent scones. Since Olivia was still working, he poured out the tea. He was about to set a cup before her when she began neatly tearing a page from the ledger.

"What are you doing?" he asked as she tossed the page into the wastepaper basket.

She pulled a face. "Some pages are easier to rewrite than correct."

He came around the desk and retrieved the page. It was the

running record of payments, one column noting debits, the other credits. Miranda had written half the entries herself, getting most of the numbers in the wrong column.

"I don't think you will find the key to a thrilling plot there," Olivia said dryly. "Not even the dullest clerk would find that of interest."

But something else was niggling at the back of his mind. He'd been looking for a clue on the written page, but he hadn't considered the clue might be the page itself. He dropped the paper back into the garbage. "Where do the contents of this basket go?"

Her look said he'd run mad. "Into a bin at the back of the house. I think it's eventually burned. Mrs. Trencher could tell you the specifics."

In other words, wastepaper went into a bin any passer-by could access if they knew where to look. "Do many Fletcher Industries papers end up in that bin?"

Olivia set down her pen. "A few pages I've rewritten. The rest are drafts of letters or other documents. And, about a month ago, father cleared out some preliminary sketches for a project that's since been finished. Nothing anyone could use for blackmail."

"Blackmail isn't the problem."

"Then what is?"

"Theft. Spies. Everything at the airfield is kept under lock and key until it's destroyed." Gideon returned to his seat. "Can you remember what the letters were about?"

"Not all of them." She sounded annoyed, as usually happened when anyone questioned her work. "I wrote letters following up late payments. One of our accounts closed, and I wrote to confirm all our business was concluded."

This was the kind of detail he'd been looking for. "Which account?"

"Harkness. Their business wound down."

Gideon paused with his cup halfway to his mouth. The Harkness Company had supplied tea, both to the house and airfield, as long as he could remember. "What happened to them?"

"People do retire, you know," Olivia replied with a chuckle. "It was good fortune that a new supplier contacted us at the right moment. That's their brew in your cup."

Gideon sipped. It was excellent Assam tea, with a faint smoky note. "Who supplied this?"

"Rutherford's Imports. I interviewed Mr. Rutherford myself. He has an interest in catering passenger flights as well."

Gideon set down the cup. "Didn't Miranda mention a tea basket on the *Leopard*?"

Olivia blinked. "What are you saying?"

Impatience surged through Gideon. Olivia was smart, but not always in a practical way. "That delivering a gift basket is an excellent excuse for a stranger to turn up at a place of business, even an airfield."

"And how is that significant?" Olivia asked.

Gideon took a deep breath, forcing himself to be precise. "Is it odd that a letter is written to close an account, a new supplier miraculously appears from the aether, and then that company delivers a sample basket unasked on the morning of the test flight, especially when we know that Featherly was almost certainly willing to admit a saboteur aboard the ship?"

Olivia paled, a sure sign that she finally understood the connection. "Oh, no."

"Quite."

"What I mean to say is that I might call all of that a coincidence on its own, except for one more thing." She looked down at the wicker basket holding the page she'd discarded. "The sketches Father threw out were of upgrades to the *Leopard*'s engine. Don't you remember, he improved the engine before the test flight?"

Gideon fell back in his chair. "And anyone who found the sketches would know exactly how to make the engine fail."

CHAPTER 24

Gideon ran from Allington House, finally in possession of a tangible lead. He knew the address of Rutherford's because it was across from his bootmaker. That, it seemed, was the only easy answer he was likely to get that day.

Clouds were gathering, the gray billows blotting out the patches of sun that had brightened his walk with Latimer. It would almost certainly snow before the day was done. When he finally found a cab, he was thoroughly chilled.

Before setting out, he'd paused just long enough to question Mrs. Trencher about the paper bin at the back of the house. The bin was kept in an unlocked cellar accessible from the garden, along with rakes, hoes, and old rags. The housekeeper was vague on when it was last emptied, or who had handled it. He was fast learning that investigative work had far more tedious dead ends than brilliant deductions.

When the cab set him down in the fashionable shopping district, the lamplighters were at work even though it was only mid-afternoon. Rutherford's Imports was a narrow brick building that announced its presence in large gold lettering above the door. Gideon started toward it. He was nearly there when he saw Layla leaving the shop, a string bag in one hand.

"Hello, Mr. Fletcher," she said cheerfully.

He smiled, touching his hat brim in greeting. "Layla, you are a ray of springtime on a winter afternoon."

There was no sign of the hunter in her today. Layla was dressed as he was used to seeing her, in an elegant walking dress and feathered hat atop her mass of strawberry blonde hair. She was the loveliest of Mrs. Randall's women and even as they stood there on the street, heads turned her way.

"How are you, sir?" she asked.

The last time he'd been near Hellion House, Huntley had dragged him there after the fight with the Threshers. It seemed like a thousand years ago, so much had happened. In truth, it had only been days.

"I am doing well, thank you." Gideon indicated her parcel. "Shopping for yourself?"

"No, no, Mrs. Randall sent me on an errand. She has a dinner party planned for important guests and wants every detail perfect."

His curiosity stirred, but he set it aside. "I hope it goes well."

"Thank you, I'm sure it will. Nothing at the house is ever left to chance."

Gideon was ready to end the conversation, but then paused. "I'm here to speak with Mr. Rutherford. My sister describes him as a tall, thin man with short-cropped brown hair. Is he in the shop today?"

"That's the younger Mr. Rutherford, not his father." She lifted her chin, indicating the interior of the shop. "He's at the counter right now."

"You are, as always, a gem. Give Mrs. Randall my compliments."

With that, he entered the shop. It was empty except for the man at the counter in a shopkeeper's apron. The younger Mr.

Rutherford, he presumed. Gideon locked the door behind him and turned the "open" signed to "closed." His last glimpse of Layla was her astonished expression. He pulled the blind of the shop window down.

"Excuse me, sir, what do you think you are doing?" demanded the shopkeeper.

His face reminded Gideon of a rodent, with close-set eyes and no chin. Gideon looked him in those rat-black eyes. "My name is Fletcher. It was my family's airship that recently burned."

Gideon had taken a gamble coming here, but it paid off. The look on Rutherford's face was all the confession he could wish for.

"I-I'm so sorry to hear that, Mr. Fletcher." The man's throat worked convulsively, as if he were about to choke.

Gideon leaned on the polished oak counter. "You have a beautiful shop, Mr. Rutherford, with a lot of lovely things."

The entire wall behind the counter was crowded with teas, chocolate, exotic nuts, and spices. All of it had to arrive in Londria by sea or air, and all of it was costly.

The man regained a little of his composure. "Thank you, sir."

He took a step to the left, as if to leave his post and reopen the door, but Gideon stopped him with a glare.

"So tell me, Rutherford, what made you participate in the murder of the men and women aboard the *Leopard*?"

"I don't know what you're talking about," he spluttered. "I merely opened an account to supply your family's business."

"Who suggested you do that?" Gideon asked. "Who took the basket to the *Leopard* that morning? They needed to be an expert mechanic to sabotage the engine that quickly, so I doubt it was anyone in your employ."

"No," Rutherford replied. "I refuse to have this conversation." This time, he came around the counter, his step determined.

Gideon got in his path. "Someone put pressure on you to

provide their cover. A big reward for a simple act no one should ever suspect. Did they approach you or your father?"

"Leave him out of this," Rutherford snarled.

"Who was it?" Gideon was losing patience. The heavy, spiced atmosphere of the store made it hard to breathe. Hooking his fingers around the strap of the apron, he pulled Rutherford close.

"Who. Was. It? I want a name."

The man's lip curled. "What good do these questions do? The law doesn't apply to everyone in this city. Even if I could tell you, there's nowhere to go with the answers."

"Maybe," Gideon snarled. "But law and justice are two separate conversations."

A pitying expression crossed Rutherford's face. "You'll see precious little of either. Ever since *they* decided I was useful, there's been a spy outside my door. They know how to make a man keep his word."

The sound of cracking wood made Gideon spin around. The shop door flung open in a shower of splinters as the lock gave way. Four men in the scarlet and gold uniforms of the Conclave guard overwhelmed the small shop. Gideon's stomach turned to lead.

Rutherford retreated until he hit the wall, making the jars on the shelf behind him wobble.

One of the guards stepped to the forefront, the shop's muted lights glittering on the gold braid of his jacket. Gideon realized he knew the man. He had hauled prisoners to the Citadel many times before.

"Captain Hagen," he said, struggling to keep his voice firm.

The captain gave a slight bow. "If you will come with us, Mr. Fletcher."

～

Later that afternoon, Miranda returned home from the airfield with her father. For an hour or two, he had been the old Norton Fletcher, enthusiastic and full of ideas. Now he had retired to his rooms for a light meal and a nap.

Miranda longed to do the same but instead sought out Olivia to receive a summary of Gideon's visit. She had just reached the doorway of the drawing room when she heard Kitteridge's voice coming from within.

"I must speak to Miss Miranda immediately," he said.

"I'm sorry." Olivia's tone showed how little she liked demands. "If you would care to have a seat, Mr. Kitteridge, I shall send someone to find out if my sister is at home to visitors."

"It's all right," Miranda interjected as she entered the room. "I'm here."

Relief spread across his handsome face, followed swiftly by apprehension, as he cast a quick glance at Olivia.

Olivia caught the look and raised her brows. "Miranda, do you wish me to leave?"

"What brings you here, Mr. Kitteridge?" Miranda asked, sensing something was terribly amiss.

"It concerns your brother."

"Then I'm staying." Olivia sat forward in her seat.

He took a step toward Miranda, as if wanting to comfort her, but then stopped himself. She remained rooted to her spot by the door, transfixed by foreboding.

"I was at Hellion House in anticipation of a dinner party when one of the women arrived in a panic," he began. "She was at Rutherford's Imports when Mr. Fletcher arrived. It was clear he meant to have words with the proprietor. She grew concerned and remained nearby in case there was trouble."

"He suspected Rutherford of involvement in the fate of the *Leopard*," Olivia put in. "That's what came of our meeting this afternoon."

"A tea merchant?" Miranda asked, but then signaled Kitteridge to go on.

"To come to the point," he said, "it was not long before guards arrived from the Citadel and took your brother away."

"Why?" Miranda cried, her mind refusing to picture the arrest. "What did he do?"

"He solved the case," Olivia said in a small voice. "Or at least he solved enough of it that the Conclave has silenced him."

Kitteridge regarded Olivia, his expression grave. "I'm afraid you are correct."

Olivia, already pale, blanched. A heavy silence followed as dread settled over the room. It was Kitteridge who finally broke it.

"I came here directly for two reasons. The first regards the safety of this house. Layla—the woman I spoke of—is observant. She believes there were spies watching Rutherford's premises. That may be how the guards became aware of Mr. Fletcher's presence so quickly, but it's also possible that they were following him."

"You think the Conclave might come here," Miranda guessed.

Kitteridge nodded. "Miss Olivia, the Conclave is far less likely to confront your uncle, the Earl of Havelock. Would you be willing to take your father there tonight and remain for a day or two?"

"Of course." Olivia rose, her hands shaking slightly. "I'll get started at once."

Impulsively, Miranda embraced her. She felt her sister's muffled sob, but then Olivia squirmed.

"I need to go," Olivia said quickly. "It might take some time to prepare if Father's already asleep."

"Will you be all right?" Miranda whispered in her ear.

"I'm best if I have a job to do. Otherwise, I shall run mad."

Miranda released her. Olivia left the room, her face carefully controlled, though tears stood in her eyes. Miranda blinked rapidly, certain she'd cry if her sister broke down. Already her chest ached, as if her breastbone had broken free of her ribs.

"Stay strong, Scorpion," Kitteridge said softly.

Miranda closed the door, damning the social rules about unmarried couples being alone. She needed a private word with Kitteridge.

"And the second reason you came here?" Miranda asked, her voice rough with unshed tears.

He took her hands, his gray eyes serious. "Mrs. Randall requests your presence at Hellion House. Mr. Fletcher is dear to her. She won't give him up without a fight."

Miranda's breath caught. She'd always wondered about Gideon's relationship with the woman, but that was the least of her problems now. "Will we even have a chance to fight for him? I've seen the Conclave's public trials. They're a mockery of the law."

The bleak despair of their victims had ripped at her soul. As if her body couldn't hold the full measure of her fear, she began to shake.

Kitteridge squeezed her hands. "Courage, Miranda."

She swallowed hard. "What does Mrs. Randall think we can do?"

He gave an encouraging smile. "She has friends everywhere, and many owe her favors."

"She can't risk it. It's enough that the Fletchers will be ruined. Gideon tried to distance himself, but it's obvious we're still close." As if her words released a dam, she began to weep in jagged, hiccupping sobs. Kitteridge pulled her close, carefully folding her in his arms. His strength was evident even in his gentle touch, but he kept still, letting Miranda take what she needed from his embrace.

She desperately needed his warmth. Resting her head against his chest, she wept until all she was aware of was the steady pounding of his heart.

"You don't need to face this alone. Go to her," he said softly. "Go as the Scorpion. That's who your brother needs."

"Will you be there?" she asked, finally pulling away.

He dropped his gaze. "As I've said before, I am always at your back."

Temper surged like a sudden flame. "But only in the shadows."

His smile was apologetic. "It's where I work best."

Miranda struggled in silence, unsure what she wanted from this man. Promises? His constant presence at her side? A magical ability to make everything all right?

She cursed herself. She wasn't a needy little girl.

Maybe she was right then.

He brushed her cheek, catching a lingering tear. "You already have all my admiration. You will have my every assistance, however plans unfold."

It still felt as if he was already fading into mist. Kitteridge never stayed long.

But that couldn't matter. Gideon needed help, and that meant finding her courage. Kitteridge was right.

As she gathered herself, their last conversation came to mind. There had been a question she'd hesitated to ask, but this was no time to hold back.

"What is Doomsfire?"

His eyes widened. "Where did you hear that word? Never mind. Forget you did."

Disappointment frosted her emotions. "How much are you not telling me?"

He took a step back, gathering his hat from where he left it on a chair. "Right now, your brother is all that matters."

"True," she said, her voice cracking on the word. "Thank you for delivering Mrs. Randall's message."

"Miranda," he chided. "I value you more than you can imagine. Please accept what I can give and ask no more."

Whatever she wanted from him, this wasn't enough. Her world was ending, and half-measures would not do.

"Pray excuse me, Mr. Kitteridge," she said, grasping the door handle. "I must get ready to visit Hellion House."

His face fell. He'd heard the dismissal in her words.

Kitteridge gave a curt bow and left.

CHAPTER 25

Once the guards hauled Gideon outside Rutherford's, all civilities ended. They pulled a hood over his head, bound his hands, and thrust him into a carriage.

"Where are you taking me?" he demanded as the vehicle lurched forward.

His question was met with a hard blow to the ribs, probably from the butt of a guard's rifle. The knife wound across his abdomen flared with pain. After that, Gideon didn't speak.

The hood was suffocating and smelled of bad breath. How many prisoners had worn it before him? Had they all been arrested after a lunch of pickled herring? It didn't help that he couldn't see where the vehicle was going, which gave him motion sickness.

Worse still, the hood negated any chance of being recognized by someone on the street. People vanished in Londria all too often, and for every case he solved, two more went unanswered. He was in danger of becoming one more mystery.

The carriage lurched to a stop. Nothing seemed to happen for ages, just distant shouts and the jangle of the harness as the horses grew restless. Then the carriage door flung open, and he was hauled into the frigid air. Rough hands shoved him into motion. They entered a building—a large one, judging by the echo of their footfalls. Terror surged as a heavy door crashed behind him. He struggled, flinging his weight forward to break free, but another blow with the rifle butt knocked him down.

His hands—cold and numb by this point—were unbound and the hood stripped from his head. He'd barely blinked his eyes into focus when another door slammed, and he was plunged into inky darkness.

He knelt on a stone floor, unmoored from any point of reference. Wherever he was, it was cold with a penetrating damp that implied he might be underground. The faint mineral smell of the air reminded him of a cave.

Cautiously, Gideon got to his feet and rubbed his hands, working the feeling back into his flesh. He'd reopened the wound beneath his bandages during the arrest, and it had begun to throb in time with his pulse.

He reached out, his fingertips brushing a stone wall. Was this the Citadel? The House of Questions had been destroyed, but the building had many wings. The mages wouldn't run short of space to use for a prison and a place of torture.

He worked his way around the chamber by touch, discovering three stone walls and one metal door. Once he ran out of surfaces to explore, all he could do was wait. There was no furniture, no window, not even a rat for entertainment.

He quickly lost track of the passing hours. Time allowed panic to build. Was this it? Would he end his days like a bug in a matchbox, collected and then forgotten until it turned to rot and dust? Or was this temporary, a ploy to make him obedient and regretful of his misdemeanors?

Hunger came and went. Without warning, the slot in the metal door clanged open, followed by a flood of blinding light. He cursed in protest, shielding his eyes with his hands.

Keys rattled and the metal door swung open. Several burly

figures pushed into the cell, one with a lamp that blinded him even more. He glimpsed gray menials' robes before another hood was pulled over his head. They dragged him down a long hall, up steps, and the along more corridors.

The air grew warmer, and despite the hood, Gideon was aware of voices and the sound of others hurrying past. There was even a snatch of a male chorus chanting. No one other than the mages—and their prisoners—set foot inside the Citadel. At any other time, Gideon would have burned with curiosity, but his mind froze with fear.

The menials hauled him up more stairs, then shoved him forward as they snatched off the hood. Again, he heard a door rattle shut, but this time he was left with light and air. The door had bars like a cage, allowing him a view of his prison.

Gideon took a swift inventory as the menials left. The cell had a long bench bolted to the stone floor, but nothing else beyond a bucket for personal needs. Outside the bars was a narrow walkway with a metal railing, then a drop into thin air. Gideon pressed against the bars to get a better view.

His cell was one of dozens—maybe more?—arranged in circular tiers around the hollow core of the Citadel's tower. Each row had a stone walkway, or balcony, that ran in front of the cells. When Gideon looked up, the tiers ascended beyond his range of vision, vanishing about where the belfry would begin. When he looked down, he saw he was only three rows from the bottom cells.

Vertigo made his head swim. There was a considerable drop from the lowest circle of cells to the floor. An enormous, arching tripod formed of marble filigree stood directly below, its apex not quite reaching the level of the lowest cells. Perched at its center was an egg-shaped crystal half as tall as a man. It burned with a blinding, blue-white fire that seemed to shift and swirl with a semblance of life.

Was this the Doomsfire that Miranda had been seeking?

Thick bands of silver extended from the tripod like the arms of a sea star, stretching across the floor and beyond Gideon's line of sight. They had to be the same silver pathways that formed the core of Londria's main roads, which ran like the spokes of a wheel from the Citadel to the wall.

Despite everything, Gideon felt a moment of awe. This had to be the heart of the Citadel's magic. The light of the glowing crystal beat with a slow, steady rhythm. Each pulse sent a surge of white energy down the silver bands to the periphery of the city. This was the mage-magic that held the barrier against the Unseen.

"Flaming hell on a propeller," Gideon breathed.

"You have no idea, sir," said a voice from the cell to his left.

"Who's there?" Gideon asked.

"Featherly, sir. I knew it was you when you swore."

"Featherly?" That was the last answer he'd expected. His hand went to his stomach, where fresh blood soaked the bandages over his wound.

"Yes, sir."

"How did you get here?"

"Strang." The word was bitter. "He was tying up loose ends. Vortigern was the first, then me."

"I'm sorry," Gideon said, though he wasn't sure how much he meant it. The lad had tried to kill him, after all.

"No, I'm sorry, sir," Featherly said. "I had debts to pay. When there was a chance to get out from under that, I let my sense of right and wrong turn upside down."

Gideon grimaced. Trouble had a way of making men sorry for their deeds. In other circumstances, Featherly might never have confessed.

"You're forgiven," Gideon said, unable to keep the weariness from his voice.

"Thank you, sir," Featherly murmured. It was the voice of a

man staring into his personal abyss. "I wish I could apologize to my wife."

"You will." Gideon said it without much conviction. Their chances were slim, but if he survived and Featherly didn't, he'd ensure Featherly's family thrived. Maybe then this tragedy would end.

Silence stretched between them.

"Tell me what happened." Gideon ran his hands over the bars, searching for a weakness. There had to be a means of escape.

"I meant no harm, sir, really I didn't. I was on the night watch at the airfield. This man paid me to let him on the *Leopard*, and with another mouth to feed, I needed the coin. I should have known nothing comes for free." Featherly stopped, then sucked in a heavy breath. "I thought he was just some bloke wanting our designs. He took measurements of the engine and compared them to these drawings he had. Then he went away, and I never thought anything more about it."

The drawings had to be the sketches Olivia had mentioned. The intruder had been verifying their accuracy.

"Except your man tried to get in another night." Gideon probed the junction of doorframe and rock. It was solid. "Higgins put extra watchmen on after that."

"Yeah." Featherly sounded very young.

Gideon's anger suddenly melted into a profound sadness. He wanted to tell the boy to stop talking, to spare them both, but there might not be other opportunities for confession. And, the truth still mattered. "Go on."

"The day of the test flight, this same bloke, he arrives in the wagon from Rutherford's. When I let him on the ship, he had whole pieces of another engine in the cart. He swapped out everything he needed to just before the flight."

"There wasn't time for that," Gideon said, examining the cell's lock. "And where did he get the equipment?"

"He brought what he needed to with him. I know it shouldn't have been possible, but he did it right quick."

Had he used magic? Gideon had never heard of a mage building an engine—or any honest work, for that matter—but it wasn't impossible. "And then?"

The young man made an inarticulate sound of misery. "I ran before the ship took off. When I saw what he was doing, when I knew the ship would burn, I lost my nerve."

Gideon said nothing after that, imagining the horror that had come afterward. No tirade, no accusation he could make would change that. He cleared his throat. "Did this mystery engineer have a name?"

"He never said. After that, Dr. Strang found me. I'd never seen him before, but he said he knew what I'd done, and I had better join his crew unless I wanted to face the law. It was him who gave the order to attack you, sir."

And the hot kiss of the boy's blade had nearly ended Gideon's life. "Why did you do it?"

"After what I'd done," Featherly began, tears fracturing the words. "I thought it didn't matter what low act I sank to next."

Gideon gave up on his examination of the door. "What about the other Threshers? Are they all being promised something?"

"More like threatened with something," Featherly said, sullen now. "Except Dr. Strang. He was promised dead things."

Gideon's stomach chilled as he remembered the professor's description of his work. "What kind of dead things?"

"From here. They promised him bodies."

The conversation cut off as a deep, hollow note reverberated through the Citadel, reminding Gideon of a dinner gong. Black-robed acolytes appeared from somewhere outside his field of vision. Two of them approached the tripod. To Gideon's surprise, they bent down, doing something to the mosaic marble floor beneath. It was only when he shifted position that he saw a trap door sat directly below the tripod and its glowing crystal egg.

More happened that he couldn't see properly, but soon the acolytes were guiding people from wherever the trap door led. Gideon squinted, unable to make sense of the activity. The prisoners—they had to be prisoners—were bound in coils of silver chain that looked like an extension of the silver spreading from the tripod. As they emerged, each figure was stripped of their bonds and taken away. Other acolytes were chaining up new prisoners and forcing them down to wherever the trap door led.

It looked like a bizarre exchange of shift workers—except the prisoners finishing the shift were infinitely worse off than their replacements. Some were carried away, seeming too weak to stand. Others struggled, whimpering in pain. Their backs and limbs were warped, their hair falling away in ragged clumps.

Gideon gave a wordless cry. *Unseen.* There were Unseen imprisoned inside the Citadel. No wonder Miranda had encountered one here. Had it escaped from whatever ritual he was witnessing?

With mounting revulsion, he saw one of the prisoners fall, his —its—frame seeming to collapse inward even as Gideon watched. The creature twitched, attempting to stand, but couldn't control its limbs.

It looked neither human nor Unseen, but something between.

"Bloody hell," Gideon murmured. Was the Conclave *making* Unseen?

The thing got to all fours and rushed an acolyte. The mage thrust his staff toward the creature, unleashing a bolt of power that sent it tumbling backward. After that, it lay inert.

Gideon sunk to the floor, overwhelmed. This was a betrayal he hadn't begun to suspect.

"They change the prisoners every eight hours," Featherly said bleakly. "Only the mages get near the fire. They need spells to protect them from the crystal's light. And the bites."

Gideon tried to answer, but only made a strangled noise.

"I know, sir. That's why there have never been visitors

allowed inside the Citadel. At least, that's what Dr. Strang said when he brought me here."

Gideon's gorge rose. He forced it down with an effort that left him sick and sweating.

Hours passed. Gideon lay down on the bench, barely noticing when a menial pushed a cup of water and a hunk of bread through the bars of the door. Some time after that, acolytes began circling the tiers in groups of three or four. They put some prisoners into cells and took others out. Gideon rose from the bench, anxiously watching the process. Those entering the cells looked as if they'd returned from below the trap door—weak, stooped, some bleeding from the mouth. Those they took, no doubt gathering the next lot of victims, screamed bloody murder.

Featherly was among them.

Gideon pounded his cell bars and bellowed in protest, but he might as well have been a phantom. The acolytes refused to look his way.

Gideon flung himself on the bench, his head in his hands.

CHAPTER 26

$\mathcal{N}$alin landed face down with a grunt, her outstretched claws just inches from the toes of Sidonie's boots. Her long white hair spread around her, turning black where it picked up streaks of the watery mud. Sidonie winced inside, but kept her expression neutral.

Sidonie and Masson stood next to the remains of last night's bonfire of bones, which had burned down to ash and died in a drizzling rain. The entire settlement stank of blood and char. Partial skulls and spurs of wood and bone still erupted from the lifeless cinders, the wash of moonlight giving the scene the look of a fanciful shipwreck. All that was missing was a scatter of stolen treasure.

Nalin raised her head, showing her teeth. She had the same quick, almost feline movements as Masson. Sidonie wondered if this was a hallmark of full-blooded Gentry, as only some seemed to have that degree of inhuman grace. She'd have to ask about Nalin's parentage someday, if she survived the next half hour.

Masson gave a curt wave to the Gentry soldiers who had delivered Nalin. They retreated a respectful distance, but didn't leave the clearing. It had taken four of them to haul her there, and a few had dire-looking wounds.

Masson put one boot over Nalin's hand, prepared to crush it with a shift of his weight. "I said she was mine alone to kill."

Nalin's gaze turned to Sidonie, who was dressed in her black velvet finery. Sidonie had twisted her hair into a fantasy of braids and sparkling combs, creating the impression of a crown.

Resentment twisted Nalin's features into a snarl. "Forgive me, Masson. I thought her weak."

"I am not weak," Sidonie said, speaking simply and clearly. "I felled two opponents before leaving. You were one of them."

She'd learned a few tricks from the politicians and lawyers who had visited Allington House. One was to keep her voice just quiet enough that others were forced to listen.

"I followed the path into Londria on my own and returned with loot," she continued. "I was clever and escaped the city without being seen. In one night, I completed all the tests you give your warriors. I have earned my place here."

Masson's hand touched the curve of Sidonie's back, a small possessive gesture. She stifled a shudder. He had chosen her on sight, crushing lives for the sake of his fantasy bride. He wanted the beautiful, terrible queen of the Gentry at his side, and she could not afford to disappoint.

Sidonie intended to draw that fantasy out one move at a time, dancing just out of reach. It was the one piece of leverage she had until she learned how to master this brutal world. When she did, Masson would pay.

She swayed against his side, gazing down at the foe beneath his boot. Nalin's glare was pure poison.

"I shall kill her for you," Masson said, the words almost tender.

A sickening thrill ran through her, muddling her thoughts. Life and death and the power to command it made a heady elixir. She studied Masson's cleanly drawn profile, the high forehead and sharp jaw. He was wooing her and paying the price with the goodwill of the Gentry. Nalin had many friends, and now with Sark dead, too many Gentry had perished in the last few weeks.

Sidonie summoned her common sense. "I thank you, my lord, for such a generous gift, but is that the best use for her?"

Masson's expression fell, but it was clear he was intrigued. "What would you have me do?"

Sidonie bent, careful of her hem in the mud, and lifted Nalin's head by the hair. The female's gaze bore into her.

What to do, indeed? It would be folly to let Nalin go unpunished and even worse to embarrass her before the tribe. The last thing Sidonie needed was an enemy with motivation to strike again.

"She did try to kill me," Sidonie agreed, baring her own fangs. "She said I was weak and worthless. A distraction you could not afford, my king."

Masson growled. Nalin stiffened and shrank at the sound.

Sidonie released Nalin's hair, letting her face fall back into the muck. "That does mean she values your welfare, my king. That is not something to waste. Loyalty is of value in a fighter."

Sidonie heard Nalin's intake of breath—and inwardly smiled. The female was eager to make her mark in the tribe. She could choose to plant a knife in Sidonie's back or to guard it. Better to give her a reason for the latter.

Sidonie straightened, wiping mud from her hands. "Sark is meat for Goblins. You need a new captain of the patrols. Assign Nalin that task so that she may earn your favor once more."

Slowly, Masson withdrew his foot from Nalin's hand. "A captain ranks high. They may choose their plunder from the city. They must fight hard to keep that post."

The female rolled over, bewilderment suffusing her mud-streaked face. She looked from Masson to Sidonie with obvious confusion.

"Is this real?" Nalin demanded.

Sidonie gave a regal nod to Masson, leaving the final decision with him. He could make the magnanimous gesture that would please the tribe. Nalin knew it was Sidonie's idea, and that was what mattered for now.

Masson turned to the guards who had brought the female. Three were still nursing their wounds. "Let it be known that Nalin is your captain."

They mumbled, but the sound was largely positive. The guards ran by fear and a bloody code of honor. A fearsome captain was expected.

Nalin got to her feet and bowed low before striding toward her new troops. She cuffed one on the back of the head, making him stumble. The others cheered.

"Others would fear you if you had taken her blood," Masson said to Sidonie.

"I can always do that later." She hooked her arm through his. "Nalin knows that. It will make her work hard."

Masson gave a low chuckle. "You are wise."

For the last minute or two, the Caretaker had been standing a dozen yards away. As Nalin departed, he approached, regarding Sidonie with interest. No doubt he'd followed every nuance of the scene.

"A fascinating move, madam," he said to her. "You are developing a reputation for doing the unexpected. I suspect your trip into the city will serve as a model for those wishing to attract the notice of the king."

"No," Masson said sharply. "Once is forgiven. No more."

An alarm sounded in Sidonie's mind. The Caretaker was warning her or stirring up discord. Knowing him, both might be true. It was time to steer the conversation in another direction.

"I don't understand how it was possible for me to get under the wall," Sidonie said. "Why can we get past the barrier?"

Masson and the Caretaker exchanged a look. Sidonie guessed there were secrets involved.

"She should know," the Caretaker said.

Masson frowned, cocking his head as if he sensed something beneath the suggestion.

"Understanding has value here."

Masson's expression shifted as he made his decision. He beckoned to them both. "Come."

Sidonie followed his lithe form as it darted between the trees. The Caretaker brought up the rear. They followed the track that led from the remains of the bonfire through the trees to Masson's abode. She'd not been in his house yet. He guarded his private den with the ferocity of a wolverine.

Like the other Unseen dwellings, the single-story house was a mix of brick, fieldstone, and wood, but it had glass in the windows and a door that shut. She wondered if a carpenter had died to build this palace, because the roof looked sound, and she'd seen the chimney smoke from a working fireplace.

When Masson opened the door to let them in, warmth enveloped Sidonie. Masson lit a candle from the fire, illuminating a large room with a wooden table and chairs. At a glance, it looked like a combination kitchen and sitting room. There was a second room, presumably for sleeping quarters. Masson's strange pale eyes studied her reaction to the place.

"Very comfortable," she said because, compared to her cold, bare cottage, that was true.

They sat at the table, an oddly human action. For a moment, she longed for the comfort and custom of tea. Then she caught the scent of something raw and enticing in the larder, and only came back to the conversation with an effort.

"Relations between the Unseen and the Conclave are old and complex," the Caretaker began. "As I said before, we have survived as a species by mixing our blood with those who also have a predisposition for magical gifts. The mages are our opposites, but they are also our cousins."

Masson made a derisive noise. "They are weak."

"But dangerous," the Caretaker said. "They caused the Great Disaster. Mages attempted to discover the life-source of magic and instead unleashed an uncontrolled alchemical reaction on every living thing, including themselves. The descendants of those alchemists are our ancestors."

"Mages became the Unseen?" Sidonie asked in astonishment. *That* hadn't been part of her history lessons.

"Indeed," the Caretaker replied. "Not all of them, of course, but enough to give those who remained a mighty scare."

Sidonie chuckled, an involuntary, bitter sound. Since arriving in this settlement, she'd heard much about how the Unseen were bred or created, and she was coming to understand why. Their origins defined them.

"Mages became the Gentry. The Goblins came later." The Caretaker's brows pleated in a frown, as if condensing volumes of information into a few words. "The substance the mages created was preserved by those who survived. Londria's Conclave has a portion of it, as do other settlements."

"What does it do?" she asked. She had theories, but wanted to hear what the Caretaker and Masson had to say.

"They call it the Doomsfire," the Caretaker replied. "It is the source of much of the Conclave's magical power."

"But mages existed before," she said. "Otherwise, they could not have caused the Great Disaster."

The Caretaker gave a thin smile. "They did, but magic before the Doomsfire was rare and difficult. It required decades of study and great sacrifice. In contrast, the Doomsfire consumes rudimentary magical power and amplifies it a thousandfold. It makes spells simple, so simple that the old ways withered from disuse. Now, after centuries, the Doomsfire is weakening, and the mages have forgotten their skills and knowledge of the craft."

Sidonie grew light-headed. Why was she hearing about this here, among the monsters of the forest, instead of inside the city?

Without magic, the barrier would fail. Who in Londria knew about this? Was her family safe?

She cleared her throat with difficulty. "So, is that why we can cross a wall that is enchanted to keep us out?"

"In part," the Caretaker replied. "The Doomsfire is fueled by the presence of magic. There used to be many more mages, and thus more active magic to feed the fire. Their numbers dwindle now."

"Weak," Masson repeated, snatching a bug from the air with eerie speed.

Sidonie imagined *many more mages*—and didn't like the picture. She'd crossed the streets to keep out of their way. "Everyone hates the Conclave. I'm not surprised no one chooses it as a career."

"Few ever chose," the Caretaker said. "It used to be customary for the noble families of Londria to be tested, and the most magically gifted child from each generation would be taken to serve the Citadel."

"Perdition," she breathed. Which Fletcher would that have been? Miranda? Olivia? She couldn't imagine any of them in an acolyte's robes.

The Caretaker waved a hand. "After a time, nobles paid off the mages with cellars of wine and feather beds, so they would leave their darlings alone. Some youths are still pressed into service, but not enough to feed the fire. That in turn starves the aging Doomsfire still further."

"And the Conclave allows this?" Sidonie murmured.

"The Conclave is arrogant. Instead of giving up their comforts, they feed the life essence of prisoners to the fire. It is poor substitute at best, and such foolishness creates the very creatures that swell our armies."

"The Goblins?" she guessed.

The Caretaker nodded. "Some survive and escape to the Outlands."

A wave of sickness swept over her. "This is madness. Their ability to protect the city is fading at the same time they are creating more of a threat."

"Precisely," the Caretaker agreed.

"So we bargain." Masson leaned forward, eyes bright. "We tell the Conclave to let us take what we need, and we won't come all at once. We live; they live. If they refuse—we make blood run in the streets."

Sidonie gaped. "How long has this agreement been in place?"

"Many years," the Caretaker replied. "Though I have heard that purist elements inside the Conclave seek to end it. That would be unfortunate for all concerned."

Sidonie caught the implication at once. Although an Unseen could go days between meals, a steady supply of prey was essential. Any semblance of civilization depended on it. Take food away, and the Unseen would quickly revert to beasts.

"Which brings me to this." The Caretaker drew a letter from inside his dark coat. "A courier brought it from our informant an hour ago."

"You have a network inside the city?" Sidonie exclaimed.

A flicker of a smile crossed his face. "One that is rarely used, but it seems this is a special occasion."

He handed the letter to Masson, who unfolded it, then sniffed the paper and handed it back. "The news must be big if that one wrote."

The Caretaker passed the letter to Sidonie. "The informant understood you'd want to know."

She desperately wanted to ask who had written, but began to read instead. Within seconds, the paper slid from her fingers.

"Gideon," she breathed. "He's in the Citadel."

Her vision blanked with fury. She'd seen prisoners dragged away by Captain Hagen and his guards. She'd cowered in the attic with her sisters, waiting to be caught and thrown in a dungeon herself. A mere human then, she hadn't found the courage to fight. Now she was more.

Gideon would not vanish. She would drag him free by tooth and claw.

Masson shrugged. "He is your old life. War with the Citadel means risking our path beneath the wall."

She sprang up, leaning across the table so that her claws dug into the wood. "He is mine. We must save him."

He grabbed her chin, pulling her close so that their noses all but touched. "Why would I take that risk, my queen? How does it benefit me?"

Sidonie felt the prick of his claws against her cheek, but that was nothing compared to the burn of his gaze. They were equally matched, fierce will against fierce will. She hated him, and yet this intoxicated her.

"What will you give me for your brother's life?" he asked with a predator's smile.

He had been waiting, watching for a moment like this, like a cat outside a mouse's hole. He had her under his paw.

I will give you anything. She was still a Fletcher, still Gideon's twin.

But she was also something else. "If you make me beg, my lord, I will make you pay."

Masson pulled her still closer. "Promise?"

"Your blood. My lips."

The Caretaker gave a gentle cough. "The risk is worth it, my king."

They broke apart, slowly resuming their seats. Sidonie's cheeks burned, but so did her temper. With blinding clarity, she saw the Caretaker's calculations, and how he had carefully set the stage so he could use her grief to force Masson's hand.

The Caretaker responded to her glare with a smirk before turning to Masson. "Londria is a tinderbox of discontent, my liege. Gideon Fletcher is an independent spirit, a young and popular heir to an important employer. The abduction of such a man may well ignite rebellion."

"So?" Masson replied.

"The Conclave will be distracted, my king," he said. "They will be fighting others. We will have the advantage of surprise."

"So?" Masson said again as he leaned back in his chair, his eyes still on Sidonie.

She gathered up the letter. Her brother's name seemed to burn on the page. She could not turn away. "The risk is acceptable."

"Indeed," the Caretaker said. "This is our opportunity to tear the Conclave to shreds. Then we take the city."

CHAPTER 27

When Miranda arrived at Hellion House, Layla escorted her to the private dining room. Access was through a very ordinary-looking door up one flight of stairs from the main reception rooms. It was the perfect place to gather in privacy, well away from the other guests.

As Miranda entered, conversation ceased. She scanned the faces turned her way, recognizing a few men and women from her father's house parties. One was high in government, another from the military, and another from the courts of law. Unease prickled through her. She wasn't sure what she'd expected to find here, but this wasn't it.

Mrs. Randall sat at the head of the table, her face set in determined lines.

"Thank you for coming," she said to Miranda. "Please take a seat. Ladies and gentlemen, meet the Scorpion."

A subdued murmur of greeting passed around the table. Those few who recognized her goggled, but most perceived only the Scorpion's reputation made flesh. The scrutiny unsettled her, and she took the closest empty chair so that the meeting could move on to other things.

The room was elegantly furnished in shades of blue and burgundy. The gold-fringed drapes were closed, giving the candlelit gloom a claustrophobic feel. An oval table large enough for a dozen diners filled the space. The remnants of an appetizer course still cluttered its surface.

"Please continue," someone said to Mrs. Randall, as if Miranda's arrival had interrupted something.

"As I was saying," Mrs. Randall said, "we have gathered here, privately and securely, to pool our expertise and knowledge for the good of Londria and its people. We have debated, argued, considered, and proposed strategies to address all elements of our current problems. Tonight has been no exception."

"And?" the same speaker prompted.

"While this group has long sought an answer to the Conclave's overreach, the destruction of the *Leopard* makes it clear we can wait no longer. It is time for action."

Several guests pounded the table in agreement.

Miranda straightened in her chair. These people came from all corners of Londria's governing class. She'd always wondered why no one in power pushed back against the Conclave. Apparently, this group was working in secret to do so.

Her admiration for Mrs. Randall was already high, but it rose another degree. Choosing to meet at Hellion House was ingenious—no one would look for a war council here.

And if anyone had answers to Miranda's many questions, it would be someone in this room.

"I still don't understand why someone sabotaged the *Leopard*," she said. "Or why it was so important that Gideon was taken. It can't simply be that it infringed on the Conclave's responsibilities."

The military man—Vice Admiral Taylor of Londria's navy— spoke up. She'd always thought his lined face was kind, but tonight she saw sorrow in it. "Because, my dear, the mages rely on a truce with the Unseen. They allow the monsters to take a few victims in return for peace. Any new aggression against the Unseen will trigger a wholesale attack the Conclave might not be strong enough to repel."

Miranda heard her own outraged gasp.

"There is a growing segment of the Conclave who believes in a return to the glory days of the Citadel," Mrs. Randall added. "They think obedience to the Conclave's laws will give them enough power to crush the Unseen once and for all."

"Utter nonsense," the Vice Admiral grumbled. "No reasonable person believes that."

"Then it seems many are unreasonable," Mrs. Randall said. "This splinter group has grown bold enough to seize the heir to Fletcher Industries off the street and condemn him without trial."

"They've condemned him without trial?" Miranda's words barely made a sound. Shock had robbed her of breath.

Another figure had entered while Taylor had been speaking. "They've taken Fletcher?" The man was brown-haired, stocky, and wore round, green-tinted spectacles. As he came forward, his long coat swung in a way that suggested hidden weapons.

"Indeed, they have," Mrs. Randall said evenly. "Thank you for coming, Mr. Huntley."

Miranda struggled to rally, still reeling with the news about Gideon. Still, curiosity prompted her to study the man. So this was the leader of the Anathema Club.

His gaze swept over her, taking in her armor with a lifted brow.

"Scorpion," she said.

"Crazy bastard," he replied, pointing to himself, then turned back to the head of the table. "Right then. The robed nasties took my friend. What are we doing about it?"

Miranda instantly liked him.

"One moment." The speaker was a tall man in his forties.

With a jolt, Miranda recognized Mr. Liddell, an official high up in the Ministry of Outlands Affairs.

"What?" Huntley demanded, stiffening with impatience.

Liddell gave him a narrow look. "Our gracious hostess has masterfully summarized the question we face, but that is all. We have yet to agree on a course of action, and when we take action, it will be for the entire populace and not one individual."

"Our one advantage is surprise," Vice Admiral Taylor jumped in before Huntley could object. "I don't question the integrity of anyone in this room, but I say if we take action, we do it tonight. That leaves no time for information to leak."

"What about preparation?" someone asked.

Taylor made a derisive noise. "My lads are always prepared. That's why you pay us."

More table-thumping followed.

"You misunderstand me. I have been given full authority by the Prime Minister to speak on his behalf," Liddell said. Everyone turned his way. "His lordship is in full agreement with a direct attack. It's time the people of Londria established their sovereignty beyond the Citadel's influence. The mages have no authority to make demands on the population, much less snatch them up like marauding pirates."

"On behalf of the University Chancellor, I agree," a woman said. Miranda knew her face, but couldn't put a name to it. "The reformers among the Conclave have announced they will resurrect the practice of tithing the One Hundred families for their children. The university's records are filled with names that were crossed out, a poignant testimony to their families' loss. I will not stand for the return of such barbarity."

The conversation continued around the table, and a vote to tame the Conclave was carried. An electric sense of possibility rose as the last bottles of wine were emptied for a toast. Miranda rose when the others stood.

"To a free Londria," said Mrs. Randall, the candlelight gleaming on her crystal goblet.

"Londria," the others chorused.

"Now go, my friends," she said. "You each know best what you must do to prepare."

A great rustling began as the diners pushed their chairs back to leave. Miranda opened her mouth to protest. No one had made a real plan yet.

Mrs. Randall caught her eye. "One moment, if you please."

Miranda held her tongue.

"Mr. Huntley, if you would remain," their hostess said, raising her voice to carry over the commotion. "Vice Admiral, you as well."

It took no more than a minute for the others to depart. The rest moved down the table to sit closer together.

"How long have you been holding these meetings?" Miranda asked Mrs. Randall.

"A little while," she replied. "But that's a tale for another time. Right now, we have plans to make."

"What is that lot actually going to do?" Huntley asked, jerking a thumb toward the door.

"They do their part," the Vice Admiral said with a shrug. "Law and the public opinion. The rest of us do the actual work. But it's good to have the important people on our side when it's time to count the corpses."

Miranda swallowed hard. Since the *Leopard*, counting corpses had become all too real. But then, so was Gideon's peril.

"One thing I don't understand," she said. "If the Conclave is having difficulty holding the wall against the Unseen, why not simply ask for help?"

"Help has been offered," the Vice Admiral said. "They treated our overture as an insult. Now we make cooperation their only way forward. We have deferred to their power for so long that it has become a dangerous habit."

"One they reinforce with arbitrary arrest and torture," Huntley reminded him.

"That's why we will negotiate in the open. We need the

Conclave, but not as our overlords." The Vice Admiral turned to Miranda. "And you, my dear, have a role to play."

"I have one small ship," Miranda said. "I'm good with an aether rifle, but that's hardly enough to take the Citadel. I flew over it recently. It's vast."

"Can you draw a map?" Huntley asked. "I've never seen the layout."

The Vice Admiral produced a notebook and pencil from his inside pocket. Miranda began to sketch. She wasn't a talented artist, so she abandoned style and concentrated on getting the proportions right.

"I don't know what's inside, just the outline of the building's footprint," she said.

"The original structure was a cathedral." Mrs. Randall nervously toyed with the fine gold links of her bracelet, caught herself doing it, and folded her hands. "That gives us some idea of the basic layout."

"There will have been alterations since the building was taken over," Vice Admiral Taylor said.

"No one knows what they do in there," Huntley grumbled. "It's a blind box. We'll have to find out when we get inside."

"Who said anything about going inside?" the Vice Admiral asked.

Huntley glowered. "I don't know what the rest of you have planned, but my crew's job is to get in, free Fletcher and anyone else handy, and retreat."

They all stared at Huntley.

The Vice Admiral shook his head. "You're mad to think you'll come out again."

Miranda struggled. She desperately wanted Gideon back, but she didn't want Huntley dead, either. "Can't we ask them to free the prisoners once the attack is done?"

Huntley pulled off his glasses and pinched the bridge of his nose. "Do you think, once the shooting starts, that they'll leave the prisoners alive? This is the Conclave. We've all seen them at work."

A long, uncomfortable silence followed.

"The rescue has to happen first," Huntley said more quietly.

"I'm afraid you're right," Mrs. Randall agreed.

Huntley turned to Miranda, as if getting back to the real business at hand. "Where are the entry points?"

Miranda sucked in a breath, wishing she had a solution that would keep both Huntley and Gideon safe. She wished she wasn't so selfish, but Gideon was her brother.

"Not counting the front door, I saw entries here, here, and here." Miranda made three marks on the sketch. "There's also a roof entry over here."

"Good," Huntley said. "The next problem is getting close to the building without getting caught."

"Two things you should know," Miranda said. "One is that guards patrol the plaza, although they are not thick on the ground at night. The other is that there are wards, even against an aerial approach."

"How strong was it?" Taylor asked. "There are wards meant to fend off dragons. Could it have been one of those?"

"I don't know. My ship is small, but we still got free. That said, it was a close call."

Huntley rubbed his chin in thought. "Did the ward cover the entire building?"

Miranda replayed the journey in her mind. "No, we didn't trigger it at first. Only when we got near the tower. A runabout could drop you safely on the outer edges of the roof."

"That won't work," he replied. "My plan was to go in through the openings in the belfry."

"The ward reacts to airships, not someone on the roof," Miranda said. "We found an Unseen lurking up there."

Mrs. Randall made a startled noise. "*On* the Citadel?"

Miranda shrugged.

"Even if you get past the outer defenses, what will you do about wards and spells inside the building?" Taylor asked Huntley. "There will be resistance from the mages."

"One of the River Rats will go with you," Mrs. Randall said. "They understand magic better than the rest of us."

Huntley shrugged. "If they can fight, send them along."

"One other thing," Miranda said. "I've heard there is something inside called the Doomsfire. I don't know what it is, but it's important."

The term prompted nothing but puzzled stares.

"How did you hear about it?" Huntley asked.

"A River Rat," she said.

"Then we'll leave it to them." Huntley tore the map from the notebook and stuffed it in his pocket. "So drop us off, give us an hour, and if we don't make it out, carry on without us."

"But what about the rest of the attack?" Miranda asked. "Besides dropping off the rescue party, what am I supposed to do? Like Mr. Huntley, I'm here to save my brother."

"You're his sister?" Huntley exclaimed. "Dear God, the Fletchers are a feisty lot."

"My men and women will be cordoning off the Citadel, both to protect the city and to prevent any means of escape," the Vice Admiral said, ignoring Huntley's outburst. "The last thing we need is the mages running and regrouping somewhere else. We want them at a disadvantage. We have ground and air forces, but the Conclave is prepared for conventional attack."

"This doesn't sound appealing in the least," Huntley observed.

The Vice Admiral harrumphed. "All we need is the element of surprise. To that end, the Scorpion's job will be much bigger than playing cab driver to a gaggle of madmen."

Miranda looked from one face to the next. "What is it?"

Mrs. Randall took a delicate sip of wine, as if her throat had just gone dry. "Gideon mentioned that there was a second ship like the *Leopard*. We understand that it's ready to fly."

Miranda's mouth fell open. "Are you asking me to burn down the Citadel?"

Vice Admiral Taylor held up his thumb and forefinger, indicating a tiny amount. "Just a little toast around the edges to encourage conversation."

Miranda went cold, and not only with the prospect of confronting the Conclave. The very mention of the *Leopard* made her relive the sensation of falling from the sky. This journey would be on a nearly identical ship.

The door flung open, startling Miranda so badly she nearly upset her wine glass. Layla rushed into the room, puffing as if she'd run up the stairs. She had changed from her afternoon dress into fighting leathers.

"We have a problem," she announced. "Word has come from the River Rats. They've been watching the waterways."

"What do they say?" Mrs. Randall asked.

Layla's face drained of color. "Unseen are entering the city. Scores of them. More than they've ever seen before."

"I WARNED YOU, but you insisted on digging yourself into a deeper and deeper hole."

Gideon looked up to see Latimer standing outside his cell door. He looked smaller without his cloak, everything about him neat and carefully fastened. With his dark hair brushed back from his narrow face, he reminded Gideon of an evil otter.

"And now that I'm here?" Gideon asked.

"You wanted answers," the councilor continued. "Now you have them. I saved a place beside your young friend for just that purpose."

"You killed him."

He waved a soft, fine-boned hand. "Oh, he's young and healthy. He'll be back once or twice before he's done."

"What exactly is going on here?" Gideon demanded.

"Now that you've heard the young lad's confession, are you asking for mine?" Latimer gave a thin smile. "I don't owe you a thing."

Gideon grabbed the bars, putting his face inches from the mage's, but he couldn't find words for his outrage.

Latimer gave a soft laugh, his dark eyes full of scorn. "Where do you think the Unseen come from? The original disaster created the rulers of their species. Use of the residual magic made, and makes, their foot soldiers."

"Why are you doing it?"

"Londria demands the protection of the wall. Without it, humanity would perish. But that means magic, and to have magic the Doomsfire must be fed." Latimer licked his lips, as if suddenly nervous. "So we give it the life essence of Londria's criminals. Radicals and malcontents. Beggars. Servants with nothing more to give."

These weren't the missing victims from Gideon's walls. He wondered if law enforcement had even heard about these cases. Who investigated the disappearance of a beggar? "You make them monsters."

Latimer made a regretful face. "The overwhelming hunger of those who survive is a futile attempt to reclaim the essence they surrender. Until the Conclave regains its full strength, this is our only recourse. For centuries now, the more power we feed to the wall, the more of our enemy we create. It is a devil's bargain."

That stopped Gideon's words in his throat.

"So much for the great investigator," Latimer scoffed. "You never glimpsed the truth."

Gideon's knuckles turned white where he gripped the bars. This was why Latimer was here, gazing at the sight of his quarry behind bars. He'd come to prove he was smarter.

"Citizens support the Citadel," Gideon said, anger twisting

inside him. "Mages keep Londria safe. Or you should. I've seen ordinary people torn to pieces inside the city walls."

"So have I." Latimer's ears colored, as if this was his personal failure. "That should never have happened. We shall prevent such tragedies in the future."

It was Gideon's turn to give a mocking laugh. "How?"

"More Threshers." He frowned. "More mages drawn from the best of Londria's families. More obedience. Reformers among the Council guarantee a revolution before long."

"I can't wait for the world you will create." Gideon didn't bother hiding his sarcasm.

"Then enjoy the anticipation while you can." Latimer backed away from the bars. "Once you visit the pit, well, without protective spellwork, not even a mage lasts long that close to the crystal."

With that, Latimer left.

Featherly was brought back later that night but made no sound, even when Gideon called his name over and over again.

Gideon did not sleep.

CHAPTER 28

The Unseen were crouched outside the same tunnel Sidonie had used to enter the city. About half their party had already crossed into the cemetery, where Nalin and her guards organized the arrivals as they came through.

Without warning, the wall flashed with crackling blue light, spiderwebbing around a Goblin trying to scale the stones. Illumination flared behind the creature's flesh, its shadowy skeleton stark for the few seconds it took for the meat to sizzle to ash.

Sidonie wrinkled her nose at the stink. "You told them to use the tunnel, not to climb."

Masson shrugged. "Always, there is one."

A scatter of other Goblins who'd been racing to hurl themselves at the stones backed away. One paused to experimentally touch a finger to the wall. Blue sparks flew and crackled. The Goblin yelped, sucking its finger as it loped away on three limbs.

Sidonie hoped that wasn't a sign of how the night would progress.

With a hand on her back, Masson guided Sidonie into line. When her turn came, she half-reluctantly crawled beneath the massive stone barrier, on the lookout for spiders.

Masson's plan required them to remain hidden for as long as possible, so the moment Sidonie emerged from beneath the wall, she ducked behind a headstone. A moment later, Masson joined her, the long line of his body grazing against hers.

The magnetic excitement of the night made her skin crawl, as if her physical form was too small to contain her. The stakes were impossible. There were a lot of Unseen, especially with the number who had come for the Midwinter bonfire, but Londria was a huge city.

She was both impatient to begin and afraid of the consequences.

"You know that many of your people will die," she murmured, leaning against the cold marble of the gravestone.

"Not all," Masson replied.

The Caretaker's elegant form glided out of the tunnel, his long silver mane unruffled. Two Goblins followed him with the slavering obedience of nightmare pets. Sidonie stifled a hysterical giggle at the sight.

Not long ago, she would have been entertaining guests at this hour, dancing and drinking champagne. As long as she could remember, she'd loathed the banality of violence. Yet it hadn't occurred to her to stay behind tonight. She hungered for blood like the rest of the monsters, and that desire terrified her to the core.

"Will the deaths be worth it?" she asked.

Masson rose from his crouch a degree, checking on the progress of the new arrivals before sinking back to the grass. "I have held the Gentry back, trying to be wise. Now the mages turn on us."

The moonlight caught the side of his face, turning him to another stone angel among the graves.

"Is that what this is?" Sidonie asked. "Vengeance?"

He smiled, destroying the angelic effect. "A king cannot leash his people forever. Not for allies who break their promise."

She balked, still human enough to think of the innocents who would die by fang and claw. He saw it in her face.

"The city is our hunting ground," he said. "We are wolves in the forest."

She leaned into him then, bringing her lips to his ear. "Protect my family."

"Once, I planned to give you your brother. To make him one of us. Would that please you?"

Temptation flared, but then Gideon would not be the same as he was—any more than she was. Sidonie shook her head. "My family is off limits. Give me that much."

He pushed his fingers into her hair, cupping the curve of her head. His breath was warm against her face. "And my reward for that?"

The wildness of the night rose in her, making it hard to remember who she was. Masson was near, sharing her hungers. Possessiveness ran through her, making her reach for him. It wasn't love or even liking. Her heart was too broken for either. But it was a fierce, primal kinship.

A shout rang out. In an instant, Masson sailed over the headstone as if he were on springs. Sidonie followed a beat later, her feet flying over the frozen grass.

Two figures ran ahead, scrambling toward the road. They wore shapeless dark jackets with wide-brimmed hats pulled down low over their faces.

River Rats. The Caretaker had said they sometimes kept watch on the Unseen's secret passages.

Sidonie glimpsed the road ahead. A two-horse carriage waited, the driver turning in his seat to see how his friends fared. The horses, sleek, white-stockinged creatures, fidgeted and whickered, clearly sensing the predators approaching.

The Gentry, with their longer legs, quickly outdistanced the Goblins. Drunk on the excitement of the chase, Sidonie ran faster, but the competition was fierce. Every Unseen wanted the taste of fresh kill.

One of the River Rats leaped into the vehicle, reaching back for his friend. The straggler was halfway in when the nearest Gentry grabbed his coat. Cloth ripped, followed by the Gentry's frustrated snarl.

The driver—a third River Rat—rose in his box, bringing his whip down on the Unseen. The attacker fell back with a yelp, and the passengers tumbled into the carriage. A second later, the horses sprang into a gallop. More Unseen clung to the driver's box, skidding in the dirt. Then Sidonie caught the flash of a curved blade, and an Unseen bounced as it hit the road, rolling into the ditch. The first blood had gone to the enemy.

A moment later, a black fog billowed behind the carriage, hiding it from view. It smelled of cold mud and rain.

Sidonie stumbled to a halt. "What is that?"

"Magic," Masson said. "The River People's power is as old as ours."

"Perdition," she muttered.

Masson's fingers circled her arm. "They will warn the city."

"What do we do?" she asked.

"We run faster."

Masson turned to the Unseen swarming over the cemetery. He spread his arms, a long-limbed raven against the glitter of the winter stars.

"The Citadel," he roared in his rasping voice. "No one escapes."

"It's inside my skull," Featherly whispered.

Gideon sat by the barred door, with his knees drawn up to his chest. He could barely hear the lad, who sounded as weak as any invalid. Gideon raked his hands through his hair, desperate to banish the sight of those pitiable, twisted forms emerging from beneath the Doomsfire.

"What do you mean?" he asked.

"I close my eyes and the light's still there."

Was that an early sign of madness? Gideon had no experience with any of this. And why would he? He killed the Unseen if he could and ran from them the rest of the time. In no fevered nightmare did he imagine a torture chamber where they were made.

"I must deserve it," Featherly mumbled.

Gideon touched the wound beneath his shirt where Featherly's knife had gone in. It still itched and ached. He'd believed in punishment once, but he'd lost any faith in simple retribution. It was too crude an instrument for this world.

"The only thing you deserve is a way back to yourself," he said.

Featherly sobbed, a rattling, dry sound that was nearly a cough. Gideon struggled to find something to say. It was hard to think because he was afraid, hungry, and desperately thirsty. Still, he tried.

"With all these cells, it will be a long, long time before you need to visit the fire again."

"They don't take turns like that," Featherly spat in a bitter voice. "They use up the bottom rows first, then the others move down into empty cells. Besides, most of the ones above us are empty. Prisoners die as fast as they come."

From the little Gideon had seen, the death rate was a blessing. If the mages lost one or two every day, that was fourteen a week. That was far more than his missing persons work covered, but he only dealt with the cases Palmer knew about. In a city the size of Londria, there were plenty of poor who had no voice. What had Latimer said? Beggars, criminals, and used-up servants? Who would notice if they disappeared a few at a time?

The gong sounded, and the exchange of victims through the trap door commenced. Featherly's weeping began again.

Gideon leaned forward, looking up into the tower and wondering how many cells above them were indeed occupied. It was hard to tell—the angle was bad and the shadows deep. High in the belfry, he saw a flicker of motion. A trick of the eye? A bat? A cloud of bats?

Gideon's pulse leaped. Four silent figures were descending from the belfry, each on a knotted rope. Huntley hung on his like a disgruntled bear, an aether rifle slung over his back.

"The bloody brilliant madman," Gideon murmured under his breath.

A River Rat dangled a few yards to Huntley's right. Moving at a faster pace, the two chess-playing gentlemen from the Anathema Club seemed to slither down theirs with the strength and grace of circus performers. Gideon's stomach flipped as one rotated so that he hung upside down to survey the scene below.

It was a rescue mission. Emotion lodged painfully in Gideon's throat, threatening to choke him. He sucked in a breath, wanting to weep or cheer, but needing to keep absolutely quiet.

Slow and steady, Huntley was the first to find his footing on the walkway outside the cells. He anchored his rope on the handrail and began hurrying along the circle of cells, searching the faces of the prisoners. A low whisper rose as the inmates noticed something was afoot.

Gideon waved both arms to attract Huntley's notice. With a jolt of recognition, his friend broke into a run, skidding to a halt outside Gideon's door. He aimed the aether rifle at the lock, delivering a brief blast with a soft *thwap*. Gideon was unsure if the lock was magical or mechanical, but it surrendered at once. Huntley tugged, and the door swung free.

Gideon sprang from the cell, nearly stumbling when Huntley thumped his shoulder in greeting.

"Let's be scarce," Huntley whispered.

Gideon pointed to Featherly's cell. "Get him out, too."

Wasting no time, Huntley shot the lock. Featherly rose from where he crouched at the bottom of the cell, haunted and hollow-eyed.

"Him?" Huntley asked when he saw the lad's face. "You want to save a Thresher?"

"I do." Gideon dragged Featherly out of the cell by one arm. "He's going to prove he deserves a second chance."

Featherly visibly struggled to gather himself. He braced against the railing, as if standing was difficult, but his gaze was bright. In that moment, Gideon glimpsed the aeronaut he'd once been.

"Where to?" Gideon asked.

Huntley pointed to a dark-clad figure ghosting along the walkway. "The River Rat knows a way out. We follow him."

The two acrobats—Gideon recalled their names were Wilmington and Barnard—were moving swiftly along the rows of cells, blasting the locks.

"That's more prisoners than we expected." Huntley muttered darkly. "I thought there'd be half a dozen at most."

"We can't leave anyone here." And yet Gideon understood his worry. More people meant more problems.

As he released them, Barnard pushed the prisoners forward. They quickly fell into line, descending from one level to the next along a series of narrow staircases. Eventually, they gathered on the wider, lowest level.

Wilmington brought up the rear, opening the last few cells. Gideon found it hard to estimate numbers, but there were perhaps fifty inmates, some barely strong enough to move but all clearly desperate to escape.

Huntley led Gideon and Featherly toward the throng.

Gideon tensed, expecting disaster.

So many people should have been making noise. No matter how careful, there would be shuffling, muttering, the rustle of cloth. The acolytes would notice—and yet they hadn't. When he strained his ears, all Gideon could make out were the footfalls of his two companions. It was as if sound suddenly refused to carry.

Then he recalled the River Rats—known for their ability to go anywhere, anytime, without being caught. It was well known that they had their own variety of magic. How long would it be before the Conclave noticed an unfamiliar spell?

The prisoners crowded around a door on the west side of the steeple tower, the River Rat and Barnard in the lead. It was likely the same door the guards had marched Gideon through, hooded and bound, before the mages had locked him in a cell.

A door that led in also led out. Anticipation stirred.

He risked a glance over the rail. The acolytes were busy retrieving the last group of victims from below the trap door. The next lot were already herded into a tight group, ready to go in.

Barnard tried the door and found it locked. He raised his rifle.

At the same moment, Wilmington opened one of the last occupied cells. The crazed prisoner, more Unseen than human, rocketed forward with a piercing shriek.

The River Rat's silencing spell failed.

The acolytes stared up into the tower with naked horror. One opened her mouth in sheer astonishment, gulping air before she stabbed her staff into the air.

The walkway exploded beneath Gideon's feet.

"So, Miss Miranda," Higgins said as he approached her. "I see the Scorpion has come out tonight."

She had arrived directly from Hellion House to the airfield, dispatching messengers to rouse whatever crew they could find. Now she stood before her fellow aeronauts in her leather armor. Most of the aeronauts already knew the Scorpion's identity and for those who hadn't—well, it was a secret no more.

Miranda cleared her throat, fighting back emotion. "There is no option but to act, and swiftly."

They stood a few yards from the base of the mooring mast and the ladder that would take her on deck, and then back into the air. Sweat slicked her skin, making the chemise beneath her armor cling despite the cold. She raised her eyes to the gondola poised above her, perfect in its weightless grace.

"What about the wards around the Citadel?" she asked.

"If the runabout got free of their spell, this lady won't have a problem."

No name graced the side of the vessel yet, but the crew called it the *Leopard Ascending*. It floated on its mooring mast, eclipsing the stars. On the cusp of its first launch, the vessel was newborn, as perfect and incomplete as a blank page. Now its baptism would come by literal fire.

The old *Leopard* had been a little smaller and years older, but the configuration had been the same. She would know this new ship because she'd flown on its sister. Flown, and burned, and fallen.

The ground beneath her seemed to drift. She jerked her gaze down to the grass, needing to know it was solid. Making fists of her trembling hands, she gulped down the ice air. She wasn't afraid to fly. She couldn't afford to be.

"Miss Fletcher?" Higgins asked gently. "Yale says all is ready. We loaded all the canisters of the incendiary concentrate we could put our hands on. Between the Citadel and the Unseen loose in the city, we'll need it."

Miranda's stomach gave a dizzying swoop, remembering her shipboard battle with the Unseen. "Are we tempting fate, defying the Conclave again?"

The lines the wind and sun had etched in his face deepened. "A mission is less about what you do than about why you do it. Are they worth defying?"

She'd seen the Citadel from the air, knew exactly where to drop their fire. But if the mages saw them first, there would be war. Everything Mrs. Randall's council said about taming the Conclave was true, but in the midnight chill of the airfield, nothing mattered but human blood and bone.

The aeronauts had gathered at the airfield in haste, uniforms half-buttoned and hair uncombed. None muttered about the untried ship or the hasty call to arms. They'd come out of loyalty to the Fletchers and their fellow crew.

And she was the Fletcher on the airfield. Each one of these aeronauts—Higgins, Yale, and the rest—was her responsibility. She could spare them and condemn Gideon or risk all in hopes of getting him back. Neither was a good answer, and the decision weighed on her like an iron cloak.

And that didn't even touch the greater mission the Vice Admiral had asked of her.

"I think I understand what it feels like to be a captain," Miranda said softly. "It's full of brutal choices."

"Keep in mind we're all here because we want to be."

She put a hand on Higgins' shoulder. "Thank you from the bottom of my soul for coming."

"I had to. The bastards burned my ship." He jerked his head toward the ladder. "Shall we go?"

She looked up again. The bottom fell out of her stomach once more, but she was getting used to the sensation. "Yes. The bastards took my brother."

With that, she began to climb. Once they were aboard, the *Leopard Ascending* prowled into the sky, swift and silent as its namesake. Miranda could feel the power of its engines, though they ran on minimal power to keep their approach quiet. This ship had been designed as an improvement on its predecessor, and it showed in its stability and quick response.

Miranda took up her usual position, Viper in hand, and watched over the side. Layla's warning about the Unseen preyed on her mind. The Vice Admiral claimed his troops would be armed and ready to fight, but few would understand how deadly the monsters were—or how good at hiding—without firsthand experience.

At a distance, the *Scorpion* passed them on its way back to the airfield. A light flashed twice, and Miranda sighed in relief. That was the signal that Janey had successfully delivered Huntley and his crew to the Citadel.

Huntley had asked for an hour to complete the rescue mission and run for safety. Miranda had arranged with the Vice Admiral to signal the ship from his position south of the plaza. If he hung a green lantern from the tallest lamp post, the rescue was complete and the ship was free to begin its attack. If the lamp was red, the rescue wasn't over.

There was movement in the streets. Miranda set down her rifle and pulled a spyglass from inside her jacket, extended the brass tube and twisted it into focus. Troops were streaming toward the plaza, but they couldn't all be the Vice Admiral's men. They wore uniforms of every kind, and some looked like sailors from the merchant vessels. In fact, some didn't wear uniforms at all, but were pouring out of taverns, meeting halls, and houses. They were shouting, with fists raised in the air.

Her chest ached with fear for them, and a fierce pride. This wasn't just men and women following orders. This was Londria rising. This was a judgment on the mages.

The *Leopard Ascending* adjusted course to approach the Citadel. For the second time, she sailed above the rambling structure with its many wings and great tower, the spire below like a claw pointing to the clouds. She adjusted her spyglass again, hunting for the Vice Admiral's signal. She found the lantern, and it was red. Huntley and Gideon were still inside.

She caught movement on the north side of the plaza. "Unseen!"

Higgins was at her side in an instant, pulling out his own spyglass.

"Down there," she said, pointing. "Hordes of them."

They were sifting out of the shadows, as if the darkness itself was spawning them. She glimpsed a handful of the tall, eerily beautiful ones, moving so fast she barely saw them at all. Those were outnumbered by throngs of their twisted, ugly brethren.

"What are they doing this close to the Citadel?" she wondered aloud. "Why aren't they attacking the crowds?"

Higgins lowered the spyglass and frowned. "They have a purpose. They want something."

As if given a signal, the misshapen horrors lunged at the building, leaping and flailing with wild fury. They crashed into the heavy doors at the side of the Citadel, only to bounce back when the iron-bound oak refused to budge.

Miranda shouldered her rifle. They were still too far away for a decent shot, but one thought pounded in her brain: Gideon and Huntley were still inside.

A keening cry rose from below, loud enough it reached the ship. With the next rush at the door, the Unseen broke through.

~

Gideon flung himself back from the edge of the crumbling walkway. Another acolyte raised her staff, smashing a section of the rail. Chips of stone sprayed over the throng of prisoners, cutting exposed flesh.

Gideon crashed against the bars of a cell, noticing too late that it was next to the prisoner that had warped into an Unseen. Claws flashed, and he ducked, elbowing the prisoner in the jaw. With a shriek of frustration, it coiled to make another lunge.

Wilmington fired his air rifle, vaporizing the screaming creature's head. The body flailed, the stump of its neck smoking, as if nothing would deter its attack. Wilmington planted a boot in its chest, thrusting it back into the cell. The remains toppled and slumped to the floor.

Gideon's gut lurched. Not long ago, that had been an ordinary human.

Another section of the walkway shattered and fell. The gong that had signaled the exchange of prisoners beneath the crystal sounded, but this time it was a constant thunder. The acolytes were summoning help.

Already agitated, the prisoners panicked. They had surged away from the mage's explosions, ignoring the River Rat's directions. Then Wilmington's shot sent them stampeding toward the narrow stairway to the main floor—and straight into the mages.

The River Rat shouted orders, but no one listened and no magic could counteract the prisoners' stark terror. Huntley grabbed Gideon's arm, but it was impossible to resist the crowd.

The current of bodies swept them toward the stairs, Huntley just managing to press an aether pistol into Gideon's hand before someone squeezed between them. Gideon checked the weapon to find the aether canister was full. At least something had gone right.

And then the crowd stalled. The stairway was a bottleneck, with room for only one to descend at a time. This didn't stop the agitated throng from pushing forward, squashing those waiting their turn. Gideon fought to keep his balance and wormed his way to the left, where the rail surrounding the walkway met the stairs. One of the ropes that had carried Huntley's crew from the balcony dangled there, within tantalizing reach. He stowed his pistol in his belt and stretched out his arm, fingertips brushing the rope. With something between a hop and a lunge, he grasped it, then hauled himself hand over hand out of the crush, eventually balancing his feet on the edge of the walkway's rail.

It made him an easy target, but he only needed a second to see what was happening below. The steady, pulsing light of the crystal flowed along the silver channels in the floor. Its illumination backlit a pair of acolytes waiting at the bottom of the stairs. The two snatched the prisoners as they emerged at the marble feet of the great tripod. With no way to retreat and a steady pressure at their back, their victims were helpless to resist.

The acolytes tossed the recaptured prisoners beneath the tripod. By their limp forms, they were either dead or deeply stunned—Gideon couldn't tell.

With a steadying breath, Gideon raised his pistol. As the next prisoner stumbled forward, an acolyte reached out, a spell sizzling in his palm. The blast from Gideon's aether pistol seared through robe and flesh. A fist-sized hole bloomed in the mage's chest. The dead man dropped.

The mage's partner froze in shock. So did the acolyte pounding the gong. A brittle silence hung in the air.

Gideon smiled grimly. Tyrants rarely enjoyed an opponent who could fight back.

Like an uncorked bottle, prisoners scrambled from the stairway, seizing their chance of escape.

By the time the mages recovered, Gideon was already on the move. He jumped off the walkway, descending on the rope as it swung over the main floor. Huntley was already down there, rifle in hand, but he was the only member of the rescue party in sight. Wilmington and Barnard were still stuck somewhere on the stairs, and the River Rat had vanished.

Huntley placed himself between the prisoners and the mages. The prisoners hurried as fast as they could, but many were sick and all were starved.

The obvious route to safety was along the central aisle of the Citadel, which led to the main doors and out onto the plaza. Gideon wasn't sure if the doors were just doors or an entrance locked by magic, but that was only one of many problems. Centuries of additions to the old cathedral had doubled the original length of the aisle to around 800 feet—too far for some of the prisoners to walk, much less run.

The rope wasn't long enough to reach the main floor, but Gideon had few options. He dropped the final distance, managing to land at Huntley's side without breaking a bone.

Above them, the crystal pulsed with deadly radiance. Gideon could feel its presence—not quite heat, not quite a sound. He'd seen what it could do, and none of them wore the mages' protective spells.

Their only hope was to get away before the Doomsfire marked them with its power.

Gideon glanced back at the stairs to see the last few prisoners descend. Then he noticed a flutter of sky-blue robes emerging from a door hidden in the wall.

Bloody hell. The senior mages had finally answered the summons of the gong. It had been touch and go to keep a handful of acolytes at bay. Now the game had changed for the worse.

He elbowed Huntley. "Council."

Huntley responded with a blaze of aether that caught the mage in the lead. He whooped as scraps of sky-blue robe wafted in the air like feathers from a pillow fight. Gideon braced for retaliation, but the other mages scattered, vanishing into the shadows beyond the Doomsfire's light. He understood their tactic at once.

"We're in their crossfire," he said to Huntley.

His friend jerked his head toward the escapees. "That lot needs to move faster."

Gideon spun and began shouting. "Go, go, go!"

He darted toward the shuffling crowd, pulling and pushing the stragglers along. Mage fire streaked in every direction, picking off one prisoner at a time. Resistance was a fool's errand, a whisper in a gale. The only things keeping the mages at bay were a handful of aether weapons and sheer bravado. Neither would last long.

Yet surrender was unthinkable. Gideon searched for the nearest mage. Councilor Ormond was crouched behind the stone leg of the tripod. Gideon glided his way, moving with all the stealth he possessed. It wasn't enough. Ormond rose to face him, face tight with a ferocity Gideon had never expected from the port-soaked gourmand.

"Stop," Ormond said. "Stop shooting for the sake of everyone's safety."

"I don't think so, Councilor. You'll have to kill me the hard way."

Ormond's gaze flicked to the Doomsfire crystal, so fast that Gideon barely saw the nervous gesture. No wonder the mages were being careful, exterminating the prisoners a bit at a time. A careless shot might shatter their great glowing egg.

The mage held up a hand, and a cold white light coalesced above it. Senior mages didn't require something so mundane as a staff.

Ormond flicked the ball, and it hurled at Gideon with punishing speed. He spun aside, feeling the bite of his previous burn as he moved. Gideon's return shot missed by an inch, vaporizing the edge of the pillar instead. Ormond's second shot scorched his sleeve.

Gideon nearly tripped on a dead prisoner. This one was so emaciated it was impossible to tell if it had been a man or woman. He righted himself quickly. This time, his shot landed, searing Ormond's thigh. The councilor buckled with a scream. He wouldn't be walking anytime soon.

Gideon moved on. He spotted Featherly at the back of the pack, doggedly intent but falling behind. He dashed toward the lad.

A figure in a navy-blue robe swirled into sight behind the

prisoners. *Latimer.* Gideon slowed to a walk and raised his pistol, taking aim at the mage. As if sensing Gideon's attention, Latimer pounced, hooking one arm under Featherly's chin to make him a human shield.

"Let him go," Gideon ordered, certain the mage had chosen Featherly out of spite.

"He's not yours to take." Latimer gave a smile that did nothing but bare his teeth. "He belongs to the fire."

A bolt of force hit Gideon from behind. He flew forward, barely keeping a grip on his pistol. He fell flat and skidded, the marble floor jarring every bone. Instinct made him scramble up, but he only made it to his knees before his vision blurred with pain. He couldn't see his back, but he could smell charred wool and flesh. A mage had hit him—a glancing blow, or he'd be cooked.

It still hurt, blotting out the throbbing of the knife wound across his stomach. He rose, his back on fire and his left arm useless. He'd been thrown some distance, because he was at the bottom of the stairs now. He grabbed the rail to haul himself up.

When he turned, Featherly's remains sprawled at his feet, grisly in the pulsing silver light. Latimer must have thrust his power directly into the young man, because he had charred from the inside out. His entire body seemed oddly malformed, as if his skeleton had powdered. Eyes, mouth, and nose had turned to blackened ash.

Latimer was nowhere in sight.

Gideon took a last look at Featherly's corpse, wishing he had words, a vow, something—but the lad was long past anything he could say. Gideon rejoined the fray.

Barnard and Wilmington flanked Huntley, their backs to the prisoners. The group inched down the long aisle, but it was clear they would not make it—not with the prisoners in tow. Mage fire darted in bright arcs from every direction, crisscrossing their path. Already the floor was littered with dead escapees.

Lesser men would have run for freedom and left the weak behind, but the members of the Anathema Club held firm.

Gideon sprinted to catch up. They were halfway down the aisle now, but a third of the escapees had fallen.

The front doors echoed with a mighty *boom* that resonated through the Citadel. In the wavering, silver light, Gideon saw black smoke seep beneath the door. More magic?

Boom.

The mage fire ceased. They had a new threat.

Boom. The doors swung open with a sepulchral groan. The cold night air washed in the open door, pushing away the stink of ancient stone and battle.

Gideon half-expected to see a battering ram. Instead, River Rats swarmed in, the curved blades of their weapons gleaming in the uncertain light. Their first act was to surround the surviving prisoners like a living wall, putting their backs to the escapees and turning their blades to the Conclave.

"Do not approach and do not interfere." The leader of the River Rats spoke firmly to the mages, an equal to equals, but his gaze strayed in wonderment toward the crystal. After a long moment, he shook himself and continued. "We will take these people and be gone."

"You will not," said Latimer. "Your freedom ended the moment you crossed our threshold."

The words rang hollow, as if they were no more than a formula. As they spoke, the River Rats had hurried the prisoners along, some picking up the stragglers as if they were children. Gideon helped. Even so, the crowd could only move so fast. As they ran, the distance to the doors seemed to grow.

The mages had scattered, but now they gathered in a semicircle, nearly touching. Some, like Ormond, were injured, but that did not matter. They all joined.

The leader of the River Rats reached into his leather belt pouch and pulled out a handful of black dust. He flung it toward the Conclave, scattering it like a farmer sowing seed. The dust billowed into a concealing cloud of black smoke, blotting out even the crystal's light.

It was suddenly easier to draw breath, as if the cloud blocked the Doomsfire's effects. The lights from the plaza beyond the doors were enough to find his way. Still, he couldn't see the mages, or what they did next.

Fighting singly, they had been deadly. Banded together, they were a juggernaut.

At first, the air felt heavy, as it did before a storm. Then, it became harder to move. Prisoners stumbled and fell, wailing as they tried to drag themselves forward on hands and knees. Gideon's wound throbbed as if a hard weight pressed into his scorched skin. He went down on one knee. Then onto both. He curled up, bending until his forehead touched the floor.

A terrible weight crushed the air from his body.

When every ounce of his strength was gone, the black cloud shredded into a mist. Then the Conclave gathered around them like crows around the dead, their eyes bright with anticipation.

THE UNSEEN ROARED as the door at the back of the Citadel splintered. Clawed hands dug into the fractured panels and tore them off their iron hinges, hurling them onto the frozen grass. Sidonie watched in fascination.

"Why are they so hungry to get in?" she asked Masson.

"Most were reborn here," Masson replied. "They have business with the mages."

"Perdition," she whispered under her breath. She understood what it was to be ripped from her life, but at least she was still—mostly—herself. "How aware are they of what happened to them?"

He shrugged again. "Witness."

A sick fury rose in her as their wails rose to a desperate pitch. When the last of the door was torn from its hinges, the Gentry stood back. There was a pause, as if the night drew breath. Then the Goblins swarmed into the Citadel like a vengeful plague.

"They shall have their reckoning," she said coldly.

"Spoken like a queen," Masson replied, finding her hand with his.

Heartsick with horror, she didn't pull away. "Remember your promise to spare my brother."

"I do not lie. I am not human."

He flicked a signal to the Gentry to follow the slavering mob. Nalin bowed and led the way. Sidonie and Masson entered last.

Pandemonium raged inside. The wing they had entered was connected to the main body of the Citadel, but the iron-bound double doors between were sealed by magic. Goblins hurled themselves against the barrier, only to bounce back in a shower of blue-white sparks. It was warded like the wall, but on a smaller scale.

"We need a mage to let us through." Sidonie worried for the handful of Goblins who smashed themselves into the doors over and over again. A few were staggering.

"Will this one do?" asked the Caretaker in a silky voice.

As usual, he'd appeared from nowhere, making Sidonie jump. He held a white-robed figure, one hand clasping the man's throat. The mage was pale and sweating with fear, every inhalation a struggle as the Caretaker squeezed his windpipe. As cruel as it seemed, Sidonie understood. The mage would find it hard to cast spells without air.

Masson nodded, shoving Goblins out of the way so the Caretaker could march his prisoner to the offending door. As they passed, Sidonie got a good look at the mage's square-jawed face, with its wild mane of iron-gray hair.

"That's Councilor Anselm, the head of the Conclave," she said sharply. "I saw him sentence a man to his death with lies."

It had been at the trial of Joseph Ellery. Ellery had been a banker, a father, and a man with an unwanted talent for fire. Anselm had condemned him before all of Londria simply because he had a gift the mages couldn't control.

"How interesting," the Caretaker mused. "I found him creeping out one of the other exits. One might think he was afraid of us."

Or was he afraid of something else? Though the building was solid stone, Sidonie thought she heard a distant commotion.

Masson pressed Anselm's face against the door, crushing his cheek with one clawed hand. "Open the door."

The mage's eyes blazed, just as they had when he'd raged against the accused.

Masson leaned close, baring his teeth. "Open it."

Sidonie thought she smelled urine, but the man didn't move.

"Try his hand on the door handle," the Caretaker suggested. "The touch might release the ward."

"In all likelihood we don't need the rest of him," Sidonie added for good measure.

Masson gripped Anselm's wrist. The mage groped for the handle, gripping the huge loop of twisted iron. The spell released, and the door swung open. Goblins swarmed around them, snarling like curs.

With a quick twist, Masson broke Anselm's neck and tossed his lifeless form aside. Sidonie stepped over him as they passed through the door.

Ahead, the sound of fighting swelled, echoing against the stone. The Gentry wound through empty corridors, their feline grace turning predatory as the sound grew louder. Beyond the noise, Sidonie was aware of something else—a humming, pulsing energy.

They turned a corner, and she could see the light—deeper, brighter, but essentially the same as the lanterns in Masson's prison. This was the Doomsfire. She had wondered if the

Unseen had preserved a scrap of it for themselves, and now she knew.

The huge crystal stood on a tripod of carved stone, its light beating like a mother's heart. The Goblins had come to a stop and stood silent as worshippers, staring with huge, goggling eyes at its radiance. Sidonie felt the pulsing echo in her own blood. It seemed the other Gentry did, too. Even Masson's pace slowed to a halt. All of the Unseen were transfixed.

They were made by magic, perhaps *of* it, and if the Caretaker's story was true, this was a piece of its source.

She alone moved forward, but only because she desired to draw closer to the fire's beauty. Part of her longed to fall into it, like a mermaid sliding into the sea. It would be like coming home.

Sidonie tripped, barely catching herself. Startled, she looked down to see a sprawled, misshapen form. Something unspeakable had happened. There were pools of black ash where the man's eyes should be.

This wasn't a clean kill of fang and claw. This was a mage's work.

Danger. Pushing the crystal's heartbeat aside, she swept her gaze over the space. The front doors were open, and bodies littered the floor. Mages gathered around a cluster of huddled forms halfway between the crystal and the doors to the plaza.

"Masson!" she cried at the top of her lungs.

His snarl answered her.

The crystal's hold broke. Goblins poured forth like hornets from a nest. The mages spun around to face the savage wave. The figures on the floor scrambled upright, gasping for air. Six of the forms—the most ragged and wasted—did not move.

What followed was pure chaos. Goblins fought mages and River Rats battled Goblins, slashing with their wicked swords. Aether rifles guarded the slow-moving knot of ragged humans inching toward the door.

Her heart leaped when she saw Gideon's dark head. She sprinted forward, then stopped in confusion, a gulf of sorrow and shame looming at her feet. He was her twin, the other half of her soul. The need to connect was a physical pain.

But she couldn't let him see her. The grief that followed would destroy them both.

Masson caught her eye and nodded. He glided Gideon's way.

Sidonie felt the mage's touch before she saw him. She slowly turned, flexing her fingers to find him standing a few yards away. The touch had been magic, not his fingers.

He was small and young-looking, wearing the dark blue of a junior member of the council. His eyes, though—those dark eyes said he imagined himself far grander than the hand life had dealt him. Sidonie's hand drifted to the pocket of her velvet dress, where she'd hidden her stolen pistol. She'd strapped the stiletto to her thigh.

"What have we here?" the mage said speculatively.

She knew that look. It was a man seeing something he couldn't touch and hating himself for wanting it. And because he couldn't have it, he'd break it out of spite.

Sidonie longed to scrape him off her shoe.

"Is this your handiwork?" She pointed to the empty-eyed body at her feet.

"Of course."

She felt the crackle of his power the instant before he lunged. Pistol forgotten, she slid aside, lashing out with her claws. They caught his robe, but she didn't dare to pull him close for a kill. Not if he had that much power ready to incinerate her. She shoved him aside and sprinted toward the melee ahead, where the rest of the Gentry battled.

Sidonie had gone three steps when he touched her sleeve. His power spiked like ice, driving straight to her core. She stumbled, numbed by his very touch.

The mage laughed, reaching for her again.

Fear spiked, triggering something wild in her soul. With a spitting hiss, Sidonie raked her claws across his eyes, digging deep. He fell, clutching his face as blood and other wet things coursed down his cheeks.

She hadn't needed weapons after all.

Sidonie ran, skirting the dead and dying. Masson caught her, pulling her through the doors.

Unseen swarmed around the Citadel. The others—prisoners, River Rats, and mages—had fled the immediate area. Human soldiers ringed the plaza, but at a respectful distance. High on a lamp post, a red lantern changed to green.

Sidonie knew that was a signal for an airship. She looked up. Above, a vessel sailed their way, graceful as a leaf on a still pond. She knew a Fletcher vessel when she saw one. Her father's careful artistry was in every curve and line.

"Look," she said to Masson, and pointed.

His face dropped and for the first time, she saw fear in his face.

"Run!" he bellowed. "Fire!"

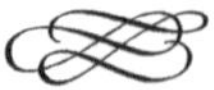

CHAPTER 31

Seconds—or perhaps years—after the Unseen broke into the Citadel, the signal lantern changed from red to green. The Vice Admiral was confirming the rescue was complete, and the *Leopard Ascending* was free to attack.

Miranda swayed against the side of the ship, taking a full breath for the first time since Kitteridge had brought news of Gideon's arrest. Her brother was safe. It was time to act.

"Captain Higgins," Miranda called, pointing to the signal light.

He turned at the sound of her voice. When he saw the green glow at the edge of the plaza, his face tightened, as if bracing himself for what was to come. He gave his captain's jacket a tug, smoothing it into place—and began shouting orders.

"Approach at speed."

The propellers picked up their pace as the ship closed the final distance to their quarry. The sound mingled with the song of the wind through the cables and the shouts of the crew as they worked.

Miranda pulled out her spyglass to survey the area surrounding the plaza below. Soldiers on the ground waved and cheered as the *Leopard Ascending* passed overhead. So did a contingent of River Rats, who lifted their fists in salute. There were thousands thronging Londria's streets.

As the ship moved into place, Miranda studied the ground next to the Citadel, a growing unease settling over her. Unseen swarmed around the perimeter of the building like ants. In her mind's eye, she saw their hungry faces lined up along the river-bank after the crash, hoping one of the fallen aeronauts would swim within reach. Her stomach flipped, the explosion and fall rushing back as clearly as if she were in the water now.

These monsters were loose in Londria. Soon they would rush the waiting crowd.

"Yale," she called. "Are we close enough to scorch these bastards?"

The crew had already mounted the iron cannons in place, and the brass tubing slung across the deck like the arms of an incendiary kraken. Yale finished fastening a valve on the canister of concentrate, then hurried to Miranda's side. He stared down at the teeming monsters and gave a low whistle through his teeth.

"We've got some cleanup to do," he said grimly. "I'll tell the captain."

As he left, Miranda readied Viper, preparing to pick off any Unseen the ship's weapon missed. It would be easy work, even in the dark. Monsters showed up well against the plaza's pale stone.

The Unseen seemed to hear her thoughts. At the sight of the ship, they all broke into a run, clearly remembering the fiery death the previous *Leopard* had brought them. She squeezed off a shot, striking one that veered toward the crowd.

"Fire pods ready," Higgins bellowed.

The six crew members in charge of the cannons took their place.

"*Fire,*" Higgins bellowed, and flame scorched the plaza below.

The crowd roared, backing away. The sound held fear, but wonder and approval, too.

The pack of Unseen split, running around either side of the

Citadel toward the back of the plaza. Fire followed them, but the aeronauts used it sparingly. With buildings and people close by, short, targeted bursts were preferable to a river of destruction. As the ship dipped within range, Miranda picked off more monsters that broke from the pack.

Higgins slowed the ship just above the Citadel's tower. From there, Miranda saw the two columns of Unseen unite again, aiming toward the cemetery and the wall—toward the place her sister had been taken.

Loathing crawled through her gut, but so did anxiety. With her heart in her mouth, she watched the pack of Unseen reach the edge of the plaza, certain there would be bloodshed. The tall, terrifyingly beautiful ones led the way, their long pale hair ghostly in the diffuse glow of the gas streetlights. Some were females. Faceless at this distance, they still reminded her uncomfortably of Sidonie. The mockery of the resemblance only fanned Miranda's rage.

She shouldered Viper, automatically adjusting for wind and distance. If Higgins held the ship steady, she could fell the leaders. Her finger was on the trigger when the soldiers parted, opening a path for the Unseen to escape. Shots fired from the crowd, picking off stragglers, but few struck the main body of the monsters fleeing toward the wall.

"What are they doing?" she cried in outrage. "They're letting them get away."

Higgins came to stand beside Miranda. "If either side attacked, the loss of life would wipe out any victory. The Unseen are not our enemy today."

As if to prove his point, eight mages emerged from inside the Citadel to huddle on the porch and gaze up at the *Leopard Ascending*. There were both light and dark blue robes among them, signifying a mix of senior and junior council members. Some were bloody or leaning on others for support. While the corpses of menials and acolytes littered the plaza, mingling with the dead Unseen, somehow these mages had survived.

"Do you suppose they're pleased that we chased off the monsters?" Higgins said dryly.

"We're the ship they forbid my father to build," Miranda replied. "By now they know Londria is in open revolt against them. I don't think anything pleases them right now."

"Then let's add to their misery." Higgins turned to the men operating the fire pods. "Ready, lads."

The ship lurched. Miranda grabbed the rail for support, her whole body recoiling as if this was another explosion. Her heart hammered so loudly she didn't hear the agonized whine of the engine for several seconds. But then it broke through to her consciousness. The propellers had stalled, even though it was clear there was plenty of steam to drive them.

Every mage had a hand raised toward the ship.

"They're sinking us," she cried.

The *Leopard Ascending* groaned. It was an eerie, mournful cry, as if the timbers themselves were in pain. Then the spire of the cathedral tower grew closer. The mages were pulling the ship down to the earth until it crumbled or crashed.

"Fire," Higgins barked.

Flame poured down once more, splashing around the plaza but not on the Citadel itself. This was the warning shot the Vice Admiral had suggested, but no warning would be enough.

Pain seared Miranda's hand where it touched the side of the ship, blue-white sparks sizzling over her skin. Cries rose around her as others among the crew leaped away from their stations in shock. One fell to the deck, convulsing. Yale scrambled to his side.

"Damn their eyes," Higgins muttered.

Miranda grabbed Viper, keeping low as she took careful aim. She didn't recognize any of the mages, so picked the easiest to shoot. Her finger hovered over the trigger. She'd never shot a human, had never dreamed of it, but this had just become a fight for survival.

The bolt of aether flew true but bounced away in a shower of sparks at the last possible instant. Miranda cursed. They'd set up a shield around themselves, too.

Her shot brought on retaliation. The vessel began a slow spin, tilting at a dangerous angle.

Seeing the ship's danger, the soldiers below surged forward, only to be repulsed by mage fire. The dismayed clamor of the crowd rumbled faintly beneath the cracks and squeals of the ship's timbers. They were breaking apart.

"Fire again," Higgins bellowed to the crew.

The weapon's controls sparked the instant Yale touched them.

"They can't keep it up," Miranda said, her voice cracking with desperate urgency. "There are only a few mages still standing, and they're hurt. They can't drag the ship down, ward it, and shield themselves at the same time. Not for long."

Miranda wasn't sure if that was truth or wishful thinking, but she resumed firing anyway. Her aim wobbled as the vessel tilted and spun, but that barely mattered. As long as she hit the shield, the mages were forced to waste their power. As soon as they understood what she was doing, three other aeronauts grabbed guns and began to fire.

The mages' shield sparked and flared until they faded behind a blinding white brightness. Miranda changed aether canisters and kept firing even as the deck swayed beneath her.

Her whole attention was on her task, so she wasn't aware when her plan bore fruit, but suddenly the wards binding the *Leopard Ascending* gave way. A fountain of flame belched from its cannons. This time, there was no room for precision. The fire bathed the roof of the Citadel, slithering in a liquid brightness over the tiles.

The ship shuddered, but after a furious clank, the propellers began to spin again.

"Keep firing," Higgins roared to the crew. Then he turned to Miranda. "You're brilliant, lass. You've saved us."

She wasn't sure about that. The ship was still losing altitude, the spire looming closer and closer to their hull. The next wash of fire caught more of the Citadel's sprawling wings this time. The lead gutters around the roof began to melt. Smoke rose in a hellish cloud, burning and foul.

The ship kept spiraling downward. The mages were dragging them into hell.

"Again," Higgins ordered, his face flushed and shining with sweat.

Miranda scrambled to help Yale as he switched a spent canister for a fresh one. He'd been right to bring all the incendiary concentrate they had.

"*Fire,*" Higgins bellowed.

Miranda fell to one knee as the deck leveled without warning. Yale gripped her arm as the vessel leaped like a balloon released from a child's hand. It gave one final rotation and then gently drifted just west of the Citadel. Cold, sweet winter air fell over them like a clean blanket.

Silence hung over the crew for a long moment. The only reason they were alive had to be that the mages were not. The enormity of what the crew had done—of what had been done to them—was too huge for Miranda to grasp. How had they gone from a rescue mission to this?

She struggled to her feet and gaped down at the Citadel. For a breathless moment, Miranda stared at the rose window, alight from within. In all her life, she'd never seen the beautiful kaleidoscope of colors. It had taken destruction to reveal them.

Fire gobbled the old cathedral. The beams and timbers of the Citadel stood out against the flame like a skeleton, then dropped away into ash. A heartbeat later, the tower folded and crumpled like a spent match. A collective cry rose from the crowd and the crew alike.

But the spectacle wasn't over yet. A deep, sepulchral explosion sounded from within the flames. As if it were melting from the inside, the Citadel imploded in a rumble of stone, burying its secrets in the earth.

Deathly silence hung over the plaza, broken only by the crackle of flames.

"We're done," Captain Higgins said softly. "Mr. Yale, take us home."

The *Leopard Ascending* docked as dawn streaked the sky. Miranda shook with exhaustion as she crawled down the ladder to solid ground. She was vaguely aware of people waiting on the grass, but she was tired enough that she had no attention to spare.

"You never did do anything by halves," said a familiar voice.

She looked up, suddenly faint with joy. "Gideon."

Her brother pulled her into a rough, one-armed embrace. He stank of smoke and sweat, but he was warm and he was *here*, whole and familiar.

"I don't know what to say except thank you." He gave an odd, strangled cough. "I was as good as dead."

He was hurt, though he wasn't admitting it.

"How about saying you'll think twice before getting yourself arrested?" she said tartly. "You caused a great deal of bother."

He kissed her cheek.

Miranda's eyes filled, but someone else was coming toward them. She swallowed back her thousand questions and wiped her eyes.

"Miss Fletcher."

"Vice Admiral Taylor," she said, scraping up the strength to stand straight.

Taylor looked as weary as she felt, but there was pride in his gaze. "I won't trouble you with anything but thanks and congratulations," he said. "You and your brother here have my utmost respect for everything you've done tonight."

"Thank you," Miranda replied. "But the credit goes to Captain Higgins and his crew."

The Vice Admiral smiled. "A good captain is a treasure, and so is a good ship. Tell me, Miss Fletcher, is your father taking orders for more vessels like the one I saw tonight?"

CHAPTER 32

"**A**re there no mulling spices?" Miranda asked Mrs. Trencher.

The housekeeper shook her head in regret. "I'm sorry, miss. Rutherford's has closed its doors, and there's nothing available anywhere in town."

Christmas Eve had come two days after the *Leopard Ascending* destroyed the Citadel. Needless to say, the holiday preparations at Allington House had been spotty.

"Is Mr. Rutherford all right?" Miranda asked.

"I've heard it's a nervous complaint, miss, though nobody knows whether it was caused by terror or relief."

With that, Mrs. Trencher left to ask the cook when the evening meal would be ready.

Terror or relief. Many felt the same mix of emotions. The populace had longed for freedom from tyranny, and now a ruin smoldered where the bogeymen's lair once dominated the skyline. Celebration mixed with shock.

The surviving mages had fled or been taken into custody. Now public anxiety focused on the spells guarding the wall. Flawed though it was, the barrier *mostly* kept the Unseen outside the city. Once the magic faded, would monsters roam freely through Londria's streets? Every other conversation was about militia and patrols.

On a more positive note, the members of Mrs. Randall's ad hoc council were as good as their word. Policy announcements and opinion pieces smoothed the shift in power from mage to government minister. Where there might have been chaos, Londria's administrative functions carried on.

Miranda tried hard to focus on the good. The people she loved—at least those still living—were safe. Her father and sister had returned from the Earl of Havelock's residence that morning, and they were about to enjoy a delicious Christmas Eve dinner. Her only regret was that Gideon had gone to his rooms above the bookshop instead of joining them at Allington House.

When she entered the dining room, her father sat in his usual place, with Olivia on his left.

Olivia had dressed for dinner in her favorite peach silk gown with a cream lace falling collar copied from the portrait of a cavalier's lady. The dashing effect was ruined by the newspaper she held in front of her face.

"Now there's talk of excavating the Citadel," she announced. "According to anonymous sources, the Doomsfire is buried beneath the rubble. The mages in custody, including our friend Ormond, claim it should be left where layers of stone will diminish its dangerous effects."

"From what I've heard, Ormond is correct," Miranda replied, taking her seat to her father's right.

"The university faculty agrees," Olivia said. "Those I've spoken to, at least. However, they'd dearly love to study it. Until now, scholars believed it a myth."

Miranda unfolded her napkin. "They should have listened to the River Rats."

"Olivia," their father said. "Put the newspaper away. No reading at the table."

Olivia gave Miranda a conspiratorial glance, but the newspaper disappeared beneath Olivia's skirts. Soup was served—a delicate consommé—and they began to eat.

"Three more orders for fire ships arrived by courier this morning," Miranda told her father. "We must hire more carpenters."

Vice Admiral Taylor had paid a personal visit to her father to congratulate him on the success of the *Leopard Ascending*. It turned out that Norton Fletcher and Atticus Taylor had flown together as youths. To Miranda's embarrassment, her father's old chum spun a dramatic tale about her role in bringing down the Conclave.

Her father had said little until Taylor left. Then, he'd insisted on giving her his personal sidearm from his glory days in the merchant air service. *It's not much to look at, but it's reliable.*

Now he gave her a sidelong look, his soup spoon halfway to his mouth. "You know our competition will try to build fire ships of their own."

"Undoubtedly," Miranda replied with a shrug.

"I wonder what they will do by way of a demonstration. You've set the bar rather high."

Olivia choked and had to cough into her napkin. Miranda merely blushed.

Jeffries chose that moment to enter, saving them both.

"Sir, we have one more for dinner," the butler said, his voice gentle, "if it pleases you to admit him."

Gideon appeared in the doorway to the dining room, a guarded look around his eyes and mouth. Her father sat back, regarding him with what appeared to Miranda like fond exasperation.

A momentary silence fell. Miranda broke it by surging from her chair and embracing her brother, careful of his injuries. A second later, Olivia wrapped her arms around them both. Gideon held both his sisters tight.

"Very well," their father said. "Set a place for my prodigal son."

He rose, shaking Gideon's hand as soon as the girls could bear to let their brother go. "Welcome home."

"Thank you. That means more than you will ever know." Gideon slid into his customary chair.

Wordlessly, Olivia passed him the basket of rolls.

Miranda couldn't have wished for a better Christmas gift than the sight of her brother's tall form at the foot of the table. Gideon and her father were both stubborn, but this was a good start at mending the family.

After an awkward pause, the conversation began to flow.

"I'm surprised that it was Kitteridge who brought word to you of what happened at Rutherford's," Gideon said as the fish course was served. "He doesn't strike me as the helpful sort."

"A frivolous young man, if you ask me," her father grumbled.

Miranda said nothing. In her heart, she acknowledged the many times Kitteridge had aided her, both with weapons and information. She didn't want to remember her angry words.

And yet every scrap of intelligence he gave her raised a thousand questions—about the One Hundred families and bloodlines and about Kitteridge himself. He was the greatest—or at least the most provoking—puzzle of all. Why couldn't he fight at her side the way she wanted him to? Why would he only work in secret? On the other hand, did she have the right to make demands of someone she kept at a polite distance—at least most of the time?

Kitteridge was the one part of this adventure she'd rewrite if she could.

"Mr. Kitteridge sent word to Havelock Hall this morning," Olivia said. "He left for Stonegate at first light. He'll be there by now."

Miranda set down her fork, losing interest in the poached salmon. It was time to change the subject away from that man. "What have you heard about any new plans to fortify the wall?"

She had addressed the question to Gideon, but it was her

father who answered. "A good question. There is some unrest over the Citadel's fall. Fools shouting about bloodshed in the streets. The Vice Admiral's men soon put a stop to it."

"I thought the fire killed the Unseen," Olivia put in.

"At least half got away," Miranda replied. She was about to say *about half too many*, but Gideon had told her how at least some of the Unseen came to be. It wasn't so easy now to speak lightly about killing them.

Their father cleared his throat, reclaiming the reins of the conversation. "The *Leopard Ascending*, once it has undergone minor repairs, will play a large part in monitoring the area beyond the wall. I understand the River Rats have agreed to protect the waterways."

"Has anyone heard what became of the Threshers?" Olivia asked. "I know they supported the mages, but might they be of any use against the Unseen?"

"Detective Inspector Palmer and his men have been on the alert, but no one has seen the Threshers," Gideon replied. "Dr. Strang resigned from the university and vacated his residence without notice. No one knows the other members' names or even how many there were."

"What about Mr. Huntley?" Miranda asked.

"The Anathema Club will carry on, and now there will be even more reason to keep their blades sharp." Gideon gave a rueful smile. "I left Huntley drinking with Palmer. We went to see Featherly's widow today."

At the mention of the young aeronaut, the conversation ended in an uncomfortable pause. When the roast goose came in, they changed topics. They chattered of airships and future plans, of old times and new fashions. Gideon sidestepped questions about his investigation work, and their father didn't press for answers. For tonight, at least, there was harmony.

Plum pudding came next, then cheese and nuts and brandy. It

was a proper Christmas Eve dinner, and they stayed together until the clock announced it was Christmas Day.

Finally, when every sentence ended in a yawn, they trudged up the stairs to bed, Gideon agreeing to claim his old room for the night. Their father retired at once, but the three siblings paused in the hallway outside their bedchambers, reluctant to part.

"I wish we could stop time," Olivia said, her voice soft with sleepiness. "Tonight was perfect. I'd like to make it stretch for a while longer."

Gideon kissed her cheek. "If anyone can find an equation to bend time, it would be you."

"I will do that." She laughed. "If I can find space in my daily calendar. There is an ironic essay somewhere in that statement." With a last embrace, she slipped through her bedroom door.

Miranda turned to Gideon. "What are your plans for the next few days?"

"I'm back to my missing persons cases," he said with a slight lift of his shoulders. "Despite everything we discovered, there are more questions. And, there are families who still deserve answers."

"Does the work make you happy?" Miranda asked.

"Yes, sometimes. There are victories, especially when lost children are found. Other days remind me to be humble."

"You chose a difficult path."

"I don't know. Maybe. I've barely taken my first steps."

She studied her brother, thinking he'd grown in ways she couldn't explain. "Good night, Gideon."

"Good night." He gave a mock salute and retreated to his old room.

Miranda had given Shore the evening off, so her bedchamber was empty when she entered and set her candle on the dressing table. Though tired, she pushed the curtain open enough to peer outside. Cold seeped through the glass, rousing her a little.

Snow fell in crazy spirals—not enough to blanket the street, but that would change by morning. The slick of rainwater on the pavement would become ice hidden beneath treacherous white.

There were things she—and many others—still wondered about the battle of the Citadel. What had the Unseen been doing at the Citadel, and why at that moment? There were endless theories, but few conclusions.

It *was* coming to light that the mages had dealings with the monsters. Perhaps they weren't the only ones? During Sidonie's abduction, Gideon had seen men in dark coats and top hats working with the Unseen. He'd assumed they'd been humans. Had they been Threshers? Monsters? Someone or something else?

There was an unsettling thought.

She released the curtain, arranging it so no draft could sneak in. The room was already chillier than it should be, as if someone had left a window open.

She went to the dressing table to take down her hair. The lone candle left the room in partial darkness, but she was too lazy to light another one just to put on her nightgown. Her fingers worked quickly, dropping the pins one by one into a china dish. When she reached for her brush, she knocked something over.

Miranda picked up the unfamiliar object, bringing it closer to the candle's glow. It was a small wooden animal, crudely carved. A cold fiercer than the room's chill seeped through her. For so many years, her sister had given her a toy just like this one every Christmas Eve. A cat, a cow, a dragon—all with the same clumsy angles, the same scrapes and scratches to add detail, the same comic expressions. The only difference was that this one had not been painted.

It was a scorpion, the knobby tail arching over its back. Her heart raced as gooseflesh crept up her arms.

Whoever had sent it knew she was the Scorpion. Lately, more

people had discovered that fact, but how many also knew about Sidonie's Christmas Eve gifts?

No one outside the family.

Tears pricked her eyes, but were they tears of sadness or fright? Gently, she closed her fingers over the creature, wondering what it meant. Explanations were few, and they all led to the same place.

The search for her sister wasn't over.

THE END

The adventure continues in *Hellion's Journey.*

Did you miss Miranda and Gideon's earlier adventures? Read the beginning in *Fortune's Eve* and *Scorpion Dawn.*

AFTERWORD

What will happen now that the mages no longer guard the wall? Who actually sabotaged the *Leopard*? And have we seen the last of the Threshers? The answers lie ahead!

Many, many thanks to everyone who has joined the journey so far. I promise more airships, mysteries, messenger dragons, and a touch of romance are all to come.

Read More from Emma Jane Holloway

www.EmmaJaneHolloway.com

Visit my website and join the newsletter for exclusive updates and previews of upcoming releases in the Hellion House series.

FORTUNE'S EVE

A HELLION HOUSE SHORT STORY

Not all monsters dwell in the woods.

. . .

The mages of the Conclave have questions—dangerous ones that put airship pilot Gideon Fletcher and his sister, Miranda, in the midst of an inquisition for illegal magic.

The Fletchers live in an elegant world of gentlemen's clubs and Society balls, but their claim to fame is making daring rescues in the perilous Outlands. It's all fun and monsters until they save a man wanted by the Conclave, and the mages turn their suspicions toward Gideon's family.

Their scrutiny brings a new kind of peril. Little does Gideon know his sisters have much to hide. Trouble has arrived for the Fletchers, and it clearly means to stay.

For those who like steampunk adventure with a touch of magic—not to mention conspiracy, monsters, airships, and an adorable baby dragon.

SCORPION DAWN

A HELLION HOUSE NOVELLA

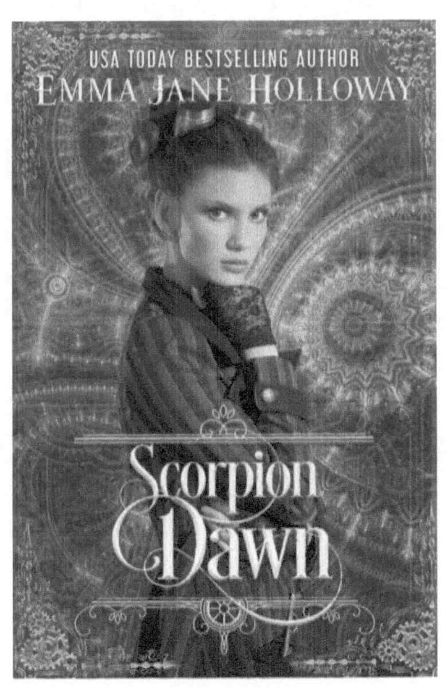

*W*hen the prey becomes the hunter ...

Miranda Fletcher lives in a glittering world of aeronauts and artists, dance cards and dandies, but terror lurks outside the city walls. The countryside is infested with hungry abominations called the Unseen, and a single crack in the capital's defenses invites disaster.

Then Miranda witnesses a murder and learns the walls aren't as secure as their magical protectors claim. But despite a string of bloody crimes, no one is foolhardy enough to question the mages, much less battle monsters at the gate.

Except Miranda. When tragedy shatters her home, she'll risk everything to get answers—and vengeance.

Sometimes the smallest creature carries the deadliest sting.

PRAISE FOR EMMA JANE HOLLOWAY

Magic, machines, mystery, mayhem, and all the danger one expects when people's loves and fears collide.

— KEVIN HEARNE

Holloway takes us for quite a ride, as her plot snakes through an alternative Victorian England full of intrigue, romance, murder, and tiny sandwiches.

— NICOLE PEELER, THE JANE TRUE SERIES

As Sherlock Holmes' niece, investigating murder while navigating the complicated shoals of Society—and romance—in an alternate Victorian England, Evelina Cooper is a charming addition to the canon.

— JACQUELINE CAREY

Splendid… the characters are thoroughly charming and the worldbuilding is first-rate

— ROMANTIC TIMES BOOK REVIEWS

Holloway stuffs her adventure with an abundance of characters and ideas and fills her heroine with talents and graces, all within a fun, brisk narrative.

— PUBLISHERS WEEKLY

ABOUT THE AUTHOR

Ever since childhood, USA Today Bestselling Author Emma Jane Holloway refused to accept that history was nothing but facts prisoned behind the closed door of time. Why waste a perfectly good playground coloring within the timelines? Accordingly, her novels are filled with whimsical impossibilities and the occasional eye-blinking impertinence—but always in the service of grand adventure.

Struggling between the practical and the artistic—a family tradition, along with ghosts and a belief in the curative powers of shortbread—Emma Jane has a degree in literature and job in finance. She lives in the Pacific Northwest in a house crammed with black cats, books, musical instruments, and half-finished sewing projects. In the meantime, she's published articles, essays, short stories, and novels, including *The Baskerville Affair* novels, featuring the niece of Sherlock Holmes.

Cover by Sly Fox Cover Designs

Editing by Jacqui Nelson